"Tell me you didn't enjoy that."

His voice was triumphant, rough with desire.

She trembled, couldn't answer, feeling the aching need inside her.

Stephen's gray eyes probed her face, the parted, trembling curve of her pink mouth, still swollen from his kisses, the wide, darkened blue eyes. Slowly he said, "So it isn't being touched that scares you. You aren't scared now, are you? What is it, Gabriella?"

Dear Reader,

The Seven Deadly Sins have been defined as Anger, Covetousness, Envy, Greed, Lust, Pride and Sloth.

In this book I deal with the sin of Anger. It is a normal human reaction to get angry when people hurt or offend us, and it helps to get over it if you tell someone they've upset you. It clears the air to tell people how you feel; it makes us understand each other better.

But what happens when anger is hidden or repressed because we are taught to feel guilty about expressing our rage? Or told that it was all our own fault and we deserved what happened? People can spend years with a secret burning rage inside them, torn between guilt and resentment. Sooner or later, that rage will either twist a personality and wreck a life, or it will break out in violence.

Charlotte Lamb

This is the sixth story in Charlotte Lamb's gripping seven-part series, SINS. Watch out next month for the final part—HOT BLOOD (#1852), the sin of Sloth.

Charlotte Lamb

Angry Desire

Harlequin Books

TORONTO • NEW YORK • LONDON
AMSTERDAM • PARIS • SYDNEY • HAMBURG
STOCKHOLM • ATHENS • TOKYO • MILAN
MADRID • WARSAW • BUDAPEST • AUCKLAND

ISBN 0-373-11846-5

ANGRY DESIRE

First North American Publication 1996.

Copyright © 1995 by Charlotte Lamb.

CHAPTER ONE

SHE began to run on the morning of her wedding-day—a cool May morning—before the sun was up.

She had been awake all night, moving restlessly around her Islington flat from room to room, unable to sleep. Each time she caught sight of herself in a mirror she saw the panic in her eyes, their blue so dark that it was almost black. She looked strange, unfamiliar, her face white against the fall of her long, straight black hair, her lips bloodless, quivering.

In a corner of her bedroom on a padded hanger hung the long white dress inside a transparent plastic bag.

'It looks like a butterfly in a cocoon,' Lara had said when she'd come round to see Gabriella two days ago. Her cousin had given her a thoughtful glance. 'Is that how you feel, Gabi? As if you're waiting to break out into a new life? I remember I did. I suppose it's the biggest change in a woman's life, getting married. Life is never the same again.' Then she'd looked more sharply at Gabriella and frowned. 'Are you OK? You don't look like a joyful bride somehow—getting cold feet? We all do, you know.'

'I don't believe you did!' Gabriella had been startled; she would never have expected Lara to have any nerves about anything; her cousin was a capable, confident, assertive woman, just as her mother had been. Nobody ever believed that she and Lara were first cousins. They couldn't have been less alike.

Lara had nodded, looking amused. 'Don't sound so surprised. I'm human too, you know! I remember I was so nervous that I couldn't eat for days beforehand. When I came out of it I was on my honeymoon and starving. I couldn't stop eating; Bob began to think he'd married a food-junkie.'

Gabriella had laughed, but she didn't laugh now as she stared at her wedding-dress. She had bought it in a bridal shop in London; it had caught her eye at once because it was so romantic—white satin and lace, Victorian-style, low at the neck, with a tight waist and a full crinoline-like skirt which had palest pink satin rosebuds scattered here and there.

It had needed some alterations—a tuck here and there—and she had had two fittings before it fitted perfectly, yet now she couldn't remember what she looked like in the dress. She couldn't think of anything but the fear which had begun to tear at her last night, like a wild animal shut inside her breast.

He had noticed, of course; he noticed everything, his narrowed grey eyes searching her face remorselessly, and she hadn't been able to hide her fear or her sick recoil. But all he had said was, 'Get a good night's sleep, Gabriella. Tomorrow is going to be a long day. Just one more day, though, and then we'll have several weeks of sunshine and peace, just the two of us alone.'

He had bent to kiss her again and she had stiffened involuntarily, hearing the echo of his words like a deadly threat. 'Just the two of us alone... alone... alone...'

At least his kiss that time had been as light as the touch of a moth's wing and soon over. She hadn't met his eyes, or looked at the hard, insistent angles of his face.

Gabriella was only five feet two but he was a big man, well over six feet, and although he dressed expensively, in smooth city suits most of the time, the body beneath was lean and spare, powerfully muscled. He had tremendous energy too. She had always known that he was a dynamic man in business—his whole career bore witness to that—but with her he had been different. She had been deceived by his coldly controlled face, and the tight rein on which he kept himself when he was with her. She had got the impression that he was not sexually demanding, that he was not an emotional or passionate man.

How could she have been so blind?

She turned hurriedly, almost falling over one of the expensive leather cases standing near the door, packed ready for departure. Gabriella stared down at them. Her cases had been packed since yesterday, to be collected on the day itself and put into the car which would take them to the airport.

Everything had been carefully planned far ahead, organised down to the last detail by Stephen's secretary, a capable middle-aged woman who had worked for him for years.

Gabriella's passport was in her handbag. Stephen had told her that she needn't bother to bring any money with her, but that had ruffled her sense of independence. She and Stephen were still arguing about her job—he wanted her to stop work when they were married, but she wanted to retain the freedom of being responsible for herself, having her own life outside her home and marriage.

So she had refused to let him give her money before they were married; it would have made her feel as if she was being bought. In her handbag she had a folder full of American dollars which she had got from her own bank; it hadn't left her much in her deposit account, but at least it was hers, so she could take it with her now.

She only had to pick up her cases and walk out, she thought. She didn't have to go through with it. She could just vanish.

Where, though? She had to go somewhere. Her mind worked feverishly. She could take a plane to... No, if she went by air she would have to hire a car and it would be too easy for him to check her name on passenger lists at the airport, and check with car-hire firms.

But would he look for her?

She shivered. He would be so angry. She had seen him lose his temper once when his secretary had had to confess to having mislaid a vital fax. She didn't want that black rage turned on her, and this was much worse than some office mistake. Stephen was going to lose face in a very public way. He would be humiliated, made to look a fool.

He would probably never want to set eyes on her, or even hear her name again.

She choked back a half-hysterical laugh which was also half a sob. No, not him. That much she

did know about him. He would want to find her
and... He'll kill me! she thought, her stomach
churning.

Think, think! she told herself, trying to clear her
weary brain. She had her car. She could just drive
out of London and head somewhere quiet and far
away... Cumbria, maybe? Or the far west of
Cornwall? Or the Fens? Britain was full of secret,
remote places, without railway stations, or hotels,
or shopping centres—little villages lost in the
countryside, where nothing much ever happened or
changed, where few people ever visited.

Oh, but wherever she went in Britain people
would read newspapers. She wasn't famous, but
Stephen was wealthy and well-known. Some reporter might pick the story up and sell it. Then there
would be pictures of her appearing, she would be
recognised, and someone unscrupulous who wanted
to earn some easy money might ring the Press and
tell them where she was, and they would tell
Stephen.

No, she must go abroad, as far away as possible.
Foreign newspapers wouldn't bother with the story.
France was closest; she could easily lose herself in
a country as large and as underpopulated as France,
but she only knew a little French, and her accent
was so atrocious that whenever she tried to say anything in shops or markets crowds of locals gathered
to hear her and laugh their heads off at the way
she mangled their language.

She didn't have enough money, either, to support
herself for very long. She would have to get some
sort of work wherever she went, and for that she

would have to be able to speak the language. She could get a job in a hotel, maybe, or a restaurant. She was a good cook—she had been well-trained—and they wouldn't insist on references if she offered to show what she could do. But she wouldn't get a job if she couldn't speak the language.

It had to be Italy, then, in spite of the fact that that was where Stephen would expect her to go. Italy, too, was a large country—surely she could hide herself in it somewhere? She would drive down to Dover and buy a ticket for the Channel ferry using cash, making it harder to trace her than if she booked a ticket in advance—she wouldn't show up on the computers until after she had left. Once in France she would make her way on the autoroute into Italy by the most direct route. If she left now she could be in France before Stephen even knew she had gone.

Her mother had been Italian, and Gabriella had been born there and lived there until she was eleven and her mother had died. She had dual nationality and spoke the language fluently. She would not stand out in Italy; she could easily be taken for a native.

She wouldn't be able to go anywhere near Brindisi, where her mother had come from—there were only distant relatives living there now, but Stephen knew about them, and would look there first. She would make for the northern part of Italy, as far away from Brindisi as possible.

She hurried into her bathroom and, dragging her nightdress over her head, stepped into the shower. The sting of the water sharpened her mind; a few minutes later she towelled herself dry and began to dress.

First she put on black lace panties and a matching bra, and then old blue jeans and a thin blue cotton sweater. She didn't want to be noticed; she would pass without comment in her old clothes, and they would be comfortable for travelling.

Her long black hair she put up in a knot at the back of her neck, but she put on no make-up, not even a touch of lipstick. She would wear dark glasses as she drove and keep them on as she crossed the Channel—that would help keep her anonymous.

She mustn't be recognised anywhere on the way because Stephen was going to be right behind her, and the very thought of him scared her stiff.

Oh, God, why didn't I face it long ago? she inwardly wailed, shivering.

What would he do to her if he caught up with her? Last night she had seen the real Stephen, the nature he had hidden from her all these months. She wasn't blinkered any more—she knew she could expect no mercy from him.

She had to let him know in advance, even so; she couldn't just run away and leave him standing at the altar not knowing what had happened to her. She sat down at a table and scribbled a note to him. There was no time to pick and choose her words, to break it tactfully; she simply told him that she was very sorry, please to forgive her, but she couldn't go through with it, and was going away.

She began to fold the note, then on an afterthought added a few more lines.

Please let everyone know and make my apologies. Try to understand, Stephen—I'm sorry, I just can't marry you after all. I thought I could, but I can't. I'm sorry, I can't explain.

She signed it with her name in a scrawl then read it and groaned. It was incoherent—he would think she'd been drunk when she wrote it, but it was the best she could do, and there was no time to try again.

She would put it into his mail-box at the apartment block on her way out of town—she knew the porter delivered all mail at eight o'clock, which was around the time the post office delivered it.

The wedding was due to take place at eleven-thirty—Stephen would have time to cancel the service and the reception before people began arriving. At least he would have help—he had a huge secretarial team in his offices; they could make the phone calls for him. Even so, she flinched from the thought of the chaos that was going to follow: the presents that would have to go back, the three-tiered bridal cake that nobody would want now, all the food for the reception.

It was going to be embarrassing and humiliating for Stephen and she felt a weary sense of shame at doing this to him as she stared down at the envelope on which she had written his name and address.

For a second she couldn't decide what to do, then the panic began to burn in her stomach again and she swung away. She could not go through with it, that was all. Whatever the consequences, she could not marry him.

To calm herself, she concentrated on little details—went through her handbag to check that she had everything she would need, then put on a light summer jacket—black and white striped. Picking up her car keys, she was about to let herself out of the flat when she saw some letters on a table; she had written them yesterday morning, and forgotten to post them. Automatically she picked them up and was about to put them into her bag when her eye fell on the address on the top letter.

At that second, inspiration hit her. Paolo! In his letter he had said that he was staying at a villa on Lake Como; he would be there all summer, until September; he was painting a series of frescos on the walls of a small private theatre in the villa, which was owned by a world-famous opera director who liked to try out future productions in his own theatre.

It was like a signpost blazing her path. That's it, I'll go to the Italian Lakes, she thought. They're hundreds of miles north of Brindisi. Stephen isn't likely to think of looking there—why should he? I've never told him how important Paolo is to me.

Dropping the envelopes into her handbag, she let herself out of the little flat on the ground floor of an old Victorian house. Her car was parked in what had once been the front garden; now, covered in asphalt, it served as a car park for the tenants of the flats into which the house had been divided.

It was five-thirty in the morning; London was grey and dim, with few cars around, and even fewer people. The street-lights glowed yellow as she headed south towards the river. She pulled up beside a red postbox which she saw on a corner, and posted all the letters except the one to Paolo. There was so little traffic that it only took her ten minutes after that to reach the apartment block facing Hyde Park with views of the cool green shade under the trees.

It had been one of Stephen's most prestigious projects, built five years ago right in the heart of London's most expensive and fashionable area, with marvellous views. Even a small flat there cost the earth.

Stephen had moved into the penthouse apartment as soon as the building had been completed; he had always meant to live there, he had told her. He had worked on the specifications of the penthouse with the architect with his own tastes in mind, and had chosen the décor, creating a perfect home for himself.

Beyond his long, beautifully furnished lounge lay a broad terrace garden; it even had small trees growing in pots, and shrubs and flowers which breathed fragrance at night. She had loved walking out there at night, watching London far below, the sound of it muted, unreal.

Being so close to the park was wonderful too, almost giving one the feeling of being in the country. On hot days you could get cool in the shade of the trees, have a picnic, or row on the Serpentine. Stephen rode in Hyde Park at weekends, on a big black Arab horse which he kept in stables near by, and in the early mornings he jogged in a tracksuit to keep fit, following the twisting paths under the trees for half an hour.

It was lighter when she parked outside the apartment block, knowing that there were unlikely to be police around at that hour. It was the work of a minute to run across the pavement and drop her letter into the chrome letter-box on the front of the locked bullet-proof glass doors of the block.

The porter seated behind his desk looked up, recognised her, looked startled, but immediately gave a polite smile, and stretched his hand out ready to press the button that would open the doors electronically, if she wished, but she shook her head and turned away.

Behind her she sensed him walking towards the doors to collect the letter she had delivered.

Please don't take it up at once! she thought, her heart going like a steam-hammer.

He wouldn't, though, surely? Not at this hour! He would keep it and take it up with the rest of Stephen's mail.

Although it was cool she was sweating as she got back into her car. She slammed the door, put on her seatbelt, and then risked a glance upwards to the soaring top of the forty-storey block, to where the penthouse rose against the early morning sky.

She had expected the high, wide windows to be dark too, but they blazed with light. Shock hit her. Stephen must be awake. Couldn't he sleep either? It hadn't occurred to her that he might be nervous too; might have doubts or uncertainties.

A shadow moved at one of the windows and her throat closed in fear. Was that him? Or was she imagining it? It was so far up that she couldn't be sure. Was he looking out? Looking down? What if he saw her? What if he had spotted the car? Was he watching her, wondering what she was doing out there, and if she was coming up? Would he come down to find out if she had left a message?

Her hands shaking, she started her engine and stepped on the accelerator, shooting away as if the devil himself were after her.

She drove far too fast in sheer panic but there were no police cars around to notice her. She shot through comparatively empty streets down to the softly moving Thames with its glittering reflections of light from the embankment and the high-rise office blocks on each bank. A few moments later she was across Westminster Bridge, and driving into the southern suburbs, unnaturally quiet at this hour, the normally crowded roads almost empty, just the odd car passing her, and a bus lumbering into the city with a few sleepy passengers, workmen on their way home after a night shift.

I won't ring Paolo from England, I'll make for Lake Como, she thought. I'll book into a hotel, and only then get in touch; that will be safest.

She had written to tell him that she was getting married and to invite him to the wedding but he had written back to say he was sorry but he couldn't make it. He had hoped that she would be happy, and he had sent her an exquisite piece of Venetian glass—a candelabra, frosty and twisting, a centre-piece for a dinner-table, he'd said. She had only received it yesterday and she hadn't yet told Stephen about it.

She didn't remember mentioning Paolo to him at all, but his name had been on the list of wedding invitations under his home address in Rome. Stephen probably wouldn't have noticed it, except to assume that he was one of her Italian relatives, and in a sense that was close in the truth. Paolo meant more to her than any of them ever had, anyway.

She arrived at Dover with half an hour to wait before she could board the ferry, and she had had time to think while she drove. So when she bought her ticket she managed to get some loose change, went to a phone box in the ferry terminal, and rang Lara.

The ringing went on for a long time before a sleepy voice finally came on the line, growling, 'Who...?'

'Lara, it's me, Gabriella,' she began, and Lara gave an outraged squawk.

'You're kidding! Gabi, what the hell do you mean by ringing me at...? Where's that damned clock...? Good grief, it's only seven-thirty! Do you know what time I went to bed? Five minutes ago! Tommy's new tooth decided to come through last night; he cried and yelled until he was tomato-red and I was as limp as lettuce. He only went to sleep as it began to get light, the little monster. So, whatever the crisis, you'll have to cope with it without me. I need some sleep before I even think about getting ready.'

Before she could hang up Gabriella said huskily, 'I'm not getting married today, Lara.'

A silence. 'What?'

Gabriella talked fast to stop her from interrupting. 'I'm going away. I've written to Stephen. I'm sorry, I can't explain—I have to go, but will you tell the others? Say I'm sorry, I'm really sorry, but I just can't go through with it.'

She ran out of words then and hung up, but not before hearing her cousin burst out, 'Where are you going? What...?'

Gabriella stared at her face reflected in the perspex hood over the phone. With her black hair pulled back off her forehead and no make-up on her face, she looked even younger, her eyes a turmoil of feelings that she had kept shut down for years and was still terrified of confronting.

I must cut my hair! she thought. It is far too long. I'll have it cut short as soon as I get to France.

She bought a cup of hot black coffee from a stall and drank it in her car, staring at the waiting lines of cars ahead of her. They finally began to move and she followed them up into the ferry, parked as commanded by the seaman in charge and went up into the ship.

She couldn't have eaten to save her life. She sat out on deck and watched the green hills of England fade into the distance as they sailed. It was a very short trip—just an hour and a half.

She drove off in Calais and followed the road system circling the old town—it was amazing how quickly one got out of Calais and got on to the motorway to Paris.

By half-past eleven—the hour when she would have been walking up the aisle towards Stephen—

she was well on her way towards Paris. After checking the map, she had decided that she could not face driving across the mountains, through Switzerland, via the Simplon Pass, which would probably be a hair-raising experience for an inexperienced driver. Instead she headed for the Autoroute du Sud for Menton and the Italian border. It was a long way round, but the terrain would be easier to handle.

She could not make the trip in one day—it was around seven hundred miles. She drove until she was dropping with exhaustion and then looked for a motorway hotel for the night. By then she was well past Lyon.

She ate a light meal in the hotel restaurant—melon followed by a goat's cheese salad—then went to bed. The room was sparsely furnished with a bed, one uncomfortable chair, and a rail for clothes, and there was a tiny shower-room with a lavatory. At least that was clean and very modern. It cost her very little, and she could have slept on the floor, she was so weary.

Even so, she woke up several times with bad dreams, trembling and sweating, remembering only Stephen's face, haunted by it.

The last time she woke it was half-past five so she showered, got dressed and went to have breakfast. It was better than the evening meal. The coffee was strong, there was orange juice and compotes of real fruit, the rolls were freshly cooked, and there were croissants and little pots of jam.

Gabriella drank juice and several cups of coffee, but only one croissant. Then she checked out, paid her bill by credit card, because it would take some time for the details to reach England, and then set off again, into a blue and gold morning, heading south. The further she went, the warmer the weather became. The landscape changed all the time, from the deciduous trees and green fields of mid-France to the cypress, olives and herb-scented maquis of Provence.

The motorway curved round from Provence towards the Côte d'Azur; the sky was a deep glowing blue, and now and then she saw the sea on her right, even deeper blue and glittering with sunlight. She drove through the low green foothills of the Alpes-Maritimes, saw the red roofs and white walls of villas lining the slopes of the hills and tumbling down towards the sea.

It looked so lovely that she was tempted to stay there a night or two. By then she was tired again, and in a mood to weep like a child, but she forced herself to push on and in the late afternoon she crossed the border into Italy at Menton, and turned up north again, away from the sea and the Italian Riviera, towards Milan and the Italian Lakes. She was turning back on herself, but the road was half-empty and she made good speed—it was still faster than trying to use a more direct route.

Driving became more difficult after she left the motorway and found herself on the narrow, twisting, traffic-laden roads running around the glimmering waters of Como, set like a blue mirror between jagged mountains.

She was almost hallucinating by then, driving like an automaton, barely aware of her surroundings and beginning to be afraid that she would crash. She must stop, must find a hotel, she thought stupidly, trying to stay awake.

She didn't know the area at all and had no idea which hotel to check into, but when she found herself driving past a hotel entrance she simply spun the wheel and turned in through the old black wrought-iron gates, followed by the angry horn blasts of other drivers who had been startled by her sudden move.

It was obviously an old grand hotel, now a little shabby but still glittering with chandeliers and marble floors, set in well-kept gardens, looking out across Lake Como which she could see through the trees running down the sides of the hotel.

There were other cars parked echelon-style on the gravelled drive; she pulled in beside one of them. Before getting out her case she walked unsteadily into the hotel reception area feeling almost drunk with tiredness.

The reception clerk behind the polished mahogany counter looked up politely and shot an assessing glance over her jeans and old jacket, his face cooling.

'*Sì, signorina*?' He had apparently even noticed the lack of a wedding-ring on her hand.

Gabriella found herself beginning to answer in easy Italian. She hadn't forgotten her mother's tongue, then! She explained that she was travelling and needed a room for a night or two, that her car was parked outside, with her luggage inside it.

The clerk looked sceptical but offered her a printed brochure which gave the prices of the rooms, perhaps expecting her to be taken aback by the high cost of staying there, and Gabriella gave it a cursory glance, nodding, not really caring how much it cost. She had to get some sleep and she wasn't short of cash, thank heavens.

'Do you have a room facing the lake?'

'A single room?'

'Please.'

'How will you be paying, *signorina*?' the clerk warily enquired.

'Cash, in advance,' Gabriella said, getting out a wallet and laying down the price of the room for that night.

The clerk considered the money. 'You do not have a credit card?'

'Certainly,' she said, showing it to him. He picked it up and checked the details on it. 'But I wish to pay cash for tonight. If I decide to stay longer, and you have a room available, I may use my credit card for any larger amounts. Is that a problem?'

He looked puzzled but shook his head, gave her back her credit card and the usual card every guest had to fill in, asked to see her passport and looked even more startled as she gave him the Italian one.

'You are Italian?' That told her that her accent wasn't quite as good as she had thought it was.

Quietly she explained, 'I was born here, but I live in Britain. My father was British, my mother Italian, so I have dual nationality.'

He handed her back the passport, a smile finally crossing his face. 'Then I do not need to keep this.' He picked up her money and handed her a key. 'I hope you have a very pleasant stay with us, *signorina*. Would you like help with your luggage?'

'Please,' she said, handing him the key of her car. 'Just the smaller tan leather case, please.'

She went to the room and immediately plunged her sweating face into cool, clear water. What she wanted was a bath, but that could wait until her luggage arrived and she could unpack clean clothes to change into.

The porter brought her case; she tipped him generously, got a broad grin and asked him to book her in for dinner for the evening.

When she was alone again she stripped and had a long, relaxing bath, put on a white cambric dress, the bodice stiff with broderie anglaise, and lay down on the bed, her muscles weak and her ears singing with hypertension.

She couldn't remember ever having been this tired before! She wanted to go to sleep, but first she had to ring Paolo.

It was surely many months since she had last spoken to him. They were neither of them great letter writers, and anyway theirs was a very intermittent friendship; it was often several years before they got in touch, but the minute they did it was as if they had never been apart.

She had always been able to tell Paolo everything. At least she would be able to talk to him about what was tearing her apart, be open about why she could not go through with her marriage, knowing that he would understand. He was the one person in the world whom she had ever told about the past.

Paolo had lived next door to her when she was a child. He was four years older than she and had been a short, dark, silent boy, always painting and drawing and making clay figures. They had been thrown together because their mothers had been friends and neither of them had found it easy to get on with their own classmates.

Gabriella, shy and nervous, had found Paolo's silences reassuring; he was sensitive and intelligent, and very different from the other boys in his class at school. They had mostly been bigger, cheerfully down-to-earth, and had made fun of his passion for art, despised him because he didn't love football and fighting, and bullied him a little too. Paolo had kept away from them whenever he could; he had already had a sure sense of what he wanted and had known that it would take him away from Brindisi.

When Gabriella's mother died, her grieving father had taken his daughter back to England so that he could be near his only living relative, his mother. Jack Drayton was himself a man in poor health; he had only survived his wife by three years and had usually been too ill to see much of his only child.

Gabriella had been sent away to boarding-school, although she'd spent her summers with her father's brother Ben and his family. They had given her a couple of very happy years until it had all crashed down again. Sometimes she'd thought that every time she began to be really happy fate intervened—something always happened to wreck it.

Her uncle Ben had died suddenly the summer that she was fourteen. Afterwards his wife had sold their home, taken her children and gone back to Scotland, to the village where she had been born. After that, Gabriella had stayed with her grandmother, her father's mother, in the summer.

During all those years, Gabriella had written to Paolo and got back scratchy little notes from him, but she hadn't actually seen him again until he had come to England on holiday five years ago. She had still been at school, and was spending the holidays with her grandmother in Maidenhead on the River Thames—and she had been thrilled to see Paolo again.

He had stayed in London for a fortnight. Gabriella had shown him around, taken him to Windsor and Hampton Court, Kew Gardens and as far afield as Stratford-on-Avon, so that he could visit the theatre and see Shakespeare's birthplace and Anne Hathaway's cottage.

Paolo had just left art school in Milan and was going to be taking up a career in TV, set-designing. At twenty-one, he had been far more sophisticated and worldly-wise than the seventeen-year-old Gabriella, yet somehow they had picked up their brother-sister relationship where it had left off six years earlier without any difficulty.

When he'd gone back to Milan he'd rarely written. Neither had, but she'd known that when she saw him again they would still talk the same language—indeed, understand each other without words.

Smiling, she picked up the phone and dialled his number. The ringing went on for quite a while before his voice came on the line.

'*Sì?*' He sounded impatient; perhaps he was very busy.

'Paolo?' she whispered uncertainly, and heard his intake of breath.

'Where are you?'

His swift reply told her a lot. 'You know?'

Paolo didn't bother to ask what she meant. His voice dry, he said, 'He rang me last night. Even over the phone he was quite frightening. I don't know what he does to you, but he turned my blood to ice. I got the distinct impression that if he found out I'd lied to him he would tear my head off my body and then dance on the rest of me.'

She half laughed, half sobbed. 'How did he get your number?'

'I think he was trying everyone you ever mentioned to him. No stone unturned, Gabi.'

She had known what he would do. Wearily she said, 'I barely mentioned you to him.'

'*Mia cara*, I was on your guest list!'

'Yes, you were, but how did he find you so quickly? I gave him your address in Rome.'

'Unfortunately, he—or one of his staff—knew I worked for TV in Rome, and tried them. Of course, they knew where to find me; I'd left my summer address with them.'

She sighed, closing her eyes. 'Thank God I didn't ring you before I left—at least you really weren't lying when you told him you didn't know where I was. Do you think he believed you?'

'I think he must have realised that I was surprised. Yes, I think he believed I didn't know where

you were, but I may have spoilt the effect later—I
lost my temper, I'm afraid.'

Anxiously she asked, 'What did you say to him?'

'I told him I wouldn't tell him even if I did know
where you were, but I hadn't heard a word from
you so I didn't have to lie and I said that if you
did get in touch I certainly wouldn't tell him so he
could shove off.' Paolo sounded triumphant. 'He
didn't like that, I'm glad to say. I did not take to
him, *mia cara*—in fact, I disliked him intensely
from the first word he uttered, and, whatever happened, I'm on your side.

'Come here if you want to; I'll give you sanc-
tuary. You'll be quite safe here—the grounds are
patrolled by mad packs of hounds at night and the
gates and walls are electrified—he won't get in.'

Her pale mouth curved into a smile. 'You're a
darling, Paolo. Listen, your phone might be bugged
by now—he's quite capable of it and he can afford
to hire detectives who'll do that. I'll write. I'm OK,
don't worry. Bye.'

She hung up and lay staring at the ceiling. She
would go down and get a postcard of the hotel; she
had seen some on the reception desk. She would
write a few apparently innocent words on it.
'Having a lovely time, wish you were here!' She
would sign it, not with her name but with the word
cara. It should reach him tomorrow. Paolo was
quick-witted; he would understand at once and
come to the hotel to find her.

She only hoped that Stephen had believed him
and was looking for her somewhere else.

CHAPTER TWO

GABRIELLA woke next morning to the sound of a church bell chiming seven. An echo came from across the lake—or was that another church telling the hour? For a moment she lay there, dazedly remembering the incoherent dreams she had been haunted by all night—Stephen's hard, dark face, his mouth, the heat of his body moving against hers, his hands...

Perspiration broke out on her forehead. With a low groan she sat up in bed and looked around the room. The walls were whitewashed. Last night they had looked rather stark, but this morning they were coloured pinky gold by the sun. She had not closed her shutters last night and had left the window slightly ajar; a gentle breeze was now ruffling the floor-length white gauze curtains.

Gabriella slid out of bed in her thin silky nightdress and walked over to the window, pushed it right open and went out on to her balcony, to be struck dumb by the beauty of the view.

She stood there, staring, blue eyes wide; she hadn't expected anything like this. Her gaze moved over the ring of mountains, their indented line blue-hazed, majestic, stretching away out of sight, the morning light moving on their peaks where here and there snow still covered the upper slopes, a cloudless sky floating above them and below, on the surface of the lake, their shimmering reflections, white, gold and soft rose.

Como was not a huge lake; it had a domestic intimacy, and she could see the other side of it clearly enough to make out houses, red-roofed and white-walled, gardens with cypress and fir trees, and, on the winding roads along the lakeside, cars moving.

The hotel gardens ran right down to the lake to where she saw a wooden jetty, with a few people waiting on it—men reading newspapers, schoolchildren, women with shopping baskets chatting to one another. On the lake a small ferry boat was chugging towards them at a sedate speed. She watched it dock, nudging the old tyres tied along the jetty. A sailor tied up and the passengers boarded, greeting the jerseyed sailors on board like old friends—which they probably were.

The boat cast off again, crossing the lake again. Gabriella watched it leave. She could see why people who lived here would use the ferry if they wanted to cross the lake. Driving around those narrow, twisting little roads would be hair-raising even in daylight. That's what I'll do, she thought; I'll leave my car at the hotel and explore the lake on the ferry.

She heard cheerful, murmuring voices outside in the corridor, then the whirr of the lift descending—other people going to breakfast, obviously—which reminded her that she had ordered a breakfast-tray in her room for eight o'clock. Taking a last look at the view, she turned reluctantly away into her bedroom.

She showered, slid into a towelling robe hanging on the door and sat on the bed to blow-dry her long, silky hair; it took quite a time, so in the end she left it loose, to finish drying naturally, and dressed in a dark blue linen shift dress, leaving her slender legs bare but sliding her feet into white sandals with a tiny heel, a few fine straps of leather criss-crossing the foot, buckled at the ankle.

A few moments later the room-service waiter tapped on her door. He was a young boy in a spotless white uniform, as slender as a girl and doe-eyed. He gave her an appreciative look, young though he was—he was, after all, an Italian and enjoyed the sight of a pretty woman. 'Your breakfast, *signorina*,' he said smiling as she admitted him.

'*Grazie*,' she said, leading the way out on to the balcony. In Italian she told him to put the tray down on the small white table.

'A lovely morning for you,' he said, as if he had produced that too. His dark eyes admiringly flicked over her from her black hair to her long legs. Clearly he was in no hurry to leave. 'Is this your first visit to Como?'

'Yes, and I've never seen anything so beautiful. Where does the ferry go?' she asked, pointing to the jetty where a new string of passengers was boarding a different boat.

'That one?' He gave it an indifferent glance. 'That sails between Menaggio, Bellagio and Varenna.'

'Do all the ferries have the same route?'

'Oh, no—some go right the way to Como itself, at the far end of one arm of the lake...'

'One arm?' she asked, puzzled.

'The lake is a Y-shape, *signorina*.' He pulled a pencil from his pocket and drew a rough outline on a notepad he also carried. 'Like that. Como is at the end of this upper arm and Lecco is almost at the end of the other arm. The lake divides at Bellagio, then you come down here to Novate.'

'What a strange shape for a lake! So which town is this?'

He gave her a startled look, his great dark eyes incredulous. 'This is Menaggio, *signorina*! You didn't know that?'

She grinned at him. 'I drove in here on impulse last night; I was so tired that I didn't even notice the name of the hotel, let alone the place.'

The boy was in no hurry to leave. 'Where do you come from? I don't recognise your accent. You sound southern—are you from Naples?'

She laughed. 'Close—I was brought up in Brindisi.'

Another waiter appeared below, on the terrace steps, and whistled piercingly. The boy looked down, startled, was given a peremptory gesture and an angry glare, and hurriedly turned away.

'I must go... Excuse me, *signorina*.'

He vanished and, smiling wryly to herself, Gabriella sat down and considered her breakfast-tray—a glass of orange juice embedded in a bowl of crushed ice, a silver coffee-pot, rolls, a couple of little cakes, butter, a pot of jam, a bowl of fresh black cherries and some frosted green grapes.

She didn't touch the cakes, but she ate a roll and some of the cherries, drank all the juice and a couple of cups of coffee while she gazed down at the lake, watching the changing reflections until a passing boat sent wide ripples to break them up. People on the jetty were talking to each other cheerfully, their voices drifting to her on the warm air. She thought that it must be nice to live in a small place where you knew everyone; big cities like London could be lonely places.

The telephone made her jump. She turned her head to stare at it in terror.

Who could be ringing her? Nobody knew she was there. Her heart began to beat agonisingly; her skin tightened and turned icy cold. She was trembling as she got up, knocking over the chair she had been sitting on.

The phone still went on ringing; maybe it was the hotel reception desk asking if she was staying another night. Slowly, reluctantly, she crossed the room and stretched out a shaky hand.

'Hello?' Her voice was low, husky.

'Signorina Brooks?' an Italian voice asked.

'Yes.' She was waiting on tenterhooks.

'A Signor Giovio to see you, *signorina.*'

She let out a quivering breath, closing her eyes in sick relief. It was only Paolo; he had got her card already and understood its message. She had known he would—he was much too quick not to have got it at first glance. 'Oh . . . my cousin, yes; tell him I'll be down in a moment.'

She brought her tray into her bedroom, then closed the balcony doors and almost flew downstairs. Paolo was waiting for her in the lounge which led out on to the garden terrace.

The room was enormous, with high ceilings from which glittered chandeliers and marble floors across which deep white sofas were scattered. One end was entirely made up of windows, stretching from ceiling to floor, draped in the same white gauze curtains as those which hung in her room; through them you could see the hotel gardens leading down to the lake and they allowed the sun to flood the great room with light.

Paolo stood by them, gazing out. She stopped to stare at him while he was unaware of her. He hadn't changed much since they'd last met although he was clearly a few years older. He was still a slight figure, his face in profile bony and memorable— not handsome but striking, his sallow skin deeply tanned and his hair jet-black, softly waving down to his shoulders. He was wearing a lightweight pale blue suit; elegantly casual, it looked expensive. Did he buy designer clothes now?

As if becoming aware of her presence he turned, their eyes met and a smile lit his thin face. 'So, there you are!' he said in Italian, holding out both hands, and she ran to take them.

'I knew you'd understand the card.'

'Of course,' he dismissed, shrugging. His slanting eyes skimmed her face. 'You don't look as terrible as you sounded last night. Sleep well?'

She nodded but perhaps the memory of her bad dreams showed in her face, because Paolo frowned.

Some other guests wandered into the room, giving them curious looks. Gabriella opened the tall glass door into the garden.

'Let's walk by the lake. I'm dying to get a closer look at it. Isn't it breathtaking? How long have you been here?'

'A couple of weeks.' Paolo fell into step beside her as she began to descend the stone steps towards the lakeside. 'Are you going to tell me about it?'

She stopped on the jetty and leaned on the wooden rail, staring out towards another town on the far side of the lake. 'Where's that?' she asked, pointing.

'Varenna,' Paolo said in a dry tone, knowing that she was delaying any more intimate talk.

'Is it worth visiting?'

'It's small but pretty; there are some nice gardens to see. Are we going to talk about the scenery or are you going to tell me why you ran away?'

She went on staring across the lake and didn't answer.

Paolo drew a folded newspaper from under his arm and offered it to her. Frowning, Gabriella took it, looked at the front page and with a leap of the nerves saw that it was an English paper.

'Page five,' he said.

Hands trembling she turned the pages and saw her own face, grey and blurred, in a photo which she didn't remember being taken—she and Stephen arriving at a theatre for a very starry first night. Feverishly she skimmed the story; it was short on facts but those it had were mostly about Stephen and it pretended sympathy for him at being left at the altar.

Somehow the reporter made her sound like a bimbo—a gold-digger who had probably run off with an even richer man, although none was actually suggested. The story did, however, claim that she had not sent back her engagement ring, which was worth hundreds of thousands of pounds, and added that she had got other valuable jewellery out of Stephen, all of which she had also kept.

She crushed the paper in her hands and looked at Paolo, stricken. 'You bought this here?'

He nodded. 'There's a good newsagent who sells a few foreign newspapers. This was the only popular English paper on sale this morning but he said he'd had half a dozen copies of this one. If you look at the date you'll see that it was out in England yesterday.'

Pale, she said, 'So others may have read the story.'

Paolo nodded grimly and took the screwed-up paper, smoothing it out again to study Stephen's face in the grey photo. 'Is it a good likeness?'

She glanced at the hard face, the fleshless cheekbones, the cool grey eyes, that insistent jawline. A little shiver ran through her.

'Yes.'

Paolo screwed the newspaper up again and tossed it into a nearby refuse bin.

'What did he do to you?'

She gave a choky little sigh. 'Nothing—nothing at all. Poor man, he must be utterly bewildered—that's why I couldn't tell him face to face.'

'That would have been an idea,' Paolo said without inflexion.

She flinched as if from an accusation, guilt in her eyes, and shot him a distraught look. 'I know—I know I should have, but I couldn't, I just couldn't talk to him. He would never have understood unless I told him . . . and I couldn't talk about it, Paolo; I still can't talk about it.'

'Ah,' he said on an indrawn breath. 'So. That is what it is all about.'

She turned to look at him, her eyes glistening with unshed tears. 'Oh, you're so quick; you always know what I'm talking about. That's why I came here to find you—at least you'll understand. I can talk to you without having to dot every I and cross every T.'

He touched her cheek with one fingertip. 'I had a suspicion that this might be behind it, but it's years ago—you should have had therapy, you know, talked it out with a professional.'

'I couldn't.' Her pink mouth was stubborn, unhappy. The breeze blew her black hair across her cheek and she brushed it away angrily.

'That's just why you ought to try!'

'Anyway, nothing really happened. I'm not the victim of some horrible crime.'

'Crimes of the heart can be as disastrous.'

Another sigh shook her. 'Yes. Don't let's talk about it.'

He grimaced. 'OK. Tell me how you met this guy Stephen Durrant, then—tell me about him. He didn't make a great impression on me on the phone.'

She turned and walked further along the lake, under a line of magnolia trees in bloom, their flowers perched like great white birds on the glossy green leaves.

'Stephen heads a big property company...DLKC Properties. I don't expect you'll have heard of them.'

'I have,' Paolo said, shooting a narrowed glance at her. 'So he's behind them, is he? I thought they were an international consortium.'

'They are, but Stephen is the main shareholder.'

'He must be very rich, then. They weathered the storm when property took a nosedive a few years back. A lot of other companies were wiped out but DLKC survived intact.

'A friend of mine bought a flat in a block they built in Tenerife—it was brilliantly designed, and a nice place to live, I thought. The landscaping was excellent—well laid out gardens, a nice-sized pool...' He stopped and grinned down at her. 'Sorry; you know how obsessed I am with design.'

'I remember,' she said, smiling back. 'And you know I love my work too. I'm always sorry for people who don't enjoy their job.'

'Does Stephen Durrant enjoy his?'

She couldn't put Paolo off the scent. She looked at him wryly.

'Stephen lives for his work; he rarely has time for anything else.'

'Including you?'

She looked away, across the lake. 'He made time for me. When he remembered.'

'Ah,' Paolo said again. 'Did that make you angry?'

'Angry?' She was taken aback by the question. 'Why should it?'

But hadn't she resented the fact that Stephen had so little time and saw her so rarely? At the same time, though, she had been relieved, because she was afraid of him getting too close, becoming too important to her. Afraid of him, of herself.

Why are you such a coward? she thought wildly. Why are you so scared of everything?

'He has a reputation as a bit of a hard man, doesn't he?' murmured Paolo, watching her troubled face.

She turned away, picked a leaf from a bush and crumpled it in her cold hands, inhaling the aromatic scent of the oils released.

'Well, he's very successful. I suppose most successful people are pretty tough.'

Paolo nodded thoughtfully. 'Is he a self-made man? He sounds like one.'

'He built his business up himself, but he inherited a small building firm from an uncle when he was twenty.'

'How old is he now?'

'Thirty-six.'

'Did the age-gap bother you?'

She shook her head. 'I've never been interested in anyone my own age; I prefer older men.' She stopped dead, catching Paolo's eyes, and flushed scarlet, then went dead white. Hurriedly she walked on and he caught up with her.

After a moment or two he said, 'But you're scared of Stephen, aren't you?'

'If you knew him, you'd be scared of him.'

'Then why in God's name did you agree to marry him?'

'I don't know,' she wailed, her face working in anguish.

'Surely to God you knew how you felt about him, Gabriella?' Paolo sounded impatient, angry with her, and that made her feel worse. She was terrified of angry scenes, of someone looking at her accusingly, blaming her. Tears stung her eyes.

'I felt...safe...with him...' she whispered, and Paolo was silent for a moment.

'What changed?'

She didn't answer, looking away.

Paolo said, 'I take it that he is in love with you?'

Her long black hair blew across her face again, in blinding strands, and she didn't push it away this time. Her eyes hidden, she whispered, 'I don't know.'

Paolo's voice hardened. 'Oh, come on, *mia cara*, you must know how he feels about you!'

She knew Stephen wanted her physically—that fact had been blazingly obvious when he had lost control and started making love to her with that terrifying heat. She shivered. He had never been like that before. Why that night?

But she knew why; she had known at the time although in her sheer blind panic she hadn't allowed herself to think about her own guilt. Now she did, and Paolo frowned as he watched her changing, disturbed face.

'Don't look like that. It can't be that bad!'

Can't it? she thought, staring across at the sunlit, white-capped mountains and remembering her mood that last evening. She had been edgy, shy, uneasy, but she had tried to hide it because she and Stephen had been the guests of honour at a pre-wedding party given for them by Stephen's elder sister, Beatrice, in her beautiful Regent's Park home. In her late forties, she was the wife of a senior civil servant in the Foreign Office. Gabriella had only met her half a dozen times but she liked her, in spite of her formidable manner, which Beatrice had in common with her brother.

Beatrice didn't resemble Stephen physically—she was small and fair and blue-eyed. Stephen said that she took after their mother. His younger sister, Anne, had married a Spaniard and lived in Barcelona—she had been at the party too, but Gabriella hadn't seen much of her. There had been so many people there and she had known only a handful of them—mostly friends of Stephen's whom she had met before.

She had never met his nephew Hugo before; she wished to God that she hadn't met him that night.

'Talk to me,' Paolo said and she started, looking round at him, her face chalky white and her eyes lost and childlike. He drew a sharp breath. 'For heaven's sake! What on earth happened to put that look in your eyes?'

She swayed and he put an arm round her, glancing behind them. 'Come and sit down,' he said, leading her towards a wooden bench at the edge of the hotel gardens. Her legs were trembling so much that she was glad to sit down. She leaned back, closing her eyes.

After a minute she said huskily, 'I realise it sounds stupid, but then I have been stupid with Stephen. I don't really know him. I should never have got engaged, and honestly, Paolo, I don't know how he really feels about me; I can't remember him ever saying he was in love with me.'

Paolo looked incredulously at her. 'Not even when he proposed?'

She shook her head.

From the beginning she had been very ambivalent about Stephen, about their relationship—not sure where it was going or if she should be seeing him at all. When she was with him she was never bored, though; time flashed past, although she could never remember afterwards anything that he had said or anything much that had happened. Looking back on all those evenings with him, she could only remember his face, his grey eyes, his deep voice murmuring.

If he went abroad, and she didn't see him for a week or so, she thought about him all the time. She didn't understand him, yet she couldn't forget him, and although she kept telling herself that she would stop seeing him she never did. When he rang to invite her out she always accepted if she was free, and Stephen knew which nights she worked so he usually made sure to ask her out on her free evenings.

On his thirty-sixth birthday he had taken her to dinner at a very exclusive Mayfair restaurant, whose chef was something of a hero of hers. The food had been marvellous, and she had drunk more wine than usual and felt as if she was floating. Stephen had watched her across the table, his eyes half veiled by heavy lids, and she had been hypnotised by that deep stare, gazing back in sleepy languor while they sipped superb coffee.

'You look lovely in that dress; you should wear white more often,' he'd said.

The compliment had made her flush, and she'd lowered her eyes.

Stephen had stretched a commanding hand across the table and taken her hand, moving his thumb softly up and down against her wrist.

'Gabriella, turning thirty-six has made me stop and think about the way my life is going. I've been too busy building up my business to have time to think of marriage, but since I met you I've realised how much has been missing from my life for years. Living alone isn't natural for human beings—we need each other too much—but I was always so busy that I never had time to see just how lonely I was.'

She had stared, struck dumb. What was he saying? Was he going to ask her to live with him, share his bed, to move into that huge penthouse apartment of his? He couldn't be asking her to marry him!

She had never quite known why he kept seeing her, or what he wanted—and she had been so shy with him that she hadn't dared ask. She had hoped, stupidly, that their relationship would go on in that undemanding, tranquil way.

The moment that he had proposed had been the end of her illusions, although it hadn't dawned on her at once that everything had changed that night. She had been too bewildered.

'I'll be forty in a few years, and the clock is ticking faster. I want a family while I'm young enough to enjoy them,' he had gone on quietly. 'How do you feel about having children? I've noticed you with your cousin's baby; you seem to love looking after him—do you want some of your own?'

Her eyes had glowed. She adored Tommy, her cousin Lara's baby, and she had given Stephen an instinctive, unthinking reply. 'I love children, especially when they're babies; I love to hold them, all milky and smelling of talcum. I envy Lara having Tommy. She says she doesn't want any more—it's too much like work—but I'd like at least four. I was an only child and I was always lonely. I told myself then that I'd make sure that I had more than one child.'

Now she thought, Why did I say all that? I knew what he might be going to say—why didn't I lie, tell him that I didn't want children and he should ask someone else? Why did I babble on like that, misleading him, giving him the wrong impression?

Did I secretly want to marry him? Or was it the same old weakness that has always haunted my life—the inability to recognise danger, to avert catastrophe?

He had picked up her hands and held them loosely, watching the way that her face lit up as she talked about babies, and, when she had finally run out of words and stopped breathlessly, he said, 'Then will you marry me, Gabriella?'

She looked now at Paolo and gave a long sigh. 'I thought he was marrying me because he wanted a family.' That was the truth, wasn't it? Wasn't it?

Paolo's brows shot up. 'Then you realised that you would be sleeping with him?'

She blushed. 'Yes, but...' Knowing something with your conscious mind was one thing; realising it at the very deepest level was another. It all depended on how you perceived a situation. Stephen had asked her if she wanted children and she did; she loved the idea of having a baby of her own, and finally belonging to a real family again. That had been one aspect of his proposal and their engagement—she had closed her eyes to another aspect of it.

That was why when Stephen had lost control and all that passion had flared out of him she had gone into blinding panic.

If he had acted that way on the night that he had proposed she would have run like hell. But he had been so different then; he had told her softly, 'I'll make you happy, Gabriella!' and she had been lulled into false optimism by that gentleness, the apparent lack of passion. She had drifted into engagement without realising what dangerous waters lay ahead, had let him put his ring on her finger, had let him arrange the wedding, had sat and nodded when he'd made suggestions, had allowed his personal assistant to organise it all, even the invitations to her few friends and family.

The closest of her family were all dead, of course. She only had distant relatives, and her bridesmaids were to have been one of Stephen's nieces and two of her old college friends—and Lara, who was to have been matron of honour in warm peach silk. The rest on the enormous wedding guest list were Stephen's friends and colleagues—some of them wealthy and influential. What would they all be thinking? What would Stephen have told them? Perhaps they would jump to the conclusion that she had run off with another man.

'He suspects you've run off with another man,' Paolo said, as if picking up on her thoughts—as he'd sometimes done in the past, she remembered. They had some sort of mental link; it had always been there, even when they were children. Thoughts flashed from one to the other like electric sparks.

She looked up at him anxiously. 'Did he say so?'

'I picked it up from his voice. *Mia cara*, that is a very jealous man, jealous as hell—I could smell the fire and brimstone down the telephone line!'

She flinched. Yes, Stephen probably did suspect that she had run off with someone. When someone fled from marriage to one man, it was usually to go to another. But jealous? Stephen? Was he? That would be yet another shock discovery, if it was true. I hardly know him at all, she thought; he's as much a mystery to me as he was the day I met him.

'He'll want explanations, answers,' Paolo warned her. 'And you had better have them ready. I have a shrewd idea that he will keep looking for you no matter how long it takes, Gabriella.'

She got up and began to hurry back towards the hotel as if running away again—and that might have been the best plan. Now that Stephen had found Paolo he might hire a private detective to check to see if she was in Como. But there were other places she might go, and he had no idea how close she and Paolo were. Surely he would hunt elsewhere first?

'Will you stay here long?' asked Paolo, reading her mind again, and she shrugged.

'Maybe for the summer. I thought I'd get a job. In a tourist area like this there should be plenty of work available. Do you know anyone with a restaurant or a hotel who needs a chef?'

He shook his head. 'Not offhand, but I'll ask around. I know a few people here who might come up with a suggestion. Come to the villa for lunch.'

'You're a darling, Paolo—another day, thank you. I need to be alone for a while. It helped to talk to you, but I want to take the ferry over to Bellagio and have lunch there; it will give me time to think. I've done far too little of that over the last few months. I want to clear my head and work out what I really do feel.'

'How about dinner tonight, then?'

'I'd love that.'

'Eight o'clock? I'm dying to show you the Villa Caterina Bella. You ought to see it first by daylight, though. The gardens are superb—people come from the other side of the world to see them—and the house itself is a dream—a nineteenth-century fantasy built for a woman who died a few months after it was completed.

'She was the Caterina of the name—a dancer, the mistress of an Italian prince who bought the house for her. He was married to someone of his own class, very respectably, with half a dozen children, when he fell madly in love with a ballet dancer. She was already sick; he hoped that she would regain her health here, by the lake, in the mountain air.

'He made the villa pure paradise for her, but they only had a short time together here before she died of tuberculosis. She's buried in the cemetery here—within sight of the villa and the lake.'

Tears filled her eyes again. 'What a sad story; don't tell me such sad things!'

Paolo looked down at her affectionately. 'Sad but beautiful. Like you! I'll see you tonight at eight, then.'

When he had gone Gabriella went up to her room, collected a light summer jacket, then walked down to the ferry and took the boat across the lake.

She spent the rest of the morning in Bellagio, exploring the shops—some of them hidden away up steep steps—staring at jewellery and leather goods, silk scarves and glass lampshades. She found a hairdressing salon right at the top of the steps; two women were working in it, one dying a customer's hair blonde in streaks, the other just finishing blow-drying another's hair.

Gabriella had her hair washed by a teenager who was learning the business, while she waited for the younger hairdresser to be free. When she told the girl what she wanted the Italian was dumbstruck.

'Cut this?' the girl repeated, running her fingers through Gabriella's long, wet, silky hair. 'You can't be serious? It would be a crime. I wish my hair was this long and looked this good.'

'I'm tired of it; I want it off.' Gabriella lifted her hand to shoulder-length, gesturing. 'Would you cut it in a bob, this long? With a fringe.'

The older hairdresser—a short, plump woman in her forties who probably owned the shop—came over then to plead with her. 'But it suits you long. Believe me, it suits you better the way it is now; you have that sort of face. Long hair is perfect for you.'

'And it will take you years to grow it this long again, you know,' said the younger girl, who wore her own hair in frizzy ringlets which hung right down her back, almost as long as Gabriella's.

'I know, but I'm sick of long hair. I want to change myself,' Gabriella stubbornly insisted. 'I want a complete new look.'

The two women exchanged quick, shrewd looks.

'I hope he's worth it, then,' the older one said, shrugging and walking back to her own customer, who had listened with open curiosity to the discussion.

'No man is!' she called across, looking faintly comic in a space-age foil bonnet with wisps of yellow hair poking through it. 'You'll get over him and then you'll regret having cut your hair off! Don't do it!'

Gabriella looked up at the assistant standing behind her chair. 'I'd like it shoulder-length,' she repeated obstinately, but it made her feel odd to watch the curls of black hair falling to the floor as the scissors snipped and slashed. The teenaged assistant swept it all away a few moments later while Gabriella's now much shorter hair was blow-dried.

She felt strangely light-headed and unfamiliar as she left the shop some time later. Her black hair now swung in a short, graceful bell, the tapered ends shaped to frame her face. She kept catching sight of herself reflected in shop windows, and each time was startled.

She ate lunch at one of the restaurants close to the jetty. From there she could see Menaggio and the cream and gold façade of her own hotel, and could watch the boats coming and going at the jetty. She had managed to get a timetable and had decided to return at around four.

First, having eaten a leisurely, light lunch, she walked further along the waterfront and visited the Villa Serbelloni, which had now been turned into a hotel. The gardens rising in front and behind the great cream-painted building were steep and tiring to explore, but were so beautiful that she spent the rest of the afternoon there, among the towering rhododendrons and camellias, the magnolias and azaleas, their flowers a mass of colours—pink, gold, deep red, orange, violet—a dazzling array. There was a drift of fragrance from roses all around her as she walked, and the busy hum of bees rifling the petals.

Among the shrubs and flowers she found a topiary garden too—sculptured shapes in yew, dark green and secretive, and, rising against the summer sky, the usual cypress, twisting like green flames into the blue air.

She had to hurry to get back to the jetty in time to catch the boat. She had saturated herself in peace and tranquillity and beauty all day; she was pleasantly tired, her mind at rest for a while. She enjoyed leaning on the rail watching Bellagio disappear, and then turning to watch Menaggio coming closer. A delicate opalescent mist had begun to drift along the lake; it gave a new mystery to the distances, the little lakeside villages and towns—they appeared and vanished without warning as if they were fairy places.

When she got to the hotel the receptionist stared, eyes widening. 'Your hair... It's... You've had your lovely long hair cut, *signorina.*'

'That's right,' she said coldly, taking her key, and walked away before he could say what she could feel he was going to say.

Back in her room, she had a bath and changed into one of the new dresses that she had bought for her honeymoon—a heavy cream silk dress, expensively simple in style but a delight to wear because it felt so good on her skin.

Paolo arrived a little early but she was waiting for him downstairs; as she got up and walked towards him he looked at her, then did a double take.

'What on earth...? Gabriella, what in the name of the Madonna have you done to yourself?'

Her lower lip stuck out childishly. 'Cut my hair! I was sick of having long hair—it's so much work; it takes so long to wash and dry, and comb, and brush... I was fed up with it; it's been long for years. I wanted a change.'

She knew she sounded petulant but she couldn't help that. Paolo looked at her with his wry smile, shrugging.

'I see. It was a symbolic act, was it?'

A little defiantly she grimaced at him. 'Don't be clever with me, Paolo. Shall we go?' She put her hand through his arm. 'You look stunning, by the way.'

He was breathtaking—wearing a magnificently tailored white dinner-jacket, black tie, black trousers; the combination emphasised his Italian colouring, his slim figure and his golden tan. Other women, walking past them on their way to the dining-room for dinner, stared at him with fascination and desire but he seemed oblivious of them.

He grinned down at her. 'That's it, get round me with flattery! I still regret your lovely, lovely hair. Something else to blame that man for! Come on, I'm parked outside.'

When they left the hotel she was stunned to discover that he was driving a Lamborghini—a long, gleaming white model which was parked right outside the hotel and being currently admired by the receptionist, a hotel porter and a couple of the waiters from the dining-room.

They fell back as she and Paolo appeared; she recognised the rather supercilious receptionist who had been so reluctant to let her check in the night before. He hurriedly smiled and bowed when he caught her eye. Behind him hovered the boy who had brought her breakfast. Gabriella smiled at the boy warmly, pretending not to notice the way he was staring at her new hairstyle. She didn't want him commenting too!

Paolo ceremoniously put her into the passenger seat; the hotel staff watched her long, slender legs swing into place before Paolo closed the door on her.

They drove out of the car park just as another car drove into it, forcing Paolo to slow down. Gabriella glanced at the dark green Jaguar XJS and froze, recognising it. Stephen had a Jag that colour—the colour known as racing green.

Oh, but it must be a coincidence. It couldn't be his car! He wouldn't have had time to get here. Her glance flashed to the number-plate; her heart almost stopped. It was!

Then the driver turned his head, and she couldn't breathe. She slid down in her seat, hoping he couldn't see her.

Paolo was out of the car park a second later and let the throttle out; the Lamborghini shot away along the empty road which was veiled in soft, pearly mist.

He looked sideways as she gripped the edge of the seat, her knuckles white with strain.

'Am I going too fast for you? There isn't much traffic around this evening. I'll slow down if another car shows up, don't worry.'

'It was him,' she said shakily.

'What?' Paolo's brows met.

'Stephen—in the green Jag. It was him.'

Paolo was looking bewildered. 'The green...' Then his face sharpened in understanding. 'Oh, in the hotel car park? The sports car? Has he got a Jaguar sports? Gabi, you're beginning to be paranoid; don't start seeing him all over the place.'

'I saw his face,' she told him angrily. 'I'm not crazy, Paolo, and I'm not imagining things. I know that car. But how did he get here in it this fast? You said he rang you from London last night.'

'I said he rang me last night; I've no idea where he was ringing from. But he could have come down on the train.'

'No, that is his car, I tell you. I saw the number-plate.'

'Darling, you can put your car on a train.'

She hadn't thought of that. 'Of course you can,' she said, slumping wearily back in her seat. Stephen had found her, tracked her down. For a second she was pole-axed, hopeless, then she sat up with feverish determination.

'I've got to get away, Paolo! I'll have to abandon all my luggage in the hotel, and my car; I can't go back for them—he'll be waiting for me. But I've got my handbag, with my passport and all my money in it. I will have to run again. I'll have to catch a train... Where could I go? On to Switzerland? That isn't far, is it?'

Paolo's gaze was fixed on his driving-mirror, watching the road unwind behind them. He didn't answer.

'Will you help me, Paolo?' she asked and he looked briefly at her, his eyes sober.

'I'm sorry, *cara*, I'm afraid your chances of escape are almost nil—he's right behind us and he's catching up fast.'

CHAPTER THREE

GABRIELLA half turned to look back and saw a flash of green close behind them. She couldn't see Stephen through the windscreen of his car but fear made her nerves leap and her skin prickle. If he caught up with them . . .

She turned back, breathing in a shallow, rapid way, cold perspiration breaking out on her forehead. 'Can't you go any faster, Paolo? Surely this car must be faster than his! I thought it was a race-car! You were boasting that it could go up to a hundred and fifty without even rocking.'

'Not on public roads,' he muttered. 'But I'll do what I can—although in this mist, on this narrow road, I don't want to risk going much faster.'

He put his foot down and the Lamborghini surged forward. She watched the speed indicator swing wildly upwards and swallowed a knot of alarm. At any other time she would have been terrified to be in a car travelling at this speed but her fear of Stephen was more powerful than her fear of being killed. She threw another look backwards; the green bonnet was further away now but still there.

She turned to look at their speed and was aghast to see the needle on the indicator start to drop. She cried out in panic, 'Why are you slowing down again? He's still behind us! Don't slow down, go faster. We've got to get away from him!'

'I'm sorry, *cara*, but there's a narrow bridge up ahead—just room enough for two cars to pass, if they aren't too big. I'm not risking meeting another car head-on in the middle of it!'

The mist seemed much thicker, dense and smoky. She screwed her eyes up to peer into it but couldn't see anything at all.

'I don't see any bridge!'

'It's there—I know this road,' Paolo told her, and at that instant something loomed up in front of them.

Gabriella threw it one, stunned look—it seemed as big as a house, and inexplicable for a second in the drifting swirls of mist. Then she realised what it was, and she screamed, shrinking down in her seat.

'Paolo! Look out!'

The huge shape which had come out of nowhere was a container lorry, driving right over on their side of the road.

Paolo swore under his breath. He'd already had his foot on the brake but now he slammed the brakes full on and the Lamborghini went into a jerky slide, tyres screaming on the wet road while Paolo gripped the steering-wheel tightly, his knuckles turning white.

It all happened so fast yet Gabriella felt that it was all happening in slow motion. She sat there, rigid with terror, as they spun sideways across the road. Paolo was white-faced, with drops of sweat breaking out on his temples, his body flung forwards by the force of the car's braking, his face contorted with fear and intense concentration. The lorry driver had braked too, wrenching his wheel to get himself back on to his own side of the road, but his vehicle moved more slowly, thundering on along the road with the whole weight of it carrying it away from them.

The Lamborghini spun almost in a circle, wheels skidding, and finally came to a stop right up against a stone wall, facing the way they had come. Gabriella heard grinding metal, the car's paintwork being grazed all the way along one side. So did Paolo.

He was swearing. 'Holy Madonna... That's my bloody paintwork! It will cost a fortune to have it re-sprayed; it was perfect, not a scratch on it.'

He undid his seatbelt and threw open his door, scrambled out, then almost fell over as his knees seemed to give under him. He held on to the door, shaking violently. Out of the mist someone came running up to him—a big man, broad and burly, sallow-skinned, unshaven, black-haired, in blue dungarees and a baseball cap.

'*Signore*?' he panted in Italian. 'Are you OK? Are you hurt?'

Paolo groaned. 'I don't seem to be injured, but I'm not OK! My God, I thought that was my last hour!'

'It was the mist—I didn't realise how narrow the road was beyond the bridge. One minute there was nothing in front of me, the next minute there you were. I didn't have time to think; there was no warning.'

Paolo swung round on him, going red with rage. 'Oh, so you're the fool who was driving on my side of the road!'

'No, that's a lie, nothing of the kind! I was just a little over, maybe, but——'

'You nearly killed us, you stupid bastard. Look what you've done to my car—smashed it like a tin can. It will cost a fortune to put right.'

The other man took in the Lamborghini and his face lengthened as he assessed the cost of repairs to a car of that quality. His face reddened in sullen resentment and he glared at Paolo with bulging eyes.

'You were driving too fast, much too fast. I know what a car like this can do! You were driving as if you were on a race-track, in mist like this! No wonder I didn't see you coming; you were probably doing a hundred an hour. You just came at me out of the mist; I didn't have time to get out of your way.'

'Oh, so it's my fault now, is it?' Paolo was shaking with fury, his Italian gestures even more pronounced than usual. 'And it's a lie. I'd slowed right down to take the bridge, and I was on my own side of the road—it was you that was on the wrong side, and don't think you're wriggling out of that, because you're not. The accident was your fault; you aren't blaming me for it. You've already said that you couldn't see a thing because of the mist—and you didn't see me, so how are you going to get away with a claim that I was driving too fast?'

'I heard you!'

'Liar!'

'Who are you calling a liar? Just because you're driving a Lamborghini it doesn't give you the right to call me a liar!'

'I called you a liar because that's what you are!'

Gabriella had been so intent on their quarrel that she had forgotten Stephen for a second, then she caught the flash of headlights right ahead of them, and, glancing forward, saw the green Jaguar being parked into the side of the road close to Paolo's bumper. Then the driver's door opened and Stephen got out, his tall, lean figure sharply outlined in the pale mist.

The shock sent her into instant reaction. She was so terrified that she didn't stop to think. She fumbled with the handle of her door, opened it as far it as far as it would go and got out; she just had enough room to squeeze along the stone wall against which the Lamborghini rested.

Ahead, through the drifting mist, she briefly saw a gleam of light on dark water. That must be the lake, she realised; she could walk back towards her hotel along the lakeside.

She began to run towards the side-road which must lead down to the lake, keeping her head down, hoping that Stephen wouldn't see her. She could hear the fierce argument between Paolo and the lorry driver—they had no attention to spare for her or anybody else—and other cars were there now, slowing, stopping, beginning to sound their horns in protest at being brought to a standstill by the lorry in one direction and the Lamborghini in the other. The noise was deafening; her head ached and she couldn't think.

All Gabriella knew was that she had to get away. She got to the corner and found a narrow lane leading downwards, between small, crammed-together houses which she could barely see in the mist. She began to run flat out down towards the sound of lapping water.

The delicate cream leather high heels that she was wearing were not built for running, especially on slippery wet roads. She skidded several times and had to grab at a wall, but she kept running, her breathing thick and painful in her throat, until she almost hit a wooden railing.

Gabriella caught hold of it to stop herself and leaned there, panting, her chest heaving, listening for the sound of pursuing footsteps. Somewhere in the mist she heard the blare of car horns, raised angry voices, and then the louder wail of a police car coming, but she didn't hear anyone following her down to the lake. Stephen couldn't have seen her running away.

It was so silent down here; the mist deadened all sounds. She stood listening to the soft, hushed lap of water on the jetty which the wooden railings enclosed, the creak of the wooden platform she stood on, a gentle rippling where eddies ran close to the banks, and, further away, a faint quacking from some ducks.

She could see nothing of the other side of the lake; the mist had closed right in. She stared into it, shaking, cold and tense to the point of tears. The accident had been the last straw. She had had to get away.

Suddenly she stopped thinking about herself, realising just what she had done. Paolo. She had deserted Paolo when he was in trouble and needed her. She was his only witness, the only person who could back up his story about the lorry being on his side of the road as it came through the bridge.

She had run to him when she needed help and he'd been there for her. In fact, if it hadn't been for her he wouldn't have been driving this evening, in the mist, far too fast. *She* had urged him to drive faster. *She* had complained when he'd slowed down again.

And then she had run away—run out on him! She should go back. She ought to. She bit down into her lower lip, groaning with guilt and uncertainty. If she went back Stephen would be there...

If she didn't, though, Paolo might be in serious trouble. It would be his word against the lorry driver's.

She closed her eyes for a second, then lifted her head, squaring her shoulders. She had to face it. She had no other choice.

She began to walk back up the hill towards the road; from a distance, through the mist, she saw the police car's flashing light, saw the policeman himself, in a shiny, reflecting yellow mac, sorting out the tangle of traffic, beckoning on a line from one direction while holding back the cars from the other.

Gabriella stopped dead as she emerged on to the main road again. Paolo was standing by his Lamborghini talking to Stephen, who was a head taller, and looked tough and formidable, even though he was wearing one of his dark city suits under a dark overcoat. He was so much more muscular than Paolo. Stephen's shoulders were wider, his body leaner, harder; he managed to make Paolo look lightweight.

As she stood there, trembling, both men glanced round and saw her. She avoided Stephen's eye and looked pleadingly at Paolo; he at once moved towards her, but another police car arrived at that moment, and one of the officers in it came over to question him.

He looked at Gabriella. 'Wait there; this shouldn't take long.'

The policeman looked round at her, asked Paolo a question and got a nod.

Stephen walked towards her with the smooth lope of a predator, his eyes glittering, his face taut and deadly. Her nerves jumped and she began shaking.

Then Paolo called out to her, 'Gabriella, the officer wants to ask you some questions.'

With a gasp of relief, she hurried over to them eagerly—while she was answering the policeman's queries Stephen couldn't get at her. She felt his frustration tangibly even though she avoided catching his eye.

'You were the passenger in the Lamborghini?' the officer asked her in Italian and she nodded.

'Your name, please?'

She gave it and he shot her a sharp look. 'English?'

She explained, got her two passports out of her handbag in the car, showed them to him, told him where she was staying, and gave him her home address in London.

He asked her a series of questions about the accident and she told him that Paolo had slowed right down in anticipation of the bridge and that the lorry had been on their side of the road and going too fast.

'I wanted Paolo to drive faster, but he wouldn't; he's a very careful driver. We had no warning that the lorry was coming; we didn't see its headlights because the bridge obscured our view of the traffic coming from that direction, but suddenly there it was, right in front of us, and so big. It was like driving straight towards a wall. It all happened so fast, too; I still don't know how we avoided hitting him.'

She could see the lorry some way down the road—presumably the first policeman on the scene had dealt with the driver first, to clear the narrow road and make it possible for traffic to flow again. Cars moved past in both directions, skirting Paolo's car which was still parked right into the side of the road.

'Thank you, *signorina*,' said the policeman at last. He turned towards Paolo. 'Now, *signor*, have you got your papers for me?'

Paolo nodded, pulling out his driving licence and a clutch of other documents from the glove compartment of his car.

'Come over to my car; I'll have to use my radio to check these out on the computer,' the policeman said, taking them from him.

Paolo nodded, gave her a quick glance. 'Wait for me in the car—you must be getting cold.' He threw a look at Stephen, waiting a few feet away, and frowned. 'Don't worry,' he told her reassuringly. 'I don't think I'll be long. You'll be OK. If you need me, you only have to yell, remember. The officer and I will be within earshot all the time.'

She knew he was telling her obliquely that she need not be scared of Stephen while he and the police were there.

He walked away with the policeman; they both got into the front of the police car which was parked further up the road and Gabriella went to get into the driver's seat of the Lamborghini, only to find her way barred. She froze, not looking up, staring at the polished black gleam of his shoes.

'Please don't,' she whispered, her voice a mere thread of sound. 'Not now; I've been in a crash. I'm still in a state of shock. I know I'll have to talk to you—try to...explain...but not tonight, please, not tonight. I can't cope with you now.'

Stephen didn't answer. His fingers clamped round her arm, making her wince at the tension she felt in him. Panic leapt in her throat. God, he was so angry! She felt it pulsing and beating inside him.

He began to walk towards his own car, pulling her after him; she fought him, struggling, trying to hang on to the Lamborghini.

'I'll scream... The police are only a few feet away...' She threw a look towards the two parked police cars with their revolving lights making strange circles in the misty air, but nobody was looking towards her and Stephen—they were all too

busy. One policeman was still directing traffic.
Another had walked on through the bridge and was
slowing down traffic coming from the other direction. She saw his swinging yellow lamp as he
moved it, casting flashes of light across the inner
vault of the bridge. The policeman in the car with
Paolo was talking on his car phone; Paolo was too
intent on what was being said to spare a glance for
her.

Wildly she stammered, 'L-Let go of me, Stephen,
or I swear I'll scream the place down. I can't talk
to you tonight; I'll talk to you tomorrow; just let
me go now...'

'With him?' He laughed harshly, without
humour. 'Oh, no, Gabriella. I don't trust you. If
I agreed to wait until tomorrow you would vanish
overnight, with him.'

She was trembling violently. It was flaring out of
him again, that terrifying emotion; it was like facing
the heat and blast of an explosion. She felt her skin
wither and sear, her body shrink.

He pulled open the passenger door of his dark
green Jaguar. 'Get in.'

She was too scared to be able to scream, or even
struggle any more. The force of his emotion had
her in an inexorable grip. Her knees had almost
given way under her; she was boneless and limp as
he shoved her with a peremptory hand into the front
passenger seat of the car, and leant over her to do
up her seatbelt while she sat there numbly, her white
face rigid. The door slammed. He strode round to
get into the driver's seat and still she did not try to
move or call out for Paolo.

She was helpless, trapped in a time warp. It had all happened before; the past rushed back to engulf her.

This was exactly how she had felt on the night of the party—the night before what should have been her wedding-day. Stephen had shattered all her illusions about him when he'd taken her home from his sister Beatrice's party. His cool, controlled manner had cracked apart and underneath she had glimpsed for the first time the real man—the man he had hidden from her all those months; the man she had run from as if from the fires of hell.

She had never met Hugo before. He was Beatrice's eldest son, yet looked more like his uncle—he had inherited Stephen's dark colouring and height, which had originally come from Stephen's father, Gabriella had been told by Beatrice. It was a dominant gene which came out in all the males in that family, Beatrice had said, laughing.

'But skipped me, thank heavens! I prefer to look like my mother. Being blonde has been fun.'

'I've often wished that I were blonde,' Gabriella admitted enviously, but Beatrice looked at her and smiled, shaking her head.

'Darling, you don't need to be blonde. You're very feminine anyway—all that lovely long hair, your beautiful little face, and those gorgeous legs... Why on earth should you need to be a blonde? Don't you agree, Hugo?'

Her son gazed at Gabriella, his eyes gleaming with enjoyment. 'Absolutely! She's perfect just the way she is!'

She blushed slightly, conscious of Stephen listening without expression, his cold face set rigidly.

Hugo worked in New York in an international bank, although you would never have guessed his sedate job from his wild mood during the party. He had obviously come determined to have a good time or was he always like that—laughing, reckless, full of fun? She enjoyed talking to him, but she had to circulate, to meet as many people as possible, because she and Stephen were the guests of honour.

She spent most of the evening talking politely to strangers, most of them much older than she was: friends of the family, business colleagues of Stephen, or friends of Beatrice and her husband. She fought to hide her boredom, kept smiling until her teeth ached and her face felt like concrete; she thought that she had deceived those who did not know her, but when she met Stephen's penetrating eyes she was afraid that he'd realised how she really felt.

The younger people had taken over a large room, turned down the lights, and were dancing in the dark. She couldn't help being a little envious of them. She felt like dancing too. The sensual beat of the music wound into her head and made her body shiver. While Stephen was talking to an influential diplomat, Gabriella took her chance to slip away from a group of people discussing politics, and wandered over to look in at the dancers.

Huge suddenly rushed out of them, grabbed her by the waist and pulled her into the room.

'No, I must go back to Stephen,' she protested, but he just laughed and began dancing with her, both his arms around her, his cheek brushing against hers.

And you let him! she accused herself now. Without trying to stop him, without trying to get away, she had given in weakly, danced with him, her body moving against his with the beat of the music.

He wouldn't let me go! And I couldn't make a scene, could I? I didn't really know what to do so I let him have his own way.

Wasn't that what she always said? 'It isn't my fault. I didn't want it to happen; I didn't know what to do.'

The truth was that she had stood at the door watching the dancers, yearning to be one of them, to move to that deep, hot beat. She had felt it in her bones, in her blood, stirring deep inside her, sensuous and disturbing. She hadn't known exactly what was happening to her, only that she wanted...

Something she couldn't name, wouldn't name.

'Hey! You're good, really good!' Hugo said after a few minutes, looking down at her, his arms tightening round her waist, then he bent his head and kissed her.

It was a light-hearted kiss, warm and laughing, but a second later Stephen was there, pulling her away, his hand cruel on her arm, his face icy.

'Sorry to interrupt when you're having fun,' he bit out, his mouth moving in a cold smile which did not reach his eyes, 'but Sir Henry and his wife are leaving and want to say goodbye to you.'

He didn't even look at Hugo, and his nephew didn't argue. Stephen took her away and Gabriella's nerves were shot to hell for the rest of the evening.

Hadn't she known then that retribution would follow? Even if she hadn't guessed quite what to expect, only known that he was tense with rage— a white-hot rage which made her skin prickle with alarm.

She didn't stray from his side again. She avoided Hugo's eyes, and hardly said a word to anyone unless they spoke to her directly and she had to answer them.

Stephen drove her home. She was relieved to realise that he was stone-cold sober. Apart from a glass or two of champagne earlier at supper, he hadn't touched any of the drink which had flowed so freely. She had never seen him drink too much, actually.

He had told her once that when he was young he had gone through a phase of drinking too much and had realised that it was a waste of life. It meant that you slept away half the morning and had a headache for hours next day; it made it hard to do your job. He had realised that he didn't enjoy anything about drinking too much. Now he simply enjoyed a glass or two of very good wine with a meal, and maybe a brandy afterwards, but he never went beyond that.

He insisted on walking her to her front door, as he always did, because London was no longer a safe city, he said. Were there any safe cities anywhere in the world today? She had to admit that she was relieved that he always saw her into her flat, put on the lights for her and looked into each room before saying goodnight and going.

He never stayed, or tried to—it had surprised her at first. She had waited for it to happen, but it never did. He had never once tried to get her into bed, never asked if he might stay the night. That was one reason why she had let herself relax and trust him, why she had drifted into that engagement, why she had so nearly married him.

That night, though, he did not go with a quiet kiss; he closed the door behind them, and the sound made her stiffen and look at him nervously.

He took off his evening coat and threw it on a chair, staring at her fixedly.

Trembling, she began to back, but not fast enough. He caught hold of her shoulders and pulled her back towards him.

His name was stifled in her throat; she was too alarmed by the way he was looking at her to be able even to scream. She shook her head, though, swallowing, trying to break away while she stared back at him.

His stare was fixed on her mouth; she felt her lips burning as if he were already kissing them. He jerked her off balance until their bodies touched; his body seemed to vibrate against her and she wanted to scream.

One of his hands ran down her body, not simply touching it but possessing it. It was a slow, lingering exploration that made her blood flow hotly everywhere he touched—her throat, her shoulders, her breasts, her thighs and inwards. That was when she began to shake from head to foot, when she grew as white as a ghost.

The intimacy was a devastating shock; she drew a long, appalled breath, and Stephen bent his head at that instant, his tongue-tip touching her mouth, tracing the curve of it, sliding between her parted lips. For a second the kiss was so delicate and cool but then it changed, as if someone had thrown a match on to spilt oil. Passion flared in him; he kissed her with such heat and demand that he forced her head backwards, bent her body and fitted his own to it, his chest against her breasts, one of his legs pushing hers apart and moving between them.

She was almost fainting by then. She couldn't breathe with his mouth crushing and bruising hers. She swayed, almost fell, and Stephen pushed her back on to a couch and came down on top of her, the weight of his body holding her captive.

She didn't want to remember the next few minutes; they were illuminated in flashes in her memory—his hand peeling down the bodice of her dress, her bra coming off, his fingers cool on her naked breast, his mouth on her neck, hot and hungry, his mouth sliding down between her breasts, moving on her soft, pale skin, finding her nipples, closing around them and sucking them into his mouth, as if he were her baby.

She was dazed by what was happening, eyes shut tight as if that would make it all stop, as if it would make it less real, her bare skin quivering at the intrusion as his hand slid between her thighs, caressing, arousing, making her burn where he touched, stabbing desire and fear into her body like knives into living flesh.

Tears filled her eyes, trickled into her lashes. She tried to blink them away—could he feel it? Had their salty wetness touched his skin? Or had her tense shivers of fear reached him?

At least—at last—he stopped abruptly, said goodnight, and went. But she realised with terror and sick dismay that that was only the beginning. Once they were married he would not stop, he would not leave; he would stay and go on...

I can't! she thought desperately. I just can't bear it. Why did I ever think I could?

Yet the very thought of trying to tell him, to explain, sent those waves of panic through her. She had left it too late. In a few hours she would be his wife and the real nightmare would begin.

So she had run, knowing all the time that Stephen would be behind her, would catch up with her sooner or later.

She had hoped that she would have time to calm down to get the courage to talk to him, to explain...

Now she slid a sideways look at his hard face as he started the engine and began to drive away. How could she ever talk to him when he looked like that? She was totally oblivious of Paolo getting out of the police car, running, calling her name.

She was oblivious of everything except the naked fear of knowing that time had run out for her— she had to face Stephen's rage now, ready or not.

CHAPTER FOUR

'WHAT the hell have you done to your hair?'
Stephen grated, making her jump.

Gabriella swallowed, and muttered, 'I had it cut
yesterday.'

'Why did you do it? Long hair suited you; this
doesn't.'

'I like it,' she said defiantly. She wasn't surprised
to hear that he didn't—Paolo hadn't liked it either.
What was it about long hair on a woman that most
men liked so much? Was it because they enjoyed
touching it, playing with it, the sensual experience
of feeling it slide through their fingers?

Was that why she had had her hair cut? Why *had*
she felt that she must do it? She had grown her hair
for years. Why, suddenly, had she felt that it had
to come off? The question made her uncomfortable. She didn't try to work out the answer.
She didn't want to think about it.

'Where are you taking me?' she whispered, but
he didn't answer, his gaze fixed on the road and his
profile stony. They were driving along the main lake
road, not too fast because of the mist and the
narrow winding of the road. Where could they be
going? Surely to heaven he didn't intend to drive
all the way back through Italy and France and
across to England? 'Paolo will tell the police...'
she began, and he gave a short laugh.

'What?' he bit out. 'That your fiancé has driven off with you?'

She fell silent. Of course Paolo wouldn't say anything to the police, and Stephen was right—what could he say, anyway?

'They would only be interested if I were a stranger,' Stephen added drily and her face tightened even further. A stranger... Wasn't that what he was, though? She had known him for months, but she knew she had barely scraped the surface of the man; they had never talked honestly, with real intimacy; they had never told each other the deep, hidden things about themselves, what they really felt, really thought. They were strangers to each other; he knew as little about her as she did about him.

Stephen shot a look sideways at her, and she felt his tension. 'What are you thinking? That that's what I am—a stranger?'

Gabriella was startled by that—he had read her mind! Paolo often did, but then she and Paolo had grown up together.

'That's what you were thinking, isn't it?' Stephen insisted curtly. 'I read it in your face. You have a give-away face, you know; every feeling you have shows on it. I saw your eyes when I said if I were a stranger, and it was obvious what you were thinking. It's true too—we are almost strangers to each other. It was only when you ran away that I realised how little I knew about you. I had no idea where you might have run off to—and when I asked Lara where you might go she couldn't come up with anywhere either.

'Oh, we both thought of Brindisi, but my people drew a blank there—you weren't staying at any of the hotels, or with any of your distant relatives. Lara couldn't tell me anything about any of your friends; neither could your friends Jilly and Petra. They seemed to me to know very little about you too—not one of them knew anything much about Paolo, for instance. My detectives had to track him down from the Rome address on the wedding-guest list.'

'You hired detectives to look for me?' It was only what she had guessed he might do but she still felt a jolt of shock at the thought of strangers prying into her life, going around asking questions about her, arousing curiosity and gossip.

'I could hardly try to trace you myself—it would have taken me forever to make all the phone calls. We had to check every one of your personal friends, which was when I realised how few really close friends you have. It didn't take long.'

She felt an ache of sadness. No, there were not many people close to her—almost none, really, except Lara and the couple of friends whom she had got to know well in the cordon bleu training-school in London where she had perfected her trade: Jilly, who was working in one of the royal households, a cool ice-blonde with impeccable taste and perfect manners, whose father ran a training stable which frequently trained racehorses for members of the royal family; and Petra, half Russian and explosive in temperament, with flashing dark eyes and spiky black hair, who had gone abroad to work for a chain of exclusive hotels and was currently working in Paris.

Stephen had met them several times—Jilly and Petra were to have been her bridesmaids; they had been at the wedding rehearsal and the party afterwards. She remembered how impressed they had been by Stephen. Jilly hadn't said much—she never did; super-cool Jilly kept her feelings and her thoughts to herself, but Petra had been ecstatic and envious.

'Darling, he's gorgeous. How did you meet him? Has he got a twin brother? I want a guy just like him. Is he very rich?'

'I believe so,' Gabriella had said, laughing because Petra always made her laugh; she had a way of saying things that was irresistibly funny even when she wasn't making jokes.

'Oh, just your luck! Sexy and rich! Whenever I meet a man with enough money he's usually bald, fat and sixty.'

'Gold-digger,' Jilly had said.

Very serious, Petra had shaken her head. 'No, darling, just practical! A girl has to think of her future. Who wants to marry a poor man?'

'If you loved one, would you marry him?' Gabriella had asked and Petra had looked sideways at her, black eyes glinting.

'Don't make my blood run cold! I just try to steer clear of poor men, that's all, especially attractive ones!'

Jilly and Gabriella had looked at each other and laughed, not taking her too seriously. Petra had been falling in and out of love ever since they'd met her, and none of the men had been rich.

Gabriella was fond of both her friends, but she had never confided in them; the friendship was on a very superficial level. That was why she hadn't felt up to ringing them to tell them the wedding was off; she had left it to Lara to warn them, and she felt guilty about that, yet she hadn't been able to face the questions they were bound to ask.

'Did you talk to Jilly and Petra yourself?' she whispered.

'Yes. They seemed genuinely taken aback. You hadn't talked to them, had you? They couldn't— or wouldn't—tell me anything I didn't already know. I asked them about Paolo and drew a blank there too. They claimed they'd never heard of him.'

'I don't suppose they have. He has only been to England once—I hadn't even left school then. I didn't know them then and I doubt if I've ever mentioned him to them.'

Stephen was silent, staring out into the veils of mist which kept blowing across the road. Gabriella suddenly realised that the car had slowed right down, was crawling along. If he drove much slower she would be able to open her door and jump out, she thought, her muscles tensing at the idea. What if she got hurt when she fell, though? And if she landed without injury, what would she do then? Run away in a strange town in damp lake mist? Where to?

She wasn't wearing a coat, just a thin silk dress, and impractical high heels, and a fine drizzle was falling in the mist. She would be soaked within minutes. And even if she did run, where would she go? Wasn't that why she had gone back to the scene of the accident a short time ago? Because she had nowhere to run to anyway?

No, that wasn't true! She had gone back because she hadn't been able to desert Paolo when he'd needed her to be a witness for him; it had been selfish and cowardly to run out on him when he was in trouble. Paolo would never have done that to her.

Her face quivered. OK, maybe that was one reason why she had gone back—but even if Paolo hadn't needed her, where could she have gone? To the hotel? Or to the villa where Paolo was staying? Stephen would have found her again immediately. A shudder went through her. She couldn't hide from him. She had known that from the minute she had begun to run. She had sensed him on her trail, had been afraid he would find her, wherever she went.

She knew that much about him. He was relentless, tenacious, insistent—a man who wouldn't give up anything without a fight.

He suddenly wrenched the wheel and the car slewed across the road, making her start violently, her nerves leaping. For a second she thought there was going to be another accident, but there was no other car in sight.

'Where are we going?' she broke out, trembling.

Ahead of them through the mist she just saw high, intricate wrought-iron gates—they had turned off the road on to a driveway. Stephen held something in his hand, pointed it, and the gates began to swing open as they drove towards them.

'Is this a hotel?'

Stephen still didn't answer. They were through the gates, which closed again behind them. She was sitting forward, tensely trying to see through the mist. Lights shone somewhere in the distance. She prayed that it was a hotel—if he had brought her somewhere so public then she was safe; she needn't be afraid what he might do.

Faintly she glimpsed high stone walls rising on the right-hand side of the car. On top of the walls was some sort of wiring—were they electrified?

Following her gaze, Stephen said quietly, 'Yes, the whole perimeter of the grounds is electrified. Nobody gets in, nobody gets out.'

'Is it a hotel?' she repeated, her hands twisting in her lap. Please, please, let it be a hotel, she begged silently.

'No, it's a private villa,' he said drily, watching her hands clench together. 'It belongs to a friend who's in Florida—she's lent it to me for a few days.'

'She?' She was startled into repeating the word, her blue eyes lifting to his face.

'The widow of an old friend,' he expanded, his gaze narrowed and searching. 'Kay has put the villa on the market; she lived here with her husband until he had a heart attack and died within minutes. She's an American, and without George she was lonely here; she wanted to go home, so she bought a villa in Florida, one of my developments. Her place is set in a large garden, with a big swimming-pool, but it is much easier to run than this villa, which needs a whole team of servants.'

Gabriella was staring at the lighted windows of the villa as they slowly pulled up in front of a double flight of stone steps leading up to the entrance. The mist made it impossible to see much of the building, except that it was of a classical design, and probably at least early nineteenth century, with rows of flat windows on either side of the columned entrance.

She glimpsed palest creamy yellow paint on the stucco walls, and white roses growing entwined along the balustrade of the steps, ghost-like and shimmering, their fragrance still hanging in the air even though the sun had sunk behind the mountains long ago.

'Is there anyone else here?' she asked nervously as Stephen turned off the engine.

'A skeleton staff of servants.' He opened his door and got out, and walked round to open her door.

She didn't move, hunched and tense in her seat.

'We can't talk sitting in the car,' Stephen coldly pointed out.

'Why not?' she whispered, and heard his impatient movement.

'Oh, for God's sake—what are you afraid of? That I may turn violent? I give you my word I won't. You walked out on our wedding on the very day itself without doing me the courtesy of explaining to my face why you felt you couldn't go through with it. I think I'm owed that explanation, Gabriella. Don't you?'

A sigh went through her. How could she deny it? Yet how could she bear to tell him anything that would explain?

He reached into the car and hooked an arm around her waist. 'Come on, Gabriella. Get out.'

The feel of his warm hand right under her breast made a wild tremor run through her whole body.

'OK!' she broke out hoarsely, trying not to betray herself by trembling. 'OK, I'll get out. Let go of me! I don't need any help.'

He released her without comment, holding the door open as she swung her legs sideways, put her feet down on the gravelled drive, got out and stood up, the top of her head coming somewhere around his chin, reminding her of how much taller he was, and how much more powerful. If he chose to exert his male strength she would have no chance whatever in fighting him, but her fear of him was not based on his physical superiority.

She wasn't afraid that Stephen might hurt her, not deliberately, not knowingly. He simply wasn't the type to hit a woman, perhaps because he was such a big man and so aware of his own strength. It was men who were aware of their weakness, men who had an inferiority complex, who wanted to hurt women, to take their revenge for their own failures.

He put a hand under her elbow to guide her, but his touch was light and cool.

'This way,' he murmured, steering her to the foot of one side of the dual staircase.

She shot a look at the top of it and realised that the front door, which had been closed, now stood open; a wide band of yellow light from within spilt out on to the stone steps. Gabriella began to climb, with Stephen keeping step with her.

They had almost reached the top when she became conscious of a man standing above, watching them. He was wearing a black jacket and trousers and a green and yellow striped waistcoat over a white, ruffled shirt. It was clearly some sort of uniform—was this one of the servants?

When they reached the top of the steps he bowed from the waist, saying something in Italian; she didn't catch the words but Stephen answered in Italian. She had known that he spoke several languages, including Italian, but he had only once used her childhood language to her, when he had first heard that she had grown up in Brindisi. Usually they spoke to each other in English and it seemed strange to hear him casually speaking Italian now.

'This is Adriano,' he told her. 'He is in charge of the house while Signora Adams is not here. Adriano, this is my fiancée, Signorina Brooks.'

Adriano bowed again. He had sleek black hair which was receding slightly at the temples and showing faint streaks of silver here and there. His thin, sallow face was very brown and wrinkled; he could have been any age from forty to sixty, but she had a suspicion that he was much older than he looked.

'Supper is laid, as you ordered, in the small supper-room,' he said, and this time his Italian was clear; she understood every word. He spoke with the local accent, she realised then. He must have been born in this region of Italy, which explained why she hadn't understood him at first—it had taken time for her ear to become tuned to his accent.

What he had said sank in slowly, though. Supper? Had Stephen been so sure that he would be bringing her back here?

'May I show the *signorina* to a room, to wash her hands before supper?' Adriano asked, and Stephen glanced at her, silently raising his brows in query.

'Yes, please,' she said, needing a few minutes alone to pull herself together.

Adriano waved his hand at the open front door. '*Per favore, signorina.*'

He stood back and she slowly walked into the villa, her eyes skating hurriedly around the large hall in which she found herself; it took her breath away as she saw the towering white columns rising up to support a white and gold ceiling lit with glittering chandeliers.

The marble floor was partly covered by a blue and gold carpet—squares of blue set with a formal spray of gold flowers, each square surrounded by a band of classical gold design. The blue was picked up again in floor-length blue velvet curtains, both blue and gold repeated in the nineteenth-century hall chairs arranged at intervals along the length of the hall—gilded wood, blue satin brocade seats.

Halfway along the hall a flight of stairs rose up to the first floor, carpeted with the same design.

Adriano bowed her towards them. 'This way, *per favore, signorina.*'

Stephen said quietly, 'Don't take too long, will you?' and walked away down the hall; she saw him vanish through an open door.

The first floor held rows of doors; Adriano showed her to one of them and waved her inside the room. It was a luxuriously furnished bedroom—rose-pink and cream, with a four-poster bed, with carved posts at each corner and a pink velvet canopy above it, a pink and cream carpet, pale cream-painted walls, an ornately gilt-framed mirror, on each side of which were gold-painted candle-holders.

Adriano trod softly across the carpet, opened a door on the far side of the room and gestured politely. 'The bathroom, *signorina*. Would you like me to wait for you——?'

'I'll find my own way back downstairs,' she interrupted, and he bowed again.

'Of course. Excuse me, *signorina*.'

He went out, closing the door behind him, and Gabriella felt the terrible tension leak out of her. She was alone, for a moment or two. She walked into the bathroom and closed the door, locked it and stared blankly around the room.

It was furnished in the Victorian style. It looked original, not reproduction; it had that solid feel to it, the walls fully tiled in white and black in a diamond pattern, the bath huge, wide and deep enough almost to drown in, sheathed in a case of heavy mahogany with a high polish, the inside white enamel, with elaborate gold taps, above which, on the wall, was coiled a very old-fashioned hand-held shower.

Gabriella sat down on the cork-topped bathroom stool. In the mirror on one wall she saw her pale face, her eyes huge, pupils enormous, her black lashes damp and sticking together as if she had been crying. But she hadn't, had she?

Maybe her lashes were damp from the mist she had run through down to the lake? She brushed a hand across them, angry with herself. She had to get herself under control. She had to explain to Stephen, to tell him why she had walked out on their wedding-day, and it was going to be one of the hardest things she had ever had to do in her life.

Her eyes met their reflection again, and there was anguish in them. Not the hardest, of course.

She wouldn't think about that now. She needed all her courage to face Stephen; she couldn't use it up in thinking about the past.

She got up, shivering, used the lavatory, and washed her hands and face in the solid white enamelled basin, grateful for the touch of cool water on her skin. She particularly splashed water on her eyes for some time; after that she felt a little better.

She combed her hair back into shape, renewed her make-up, inspected herself from head to foot—she looked normal enough. How was it possible to look so ordinary when what was happening inside you was cataclysmic?

Well, she couldn't stay in here forever. Sighing, she unlocked the door and went back down the stairs. Adriano was waiting at the foot of them; he gave her one of his bows, plus a polite smile—she detected no touch of curiosity in his eyes. But then as he didn't work for Stephen he had no idea what this was all about; why should he be curious?

'Please follow me, *signorina*,' he murmured in his local Italian, and she obeyed, her legs unsteady as she walked along the wide strip of blue and gold carpet, staring at paintings on the wall, gold-framed canvases which she thought had an eighteenth-century look—large, bosomy women in satin and sallow-skinned men in dark suits staring out with arrogant self-confidence, behind them Italianate backgrounds—hills and trees and ruined castles.

'Are those family portraits?' she asked Adriano, who glanced up at them indifferently.

'They have always hung there, *signorina*; they are portraits of the ancestors of the man who built the villa, an Italian manufacturer from Milan, but he had no children so the portraits were sold with the villa when he died. Some people say the portraits weren't even genuine—he had had them painted to invent a family background for himself. He was a self-made man, from the back streets of Milan. He had made a fortune and dreamt of starting a dynasty. When his first wife, whom he blamed for being barren, died, he hurriedly married a second wife, almost half his age, but she had no children either, so it must have been him who couldn't father a child.'

'How sad.'

Adriano shrugged and threw open a door, bowing her through it. She stopped on the threshold, staring at a small table in the centre of the shadowy room, at the soft gleam of candlelight on silver and crystal, a bottle of wine in a silver wine-cooler, at Stephen standing by a massive stone fireplace, one polished shoe on a brass hearth-surround, watching a log fire sending flames leaping up the blackened chimney. He turned to look towards her, but it was to Adriano that he spoke.

'I'll ring if I need you. Thank you.'

Adriano bowed, and silently closed the door.

'Don't just stand there, Gabriella; come and sit down,' Stephen added drily, moving away from the fireplace to the table. He pulled back a chair for her and she sank on to it, glad to sit down because her knees were shaking. Stephen took her white damask napkin and flicked it open, laying it across her knees.

In front of her stood a large silver dish filled with crushed ice not yet beginning to melt, into which had been pushed down a crystal bowl containing half a melon, hollowed out and then refilled with prawns and strawberries and small balls of yellowy-greeny melon.

'A glass of white wine?' Stephen had picked up the bottle from the wine-cooler and was holding it over one of the glasses arrayed in front of her.

'Thank you.' She watched the clear golden wine fall in a stream into her glass. She almost never drank, but suddenly she needed something to dull her senses, an anodyne, to make it easier for her to talk to him and give him the answers he was going to insist on. She picked up the glass and sipped; the wine was crisp and dry on her tongue.

It gave her the courage to blurt out, 'Paolo is going to be worried. I should get in touch with him to tell him where I am and——'

'I rang the villa where he's staying and left a message,' Stephen said curtly. 'Forget about him for the moment—eat your melon.'

She took a spoonful of fruit; it was very chilled. She ate it slowly, staring as if hypnotised at the double-branched candelabra in the centre of the table; the candles burnt with a flickering light.

'Is this too cold for you?' asked Stephen, and she shook her head and drank some more wine.

'How did you get here?' he asked and she gave him a startled look.

'I drove.'

'All the way from the Channel?' His black brows rose in sardonic disbelief. 'Why didn't you take the TGV to Nice and drive on from there? It would have halved the time you took, and made it a much less exhausting trip. You could have slept overnight in a cabin, had breakfast while they got your car off the train and felt quite fresh for the rest of the journey.'

'Is that what you did?'

'Of course. I did consider flying, but I dislike hired cars.'

They had both finished their melon so he got up and removed the silver dishes, placing them on a trolley waiting discreetly on the other side of the room. He brought back from it two plates which held chicken masked in a smooth, cold, creamy sauce. After that he produced a large bowl of mixed salad and a bowl of hot new potatoes decorated with sprigs of mint and tossed in butter.

'Can I help you to salad and potatoes?'

'I'll do it, thank you—can I give you some?' she said, picking up the salad servers.

'A little of each, thank you.' He refilled her glass while she was piling some salad and several small golden potatoes on to his plate. 'That's perfect, thanks,' he said.

It was all so polite and remote, as if they had never met before. Gabriella wanted to scream. What was he waiting for? When was he going to start the inquisition? She knew now how it felt to be stretched on the rack; she was in agony before he had even asked a single question.

He shifted in his chair and she started, her nervous gaze flying to his face. His brows met; he looked at her angrily.

'Stop it!'

'What?' she whispered, white-lipped.

'Jumping every time I so much as breathe! What on earth do you think I'm going to do to you?'

She looked down at the food on her plate, swallowing convulsively on a wave of sickness.

'I... Nothing; of course I don't... I...' Her stammering died away and was succeeded by silence.

Stephen watched her. 'Tell me about Paolo.'

It was going to begin now. She took a breath to steady her voice. 'He's a painter, a set-designer for TV and the theatre. He lived next door to me when I was a child, in Brindisi. His mother was my mother's best friend, until she died...my mother, I mean...and we left, my father and I, for England.'

'But you kept in touch with Paolo?'

'We wrote and exchanged Christmas cards.'

'He's older than you, obviously.'

'Yes. By four years.'

'Have you seen him again since your mother died and your father took you back to England?'

The questions came tersely, in a cool, clipped voice; she answered them more slowly, huskily.

'Yes, I told you—he came to England while I was in my last year at school.'

'How long did he stay?'

'Only two weeks.'

'How old were you?'

'Seventeen.'

Stephen drank some more wine, his frowning stare fixed on the candle-flame; she risked a glance at him and saw the flame reflected in his eyes, making them glitter and shine with fire. Gabriella shivered. His gaze flicked to her face then and she hurriedly looked away, a pulse beating in her neck.

'You're in love with him,' Stephen curtly accused, and she stiffened, shaken.

'No! Of course not. He's my friend, that's all.'

His eyes bored into her. 'Yet when you ran away from me it was to him!'

She answered before she thought how to choose her words. 'Because I trust him!'

Stephen went rigid, turned white then dark red. 'What have I ever done to you to make you think you can't trust me?' His voice was bitter and stung like a whip.

She was frozen, her eyes wide and terrified, filled with shifting emotions; Stephen stared into them, his mouth hardening.

'This is about what happened after my sister's party, isn't it?' he said harshly, and her eyes answered for her. His frown deepened, his voice roughened, hurrying out the questions as if his patience had run out. 'You're going to have to tell me sooner or later, Gabriella. Is it just me who turns you off—or are you scared of sex? Did something happen to you? Someone hurt you some time? Tell me about it, for God's sake; don't just sit there staring, like a rabbit in a snare. You're not making a sound but I can almost hear you screaming. My God, Gabriella, I'm not a monster—do you think I want to feel you shrinking and trying not to faint every time I touch you?'

CHAPTER FIVE

'I'M SORRY,' Gabriella whispered, filled with guilt at what she had done to him. She had never meant to hurt or harm him. She hadn't thought he would care so much. After all, he had never once said that he loved her. Stephen's proposal had been more like a business proposition—a suggestion for a merger, practical, down-to-earth, full of common sense. He had more or less said it would suit them both, give them both what they wanted—him a settled home life with children, her stability, a family again.

All the same, she should have remembered that he was human. He might be a man with a powerful drive—in fact she had never met anyone with such energy and fixed determination—but he was still human; he was not a machine or a robot. He needed that fierce self-confidence of his to keep him ahead. Anything that undermined his confidence would damage his image of himself, and interfere with his ability to work. Gabriella didn't know much about men, but one thing she had been taught long ago, and which was indelibly printed on her mind, was that however strong a man seemed on the outside he could be destroyed by his own feelings; he could not bear rejection or humiliation.

She looked at Stephen with blue eyes clouding with tears that almost blinded her. 'It—it isn't you,' she stammered. 'It's nothing to do with you... Oh,

it's such a mess, and it's all my fault. I'm sorry; I
never meant this to happen...'

She pushed her chair back and blundered across
the room, only to collide with a small table on which
stood a silk-shaded lamp with a finely embossed
glass base. The table crashed over, and with a noise
like an explosion the glass base of the lamp shattered into dozens of glittering pieces.

Gabriella stood stock-still, staring down at them,
horrified. It was somehow the last straw, that
stupid, pointless destruction. Was that all she could
ever do—hurt people, wreck things, destroy? 'Oh,
no, your beautiful lamp... I'm sorry, I'm sorry,'
she groaned, getting down on her hands and knees,
and began frantically trying to pick up the pieces.

The shards of glass were dagger-sharp but she
was so distraught that she didn't even feel it when
she cut herself, or notice the blood welling out of
her skin.

'What the hell do you think you're doing?'
Stephen said fiercely from above her a moment
later, grabbing her by the shoulders and hauling
her to her feet. 'Leave it! I'll get Adriano to pick
it up!' Then he took hold of her wrist, lifted her
hand, and broke out angrily, 'You've cut your hand
open—look at it!'

She looked at the bright red blood seeping
through her skin and swayed, paper-white.

He made a rough, angry sound in his throat—a
growl of rage—then suddenly she found herself
being lifted off the ground, his arm around her
waist, another hand under her knees. Alarmed, she
clutched at him with the hand that wasn't injured,

fingers closing on his shirt; she gave a frightened glance upwards, into eyes that glittered like the dagger-points of glass on which she had impaled herself.

'What are you doing?'

'That hand needs medical attention,' he bit out, still sounding very angry, 'and you looked as if you were about to faint.'

'No... I... I'll be fine... Put me down, please...'

He ignored that, strode across the room with her, shifted her weight to free one hand so as to open the door and then paused as he came face to face with Adriano, who looked at them impassively, as if not surprised to see Stephen carrying her.

Had he been listening at the door? Gabriella dazedly wondered. She was feeling very odd, light-headed. Maybe Stephen was right; maybe she was a little faint.

'Is there a first-aid box anywhere?' Stephen coolly asked Adriano, without putting her down. 'There has been an accident—one of the lamps has been broken, I'm afraid—and the *signorina* has cut her hand on a piece of glass.'

Adriano's glance went to her injured hand hanging down beside her, then he looked past them into the room to assess the damage. He didn't comment, but merely said, 'I will bring you the first-aid box, *signor.*'

'I'm taking the *signorina* upstairs. She must have the hand washed before I dress it—there could be pieces of glass embedded in the skin; I may have to use tweezers to get them out, and a magnifying glass to make sure I don't leave any tiny fragments behind.'

'Perhaps I should try to get hold of a doctor, *signor*?'

'First I'll see what I can do. It may be necessary to call a doctor if I can't get all the glass out.' Stephen shot a look over his shoulder at the table laid with their food. 'Oh, and when you've brought me the first-aid box clear all that food away, Adriano—we won't be eating any more. You can make some strong coffee later, when the *signorina* is feeling better.'

He walked away along the hall. Aware of Adriano watching them, Gabriella couldn't struggle or try to get down. She waited until the other man vanished from sight. Her head was near Stephen's chest; she could hear his heart beating, a deep, resonant echo of her own, hear his thickened breathing, feel the warmth of his body under his shirt. He was too close; she was too aware of him. She had to get away, but she couldn't embarrass him with the other man staring at them—Stephen would hate it if she did. She had humiliated him enough.

I'm a disaster, she thought miserably, I do nothing but smash things, hurt people, make a mess of my own life and everyone else's. Oh, God, I wish I were dead.

And then she felt a strange, angry surge inside her, a feeling she had had before, had forced down out of sight many times, because she knew she had no right to feel rage or resentment—she was the one who was guilty; she was the one to blame. The feeling was stronger this time; she couldn't push it down, deny it—the rage was making her head pound, her skin burn.

As Stephen reached the foot of the stairs she burst out, 'Put me down! I can walk; I've only cut my hand; I'm not a cripple!'

He looked down at her, frowning grimly. Her face had flushed, turned dark red; her eyes were feverish with anger.

'Put me down!' she repeated hoarsely, and that time he obeyed, lowering her until her feet touched the ground. But his stare darkened, fixed on her face. Stephen was angry too. Rage flashed between them like summer lighting across meadows. His hands clenched at his sides; his skin ran with dark colour.

Gabriella was frightened for a second, then she lifted her chin in a gesture of defiance. 'Now please get me a taxi; I want to go back to my hotel.'

His mouth barely parted to bite out his answer. 'Not until I've dressed that hand.'

'I'll have it done at the hotel!'

'You'll have it done here,' Stephen said brusquely. 'Upstairs, in a bathroom—it must be washed and any glass fragments taken out before it is bandaged.'

She opened her mouth and he put his hand over it.

'Don't argue, Gabriella! Either you let me do your hand or we call a doctor. Which is it to be?'

She raged helplessly, her eyes seething over that muzzling hand. She didn't want a doctor; he would ask questions, be curious. No, she had no choice, had she?

'Very well,' she accepted, with resignation. 'You do it—but when you've finished I want that taxi, please! I am going back to my hotel.'

She began to climb the stairs, wishing that her legs wouldn't tremble so much under her. Stephen stayed a stair behind her and once, when she almost missed her step, she felt him put out a hand to catch her. She stiffened and hurried on upwards.

At the landing he caught up with her and said curtly, gesturing to the room she had used earlier, 'We'll use the bathroom in there.'

Wordlessly, she walked into the bedroom and through it to the bathroom. Stephen pulled a cork-topped stool out for her to sit on beside the basin. He held her hand under lukewarm, running water to wash away the blood, then gently dabbed the site of the wound dry with some cotton wool from a large glass jar.

Adriano arrived a moment later with a large first-aid box with a big red cross on the lid. He held a magnifying glass and a pair of tweezers.

'If there anything else I can do, *signor*?' he asked, lingering, staring at Gabriella's palm.

Stephen shook his head. 'No, thanks, Adriano— except make that coffee. We'll want it in about fifteen minutes.'

When Adriano had gone Stephen spread her hand out on the edge of the basin and stared at the palm through the magnifying glass, frowning.

'Keep absolutely still! This may hurt a little, but try not to jerk your hand away.'

She shut her eyes, tensing; the fear of pain was worse than pain itself, she thought wryly. She felt the cold, metallic touch of the tweezers and a faint stabbing as Stephen pulled a piece of glass out of the wound. She held herself still, not making a sound. He extracted several other fragments.

'The tweezers are too clumsy; I'm going to have to use a needle,' he said a moment later. 'You're being very good. I'm sorry if I'm hurting, and it may hurt even more when I use the needle, but I'll be as careful as I can.'

He sterilised the needle by putting the point of it into disinfectant for some moments. Gabriella opened her eyes to look at her palm; the blood was still welling up slightly but it wasn't bleeding as much as it had been.

'Ready?' Stephen asked gently, taking the needle out of the disinfectant.

She nodded, shutting her eyes again. He was quite right—the needle did hurt more; she felt the fine point of it probing her torn and tender flesh and had to bite down on her inner lip to stop herself crying out. It was a terrible relief when he finished, and washed her hand again under the tap. He took a final look at it through the magnifying glass.

'I think I've got it all out,' he said quietly. 'But there may be an odd tiny piece I can't see; don't you think you ought to go to a hospital casualty department to have the hand X-rayed, to make quite sure?'

'No, I'll be OK.'

'Why are you so obstinate?' he muttered, then carefully cleaned her wound again with a mixture of disinfectant and water before drying it and bandaging it.

Now that he had finished Gabriella was released from her tension; she relaxed, trembling, and Stephen gave her a sharp look.

'You aren't going to faint, are you? You're very pale.' His arm went round her, lifting her before she knew what he meant to do; he carried her out to the bedroom and laid her on the bed, then turned away to pick up the phone.

She was too shaken to protest or try to sit up again. She was incredibly tired; she shut her eyes and lay still, listening to Stephen's deep, curt voice.

'Adriano, is the coffee ready? Good, then bring it up here, please.'

He put the phone down; she felt him watching her but he didn't say anything, or come any closer. He began to walk around the room; she didn't risk a look at him; she just heard him, felt him—walking across the room and back, over and over again, with a soft pacing that made her want to scream. It was like the restless, impatient lope of an animal in a cage longing to get out.

Adriano came a moment later, carrying a tray which he placed on a table near the window. She heard the rattle of the cups, the chink of a spoon.

'Thank you. I'll pour it, Adriano,' Stephen said.

'*Sì, signor*,' the Italian said, and walked out again quietly, closing the door behind him.

Panic fluttered in Gabriella's throat as it dawned on her that she was alone in a bedroom with Stephen. She heard the chink of the coffee-pot on a cup. He came over to the bed a moment later.

'Sit up and drink your coffee.'

Shakily she obeyed, resenting the terse voice. Did he have to keep talking to her as if she were a criminal? She put out her uninjured hand to take the cup and saucer, then frowned, looking at the creamy white coffee he had poured her.

'Oh... I wanted it black. I never take cream in my coffee—too many calories.'

'This is no time for dieting,' he snapped, going back to the table to get his own coffee.

She seethed, but didn't have the energy to make a fuss over it. She took a sip and made a face at the taste. 'It's sweet!'

'You need to raise your blood sugar,' he told her, coming back towards the bed, carrying his cup and saucer. He sat down on the edge, and her throat fluttered with panic. To cover it, she drank some more coffee while Stephen lifted his own cup to his lips.

She risked a glance at him and was even more alarmed to see the strong, dark planes of his face set in a remorseless insistence. She had hoped to get away without having to explain anything but one look at that face and she knew he wasn't going to let her leave until he had answers. She had thought of him a few moments ago as a caged animal, but it was she who was trapped. She had no hope at all of escaping from this house, from these grounds, from this man.

Shivering, she drank the rest of her coffee and as she finished it Stephen took the cup out of her hands and put it down, beside his own empty one, on a bedside table.

Hurriedly, she moved to get off the bed. 'I'd like to go now, please.'

Stephen grabbed her shoulders and held her, his fingers biting into her. 'You know I'm not letting you leave until you tell me why you ran out on our wedding.'

He didn't shout, but his voice was barely controlled; she heard the anger beneath the quiet surface of it and froze, rigid, unable to move.

She swallowed, her throat dry and painful, and whispered, 'I... You...' She stopped, and tried again, even more huskily. 'That night, that last night, after the party, I realised I couldn't go through with it. I just can't marry you. I thought I could, but I can't. I'm sorry, I know you're angry; it was a rotten thing to do to you, and I'm sorry, but I really couldn't help myself. It was all a terrible mistake; I should never have let it go ahead.'

She heard his breathing, rough, irregular, felt the tension in the hands still holding her, and her nerves went crazy again. It was like being on the edge of a volcano—any minute now, she kept thinking, any minute now, it is going to blow sky-high, and take me with it.

'You still haven't told me why,' he said. 'Tell me about what happened to you.'

'Nothing happened, nothing at all!'

'It must have done, Gabriella!' he broke out, his voice harsh. 'Don't lie to me. Do you think I'm not aware of what happens inside you every time I come too close? Either you're terrified of me or you're terrified of every man you meet; it didn't take me long to realise you were scared stiff of being touched.

'Why do you think I've kept my distance all these months, while we were engaged? Why do you think I gave you a little peck on the cheek now and then, held your hand... acted as if we were teenagers instead of adults?' His tone turned angrily sardonic, his grey eyes flashed. 'Or were you under the impression that I was totally sexless? That I wasn't going to make any demands on you after we were married? Did you think I was some sort of eunuch?'

She looked helplessly at him, then gave in and told him the unvarnished truth. 'I was living like a sleep walker; I was trying not to think at all. I knew, of course, that it was madness, that I couldn't marry you, but you seemed so calm and in control. You never——' She broke off, shivering. 'I let myself be hoodwinked into thinking that maybe... maybe it would be OK, maybe it would work out.'

He repeated slowly, '"Calm and in control"?' His mouth twisted with a sombre, self-mocking sarcasm. 'Is that what you thought? Oh, I had myself on a leash OK. I didn't know what exactly the problem was, but I knew there was some sort of problem with you, and I tried hard not to frighten you. And then I lost control the night after the party—that was what scared you into running away, wasn't it? That I lost control?'

She looked down, her lashes dark on her pale skin, her mouth bloodless and quivering, and couldn't get a word out; if she said anything it might be too betraying; she might say too much.

Stephen put a hand against her face and she tensed at once, looking back at him hurriedly, with alarm.

His eyes were molten, the grey glittering, the black pupils enlarged and glistening with desire. She drew a rough breath, burst out, 'Don't!' and shoved him hurriedly away with both hands.

Stephen made a rough sound in his throat and grabbed her again, yanking her violently towards him.

'Don't push me away! Don't ever push me away again!'

Gabriella arched away from him, giving a cry of alarm, shaking her head, but as her lips parted to protest his mouth crushed down against them in fierce demand, and although all the alarm bells went off inside her again the passion in his mouth made heat begin to burn deep inside her.

He pushed her backwards, off balance; she instinctively clung to him, trying to stay upright, but his body pressed her down on to the bed. He fell on top of her, and her senses went crazy. She loved the feel of his mouth, his exploring hands as they roved from her throat down to her warm breast and the soft female curve of her body. She couldn't stifle the moan of pleasure in her throat; she wanted what he was doing to her. Sensuality beat in her, made her body quiver and her blood run hot.

His lips slid down her throat. Her ears drummed with the sound of her own blood, deafening her, making it almost impossible to think. She was deeply aware of his body lying against her, hard and masculine; every nerve in her was sensitive to him, every cell in her body clamoured for closer contact with his, and she had always felt this hungry response. It had never disturbed her; it was purely physical; it could not destroy the way emotion could.

If only it could be just their bodies moving together in this passionate languor; if only they could keep their hearts and minds silent forever.

Stephen slowly lifted his head, his eyes, half hidden by heavy lids, moving over her yielding body. Gabriella stared back at him, breathing quickly, her heart beating fast.

'Now tell me you didn't enjoy that,' he said, his voice husky, triumphant, rough with desire.

She trembled, couldn't answer, feeling the need aching inside her. He could have gone on without meeting any resistance—he could have taken her and she would not have tried to stop him. She had never been scared by the idea of going to bed with him.

Stephen's grey eyes probed her face, the parted, trembling curve of her pink mouth, still swollen from his kisses, the wide, darkened blue eyes.

Slowly he said, 'So it isn't being touched that scares you. You aren't scared now, are you? What is it, Gabriella? What sent you into panic that night? What was different that time?'

She shut her eyes and forced herself to say the truth. 'You,' she whispered.

'Me?' A silence. Then he asked, 'How?'

'You were...' She couldn't finish the sentence and stopped dead, her mouth full of the taste of ashes, the memory of anguish.

He waited for a moment, then quietly finished it for her.

'Out of control? Is that what you were going to say?'

She was still unable to speak, her memory haunted by moments she had spent years trying to forget.

Quietly Stephen asked her, 'Somebody once lost control with you, did he, Gabriella? What did he do to you? What happened?'

A tear trickled down her face, surprising her because she hadn't known she was going to cry. She lifted her arm and brushed it across her wet eyes like a child.

Stephen moved her arm away and wiped her face gently with a handkerchief. 'I realise it's hard for you to talk about it—that's crystal-clear—but you have to, Gabriella, can't you see that? You've been locking it all away inside you when you should have been talking about it...to someone, if not me. This is the sort of problem that festers if it isn't forced out. You should have seen a psychiatrist long ago; had therapy.'

'That's what Paolo says,' she said, and felt his sharpened attention, the immediate frown.

'So he knows—I suspected he did when you said you trusted him. That was why you came here to him, wasn't it? Because he knew.' Then his voice deepened, angry and harsh. 'Why could you tell him when you apparently can't tell me?'

She gave a quivering sigh. 'I didn't mean to tell him—but we've known each other so long that Paolo sometimes guesses what I'm thinking. I don't know how he does it; I suppose he picks up clues from my face.' Or made leaps of intuition, simply from knowing her so well.

'Maybe I can do that too,' Stephen said roughly. 'It's pretty obvious that something sexually disturbing happened to you. You were attacked, weren't you? Some man attacked you? A stranger? Were you raped?'

'No!' she broke out angrily, struggling away from him and sitting up. 'I told you, no! It wasn't like that.'

'Then what was it? There's something like that— there has to be! Tell me, Gabriella! Talk to me.'

His voice was harsh again, hoarse with angry feeling, and she shrank from it as from fire, afraid of contact with so destructive a force. 'If you can talk to him, you can talk to me!' Stephen muttered and she shuddered.

'When you get like that...that's when you frighten me! You're scaring me now.'

'Like what?' His brows met, his face impatient, baffled. 'Stop talking in riddles! I'm in no mood to play games, Gabriella.'

She looked at him helplessly, knowing that she had to tell him yet afraid to talk about the past. She had to open the locked door, descend into the dark cellar of her past where the ghosts were imprisoned, the memories shut away.

Gabriella didn't know if she had the courage to do it.

CHAPTER SIX

GABRIELLA'S anger came to her rescue again—a deep-burning anger which made her want to hit out at him so much that it gave her a new sort of courage, coursing like adrenalin through her bloodstream. She sat up, swinging her long, slender, silk-clad legs to the floor, her colour coming and going in her delicate face, and knocked Stephen's hand away when he tried to make her lie down again under the fringed canopy of the four-poster bed.

'No! Stop trying to push me around! That's one reason why you frighten me—you crowd in on me too much, won't give me room to breathe; you're always trying to run my life; you don't ask me what I want to do, you just give me orders; you want to make my decisions for me!'

She stood up and walked across the room, as he had done, without even seeing her surroundings, pacing the thickly carpeted floor, her head bent while she thought hard, frowning, her black hair falling forward against her pale cheeks.

Did she want to tell him? Could she bear to talk about it? He was bound to despise her, condemn her—everyone else had at the time. She would never forget the way they had looked at her; that hatred and contempt had marked her for life. She didn't want to see that expression in Stephen's eyes.

Yet would she? She didn't know how he would react. She didn't know him well enough to guess.

She swung to face him again, her blue eyes accusing. 'And another thing... I really don't know you at all, do I? You rushed me into a engagement before I had a chance to get to know you. It never seemed real to me, that engagement. You just said you were in no mood to play games. But what else have you been doing for months? It felt like a game to me; it certainly didn't feel as if I was really engaged, or that we would ever really be married. You've never talked to me about yourself; I don't know what you like, what you want, how you feel— I know very little about you at all.'

He was on his feet too, standing two strides from her, watching her with a black frown.

'You've never shown any interest before. All you had to do was ask questions, but you never asked them.'

It was true; she couldn't deny it. 'But we never talked,' she said. 'I couldn't ask questions when we never talked about anything intimate, never talked about ourselves.'

Quietly he asked, 'So what do you want to know, Gabriella?'

She spread her hands in a furious gesture. 'I don't know... Everything, I suppose. "Talk to me", you said a minute ago. You want me to tell you things I've never told anyone——'

'No one at all?' he broke in harshly.

She shook her head. 'No one at all,' she whispered, her eyes wide and burning.

'Except Paolo!' Stephen bit out and she flinched, hating the snarl of his voice, the threat coming from him.

She had learnt far too young the danger of strong emotions, of a loss of control; she feared it as a burnt child feared fire. She yearned for calm, needed to be safe. She had only ever considered marrying him because he had convinced her that he could give her that stability and security, but she had been fooling herself. She hadn't known him at all, and for that she blamed him, her eyes restlessly touching him and moving away with an angry impatience.

'I explained why I talked to Paolo! You know I did! He is my oldest friend; he's almost family, almost a brother—I know him better than anyone in the world. He was the only one I could risk talking to; there was nobody else!'

'What about your family?'

'There was only my grandmother——' She broke off, biting her lower lip, a small spot of blood showing on it a second later. Her mouth quivering, she added, 'She knew, but—but she couldn't talk about it; she never said a word to me. I certainly couldn't talk to her. We buried it, pretended it hadn't happened.'

'And that's what you've been doing ever since,' he said in a dry tone, and a shiver ran through her. He saw it and said quickly, 'Are you cold?'

She shook her head. 'A ghost walked over my grave.' In more senses than one, she thought; and Stephen frowned as if he had picked up on her thoughts.

'Don't think like that!'

'You mean 'pretend'?' She gave him a melancholy glance. 'I've done so much of that in my life. In fact, that was the worst part of what happened—having to pretend, trying to push it to the back of my mind, trying to make myself forget. Because I couldn't, of course, and neither could my grandmother. It was there, all between us, like a desert we could never cross—a great, empty, burning space where nothing lived or moved.'

'What was?' Stephen asked, but she ignored the question, barely heard it, she was so intent on remembering.

'I knew she hated me, you see,' she whispered. 'Because it was all my fault. I could see it in her eyes. She would be staring at nothing, sitting at the table, at meals, in an armchair in the evening, her face blank, and then she'd suddenly look at me, and I always knew what she had been thinking about. I could feel the bitterness, the resentment, the hatred. It's awful to know you're hated like that. It's very hard to live with, even for a few days, let alone years.'

His frown deepened. 'How old were you then?'

'I lived with her until I was nineteen. She died while I was at college. She had a stroke and couldn't talk or move, and she died a few weeks later. I sat by her bed and held her hand, and tried to talk to her, to tell her how sorry I was, that I knew it was all my fault, that I hadn't wanted any of it to happen. I begged her to forgive me, but she never even looked at me, or showed that she knew I was there. She died without ever looking at me again.'

'She was your father's mother, wasn't she?'

'Yes. My mother's parents died when I was much younger. I was very fond of them, but I never saw them again after my father took me back to England.'

Stephen was watching her intently, his eyes narrowed and silvery. 'You were eleven when you returned to England, weren't you? Did you speak English then? Or had you grown up just speaking Italian?'

There was so much he didn't know about her, so much she didn't know about him; they were practically strangers to each other. This was the first time that they had ever really talked, ever been so frank with each other.

'Italian was my first language,' she explained. 'But my father had always talked to me in English every day so it wasn't difficult for me to go to school when we came over here. I just had to have a few months' coaching in the English language before I went off to boarding-school.'

'Did you like it there?'

She shook her head. 'Not at first. I was lonely, but my father wasn't well enough for me to live with him and he found travelling difficult so I only ever saw him in the holidays.'

'How old were you when your father died?'

'Thirteen,' she said, her eyes haunted. 'I was fourteen that summer, but he died before my birthday. I was still thirteen when he died. It wasn't really a shock; I had been expecting it—we all had—for a long time. He wasn't very strong. He never really recovered from my mother's death; they were very close—her death was a dreadful blow to him. I don't think he wanted to live without her. That was why he brought me back to England—so that his family could take care of me.

'He was always ill; he had to send me to boarding-school, and even in the holidays I saw very little of him. I spent the holidays with...'

She stopped and swallowed, her throat moving visibly. 'With Lara's family. My father lived near them and I visited him on days when he was well enough, but he was too ill to have me living with him. I didn't mind that so much, after a while, because I loved being there. I liked Lara very much, and—and her family... I did miss my father, of course; I kept hoping he would get better and I could live with him all the time, but he got worse, not better, and then the summer when I was coming up to my fourteenth birthday——' She broke off, drawing a long, shaky breath.

'He died,' Stephen said quietly. 'It must have been a bitter blow to you, when you were so young.'

'It was a bad year,' she admitted huskily. 'First my father died, and then... and then my uncle Ben...'

'His brother?'

She swallowed, her slender white throat moving convulsively, and Stephen's gaze sharpened, glittering like needle-points.

'Yes. There were only the two of them. My grandmother only had two children—two sons— and they both died the same summer. She never got over it. I think she began to die too, that summer.' Her mouth quivered. 'I sometimes think my whole life has been punctuated by deaths...my mother's, my father's, my grandmother's...'

There was a silence. She stared at nothing; Stephen stared fixedly at her.

'It was him, wasn't it?' he said at last, and watched her body jerk with reaction, her white face stiffen, her eyes darken.

Tongue-tied, she just stared back at him, but he saw a tell-tale pulse beating in her neck, her hands trembling.

'What...what do you mean? Who?' she whispered.

'You know who I mean. What did he do to you?' He searched her face, his brows together, and said curtly, 'OK, I can see how hard it is for you to talk about it, but it has to come out, Gabriella. You've kept it shut inside you for too long. Why don't I just make a guess? Your uncle tried to——'

'No!' she burst out, shaking so much that she could hardly stand upright. 'Don't. You'll only make it sound...vile...horrible...and it wasn't like that. It wasn't his fault. It was mine. I was the one...'

Her head swam as emotion clouded it; tears welled up in her eyes and fell like rain, running down her cheeks, trickling into her mouth, their salt taste on her tongue. She was shivering from head to foot, her skin icy cold and totally colourless.

Stephen took the two strides between them and picked her up, carried her over to the elaborate four-poster bed and sat down with her on the edge. He pulled up the rose-pink satin quilt which covered it, and wrapped it round her, cocooning her in the thick, soft folds, his arm holding her close to him.

'Cry it out; it's the best thing you could possibly do,' he murmured, rocking her like a child against his heart, and for a few minutes she gave in to her grief, crying helplessly, burrowing into him and feeling the rock-like strength of his body there for her to hide in, feeling his cheek against her hair, his hand stroking her back.

She had had years of practice in hiding her feelings, forcing them down out of sight, pretending they didn't exist. She was an adept at it now. She was afraid of letting go, giving in, afraid that she might go to pieces altogether. She felt herself collapsing inwards like a meringue—crumbling, dissolving.

'No, stop it, let go!' she cried, pushing him away, sitting up, running her hand across her wet eyes. 'I'm fine now,' she insisted.

'Liar,' Stephen said, and caught her face between his two hands, his palms warm against her cold skin. He looked into her startled blue eyes as they lifted to scan his face. 'Stop trying to put off the moment, Gabriella. You are going to tell me what happened to you, what your uncle did, even if I have to lock you up in here and throw away the key until you stop lying to me!'

'He didn't do anything, I keep telling you!' She closed her eyes, fell silent again, then slowly began, her voice barely audible, as if she was talking to herself. 'I was so lonely—I never saw my father and my mother was dead, and school was boring. I lived for the holidays when I went to stay with

Uncle Ben and Aunt Kate; I was fond of them both and I enjoyed having my cousins to play with, being part of a family for a while, feeling I belonged.

'That's the worst part of not having parents or brothers and sisters—you don't belong to anyone. I used to watch my friends being brought to school at the start of term, or being collected at the end of it—they had families, parents who hugged them and looked sad to be saying goodbye to them, or happy to be seeing them again—I envied them so much.

'They used to groan about their parents, complain about them if they had to write letters home each weekend, make jokes about how boring and old-fashioned and fussy they were—and I'd listen and think how I'd give anything to have people who cared enough about me to fuss over me and complain if I didn't write or ring them often enough.'

'Children in happy families always take their lives for granted,' he said drily, grimacing. 'I know I did as a child. Tell me about your uncle and his family—what were your uncle and aunt like?'

He watched her face change, the shutters go up and all expression vanish.

'Never mind,' he quickly said. 'Tell me about Lara—she's older than you, isn't she?'

Relieved to be let off the hook for now, she nodded, relaxing again. 'Yes, she's three years older than me. Her brothers, Sam and Jack, are older than either of us. They're twins; when I first met them, when we first arrived from Italy, they were already in their last year at school—tall, gangling boys, identical. I couldn't tell them apart at all, but

Lara could; she told me to look at their eyebrows. Sam's turned up at the edge like wings; Jack's didn't. That was the only thing about them that wasn't absolutely identical.

'At first I used to have to stare hard to make sure which one it was—but I gradually found I could tell them apart without staring—they had very different personalities, I began to realise. Sam was kind and patient, although he tried to hide it, as if he was ashamed of it. Jack was mischievous; he had a great sense of humour and he loved to tease.'

'They weren't coming to the wedding, were they?'

'No, they both live in Australia. They're married with children. It would have been too far to come just for a wedding and, anyway, I don't know if either of them would have wanted to come even if they lived here. I haven't seen either of them since...'

She stopped again, then hurriedly went on. 'They went to college soon after I arrived in England, anyway, so I didn't see much of them after that first year. During the summer holidays they both worked abroad—in France, at hotels, one year, and another year in America, working in summer camps, coaching kids in yachting. That was one of their hobbies; they were both good with boats and very good swimmers. I think they didn't get on with their parents, either. They wanted to get away.'

'But you liked them—your aunt and uncle? You were happy living with them?'

Her face defiant, she said, 'Yes, they were kind, they made me welcome—it must have been a bore for them to be landed with me, but they never let me see that. Aunt Kate could be irritable sometimes, but she was like that with all of us. Heaven knows she had enough to cope with; three teenagers are quite a handful, and the house was big and needed a lot of work. She had help—someone came in to clean the place—but Aunt Kate did everything else—all the cooking and shopping.'

'How old was she?'

'In her forties, I suppose. She had been pretty, but she'd got plump and her hair was grey. She was a very busy woman, very practical and capable— she ran things, had her own shop, sat on charity committees and raised money, had a lot of friends.'

'Did she get on with her husband?'

She knew he had been leading her inexorably to this question; she dreaded telling him, but she had no choice any more.

'I think they were both fond of each other. They didn't quarrel in front of us, but sometimes I think they argued over money, or Aunt Kate complained that he wasn't ambitious enough. She wanted a better lifestyle than he had given her. She had some very wealthy friends and she wished she could buy the same sort of clothes, a car as good as any they had; she was discontented and critical.

'She went out a good deal in the evenings—to parties, dinner with people. The funny thing was that she went alone. Uncle Ben wasn't part of her social life. He wasn't a man who enjoyed going out much. He was quiet and private; he preferred to stay at home, read, listen to music. When he had the time during the summer he liked to go for country walks—he was very active and could walk for miles; he could walk us all off our feet—or he'd take a boat out on the river, teach us to row, or play tennis. He gave us all tennis lessons; Lara wasn't very keen, but the boys were and so was I.'

'So in the holidays you saw far more of him than of your aunt, who was always out and busy?'

Their eyes met. Her mouth was dry; she ran her tongue-tip over her lips, nodding.

'Especially at weekends,' she admitted huskily. 'He always thought of things we could all do, but quite often the others argued, didn't want to join in—they were always going off with their friends, leaving me behind.'

She stopped, and then said in a sudden flare of anger, 'He was such a good man! I've never met anyone who was so kind and thoughtful. He spent hours coaching me in tennis, helping me with my holiday projects, talking to me in French, because I was way behind my class in French. I hadn't learnt it in Italy and I had to catch up fast when I went to the boarding-school.

'Uncle Ben spent more time with me than with his own children, but that was their choice, not his. They preferred being with friends their own age.'

'But you didn't?'

She stared at the floor, shuddering, then looked up into his eyes with an angry, desperate honesty.

'I wanted to be with him; I couldn't understand them at all. His wife, his children... they treated him in such an offhand way; they laughed at him, ran him down. I adored him. I thought the sun shone out of him. He was a wonderful man. He was so like my father to look at, but he seemed to care about me, and my father no longer cared about anything. I loved Uncle Ben more than anyone in the world.

'Every summer he drove to the school to collect me for the holidays and I'd hang around watching for him through a window, and when I saw his car I'd rush down and hurl myself at him, fling my arms round his neck and cling to him like a limpet while he whirled me round and round with my feet off the ground.

'I was very young for my age, although I didn't realise it then. Oh, in some ways I was independent—living in a boarding-school had taught me to cope with taking care of myself. But in other ways I was quite childish, especially in my emotions; I was always hugging him, kissing him. It never occurred to me that I was no longer a child and it was time I stopped acting as if I were.'

'But your uncle didn't mind all this hugging and kissing?' Stephen asked drily, and her face burned.

She gave him a stricken look, looked away, whispered, 'It never occurred to me to wonder what he felt, what he thought. It should have done—I know that now—but I had no idea about men.'

'How many girls of thirteen would have?' Stephen bit out, and she sighed.

'I was more innocent than most girls of my age. I was a late developer; I was a leggy, skinny girl; I had almost no breasts and I hadn't started having periods. Maybe that's why it was such a shock.

'I think now that I didn't want to grow up—I was clinging on to my childhood because of my mother's death and seeing so little of my father. I hadn't had a chance to follow the usual path kids follow, from being just a child to being a teenager and then an adult. One minute I was a child, the next I had, in effect, no parents and I was on my own.

'I clung to Uncle Ben to save myself from having to face life as a grown-up. It never entered my head that he had different feelings, that he——' She cut off, a sob in her throat, and covered her face with her hands, shaking with tears.

Stephen held her, stroking her hair, murmuring wordlessly. 'Shh... Shh...'

'Don't be kind to me,' she groaned when she could speak without crying. 'It makes it harder; kindness is a trap.'

'Life without kindness is as tasteless as meat without salt,' Stephen said with a crooked little smile, adding, 'Dry your eyes and blow your nose, like a good little girl,' and he produced a clean handkerchief for her to use.

She vaguely resented the gentle mockery. 'I said I was a late developer—I didn't say I hadn't grown up in the end!'

He smiled at her with a charm she couldn't help responding to, a warmth that made her smile back. 'We all have to do that, Gabriella. Life doesn't give us any choice.'

'It certainly didn't give me one! One day I was still just a kid, a bit dreamy, wide-eyed and innocent; the next I was thrown into a maelstrom, and my life was never the same again.'

She gave a little sob, and put her hand over her mouth to stop herself crying again. He took hold of both her hands. 'Tell me the rest, Gabriella. Don't stop now.'

She gave a long sigh, her whole body wrenched by it. 'It was that last summer—the summer my father died. For a few weeks we had very hot weather. One day Uncle Ben and I took a picnic out into the countryside. We walked across some fields into a wood and ate our lunch in the shade.'

She shut her eyes and could see it—midges dancing under the gently moving branches, beyond in the fields the gold of ripening wheat, the dark green of elm and oak with the hot blue sky above them.

'We lay down in the long grass and listened to the birds, and Uncle Ben sat up to watch larks hanging in the sky above the field, so high up you could hear them far better than you could see them; they sounded wonderful.

'I was lying on my back watching him, sleepily, because it was so hot and I had walked a long way and then eaten and I was barely awake. He looked down at me and I smiled at him, feeling terribly happy, and then he changed...his face seemed to break up; his voice was sort of hoarse... He said he loved me, and that was wonderful, because I needed so badly to be loved. I said I loved him too, of course, and I think I went pink.

'Then suddenly he kissed me...not on the cheek the way he usually did, but on the mouth, and in a funny, worrying way, and he didn't stop. He kissed my face and my hair and my neck and my hands and he kept saying how much he loved me;

his voice sounded so weird. He was very flushed and he was shaking.

'I began to get frightened after a while, but I didn't know what to do. I just lay there—and then he...he began...touching me. I wasn't so innocent that I didn't know what he wanted to do, and I was horrified. I felt sick; I went into panic; I began screaming and fighting him off; I scratched his face and kicked...and then—and then...'

She was hyperventilating, breathing so fast that she could hardly get the words out; she wanted to finish telling him quickly; she wanted to get it over with now that she had started. She had shut it all inside her head for so long—it was a terrible relief to say it out loud, and the words just poured out of her.

'There were some people across the other side of the field—ramblers, on a walk, like us. We hadn't even noticed them coming towards us but when I began to scream they came running; they pulled him off and one of the men hit him, knocked him out. He just went limp and lay there, and that frightened me even more—I thought they had killed him; he looked as if he was dead. I felt the most terrible guilt.'

Stephen's face was grim. 'You had no reason to feel guilty!'

'Didn't I?' she asked, her eyes wild. 'Don't you see...? It would never have happened if I hadn't acted the way I did. He was lonely and unhappy and he misunderstood how I felt about him.'

'You were a child, he was your uncle. You were in his care—if there was guilt, it was his. Gabriella, try to step outside it all. How would you feel if you read a story in a newspaper about a girl of thirteen and her middle-aged uncle? Who would you think was to blame? The child or the man?'

'You'd have to know what really happened!'

He sighed, his expression hardening. 'Well, never mind. Tell me what happened next.'

She shut her eyes. 'I don't know. It was so confusing; everyone was shouting and asking questions and I was so scared. One of the ramblers went off and called the police. It never occurred to me that they might do that.

'The first thing I knew was when a police car arrived and then an ambulance. I was taken to the hospital where I saw a doctor. The two hours I spent there were——' she groaned, shuddering '—horrible. I was so embarrassed and scared. I kept telling them nothing had happened, but they didn't believe me. They made me take all my clothes off; they took them away for examination; they examined me. I was petrified.

'Eventually the police arrived and took me to the police station where I had to answer a lot more questions. My uncle was there but I didn't see him. After I'd made a statement I was sent to my grandmother's. She was so angry with me that she couldn't even speak to me at first, then she made me tell her exactly what had happened, and she called me some terrible names, said it was all my fault, and that she and Aunt Kate had seen me always hanging around him, wanting him to notice me. I'd brought it on myself; I was the one to blame, she said.'

Stephen inhaled sharply. 'Ah, so that's why you blame yourself! She put the idea into your head.'

'It was already there! I loved Uncle Ben, I was appalled at what was going on, I desperately wanted to stop it happening but there was nothing I could do—it had all gone too far. My grandmother said she couldn't bear to see me; she sent me back to school a week later. It was like being in a nightmare. I had to pretend nothing was wrong; I couldn't talk about it to anyone.

'I didn't know my uncle had been charged—I don't know what with exactly; I think they called it a sexual assault. They hadn't named me, of course—I was a minor—but I discovered later that it was the talk of the neighbourhood. Everyone knew some version of the scandal; and what they didn't know they embroidered.

'People stood outside his house and stared, and Aunt Kate sent her children away to stay with her family in Scotland. My uncle was released on bail. God knows what Aunt Kate said to him, but he killed himself, two weeks later, with sleeping pills. Aunt Kate sold the house and went back to Scotland. I never saw her again, but my grandmother let me go back to stay with her in the holidays.

'She told me Uncle Ben had written her a suicide note, asking her to be kind to me, saying it was all his fault. She said she knew that wasn't true—it was my fault—but it was the last thing he asked her to do, so she was having me back, but I needn't think she had forgotten what I'd done.'

She stopped speaking abruptly, out of breath, trembling, and Stephen watched her, his eyes sombre. 'Are you telling me that your grandmother went on blaming you for the rest of her life? How could she, when you were just a child and——?'

'He was her son,' said Gabriella. 'They both died that summer, both her sons—it broke her heart. I broke her heart.'

Roughly, Stephen contradicted her. 'He broke her heart—first by trying to abuse a child he was supposed to be protecting, and then by being so weak and cowardly that he couldn't face the consequences of what he had done.' His voice was harsh, scornful. 'You aren't guilty of anything but a normal, childish need to love and be loved. He knew you were still just a child—his brother's child. You were the last person he should have hurt like that.'

She shook her head. 'With one part of my mind I know you're right, but you didn't know him. He was a very kind man, a good man, and he did love me. I think, looking back, that he was going through some sort of mid-life crisis; I don't think his marriage had given him what he needed, and he grabbed at my love for him, misunderstood the way I felt.'

'And left you scarred for life, unable to let yourself have feelings in case you lose control the way he did that summer day in the woods. That's what he did to you, isn't it, Gabriella? Left you terrified of passion, of any intense emotion.'

She sat silent, pale and exhausted. She was too tired to argue any more; she was too tired even to cry any more. She felt as though she had been through a new ordeal more terrible than anything else that had happened to her; her body was limp with weariness. She wanted to fall on to a bed and sleep for days, drown in sleep, escape into oblivion.

'Will you take me back to my hotel, please?' she pleaded, her eyes dark-ringed. 'I can't talk any more tonight, I'm so tired. Please let me go back to my hotel. I need to be alone for a while.'

Stephen frowned at her, hesitated, then said flatly, 'Will you give me your word of honour that you won't run away again?'

She nodded. 'Yes, word of honour...' She would have said anything he wanted her to, if only to get away from him. 'Anyway, I couldn't run anywhere—I'm dead on my feet.'

She got up, staggering slightly as she began to walk, and Stephen quickly moved to put an arm round her shoulders. She was grateful for the warmth of his body, for his strength. She wanted to lean on him, but she couldn't let herself give in to the temptation—he might misunderstand.

She had promised that she wouldn't run away again, but that didn't mean she had changed her mind about marrying him. If Stephen thought he could talk her into going back with him and going through with the wedding after all he was deluding himself. Nothing would persuade her to marry him now.

CHAPTER SEVEN

STEPHEN dropped her at the entrance to her hotel. Gabriella had sat in silence all the way along the narrow, winding roads, her body limp and her mind empty. She didn't even notice that the dripping, damp mist had cleared and the night sky was deep blue, clear and full of stars. She didn't hear the murmur of the lake just below them or realise that there was no other traffic around, and that the little villages and towns were silent and dark. She wasn't thinking of anything, or feeling anything. She was far too tired.

When the car stopped she stirred and looked out of the window, realised they had arrived, and saw then the mist had gone, but without surprise or even interest.

Stephen came round to open the door. He took her elbow to help her out. She pulled away from him gently, without looking at him or saying anything. She did not want him to touch her.

She moved slowly because she knew that if she moved fast she might fall down. She was barely in control of her body. She had to concentrate on every movement like a baby learning to walk, her head bent, her face averted from him.

'I'll see you safely inside,' Stephen said, walking beside her. She felt his intent gaze on her; it was like the touch of his hand, too disturbing to be

126

borne. She didn't have the energy to cope with him, not now. 'And I'll be back tomorrow morning, at about ten-thirty,' he added when she didn't answer. 'Sleep late; have your breakfast in bed. You'll feel better after a good night's rest.'

He was giving her orders again, trying to run her life. She stirred herself, forced at last to reply. 'I'm not coming back with you, Stephen,' she told him wearily. 'I'm staying here for a while.'

'We'll talk about that tomorrow.' His voice was cool, but carried that unselfconscious arrogance which annoyed her. He was so sure of himself, so convinced that he must have his own way.

'No, we won't! I've decided to stay and I'm not going to be talked out of it!' There was a last flicker of energy in her raised voice, in the impatient little flush which invaded her cheeks. She had had enough for the moment. The last thing she needed was another confrontation, but at the same time she did not want him dictating to her. She knew what she wanted to do and she was not going to allow Stephen to bully her.

He shot a probing glance at her, read the anger and obstinacy in her face, shrugged, then opened one of the big glass doors which bore the gilded crest of the hotel on them.

'Goodnight, Gabriella,' he said, with the same cool arrogance.

'Goodnight,' she said, walking past him into the echoing marble-floored vestibule of the hotel. For a second she thought he might come with her, but the door swung shut and he vanished back into the dark blue of the Italian night.

She collected her key from the night porter, a man she had not seen before, thin and neat in his uniform jacket, in his forties, with a moustache and slicked-back black hair.

When she said her name and room number he gave her a very odd look, his eyes sharpening.

'Ah, yes. There is a gentleman waiting to see you, *signorina*. He has been waiting for three hours.'

Gabriella did a double-take, blue eyes widening, the pale skin around them stretching into a mask. 'A gentleman?' Then she realised who it must be and added breathlessly, 'Where is he?'

'In the main lounge, *signorina*.' The porter gave a little cough, veiled disapproval in his face. 'At this hour, please do not raise your voices; you might disturb other guests.'

Gabriella flushed, looked up at the old mahogany-cased clock ticking on the wall behind the porter, and was amazed to see that it was past midnight. She and Stephen had been together for nearly four hours!

Without another word, she turned away and walked through into the long lounge which led to the garden terrace. As her footsteps echoed on the marble floor there was a movement in one of the chairs and then Paolo got up, dropping the magazine he had been reading.

'At last! Are you OK?' His face was drawn, anxiety in his eyes. He came towards her fast, looked down searchingly into her face.

She managed a pale smile, nodding.

He groaned. 'I've been out of my mind. I wanted to ring the police but I didn't know what to say to them—it wasn't easy to explain why I was worried. So I've been sitting here for what seems an eternity, waiting for you. The night porter has tried to throw me out a couple of times, but I wouldn't go until I'd seen you.'

'You shouldn't have waited! You must be very tired, Paolo. You look as if you are. Didn't you get Stephen's message saying I was with him?'

'Of course I did; why do you think I was so worried?' Paolo took both her hands, then noticed the bandaging on her palm, stiffened and stared down at it, frowning. 'Gabi, what's this? What happened? He wasn't violent?'

She sighed, shook her head. 'No, of course not! I had an accident; I was clumsy—knocked over a glass lamp and then stupidly tried to pick up the pieces in a hurry and cut myself.'

'He scared you into it, then,' Paolo rightly concluded and she gave him a wry look. He knew her far too well.

'Maybe, but . . . I'm sorry, I'm really too tired to talk tonight—I'll tell you all about it next time I see you.'

'Tomorrow morning?'

She hesitated. 'He's coming at ten-thirty.'

Paolo's face tightened. 'Then I'll be here at ten.'

She shook her head. 'I will have to see him alone, for the last time, to make him understand that I'm not going back to London, I'm staying here, and . . . and that it's over . . . between us.'

Paolo's brows jerked together. 'Haven't you told him yet? About your uncle? Gabriella, you must . . .'

'I have,' she said shortly.

He watched her with fixed attention. 'You told him everything?'

Their eyes met. She nodded, her face sad and weary. 'Everything; I told him everything.'

'How did he react?' Paolo's gaze hunted over her face. 'From the look of you he wasn't sympathetic—if he hurt you, I'll kill him!'

She managed a quivering smile. 'Don't be so bloodthirsty!' Then she remembered Stephen's face while he'd listened to her and gave a grimace of surprise. 'Actually, he was very sympathetic. But I can't talk now; I'm so tired, Paolo—I feel as if I've been through a wringer, emotionally. I really must go to bed. Ring me tomorrow afternoon.' She leaned forward and kissed his cheek, finding his skin cool against her lips. He had been sitting here in the hotel for hours; anxiety had made him pale and cold. 'You must be tired too. Go home to bed, Paolo,' she said, smiling at him. 'And thank you for worrying, and for being here for me.'

'You're my oldest friend, Gabi. I'll always be here for you,' Paolo said, kissing her back lightly on the cheek, and she was very touched by the gesture, by the words.

Her spirits lifted. She walked to the lift, hearing Paolo leave, his footsteps ringing on the marble floor, the swish of the hotel's glass doors opening and closing, before the night quiet descended. Apart from the porter behind his desk, the whole hotel was asleep.

Back in her room overlooking the dark lake, she undressed automatically, folding her clothes in a pile on a chair, and went into the bathroom. A few

minutes later she slid down into bed, reached across
to the bedside lamp and turned it off. The darkness
was a deep relief. A long sigh wrenched her. She
lay listening to the distant sound of the lake lapping
at its shores, the murmur of a little wind across the
water. Her eyes closed, and she fell into a deep,
dreamless sleep—the sleep of exhaustion, of utter
blankness.

When she woke up, sunlight dappled the walls.
She felt light and cool; all the weariness had gone,
and taken with it the strain she had felt for days.
Staring out of the window, through the gauze curtains, she saw a blue sky and, beneath it, the snowcapped outlines of the mountains on the far side
of the lake. It was a beautiful morning. She felt no
urge to move, or do anything; she just lay there
contentedly staring at that miraculous view.

Yawning, she reluctantly looked round at her
bedside clock, realising that she could not lie there
all day, and was amazed to see that it was nearly
ten. Stephen would be here in half an hour!

If she wasn't downstairs he would come up here
to find her—he mustn't find her in bed!

Hurriedly, she got up and went to the bathroom,
used the lavatory, showered, quickly blow-dried her
wet hair, slid into a towelling robe, then rang
downstairs and ordered breakfast from Room
Service, having realised that they would have
stopped serving in the dining-room.

She fell easily into Italian, asking if they could
bring her some breakfast.

'*Posso avere la prima colazione in
camera, signore?*'

She hoped that they had not stopped serving breakfast altogether.

But the man who had answered the phone agreed amiably. '*Sì, signorina*, we will bring it to your room at once. What would you like?'

She ordered a simple continental meal—orange juice, coffee, croissants. She was quite hungry, she realised suddenly, surprising herself.

While she waited for the food to arrive she put on crisp white cotton underwear, white jeans and a navy blue and white striped T-shirt, slid her feet into white moccasins, then smoothed a little foundation cream into her face, brushed her mouth with lipstick and was just clipping earrings into her ears when the room-service waiter knocked briskly on the door.

It was the same boy who had told her about the geography of the lake. He beamed at her delightedly.

'*Buongiorno, signorina! Come sta?*'

'*Benissimo, grazie,*' she said, smiling back at him and still feeling light as air and free as a bird. It must have been the relief of having told Stephen the truth, of no longer having to worry about what to say to him. She hadn't realised until now just how much of a strain it had been, never talking about the past, trying to suppress it from her mind, trying to forget it had ever happened. Paolo was right; she had let the past destroy the present. The poison of her memories had darkened her entire life.

'You would like me to take the tray out on to the balcony?' asked the waiter and she nodded, opening the windows wide to let him walk outside.

He lingered for a moment or two, setting out the woven basket of toast and croissants, a white damask napkin covering them to keep them hot, little pots of marmalade, honey and jam, a white bone-china butter dish, a large silver coffee-pot, the matching cream jug and sugar bowl, the cup and saucer, before he poured her first cup for her. While he deftly worked he talked to her about a cabaret they were going to have that night at the hotel next door.

'A pop group, and dancers. My friend who works there says the girls just wear a few sequins and a couple of feathers! And he says they can kick their legs above their heads! And turn cartwheels. They're almost boneless, like rubber. He's going to smuggle me in to see the show from the back of the room. Oh, they're a go-ahead bunch, next door, not like this place. The manager here shudders at the very idea of loud music, and as for dancers like that...' The boy pulled a droll face, waving his hands contemptuously. 'He would have a heart attack if you suggested it to him!'

'Did you?' Gabriella sat down at the table and picked up her orange juice, sipping it with pleasure; it was freshly squeezed, thickened with tiny fragments of orange, but cold from a fridge and very refreshing.

The young waiter was laughing. 'Me? Suggest he had a cabaret here? He'd fire me on the spot.'

Behind them someone pushed open the door of the room, which the waiter had left ajar when he arrived. Giving a hurried look over his shoulder, the young waiter stopped laughing.

'*Scusi, Signorina*,' he said quickly and turned to go.

Gabriella looked after him and saw Stephen framed in the doorway. Her heart almost stopped; she felt a sharp kick of pain in her chest and her breath caught.

He came out on to the balcony, stepping out of the path of the departing waiter, his face impassive. The boy muttered a polite greeting, Stephen nodded to him and answered in English.

'Good morning. Could you bring another cup and some more coffee?'

'*Sì, signore*,' the waiter said, his eyes curious. He had seen her with Paolo; he must be wondering which of the two men she was actually involved with—or perhaps he thought she had both men on a string? The idea made Gabriella flush. What sort of reputation was she getting at the hotel? The thought hadn't occurred to her before, but she didn't like the obvious answer.

When the boy had gone Stephen stood beside the table, his grey eyes narrowly searching her face for clues about her mood and state of mind. He was far too clever and he saw too much; she resented that probing stare, the mind behind it trying to probe her own mind.

'You look much better this morning,' he drawled, his lean body at ease as he leaned over the back of one of the chairs. 'How do you feel?'

'Fine,' she said warily, not wanting to tell him too much.

His mouth twisted ironically, as if he did not believe her. 'Did you sleep?'

'Very well.' There was defiance in the lift of her head. She had been betrayed into saying too much yesterday—she wasn't going to do that again.

His grey eyes bored into hers, his face sardonic. 'Good. I wish I had. I got an hour or so, no more than that.'

'Sorry,' she said helplessly, not sure what to make of that answer, whether he was blaming her, accusing her, or simply telling the truth.

She tried not to stare, fighting to seem calm and indifferent, but she was neither. The moment he had walked out on to the balcony she had felt her whole body come alive. She had felt as if the sun had just come out on a grey day, flooding her with light and warmth. That the mere sight of him could have such incredible impact on her—wasn't that scary?

He was wearing casual clothes—lightweight pale grey trousers, a white sweater so fine and delicate that it was like a spider's web, and under that a black shirt worn open at the neck and without a tie. She had rarely seen him dressed so casually. It looked good on him, but then whatever he wore looked terrific. In his usual dark city suits and immaculate white shirts and silk ties he was deeply sexy; in formal evening-suits he took your breath away.

Hungrily, she absorbed every detail of the way he looked this morning—his dark hair brushed flat and smooth, his face clean-shaven. He looked cool and elegant—you would never have guessed that he hadn't slept, but then Gabriella had never been able to read what was going on inside Stephen. He had always been a mystery to her. Nothing had changed in that respect, had it? After yesterday he knew far more about her, but what did she know about him?

He had all his usual poised alertness, those grey eyes watchfully intelligent, hunting over her own face and picking up what was happening inside her. It disturbed her that he should be able to read her feelings while she never seemed able to get inside his head in the same way. She felt her pulse-rate pick up, felt her body vibrate with awareness of him and was shaken and taken aback by the intensity of her instant physical response to him.

It wasn't fair! she thought, filled with childish resentment. Why couldn't she control those feelings? She tried, God knew. She didn't want to feel that way; she would have given anything to be able to look at him without this terrifying, dizzying reaction, without her breathing quickening, her blood whizzing through her veins, her skin perspiring as if she had suddenly found herself under a burning sun.

Why couldn't she fight it? She had to; somehow she had to—if she didn't, how could she tell him to go and make him believe that she meant it? She was giving herself away too painfully with every second of the time they were together, every look she gave him, every tiny betraying response.

She tore her gaze away and looked down at the

table, at the coffee-pot, the covered basket of croissants and toast, the half-drunk glass of orange juice.

'I was just going to eat my breakfast.'

'Eat it, then,' Stephen said coolly, and sat down on the other chair beside the table, his gaze flicking over the food. 'It looks very good.'

She moistened her dry lips. 'Have you eaten? Have one of these croissants; I only want one and there are several in the basket.'

'No, thank you; I'm not hungry.'

'Neither am I.' She had been until he arrived. Now her appetite had gone.

He leaned over and picked up the glass of juice, held it to her mouth. 'You need the sugar.'

He was far too close. Their eyes met and her heart did a sideways skip. She took the glass away from him and gulped some juice, her eyes lowered, put the glass down on the table, knowing that she was trembling, then forced herself to start eating a croissant, before drinking some of the coffee the waiter had poured for her.

'Lovely view,' Stephen drawled a few moments later, and she risked a glance at him, saw him staring out across the lake, sunlight glittering on his smooth skin and the jet-black hair. Her bones seemed to turn to water. She had to put down her cup because her hand was shaking and she was afraid she might drop the coffee.

Stephen turned back towards her, and her pulses leapt again. His grey eyes gleamed suddenly with soft mockery as he observed the agitation in her face, her shaking fingers.

'What's the matter, Gabriella?' he murmured, and she felt her skin run with hot colour.

She tried to lie her way out of it. 'Nothing! I...burnt my fingers on the coffee-pot. I...you... Oh, you make me nervous! That's all.' The dry amusement in his eyes made her anger flare up again, and she snapped at him, 'Why won't you go? I meant what I said to you last night—I'm not coming back to England yet. In fact, I might stay here. I may get a job, work in a local hotel. Please leave me alone, Stephen. Go back to London.'

He didn't look amused now; his brows had jerked together in a frown. 'I'll go back to London when I'm ready,' he bit out, and she shrugged crossly at him.

'Well, that's your affair, but stay away from me from now on! I don't want to see you any more. It's over.'

'Is it?' He got to his feet, and at once she was swamped with alarm.

She got up too, tried to back. 'Don't you...' She found herself right up against the balcony rail and stumbled, almost falling over it with a startled cry.

'Are you trying to kill yourself?' Stephen muttered harshly, grabbing at her.

Off balance, having frightened herself by almost falling, she couldn't think clearly enough to stop him. His arm was round her waist, his hand right under her breast, so that she felt his fingers touching her with an intimacy that made her head spin.

She caught her breath audibly and her eyes closed. The next second he lifted her right off her feet, up into the air, and she clutched at him, dizzy and breathless.

'No, put me down... Don't...'

'And let you fall off this damned balcony? Not on your life.' He carried her off the balcony into her bedroom, ignoring her struggles. 'Keep still; you're making me angry,' he muttered with his face down against her hair, the sound of his voice muffled.

Held high, against his heart, Gabriella heard the deep, ragged beat of it under her ear.

He sat down on the bed, still holding her, so that she lay across his lap like a child, except that she did not feel in the least childlike—her emotions were far too troubled and adult.

'Let go of me,' she whispered, wishing her body would not pulse with such hot awareness of him.

'Why did you ever say you'd marry me?' he asked, taking her by surprise so that her blue eyes widened and without pausing to think she blurted out the truth.

'I don't know.'

His brows met. 'Oh, come on, Gabriella!' he bit out impatiently. 'Of course you know—you're not stupid!'

'No, I'm not,' she threw back, very flushed. 'But that night is just a blur—I can't remember much about it. It all happened too fast. We were having dinner as usual one minute, and the next——' She broke off, her eyes confused with the memories of how she had felt. 'I wasn't expecting you to propose. I hadn't thought ahead, about where it was leading—seeing you, I mean, dating you...'

His mouth was hard, angry; his grey eyes flashed. 'What the hell did you think I wanted? I hadn't tried to get you into bed, but I kept asking you out. You must have realised I wanted more than friendship. I'm not a teenager, I'm a man, Gabriella—a perfectly normal male with all the usual needs and desires.'

She was so tense that she was shaking. She had to swallow twice before she could stammer, 'I know—I... Oh, I can't explain... I was just sleepwalking...'

'Sleepwalking?' he snarled. 'What in God's name does that mean? What are you talking about?'

Tears prickled behind her lids. 'Don't keep shouting at me! How can I think straight when you keep shouting?' She tried to struggle up, get to her feet. 'And will you let me go?'

His arm tightened round her; she couldn't get free. Stephen looked down into her eyes, his face taut and darkly flushed.

'Stop fighting me, Gabriella,' he said through his teeth. 'I'm sorry if I shouted—I'll try to stay calm—but don't fight me or I won't be responsible for what happens. Now, what exactly did you mean when you said you were sleepwalking?'

She shut her eyes and lay still in the circle of his arms. The trouble was that it was so tempting to feel the warmth and security of his body against her, to be held and protected. She yearned to yield to it, but she was still so afraid—loving was far too dangerous. You could get hurt, or you could hurt someone. Love was a road that could lead you right off the edge of a precipice.

'Come on, Gabriella,' he coaxed. 'Tell me what you meant. How can I understand if you won't explain?'

'It's hard to put it into words,' she whispered. 'Of course I was wide awake—but sleepwalking is the nearest I can get to what it's like, because sleepwalkers don't see where they're going, or realise when they're in danger. They fall out of windows or down the stairs, because they aren't looking—they're walking with their eyes shut, in a daze. That's how it is with me; this isn't the first time I've sleepwalked into disaster. That's why it happened with...with him...'

She stopped, swallowing, and felt his hand move on her hair, stroking it slowly, softly, soothing her.

The gentleness undermined her even more. She wanted to cry. Her body went limp against him, leaned on him, taking in the warmth of his body through his clothes, comforted by it as well as by the caressing movement of his hand on her head.

Did he care about her? She hadn't thought he did, perhaps because she had been afraid to hope that he might; she was still afraid. It was so long since anyone had loved her. She needed love with an ache that was intolerable, yet she was afraid of what she needed because the only time that she had let herself care about anyone and known that she was loved in turn it had all ended in a horror that she could not bear to remember even now.

'Your uncle?' His voice was so low and soft.

'Yes,' she huskily admitted. 'I sleepwalked into that. I should have realised he...that... But I didn't, because I never stopped to think—I just felt so happy, knowing he was really fond of me. I didn't understand what was really going on. I was blind—and the same thing happened with you.

'I should never have gone out with you, or let things go so far, but I was in a sort of trance. I didn't have any control, any idea where I was going—I just let things drift, day after day, and when you asked me to marry you I was taken aback—I hadn't expected it—and I didn't know what to say, but I——' She broke off, swallowing, then said in a rush, 'I thought we might be happy; I hoped...I thought it would work out, until——' She broke off again, shuddering, and felt his body stiffen against her.

'Until?' he prompted tersely and she sighed.

'The party...'

'At last we're getting to the truth! You ran away because I scared you that night. That's the truth, isn't it? I lost control, and you suddenly realised that once we were married I'd expect rather more from you than a polite kiss or two.'

Her face burned. A pulse beat in her neck, another in her temples; panic ran through her and made her throat close up.

Stephen took hold of her chin and turned her face up towards him; she had to meet his gaze, her blue eyes wide with terror.

'Hadn't it occurred to you to wonder what I wanted from you, Gabriella? Why on earth did you think I asked you to marry me?' His eyes darkened, heat suddenly burning in them, and she trembled even more. 'Do I have to tell you?' The hand beneath her breast moved, slid under her navy blue and white striped top, and she drew a fierce breath as she felt the warmth of his fingers slide inside her bra to caress her naked breast.

'No, please! Don't!'

Stephen lowered his head as she cried out; a second later his mouth softly touched her eyelids, kissed them shut.

'I knew you were shy; I knew you were nervous,' he whispered. 'Why else do you think I was so careful never to panic you or go too fast? I was taking it slowly, taking my time, and it wasn't easy for me.'

Gabriella was lost in darkness, her lids fluttering but not lifting because she didn't want to see that look on his face again. It scared her too much. The desire in his eyes sent shivers down her back.

'Stop trembling,' he whispered, his mouth silkily moving over her face, brushing kisses like the flicker of a butterfly's wings on her lashes, on her cheeks, along her nose.

'Let me show you how it can be between a man and woman, when there's no guilt or fear. Gabriella ... you don't need to be afraid ...'

He carefully removed the earrings from her ears. She heard them drop on to the bedside table with a little chink.

'I...I can't...' she groaned as his mouth pressed against the lobe of one ear; then she felt his tongue slide inside, follow the curled softness of the interior, making her shiver with pleasure at the soft, warm invasion.

'I'm not frightening you now, am I?' he murmured into her ear, and his hand moved again against her breast. The warmth of his palm cupped the naked flesh, his thumb softly caressed the hard, aroused nipple. 'This isn't frightening, is it?'

A sensual shudder ran through her. No, he wasn't frightening her; this was not fear that she was experiencing. It was an almost agonising arousal, a sensuality so piercing that it hurt, but then desire was pain, as she had learnt a long time ago.

Pain and fear, guilt and anguish were the consequences of desire, and Gabriella was terrified of being dragged down into that inevitable spiral again. Torn between what she needed and wanted and what she feared, she groaned, opening her eyes, as white now as she had been red a few moments ago.

'No, please don't, Stephen. I can't bear it.'

He wasn't listening. His head was moving down her body, slowly, so slowly, until his mouth reached her throat and his lips parted, his teeth softly grazing her skin.

'Stephen . . . no, don't!'

His mouth moved on again and her whole body arched in a paroxysm of desire which pierced her like a knife as she felt his lips on her breast, opening around her nipple, sucking it into his warm, moist mouth.

The intimacy shocked her, excited her—she cried out silently, her own mouth open in a soundless, ecstatic, tortured cry of pleasure beyond anything she had ever felt in her life before.

'Give in to it, darling,' he muttered, his tongue hot on her cool flesh. 'Stop fighting me. Once you stop fighting you'll realise it was fear itself you were frightened of, not me or passion. You're still hooked into the past, still tied up with guilt over what happened to you when you were just a child. It wasn't your fault. You don't need to feel guilty or afraid. Break free; make love to me; touch me.'

He grabbed one of her hands and lifted it, pushed it under his sweater and inside his shirt, and held it palm down against his naked chest. She felt his heart beating under her fingers, the blood running through his veins, his life under her hand.

Of their own accord her fingers seemed to press deeper into him, their tips caressing his warm skin, the rough dark hairs prickling against her. She followed the downward track of the hair, and felt his breathing quicken.

Stephen suddenly sank backwards, taking her with him. Startled, she found herself on her back on the bed, with him lying above her, his knee nudging her legs apart, his muscled thigh pushing in between them.

'No...' she gasped.

He muttered thickly, 'Gabriella ... you want me; tell me you want me. You do, don't you? God, I want you, you know that, Gabriella; I must have you. Now, Gabriella, now.'

His voice was hoarse, barely audible, and she stiffened, her eyes opening again, wide and dark blue with shock.

There was something so strange in his voice—a roughness, like triumph, a harshness like rage. It was not, surely not, the voice of a man in love? Or a man who cared for the woman he was talking about making love to?

Had he come after her just to find out why she had run away, why she had jilted him on their wedding-day and left him practically standing at the altar? Oh, no doubt he had wanted to know what was behind her flight—he had been determined to find out why she had run away—but what if his motive in coming after her had not been simply to get her to confide in him? What if he had wanted more than the answer to the question why?

Had Stephen pursued her to get his revenge? Sick panic clenched her stomach.

It wouldn't be so surprising, would it? She had humiliated him publicly, made him a laughing-stock. A jilted bridegroom was always a comic figure, and Stephen Durrant was not a man to shrug off the experience of being made to look a fool. He would want to get his own back on anyone who had done that.

What if this had been his game-plan all along, from the minute he had caught up with her? It was so simple, wasn't it? He would seduce her, take her to bed and then walk away afterwards and forget all about her.

She shuddered, and he muttered, 'Gabriella, Gabriella, relax ... give in to it ...'

Give in? she thought wildly. Give in to what? If she was right, and Stephen was cold-bloodedly bent on getting her into bed in revenge, it had nothing to do with love or desire—no such hot emotions were driving him at this moment.

If she did give in—if she gave herself to him, let the sensuality of his mouth and hands seduce her— he would take her body with hatred, a cold conquest in which the only pleasure would be in the pain he meant to inflict on her afterwards.

Revenge was a satisfying of cold rage, a tortured way of dealing with your own pain by inflicting it on others. He would use her, and afterwards ...

She shivered in shame and fear at the thought of how he would tell her what he had just done to her, precisely what he really felt about her. If he had followed her here relentlessly to get his revenge it would be all the sweeter for having humiliated her in private, as she had humiliated him in public.

If that happened to her she would want to die.

She felt his hands dragging off her jeans and began to fight him, almost crazy suddenly, not caring whether or not she hurt him, kicking and scratching like a wild cat.

'Gabrella ... what the ...? Stop it,' he grunted, trying to calm her, trying to hold her down on the bed by her shoulders, his body imposing its weight on her; but that only made her more determined than ever to get away, to escape the powerful body she found so piercingly attractive and yet feared so much.

She was sobbing and yelling at him now, almost demented. 'Let me go... I don't want you to touch me... I won't let you do this to me...'

He sounded shaken, his voice deep and startled. 'Stop it, Gabriella! What's the matter with you? Why have you gone crazy like this? I'm not going to hurt you—that's the last thing I'd do... Calm down...'

'Not until you let me go!'

At that instant somebody knocked on her door with a sharp, peremptory tattoo. Stephen froze, lifting his head to listen. 'What the hell...? Who on earth can that be?'

Gabriella took advantage of his distraction to dislodge him. She bucked like a wild horse, her body writhing furiously in the effort to push him away.

With a grunt of surprise, Stephen fell backwards, but he was still holding on to her, and he dragged her with him so that they both fell on the floor with a loud thud.

Gabriella was winded for a few seconds, her heart crashing into her ribs and her breathing deafening her. Stephen was breathing fast too, his body tangled with hers, their arms and legs meshed together.

While she was trying to pull herself together, the knocking on the door came again—but louder, more peremptory, and at the same time the man outside spoke loudly, close to the door.

'Gabriella?' The voice made her start, her blue eyes opening wide. 'Gabriella, are you OK? It's Paolo. What's going on? What was that noise? Open the door.'

CHAPTER EIGHT

'WHAT'S he doing here?' Stephen glared down at her and in his eyes Gabriella read jealousy and suspicion. 'Were you expecting him? Had you arranged for him to come?'

Could he be jealous if he didn't care about her? Her mind swam with confusion again, and the usual uncertainty and insecurity. If only she knew what really went on inside him; if only she understood him. But she had never yet understood the way a man's mind worked. They were a mystery to her. Did other women understand them? she wondered. Were they so different from women? Was it quite impossible to guess what made them tick? Or was it just her? Was she too stupid to work out what happened inside their heads?

Paolo banged on the door even louder, his voice rising. 'Gabriella, let me in. What's wrong? Is he in there? Won't he let you open the door? Shall I go and get the manager to use a pass key?'

Stephen swore through his teeth. 'Damn him, he would, wouldn't he?'

'Yes,' she whispered, because Paolo was the one man she had ever vaguely understood and she knew that he would do what he had threatened. Uneasily she watched Stephen get to his feet, raking back his tousled black hair, tucking his shirt back into his trousers with an impatient gesture.

'I'll get the manager, then, shall I?' Paolo repeated.

'Wait a moment, Paolo,' Gabriella called unsteadily, fumbling with shaking fingers to tidy herself as she hurried to let him in.

'I'll do it,' Stephen muttered, but she shook her head without looking at him.

'No, I will; this is my room.' She pushed past him, zipping up her jeans, pulling down her T-shirt, smoothing her hair as she stumbled across the room to the door, to unlock it and begin to open it.

As she did so, Paolo almost crashed through it, using his shoulder to widen the gap. Behind him, in the corridor, she saw the stares and fascinated, shocked faces of other guests who had come out of their rooms on hearing all the noise and were waiting to see the outcome.

They gaped at her, taking in her dishevelled state with widening eyes. Turning crimson, Gabriella hurriedly backed out of sight again. She shut the door and looked round at Paolo, who had halted in the centre of the room, confronting Stephen, his body language as clear as a bell—shoulders set belligerently, feet apart as if poised to spring at the other man, his hands screwed into fists.

'What have you been doing to her, you bastard?' he snarled in angry, rapid Italian.

'Who the hell do you think you are, talking to me like that?' Stephen threw back, using the same language, and bristling like a dog about to bite. 'Gabriella is marrying me, not you, and whatever happens between me and her is no business of yours, so just you stay out of it.'

'I'll do nothing of the kind! I'm the closest thing to family she's got and I'm not going to stand by and let you hurt her, so get out of here and leave her alone!'

'Hurt her? What do you think I am? Gabriella, tell him I wasn't hurting you!' Stephen's grey eyes flashed to her face, the glitter in them demanding, insisting that she back him up.

She couldn't make a sound—she was too disturbed. Stephen's features tightened into a grim mask, as if she had hit him across the face.

'Gabriella! Tell him the truth!'

'Yes, tell me the truth, Gabriella,' Paolo said with angry emphasis. 'Don't tell me whatever lies he wants you to give me. I'm here now; you don't need to be frightened of him. Was he hurting you?'

She shook her head. 'No, of course not.'

She wasn't sure it was true, though. Maybe Stephen had wanted to hurt and humiliate her for what she had done to him; she knew he was violently angry with her. Every time she saw him she was aware of the rage inside him, and she was an expert on hidden rage. She had lived with it for too many years not to recognise it in others.

But he hadn't hit her or hurt her physically, as Paolo suspected; any pain he had inflicted had been to her heart, not her body, and, anyway, she did not want Paolo to get into a fight with Stephen. The two men were not evenly matched; Stephen was bigger, fitter and more muscular—he could knock Paolo into the middle of next week without even trying.

'Satisfied?' Stephen snapped at Paolo.

'No, I'm damned well not! I heard a crash from in here; I heard her cry out when I was outside that door. It was a cry of pain—she'd been hurt and——'

He broke off as someone else knocked on the door, even louder and more peremptorily than the way in which he had knocked. They all started in surprise, turning to stare at the door.

'Now what?' grunted Stephen in a voice which sounded as if he was at the end of his tether. 'Who else are you expecting?'

'It's probably the room-service waiter, coming back for my breakfast tray,' she said shakily. Who else could it be?

Stephen strode across the room and flung the door open turning basilisk's eyes on whoever was outside. Gabriella was glad that she wasn't on the receiving end of that stare. 'What do you want?' he barked.

A furious, self-important voice answered him. 'I am the manager of this hotel, sir, and I have had a number of complaints about whatever has been happening in this room!'

Gabriella's heart sank.

'You'd better come in, then,' Stephen said curtly, stepping aside to let him pass.

The manager strutted into the room—a short, tubby, grey-haired man in a well-cut dark suit and silvery tie. He looked at Gabriella with disdain, running a look up and down her faintly dishevelled figure, and then gave the two men the same sort of glance, his nostrils pinched, his mouth set in an expression of distaste and offence.

'This is a respectable hotel; we do not expect our guests to have fights in their rooms, or shout and yell at each other. You have upset all the other guests on this floor.

'My reception clerk told me he had doubts about accepting the young lady as a guest when she first arrived because she did not seem to be the sort of client we wish to welcome to our hotel. However, she said she was touring, and was very tired, and would only want the room for one night—and he felt sorry for her. But it seems that he was quite right in his first impression.' He turned back to Gabriella, sniffing again. 'I shall have to ask you to leave my hotel at once.'

Gabriella was stricken with shame and embarrassment; she went white then red, wishing the floor would open up and swallow her. The feeling was bitterly familiar. This had happened to her before. Long ago, when she was still a child, she had been looked at with this terrible distaste and contempt, and she had wanted to die.

Stephen bit out fiercely, 'How dare you speak to her like that? You'll regret this! Get your things, Gabriella; I'm taking you back to England——'

Paolo broke in over his voice, 'No, she is not going back to England; she is coming to stay with me, at the Villa Caterina Bella, aren't you, Gabriella?'

The manager started violently, looking like someone who'd been hit round the face with a fish. He stared at Paolo, his black eyes round and incredulous. 'The Caterina Bella? You are not the owner of the Caterina Bella! What are you talking about?'

'I didn't say I was the owner. I said I was staying there—not that that is any business of yours!'

The round black eyes grew even rounder. 'You are a friend of...?'

'Yes,' said Paolo with curt unfriendliness. 'I work with the maestro—we are old friends. He has lent me his villa for a while, but he will be joining me shortly. I know he will be very shocked to hear how you have treated my cousin.'

'Cousin...?' repeated the manager unhappily, swallowing. 'The young lady is your cousin?'

'Yes.' Paolo turned to her. 'Pack your case, Gabriella; I will take you to the villa at once.'

Flushed and gabbling, the manager broke in, 'No, please. I see now that there has been a misunderstanding. A family quarrel...well, of course, that is different. I thought the young lady was entertaining men in her bedroom and...'

He gave her a sideways look, very red, shrugging apologetically. Gabriella then realised what he had thought she was; it was even worse than she had realised, even closer to meriting the disgust she had once seen in her grandmother's eyes, the hatred she had seen in her aunt's face. Burning colour rushed up to her hairline.

'Please forgive me!' The manager bowed to Gabriella. 'I am very sorry, *signorina*, if I have offended you. It is all the fault of my receptionist; he gave me the wrong impression...and the complaints of other guests... You know, a hotel like this has to be so careful—we cannot afford to get the wrong reputation. Please overlook what has happened. I hope you will stay on with us, and give us a chance to make up for this very stupid mistake.'

She made a helpless gesture. She was still upset and embarrassed, but she was too honest not to see his point of view. He was doing his job, protecting the reputation of the hotel. This was a discreet, civilised place. The air of tranquillity was soothing. That, after all, was what she had loved about it from the minute she had arrived, and she could understand why the hotel would not want that peace torn up by uproar and scenes, offending all those guests who had come here, like her, in search of a restful holiday.

She had seen the looks on the faces of the people in the corridor a little while ago. Most of the guests were middle-aged. This was that sort of hotel. It did not want children running up and down the corridors; it did not have a cabaret at night, or encourage loud music in the rooms. The atmosphere of the place was maintained by insisting on quietness and courtesy.

The manager took her gesture for agreement. 'Thank *you* for being so understanding, *signorina*.' He bowed. 'And if there is anything I can do, at any time, please do not hesitate to ask.' He turned to Paolo, his face eager. 'I am myself an opera fan, *signore*, I have many times been to productions by the maestro. Such a genius! It must be so fascinating to work with him.'

Gabriella felt a bubble of hysteria form in her throat and swallowed to keep it down. One minute he was ready to throw her out, the next he was desperately eager to keep her staying here, and it was not because he had realised that he had been mistaken about her, or because she and Paolo were cousins—it was Paolo's connections that had done the trick.

That was what fame did for you. You could get away with murder if you knew the right people!

'The Villa Caterina Bella is one of our most beautiful houses,' the manager was saying now. 'Are you staying there all summer?'

'Yes,' Paolo nodded. 'I'm having a working holiday. I design sets for the maestro and I'm painting frescos for him in his little theatre. Have you ever seen it?'

'Indeed I have, several times—the villa is open to visitors, as you know, one day a week, for charity. I remember the theatre—very beautiful, a little gem,' the manager said, beaming. 'So you are painting frescos on the walls—how exciting. May I ask what sort of frescos you are painting?'

'Scenes from famous operas and views of the lakes,' said Paolo, with a dry note in his voice which told Gabriella that he was well aware of the cause of the manager's change of attitude.

'How interesting. I shall look forward to seeing them when they are finished,' the manager said unctuously. 'And the maestro will be joining you later, you said? He usually does spend the summer here, of course.'

'Yes, he plans to be here before long, to go over plans for the next season with me and the musical director, who will be joining us too, at the villa.'

Paolo sounded polite and friendly, but when he met Gabriella's eyes she saw irony in his, and he winked at her discreetly. She looked away, her mouth quivering.

The plump little manager eagerly said, 'Perhaps, when he does arrive, one evening you would all be my guests here at the hotel for dinner? I have a marvellous chef—he would create a superb meal for the maestro. It would be a great honour.'

'I shall certainly mention it to the maestro,' Paolo said blandly, and for the first time Gabriella realised the sort of world Paolo now inhabited, the way his mind had changed, had developed, how far he had come from the shy, silent little boy she had grown up with in Brindisi. They had both come from hard-working, ordinary families. They had had few toys, no other friends and they had known very little of the world in those days.

Today, Paolo lived and breathed in a very different environment. He was not the same person she had once known. It had been stupid of her to imagine he could be. The serious-minded little boy had become a sophisticated, experienced man of the world used to moving in powerful circles, used to flattery and manipulation and privilege.

She felt a pang of loss; there was a gulf between them now. Their friendship belonged to another world, another time.

The hotel manager glanced at Stephen and his manner suddenly changed again as another thought occurred to him. No doubt he had picked up on the hostility between Paolo and Stephen. His black eyes like glinting little stones, he asked, 'Perhaps...

Was this man responsible for the incident? Has he been causing trouble? Would you like him to leave, *signorina*?'

Stephen's long, lean body was as tense as a bowstring, his grey eyes hard and dangerous.

'And are *you* going to make me leave?' he asked him, his lips scarcely moving, the words bitten out between his teeth.

The manager was not a brave man; he backed, going pale. 'I . . . I shall call the porter . . .'

Gabriella had to intervene before another scene started. She hurriedly said, 'No! This gentleman is my fiancé, *signore*!'

Stephen quickly glanced down at her, his eyes narrowing at the claim. She had told him that she would not marry him. She had run away from him, yet here she was claiming him as her fiancé! A fiery spark lit his dark pupils.

She met his gaze imploringly, desperate not to have any more trouble. For a second his mouth parted, as if he was going to make some sarcastic or revealing comment, then his shoulders moved in a shrug.

'That's right; we are about to get married,' he said in a calmer tone.

The manager was taken aback. 'Married?' he repeated, dark red.

Paolo intervened again. 'Ah, *signore*—we are all Italians; we know what family life is like! The quarrels, the making up, the fights, the kissing . . . pure opera! Family life and opera are never far apart in Italy.'

The manager gave a nervous little laugh, covered in confusion now. 'You are right, *signore*. Yes, indeed, the opera and the family are both very important to us.' He gestured with his hands, gabbling apologetically at Stephen. 'Ah, *la famiglia ... Scusi, scusi, mi dispiace, signore ...*'

Stephen inclined his head without a word, his strong features grim.

'And now we must be on our way; we're lunching at the villa,' said Paolo, even more amused. He looked at his watch. 'It's gone twelve! Come along, Gabriella; my car's parked outside.'

She gave him a grateful smile—tactful, clever Paolo; he thought fast on his feet. 'I'd like to change first, though,' she said, gesturing at her rumpled clothes.

'Of course.' Paolo opened the door and gestured to the other two men. 'We'll wait for you downstairs in the lounge, Gabriella. Don't take too long, though, will you?'

The manager muttered something polite in Italian and gratefully rushed away, glad to escape from the embarrassment of his situation. Stephen gave her one long, insistent stare, then he went too, and Paolo followed him out, giving her a little grin before he closed the door.

Left alone, Gabriella sank down on the side of the bed, closing her eyes with a little moan of exhaustion. She felt as if she had been through a wringer. The last thing she wanted to do was have lunch with Paolo at the Villa Caterina Bella, but she didn't want to stay here at the hotel either.

Well, she couldn't sit here all day, much as she would have liked to. She had to change her clothes, make herself more presentable—she must look as if she had been dragged through a hedge backwards.

She stripped off her top and jeans and went into the bathroom in her bra and panties to wash again; she felt grubby, her body damp with perspiration after all that had happened since she got up. Was that only such a short time ago? It seemed like days since she had first opened her eyes to a radiantly lovely morning. She had felt so peaceful then, but that wonderful feeling of calm happiness had not lasted long, had it? Just long enough for Stephen to get here! Peace had flown out of the window once he had arrived.

She had a quick shower, which certainly improved her state of mind, then went back into her bedroom and changed into something less casual— a spring-green dress with a scalloped neckline, a close-fitting bodice, tight waist tied with a wide sash at the back, and a calf-length, full, flowing skirt. She didn't hurry doing her make-up and hair—if the manager was downstairs, or she ran into some of the other guests, she wanted to be certain that she looked her best.

It was a quarter of an hour later when she walked out of the lift downstairs. She found Paolo and Stephen standing by the window looking out over the terraced gardens towards the lake. They had their backs to her and were absorbed in conversation; for a minute she was relieved to see that they did not seem about to come to blows but then she wondered with a prickle of anxiety what they were talking about. Her?

As she walked towards them they heard her foot-steps on the marble floor and swung to face her, standing side by side.

She felt the world shift, her whole being dis-orientated, dislocated as she looked into their faces—the only two men in the world who had ever been close to her. Then the fractured pieces came together again and the world stopped swinging wildly; she saw clearly again, saw the two men she loved—one as a brother, the other as a lover—and her heart turned over in joy and pain.

Loving was both. She was still afraid of feeling like this, afraid of the way it might end. You gave a hostage to fortune when you loved someone, es-pecially if you didn't understand them. You could get badly hurt. She had been once, and it had not been her fault, yet she had been blamed for every-thing that had happened. How could she help being angry about that? She needed love so badly, yet she was afraid to reach for it because of the past—no wonder rage churned inside her every time she thought about it.

'You look lovely,' Paolo said gently, smiling at her, and she felt the angry tension draining out of her; her mouth trembled into an answering smile. The familiar Paolo she had known all her life was back—the friend she trusted, not the strange, dis-comfiting stranger who moved in a world of sophistication and cynicism. Perhaps there were two Paolos? Perhaps beneath the shell of the man who had changed so much there still hid the shy little boy who had had no other friend but her?

'Thank you, Paolo,' she said with affection and relief. She would have missed him if the Paolo she had known had really gone forever; he was the last link with a life which had otherwise vanished, the world of her childhood, when she had been happy with both her parents, safe and loved and filled with all the blind optimism of innocence.

Stephen didn't say anything, but his eyes made her pulses beat with fire as they moved over her, from her smoothly brushed head, her bright, spring-like dress to the rise of her high breasts, the curve of her waist and hips, her long, slender legs.

She took a quick, shaky breath. Every time they were in the same room he had that effect on her; she responded to him the same way she did to light, air, music—instinctively, immediately, with passion—and even fear couldn't change that. She almost wished it could, because she was so tired of getting hurt.

'You're both driving back to the villa with me; Stephen will leave his car here at the hotel,' Paolo told her, holding out his hand. 'Come on, Gabriella—I've arranged a really special lunch; you'll enjoy this.' There was mischief in his eyes and she laughed.

'What have you been up to now?'

'Wait and see!' He seized her hand and pulled her along with him, past the reception desk where the clerk stared at Paolo, getting up to bow to him.

'*Buongiorno, signore*!'

Paolo answered him with a faint smile, a touch of wry cynicism in his eyes. How did it feel to get that sort of reception once people knew you worked for someone famous? wondered Gabriella. Did it irritate Paolo? Or was he accustomed to it, resigned to it?

His car was parked right outside; he opened the rear door and held it open for Gabriella. She slid inside, and Stephen got in from the other door. Paolo closed the door again, and Gabriella flicked a sideways look at Stephen's impassive face. 'What were you and Paolo talking about while I was getting ready?'

'You,' he said coolly. 'What else?'

What else indeed? she thought, her nerves beating with tension. She'd known they had to be talking about her, but she still did not like it.

'What about me?'

Paolo had stopped to speak to the hotel porter, pointing to Stephen's car. They could hear him explaining that it would be left there for some time—Stephen was not a guest but he was visiting a guest in the hotel. The porter began to argue. Paolo fished a banknote out of his pocket and handed it to the porter who smilingly nodded, pocketing it.

Stephen said quietly, 'I took the opportunity of asking Paolo about your childhood and your Italian family—he's the only person who could tell me about all that. You never have, have you?'

The dryness of his tone made her look away. 'I told you about my parents.'

The defensive note in her voice made his mouth twist with cynicism. 'You mentioned them, but you never told me anything about yourself; I had to prise every syllable out of you. And even now there's still so much I don't know, isn't there, Gabriella?'

Inside her the dark rage flared again. 'What have you ever told me?' she threw back. 'What do I know about you?'

Paolo opened the driver's door and got behind the wheel at that instant and Stephen didn't answer her.

'I've asked the porter to keep an eye on your car,' Paolo told him in Italian and Stephen thanked him in the same language, smoothly polite suddenly, and very formal.

'*Tante grazie. Le sono molto obligato.*'

What had changed? What had they said to each other while she was upstairs changing? She felt a childish resentment; she did not want them to be friends, especially when they excluded her.

Leaning back in the corner of the car, she turned her whole body away, staring out as they drove along the narrow, meandering road through the village towards the Villa Caterina Bella. Between the white-walled, rose-pink-roofed houses on her left she saw the blue gleam of the lake and above that the brilliant blue sky, cloudless at the moment.

Rising behind it were the white-capped peaks of the mountains on the other side of the lake. As usual, there was a ferry crossing from one side to the other, from Bellagio to Menaggio.

It was so beautiful here; she wished she were in the same calm, reflective mood as the landscape she was staring at, but she wasn't. She was in the same turmoil of uncertainty and anger that she had been in for days now.

Paolo suddenly slowed and turned off the road, in front of closed, wrought-iron gates. There was a little man with a bald head and a wrinkled, weathered face clipping hedges beyond them; he looked round at the car, then came trotting forward, producing a bunch of great keys from the pocket of his navy blue gardening-apron. He unlocked the gates, pulled them open, and stood back, smiling cheerfully as Paolo drove in past him.

Slowing, Paolo thanked him. '*Tante grazie*, Giovanni.'

'*Prego*, Signor Giovio,' the old man said, closing the gates.

Gabriella sat up and leaned forward to look out, staring up through dark green cypress and yew trees to the golden stone of the romantic nineteenth-century façade of the house. Set among smooth lawns and great banks of pink and yellow rhodo-dendrons, azaleas and huge, shiny-leaved camellia bushes glowing with red and white blossoms, the villa was unreal—so lovely that it floated like a dream among its gaudy flowers, shimmering and incandescent.

They drove a little further on, then Paolo parked and turned to look at her and Stephen.

'Why don't you two wander around, explore the gardens, while I check on lunch? Walk up to the house in about half an hour and we'll be ready for you.'

'We can do that later,' Gabriella began, her nerves prickling at the idea of being alone with

Stephen again, but the latter had already got out, slamming the door behind him, and was rapidly coming round to her side of the car. She looked in agitation at Paolo. 'I don't want to stay out here with him!'

'Don't be such a coward!' Paolo told her drily. 'If you don't want to marry him, say so—but don't just try to avoid the subject. Stop hiding from life, Gabriella; face up to it.'

She flushed angrily. 'I'm not hiding from anything!'

Stephen opened the car door. 'Come on, out you get!'

She glared at him. 'Will you stop ordering me around?' But she couldn't go on arguing—it would be too humiliating. She might as well get it over with, tell Stephen firmly that she wasn't going to marry him and send him away. Giving Paolo a reproachful look, she turned and slid out. Stephen closed the door firmly and the car moved on up the drive at a steady five or so miles an hour, the wheels crunching on the gravel.

Beside the drive a path wound away between blossoming dogwood, slender trees whose branches were frothy with pink and white. Slowly she began to walk along the mossy, sandy path below the branches, and Stephen fell into step beside her.

'Paolo tells me these gardens are world-famous,' he murmured coolly. 'The colours are breathtaking, aren't they? I suppose the soil here must be very acid or these azaleas and rhododendrons wouldn't do so well. Don't they come from the Himalayas originally?'

'Is that what you want to talk to me about? Gardens?' She stood still to stare down through the trees and shrubs at the blue of the lake, glittering like a jewel in the sunlight. From up here they couldn't hear the traffic on the busy road beneath; they were wrapped in peace and beauty, yet Gabriella still felt that terrible anger burning inside her.

'Why don't you go away and leave me alone?' she burst out hoarsely, turning on him. 'I hate the sight of you, can't you understand that? I ran away because I never wanted to see you again. I just want you out of my life.'

Stephen looked as if he had turned to stone. He stared at her fixedly, his face colourless, unmoving, blank, like the face of a statue, eyeless and dead.

After what seemed an eternity he turned and began to walk away.

He was going. He was leaving her.

Agony pierced her. Tears stung her eyes. He was walking out of her life forever, and she wished she were dead.

CHAPTER NINE

THEN Stephen stopped dead in his tracks and stood there with his back to her, his black head bent as if he was staring at something on the ground. She watched him, trembling. What now? His head came up and he swung round and began to walk back towards her with long, angry strides, his whole body pulsating with a rage she could feel even from a hundred paces away.

Gabriella tensed with a peculiar mixture of alarm, hope and confusion. She was afraid of the pain loving him could bring, yet she couldn't bear to see him go, and, torn between one and the other anguish, she was in a state of utter chaos. She would have fled if there had been time, but he reached her before she could decide what to do.

The only defence she had was words. 'Don't you touch me!' she hurriedly said, and saw his eyes flash.

'Touch you?' he repeated in a horse, ragged voice. 'I haven't even started on you yet.'

This close she could see his face clearly; it looked strange, unfamiliar, the strong features convulsed with an emotion she couldn't identify for certain— was it pain or rage or desire? Whichever it was, the feelings were powerful and disturbing.

Gabriella backed and Stephen advanced in-exorably, staring at her with fixed intensity.

'You aren't sending me away like that! Hate me or not, I'm not going until I know for sure...'

'What?' she whispered as he stopped, still staring at her. 'Until you know what?'

She couldn't back any further; she felt a hedge behind her now, the leaves rustling and brushing against her.

'An answer to one question.'

'What question?'

Stephen's hands came up and reached for her, grabbed her upper arms and pulled her forward so abruptly that she lost her balance and fell towards him.

'This,' he muttered, and her pulses went crazy as she saw his head coming down.

'No...' she groaned, looking at the strong, male lines of his mouth as it descended.

'Yes,' he said huskily, and kissed her angrily, fiercely, his mouth hurting her.

She fought him, pulling her head back from the onslaught of his mouth, punching him in the chest with both hands curled into fists. He ignored her for a moment or two, his hard mouth insistent, until she began to kick his ankles.

Her toe must have connected because Stephen gave a little grunt of pain, and finally broke off the kiss, but held on to her, looking down at her furious face. Tears glittered in her eyes, her skin was dark red and she was shaking with resentment as she lifted a hand to her mouth, felt the bruised heat where his mouth had crushed it.

'You bastard! That hurt, and you did it deliberately; you knew what you were doing! You wanted to hurt me!'

'What do you think you've done to me?' he threw back, the lines of his face clenched with pain and rage. 'First you walk out on me on our wedding-day without an explanation, making me a laughing-stock in front of my friends, and now, just when I thought I was making progress, finding out what was wrong all this time, getting to know you properly at last, you turn on me as if I were your enemy, tell me to get out of your life for good, and tell me you hate me! How did you expect me to take that? Aren't I allowed to have any feelings? What do you take me for? Some sort of machine?'

She was trembling, frightened by his anger yet at the same time still possessed by her own secret rage, the mind-clouding emotion she was only now admitting that she had felt ever since she was a young girl. All those years ago she had felt guilty about what had happened with her uncle, and at the same time she had always known that she was not to blame. No wonder that, mind and body, she was a battleground of contrary, bewildering emotions that she could never resolve. No wonder rage had driven her ever since she had met Stephen and found herself trapped in another emotional conflict.

Her voice low and unsteady, she whispered, 'I don't think I know you at all.'

'No,' he bit out. 'I don't think you do either, but you're going to, Gabriella; believe me, you're going to. I don't give up easily, especially when I want something as badly as I want you.'

She bitterly threw back at him, 'Want? Want? Is that all you understand? I'm not some company you're trying to acquire! I'm a woman, a human being...'

'Oh, I know you're a woman,' he muttered, his eyes half closing, his voice huskily aroused as he looked down at her, and she felt her body quiver with passion at the expression on his face.

'S-stop it,' she stammered, trying to pull away.

'Stop what?'

'Looking at me.'

'Can't I even look at you now?' he angrily mocked, his mouth twisted and bitter.

'Not like that!'

'Like what, Gabriella?' he asked in that deep, husky voice, and his eyes were molten with desire. She stared into them, shuddering, with heat inside her. Her mind swam with confusion—she was terrified by the hunger she saw in those eyes, and yet she felt an echo of his desire deep inside her.

'As if you...'

'As if I what? Want to do this?'

He slowly bent his head and she stiffened, but this time his mouth did not hurt; he was not angry now. His mouth didn't even touch her at first; instead she felt his tongue-tip softly caress her bruised and aching lips, move very slowly, very softly, along the trembling curve of her mouth, over and over again, soothing, comforting, but above all so sensual that she groaned, her mouth parting with the deep sigh of her pleasure.

His tongue slid inside. She groaned again, her body instinctively moving closer to his, swaying into him, her mouth clinging to his, and then his arms went round her and held her even closer as the kiss deepened and took fire.

When he broke off the kiss again she didn't try to move away; she leaned on him, trembling with the passion he had unleashed. Stephen watched her through those half-closed lids; there was a dark red heat in his face and his eyes were brilliant with feeling.

'I love you, Gabriella,' he said softly, and her breathing seemed to stop.

She stared at him, her eyes stretched wide, unknowingly shaking her head; afraid to believe him.

'Yes,' he said, looking at her with the same intense passion that she had seen in his eyes before. 'I've been in love with you almost since the day I first saw you. I took one look and thought I'd found the woman I'd been waiting for all my life. You were everything I wanted in a woman, Gabriella, and you weren't just beautiful; your eyes held such intelligence, and you had a shy, gentle smile.'

Her heart beat so fast that she felt dizzy. 'You never said anything like this before,' she whispered. 'If it's true, why didn't you tell me?'

His mouth twisted. 'I'm not blind, or stupid. I knew you weren't in love with me, that the lightning hadn't struck you the way it had struck me on first sight.

'I thought at first that I'd just have to wait for you to fall in love, but then I began to realise there

were problems hidden under your lovely face. I
began to see that you were scared stiff of intimacy
for some reason. You wouldn't confide in me, and
I didn't know the right questions to ask, did I? So
I couldn't find out what made you so screwed up
inside, so frightened of showing your feelings, but
I knew you weren't indifferent. When I kissed you,
I knew I was getting a response.'

She blushed, her lashes hiding her eyes, and he
laughed softly.

'Yes. I thought at first that you were just plain
scared of sex, but there was something else, I began
to realise. I didn't dare risk trying to get you into
bed, because I didn't know what sort of hornets'
nest I might arouse, but your responses whenever
I did touch you made me hopeful—and you went
on seeing me.

'I told myself that if you didn't like me you
wouldn't date me. We seemed to get on well—we
could talk, we liked the same things... I thought,
give it time; be patient.'

Gabriella gave him a sudden wry smile. 'Patient?
You?' It was not a virtue he was famous for.
Energy, drive, determination—all these he pos-
sessed in abundance—but patience? No, never.

He grimaced, half laughing. 'I think I was very
patient with you, Gabriella. I was amazed by
myself, in fact. I tried to get you to talk about
whatever was wrong several times, but you always
got so tense that I gave up trying. But I fell deeper
and deeper in love with you, and I'm a normal

male—I was desperate to make love to you; it was driving me crazy not getting you into bed.'

She trembled at the passion in his voice, and he bent his head to put his lips against her throat, whispering close to her ear.

'God, Gabriella, if you knew how much I love you, how much I need you...'

She shut her eyes, hearing his deep, thickened voice echoing inside her head.

'I thought...if there was no hope for a future with you then I had to know that. It was killing me not to know where I stood with you. So I risked asking you to marry me,' he muttered. 'I knew it was a gamble. I was terrified you'd refuse and then stop seeing me, but I had to know what my chances were. And you accepted. That was when I realised that it wasn't sex you were so scared of—you'd never have promised to marry me if it had been. You must have known I'd expect you to go to bed with me.'

He put a finger beneath her chin and pushed her head up; she opened her eyes and looked back at him, very flushed.

'I'm right, aren't I?' he asked softly.

She nodded, her mouth too dry for her to be able to speak.

'You weren't scared of sex itself?'

'No.' She sighed. 'I wish it had just been sex...that would have been simpler to deal with! If I'd been raped by a stranger, for instance, I'm sure I could eventually have talked about it; I could have gone to see a therapist, and had treatment; I'd have realised it wasn't my fault. I wouldn't have been so ashamed of that—I could have talked it out, but the truth was so much worse...'

He said fiercely, 'Gabriella, what happened wasn't your fault!'

She looked at him with anguish, her voice breaking. 'I tell myself that all the time, but deep down I don't believe it; deep down I feel guilty. I blame myself.'

His face tightened, dark with anger. 'Because of your damned family!'

'Yes,' she said, white to her hairline. 'They never forgave me—my grandmother, my aunt...'

'They were the ones who should be ashamed! You were just a child; you were the victim; you were guilty of nothing but a child's need to be loved.'

'But I was no longer a child; they were right. I was almost a grown-up.'

'Stop telling yourself that! It isn't true! It never was. At thirteen you were still half a child, but he was a grown man; he knew he had no right to feel that way about you. He should have protected you, not tried to seduce you.'

A sob caught in her throat and Stephen held her closer, his head against her hair.

'Don't cry, darling. Don't.' He kissed her hair, put his cheek against it. 'It breaks my heart to see that look in your eyes, to hear you cry. I love you so much, Gabriella.'

She drew a shaky breath, leaning on him, clinging to him. She felt a strange, new comfort in having his arms around her, in feeling his love surrounding her, hearing the deep feeling in his voice.

'When we get back to England I'm going to arrange for you to go into analysis,' he said quietly.

'You need to talk this out; you need to face it all and get rid of the guilt, Gabriella. You can't live with it for the rest of your life. You've buried it— that was your mistake. It never works to bury feelings of that sort—they just fester and poison the whole of your life. As soon as we get back from our honeymoon you'll start having sessions with a therapist.'

She stiffened and pushed him away, looking at him wildly. 'What do you mean, "honeymoon"? I told you...I can't marry you.'

'Don't you love me, Gabriella?' he asked softly, and she froze, her eyes wide, naked with feeling.

Stephen smiled at her.

'Don't!' she cried out, trembling.

'Tell me you don't love me, Gabriella!'

She covered her face with her hands. 'I can't...'

'Can't tell me? You aren't still afraid of me, are you? You can tell me anything, Gabriella.'

'I can't love you!' she groaned, and he took her hands and pulled them down.

'Look at me when you say that, darling.'

He tipped back her head and made her look at him, and Gabriella, eyes wet and wide, stared at him with her heart in her eyes. She heard his intake of breath and then he put his arms around her and held her close against him, his head on her hair.

'I'll make you happy; I swear I'll make you happy,' he whispered, and then he pushed her hair back from her face and kissed her forehead, her eyes, her cheek, her mouth, murmuring to her all the time. 'I love you, Gabriella. I can be patient if I have to; I'll wait to marry you if you really aren't ready to go through with it yet, but just don't make me wait too long because I love you so much it's killing me.'

She began to kiss him back with passion, winding her arms around his neck, and he groaned out her name.

Suddenly he pulled back, looking down at her with wry, passionate eyes. 'We'd better go up to the house for lunch now, before I lose my head again.'

Very flushed, laughing, she let him take her hand, and they walked up through the magnificent gardens towards the Villa Caterina Bella.

Paolo met them on the top terrace, which was paved with marble and surrounded by a white stone balustrade. He was leaning elegantly at the top of the short flight of steps which led up to the terrace, and waved to them as they emerged from behind a little cluster of magnolia trees, the waxy white blossoms like chalices uplifted to the sun.

'I wondered if I should send out a search party,' he murmured, grinning at them.

'Sorry, are we late?' Stephen returned blandly, and Paolo gave him a dry look.

'A little, but never mind. Did you admire the gardens?'

Stephen looked blank. 'The gardens? Oh, yes, the gardens . . . they're ravishing.'

'I've never seen anything so beautiful in my life,' Gabriella chimed in hurriedly, and Paolo smiled at her with affectionate amusement.

'I thought you'd like them. Come and have lunch.'

To their surprise, instead of leading them into the villa he began to walk around the house. As they fell in beside him, Gabriella asked, 'Where are we going?'

'I thought you'd like a picnic today, so I've had a cold buffet laid out in one of the conservatories. We'll sit on a lawn near by and eat the food in the open air.'

'That sounds marvellous.' She paused as they rounded the house and saw the smooth green lawns and flowerbeds behind it. 'Oh, how pretty!'

'Isn't it. Very English, this part of the gardens. The conservatory is Victorian, by the way, designed by a Scotsman, rather in the style of the Crystal Palace, I gather.'

It was an amazing building—the glass arches of the roof glittered in the sunlight, and, inside, a small fountain of water sparkled as it rose and fell among the semi-tropical plants which the conservatory housed.

Paolo opened the door and they followed him inside to find that a long trestle-table had been covered with a white cloth on which was laid out a series of plates and dishes filled with food—cold chicken, a platter of various cold meats, sliced Italian salami and sausages, a game pie which had been cut into quarters, bowls of different salads including pasta and rice, boiled eggs, cheese and fruit.

'There's enough here to feed ten of us!' protested Gabriella, putting salad on to her plate. Paolo used tongs to lay slices of meat on her plate too.

'It won't be wasted. What's left will go back into the fridge to be used for my supper.' He was about to pick up some rice to put on her plate but she stopped him.

'I've got more than enough, thank you, Paolo!'

They ate their food on the smooth, billiard-table-like lawn outside, where Paolo had spread a Stuart tartan rug and dark green velvet cushions for them to sit on. They drank champagne and orange juice, had grapes and peaches to follow the salad, and afterwards Paolo produced cups and saucers and a vacuum flask of coffee.

The sun was so warm that Gabriella lay down with her head on a cushion and could almost have fallen asleep, listening to the quiet murmur of the men's voices, the splash of the fountain in the conservatory, the hum of bees among the flowers.

Suddenly she heard Paolo say, 'Why don't you get married here?' and she shot up, eyes wide and startled.

'What?'

'That's a very good idea,' Stephen said slowly. 'But it might be difficult—there are bound to be problems, marrying in a foreign country.'

'Gabriella is half Italian; she has an Italian passport. This isn't a foreign country to her—she was born and brought up here,' Paolo pointed out.

'We can't,' she protested, and Stephen turned to look at her, his eyes tender.

'It would solve one major problem.'

'What are you talking about?'

'The embarrassment of announcing our marriage *again*!'

'Oh,' she said, biting her lip.

'And knowing that people will be wondering if you're going to run off again,' he added drily.

She blushed. 'I hadn't thought of that.'

'I had,' he said, his mouth twisting. 'I would have a very uneasy feeling until I finally managed to put that ring on your finger!'

She looked helplessly at him. 'I'm so sorry, Stephen. It must have been awful for you.'

'She may be half Italian,' he said to Paolo, 'but she has managed to inherit the English genius for understatement.'

Paolo laughed. 'Ah, but the Italian side of her is far more exciting, Stephen. Don't worry. Look, why not get married here, in Como? I can fix it all up for you. The maestro's name opens all doors here—he's a living legend; he can do anything he wants to! I'll talk to him and we'll create the most beautiful wedding that ever happened in this world, and you and Gabriella don't have to do anything about it.'

'My wedding-dress is back in London!' she protested.

'It can be brought here by your cousin Lara,' Paolo quickly said. 'She'll be delighted to come, won't she?'

She couldn't deny that; Lara would jump at the chance to have a trip to the Italian lakes.

'How soon could it happen?' asked Stephen, and Paolo shrugged.

'I don't know, but it shouldn't take long.'

Stephen looked at her, his eyes dark and pleading. 'Gabriella?'

He was leaving the decision to her, and she hesitated, her mind in confusion. She wanted to be his wife, she wanted to be with him, but what if that panic swept over her again? She stared at Stephen, saw the little tic beating beside his mouth, the pallor of his skin, and love swamped everything else. She smiled at him with passion, and nodded.

Stephen let out a long, relieved, triumphant breath.

They were married three weeks later, on the lawns behind the Villa Caterina Bella, with all the arrangements orchestrated by Paolo. It was a much quieter wedding than the one which had originally been planned in London—only family and close friends flew out from England to be there, and there was a sprinkling of Gabriella's Italian relatives, who managed the drive from Brindisi to be present.

Lara was there, of course, and was the matron of honour as planned, and the bridesmaids managed to get time off from work for the wedding too.

'You certainly made this a memorable wedding!' they teased Gabriella as they helped her get ready on the morning itself. 'Running off like that, and then changing your mind again! Nobody is going to forget your wedding, that's for sure.'

'Sorry,' she said, her mind more on getting her veil to hang the right way than on what they were saying.

'I even had reporters badgering me on the phone,' ice-blonde Jilly said. 'My old dad was utterly shocked.'

Knowing that Jilly's father trained racehorses and was a friend of royalty, Gabriella could imagine his reaction to seeing his daughter's name in gossip columns, even if by association.

'She's only teasing you,' Petra comforted, her spiky black hair smoothed down for once and bearing a crown of fresh white rosebuds. She made a face at Jilly. 'Stop it, Jilly; she always takes you seriously, you know that! Don't upset her on her wedding-day—it's bad luck!'

Jilly gave Gabriella a quick look. 'Sorry, darling; I was only joking, you know! Dad sent his love and hoped you'd be very happy.'

Petra moved to the window to look out. 'Your cousin Paolo is very efficient; he's out there at the marquee, organising everything like mad. Darling, he's fabulous—is there a woman in his life?'

'Not that he's ever told me about.'

'He isn't gay, is he?'

Gabriella laughed. 'Why don't you ask him?'

'I will,' Petra decided, still lingering to watch Paolo. 'These theatrical types often are, but he's Italian.'

'What's that got to do with it?' Jilly impatiently demanded.

'You know . . . Italians . . . they're supposed to be very hot-blooded, aren't they?'

Gabriella and Jilly laughed. 'I'll tell Paolo your theory,' Gabriella said, adjusting the set of her head-dress. 'How does that look?'

'Better,' Jilly nodded.

'I bet Stephen is,' said Petra.

Confused, Gabriella stared at her. 'Is what?'

'Hot-blooded.'

Gabriella blushed, and at that second Lara arrived with an opened bottle of champagne and a tray of glasses.

'Here you are—I thought you'd feel better for a little buzz, and there's nothing like champagne for giving you that.' She poured four glasses; they all took one and Lara lifted hers in a toast. 'Enjoy your day, Gabriella, and be happy ever after.'

Gabriella smiled at them as they all sipped champagne. 'Thanks, and thanks for forgiving me for ruining your day last time, and for coming all this way now.'

'It's wonderful,' said Petra, sighing as she looked out of the window again into the gardens of the villa. 'What a romantic setting for a wedding. I walked by the lake early this morning and I couldn't believe how beautiful it was . . . seeing the sun come up behind the mountains, the red glow reflected in the lake. It's heaven here, darling, and it's heaven staying here in this gorgeous villa. Thanks for asking us to come.'

Gabriella drained her glass of the golden sparkling wine and felt the brilliance of it entering her veins. The weather was superb, the views from the villa magical—Petra was right; this was a far more romantic setting than she would have had in London.

Then Lara said, 'I'll take Jilly and Petra downstairs now, then, darling, to give you a few minutes alone before you have to come down too.'

They all kissed her and wished her luck and told her how radiant she looked, how beautiful in her wedding-dress.

Then they had gone, chattering and giggling, and she was alone, the door shut and silence descending. She was afraid to sit down in case she crushed her dress; she looked down at the full crinoline skirt with its scattered pale pink satin rosebuds, and moved to set it swaying and dipping. It felt wonderful as she walked, but sitting down in it was not easy. She looked at herself in the mirror to make a final check and barely recognised herself. That was not her, it was "the bride". With her wedding-dress she had put on a symbolic persona which hid the real person inside it. She hadn't expected that.

While she was thinking about this, Paolo knocked on the door and asked, 'Are you ready, Gabriella?' and she suddenly had a sharp stab of uncertainly, of doubt, of fear.

She wasn't ready. She wasn't sure that she would ever be ready. She froze on the spot, as white as her dress.

'Gabriella?' Paolo knocked again, his voice sounding anxious—no doubt he was wondering if she was about to bolt again.

She swallowed down her nerves, huskily said, 'Yes, I'm coming,' and Paolo opened the door and stood there staring at her.

To her dismay tears came into his eyes.

'Paolo, what is it?' she gasped.

'You look so lovely.' He took her hand and lifted it to his lips. '*Cara*, be happy.'

She wanted to cry too. A bubble of tears seemed about to burst in her throat. 'Oh, Paolo...' she whispered.

He ceremonially placed her hand on his arm and smiled at her, his mouth quivering.

'He's waiting for you, looking like a man about to be shot—if you don't arrive in one minute he's going to think you've run out on him again, so let's start now, *cara*.'

He led her down the stairs and out into the morning sunlight, into the marquee, filled with the scent of a thousand flowers, with the sound of music and the light of candles, and Stephen turned his head sharply to look back down the aisle between the chairs, his face white with the fear that she was not coming.

Gabriella had her veil down over her face, so he could not see her, but the music swelled into a triumphal anthem, and Stephen took a long, deep breath of relief as she walked down the aisle towards him.

As he later put back her veil to see her face and kiss her on the mouth she saw the brilliance of his eyes, the passion and love which had frightened her so much, and suddenly she knew the fear had gone, and with it the anger she had felt for so long, the rage against what had happened to her all those years ago. She was free of the past. As Stephen bent to kiss her she met his mouth with passion.

'I love you,' he whispered huskily, and at last she could say it too, with all the emotion she had tried to hide for so long.

'I love you too, darling.'

by
Miranda Lee

Complete stories of love down under that
you'll treasure forever.

Watch for:

#1855 *A WEEKEND TO REMEMBER*

It was only a little white lie...but before she knew it,
Hannah had pretended she was Jack Marshall's fiancée.
How long would it be before Jack regained his memory?

Available in December wherever
Harlequin books are sold.

Look us up on-line at: http://www.romance.net

HARLEQUIN PRESENTS®

HARLEQUIN PRESENTS®

by Charlotte Lamb

Coming next month:

#1852 HOT BLOOD

Kit and Liam were business partners by day and lovers by night. Without warning, tensions erupted between them—and Kit found that, beneath his calm, controlled exterior, Liam was red-hot!

Love can conquer the deadliest of Sins.

Available in December wherever
Harlequin books are sold.

Look us up on-line at: http://www.romance.net

SINS7

If you are looking for more titles by

CHARLOTTE LAMB

Don't miss these fabulous stories by one of
Harlequin's great authors:

The collection of the year!
NEW YORK TIMES BESTSELLING AUTHORS

Linda Lael Miller
Wild About Harry

Janet Dailey
Sweet Promise

Elizabeth Lowell
Reckless Love

Penny Jordan
Love's Choices

and featuring
Nora Roberts
The Calhoun Women

This special trade-size edition features four of the wildly popular titles in the Calhoun miniseries together in one volume—a true collector's item!

Pick up these great authors and a chance to win a weekend for two in New York City at the Marriott Marquis Hotel on Broadway! We'll pay for your flight, your hotel—even a Broadway show!

Available in December at your favorite retail outlet.

NEW YORK
Marriott®
MARQUIS

HARLEQUIN®   **Silhouette®**

NYT1296-R

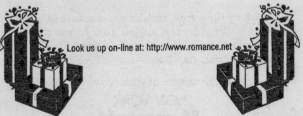

Praise for Mark Lindquist and *The King of Methlehem*

"Mark Lindquist introduces us to a chef among cooks."

—Nicholas Kulish, *The New York Times Book Review*

"*The King of Methlehem* is a tightly wound, economically written trip . . . engaging characters . . . [and] perhaps the most vividly drawn character in the novel is our very own grit city."

—Debbie Cafazzo, *The News Tribune* (Tacoma, Washington)

"[A] swift, sure-footed novel. . . .The story is thus shot through with inside knowledge . . . such details [make] this sharp book come alive."

—Adam Woog, *The Seattle Times*

". . . evocative details . . . enmesh us in Howard's mad world right up to the inevitable, satisfying conclusion. A grim thriller with an insider's view of a deadly epidemic."

—*Kirkus*

"The quality writing and flashes of gallows humor raise this above the usual tale of good guys vs. bad guys."

—*Publishers Weekly*

ALSO BY MARK LINDQUIST

Never Mind Nirvana

Carnival Desires

Sad Movies

MARK LINDQUIST

The King of Methlehem

A NOVEL

Simon & Schuster Paperbacks

New York London Toronto Sydney

SIMON & SCHUSTER PAPERBACKS
A Division of Simon & Schuster, Inc.
1230 Avenue of the Americas
New York, NY 10020

For information about special discounts for bulk purchases,
please contact Simon & Schuster Special Sales at
1-800-456-6798 or business@simonandschuster.com.

Book design by Ellen R. Sasahara

Manufactured in the United States of America

10 9 8 7 6 5 4 3 2 1

The Library of Congress has cataloged the hardcover edition as follows:

Lindquist, Mark, 1959–
    The King of Methlehem / by Mark Lindquist.
      p. cm.
      1. Detectives—Washington (State)—Tacoma—Fiction. 2. Drug traffic—Fiction.
3. Methamphetamine abuse—Fiction. 4. Tacome (Wash.)—Fiction. I. Title.

PS3562.I51165K56 2007
813'.54—dc22   2006037311

ISBN-13: 978-1-4165-3577-5
ISBN-10:   1-4165-3577-2
ISBN-13: 978-1-4165-3578-2 (pbk)
ISBN-10:   1-4165-3578-0 (pbk)

for chelsea

You never know what is enough until you know what is more than enough.

—William Blake, *Marriage of Heaven and Hell*

tweeker 1. A methamphetamine user. Tweekers are known for their extreme paranoia, flagrant dishonesty, and lack of non-tweeker friends. A tweeker will steal your stuff and then help you look for it.

If you let those goddamned tweekers come to your party, don't expect to have your stereo in the morning.

From www.urbandictionary.com

HAD TO TELL YOU LIES

I had to tell you lies to help you get to the truth.

This is the motto of Detective Wyatt James, who believes a good old-fashioned dialogue is the surest way to solve anything, though sometimes the specter of coercion is necessary to keep the conversation lively.

"Let's hear it, Marvin," he says.

"Hear what?"

Marvin squirms and adjusts the cuffs on his wrists, aggravated by the cold steel rubbing against his scabbed skin. Over long johns he wears shredded Levi's and a gray T-shirt that reads: REHAB IS FOR QUITTERS.

"Don't waste my time," Wyatt says, walking in a circle around the scrawny tweeker.

"I don't know what you want, I swear."

Sweat drips from Marvin's pocked forehead. He licks his teeth, dying brown and gray pegs poking out from swollen gums. Judging by the dental deterioration, Wyatt figures Marvin has been using for at least three years.

Though a plainclothes detective, Wyatt wears a uniform of a kind: khakis, a button-down oxford shirt, and a worn blue blazer. He looks like an overgrown college kid except for the Glock .40 on his hip next to his badge. His parents named him Wyatt after the Peter Fonda character in *Easy Rider* and, weirdly, Wyatt grew up with a vague physical resemblance to the lanky movie star.

"Have I been fucking with you, Marvin?" Wyatt asks, stopping in front of him.

"No, I guess not."

"You *guess* not?"

"No, you haven't."

"Then why are you fucking with me?"

"I'm not," Marvin says, glancing at him, then looking back down. "I swear to God."

The more they swear to God, the more they're lying.

Wyatt could conduct this interview back at the station, but he prefers the eerie atmosphere of the cook site. They are in a clearing surrounded by fir trees. On a grill mounted on rocks over a campfire is a shallow pie pan crusted with white powder and littered around the site are mason jars, porn magazines, shredded lithium batteries, cans of muriatic acid, a propane tank with blue tinting around the valve, and a plastic soda bottle with rubber tubing snaking out to nowhere.

Despite a chilly fall breeze, ammonia lingers in the air and stings Wyatt's nostrils. He is considering his next move when the wind suddenly picks up and the tree branches rustle.

Seemingly out of nowhere a dirty white Starbucks paper cup rolls toward Wyatt's feet and stops with the black and white mermaid inside the green circle facing up.

A sign.

"Howard was here?"

Marvin twitches in a nodlike motion, but Wyatt cannot be sure if this is an answer or a random tweeker jitter.

Wyatt once read about an East Indian monkey trap in which a hollowed-out coconut with rice inside is chained to a peg in the ground. The trap has a hole carved in the coconut and the hole is large enough for a monkey to reach inside and grab the rice, but small enough that the monkey cannot pull his hand back out while holding on to the rice. Even as hunters approach, the monkeys hold fast.

Tweekers remind Wyatt of these monkeys—they typically cannot let go of the rice, no matter the cost.

"Do you want to talk? Or do you want to just go to jail?"

"Talk."

"Then start talking."

"What do you wanna know?"

"The truth."

Marvin dimly weighs his options, the upsides and downsides of snitching flapping around in his meth-damaged brain like bats.

"Was the midget here?" Wyatt tries.

"What?"

Genuine confusion contorts Marvin's face and Wyatt knows he missed. He has heard that Howard sometimes works with a midget, but it could be a joke, the sort of semi-amusing information tweekers occasionally dissemble. Clearly Marvin is not in on the joke, if it is one.

"Who all was here?" Wyatt asks, quickly moving past his misstep.

"Just me and him."

"Just you and Howard?"

"Yeah."

"Tell me what you know."

"Like what?"

"Let's start with what he looks like."

"He's . . . short, I guess."

"How short?"

"Five-foot-six or so."

"Complexion?"

"You know, the usual. Very white."

"Hair?"

"Long, dark blond."

"Facial hair?"

"Just kinda unshaved. And a goatee."

"Age?"

"Around thirty. Maybe forty."

Wyatt looks at him, not pleased with this answer.

"I don't know," Marvin insists, convincingly. "It's hard to tell sometimes."

"Tats?"

"I don't remember."

"Anything else about him you do remember?"

"Well, he always wears black cowboy boots."

"Good. Anything else?"

"That's . . . it."

"What about his real name?"

"I don't know his real name. Nobody does. I swear."

"How about his mom? Does his mom know his name?"

This flummoxes Marvin.

Patience is key to questioning a suspect, but Wyatt does not have much of that these days. He attributes this to his assignment to the meth lab team, which he mistakenly thought would be a low-stress break from homicides but instead has been a grim tour through doom and decay.

"Quit fucking with me, Marvin."

"I'm not, I swear."

Waiting for Marvin to crack, allowing time for meth paranoia to build as Marvin continues to come down, Wyatt steps around the site. He kicks the Starbucks cup, stops at a boom box on the ground, leans over, clicks it on.

"Ain't found a way to kill me yet . . ."

Alice in Chains from the *MTV Unplugged* recording, which Wyatt also owns.

"I went to high school with Jerry Cantrell," Marvin says. "Spanaway Lake. Not far from here."

"Yeah," Wyatt says, turning off the CD. "I know where Cantrell went to high school."

"He was in choir," Marvin adds.

"Do I seem like I give a crap about Jerry Cantrell right now?"

"No," Marvin says, shaking his head.

"If you don't fuck with me, I won't fuck with you. But if you *do* fuck with me . . ."

Though Wyatt has never beat a suspect, it happens so often and gratuitously on television and in the movies that he figures the scare factor can work for him. He steps directly in front of Marvin and puts his hand behind his back and slouches and tilts his head, mirroring Marvin's posture, a standard technique for establishing rapport.

"What kind of criminal history do you have, Marvin?"

"Just misdemeanors. No felony convictions yet."

"*Yet.* Well, I guess it's good to leave yourself something to work toward."

Wyatt smiles, and then so does Marvin, lopsided and snaggle-toothed.

"There are some advantages to being a nobody, Marvin. Namely, we don't care about you. We don't care if you go to prison or walk. You get what I'm saying?"

Marvin nods. Wyatt nods along with him, encouraging him in the direction he is leaning, *pull your hand out of the coconut.*

"So where can I find him?"

Marvin's eyes blink and dart rapidly, as skittish as the brain behind them, avoiding Wyatt's gaze. Raindrops start falling, pinging on pans and the blue tarp.

"Time's running out, Marvin."

"He won't find out I told?"

"This is confidential background, just between us."

I had to tell you lies to help you get to the truth.

"And if I tell you?"

"Truth is its own reward."

Though Marvin suspects Wyatt is hustling him, even mocking him, he decides it does not matter.

Nothing matters, except staying free.

THE LAST TYCOON

With freakish focus Howard methodically pops Sudafed pills from blister packages into a blender, *pop, pop, pop,* his filthy fingers trembling with anticipation like a poker player with the winning hand. His eyes are red, pupils dilated, skin pale, blond hair long and stringy and dirty.

Piling up behind him on the floor of the kitchen area of the double-wide trailer are dozens of crumpled blister packs. In the corner sits Amber, a skinny tweeker transfixed in front of a television. She is doing exactly what Howard told her to do—staring at a black and white image of an empty rural road, looking for signs of trouble in the dim light of dusk. Howard, who prides himself on superior security precautions, wired the television to a camera he set up on a post at the end of the dirt and gravel driveway.

Amber's four-year-old girl sits nearby on the floor in a purple jumper, eating potato chips and playing with the bag, mesmerized by the crinkling sound. She occasionally glances up at the television or the adults.

"Mom?"

"Sssshhh."

Rain patters lightly on the aluminum roof. Howard cooks regularly at Amber's trailer, which is parked on the property of a couple in their seventies who allow Amber to keep her trailer on the three-acre rural lot because they know her mother, who works as a waitress at a Sizzler in Puyallup. The couple is clueless, oblivious to the occasional chemical odors and the poisonous meth waste Howard has been dumping onto their land.

As soon as Howard pops the last of the blister packs, he turns

the three-speed blender on high. The pills disintegrate into powder and the blender pitcher fills with a cloud of white dust.

He feels a Pavlovian rush as the process begins.

Two mason jars with coffee filters set in the mouths are ready on the kitchen counter. He pours the powder in the filters, then adds HEET, America's "#1 selling brand of gas-line antifreeze," through the powder. This filters out the binder from the pseudo pills.

He pours the pasty mess from the mason jars into a twelve-inch frying pan set on simmer, which evaporates the methanol and leaves purified pseudo powder in the pan.

"How's it going?" Amber asks, hand tapping her thigh.

"Shut up. Watch the monitor."

When Howard started cooking a few years ago, he burned out a friend's trailer, and then a shed, and then a motel room, and then his girlfriend's apartment. He subsequently refined his technique.

He uses the so-called Nazi method of production because it is the easiest and quickest: extraction, reaction, and gassing. Contrary to tweeker lore, the modern Nazi technique was not developed by Nazis or even used in the Third Reich.

Though the Nazis did feed their World War II troops uppers that included methamphetamine, as did the Japanese and the Allies, the labs of that era were designed for mass production and employed a process far more complicated than the one practiced in mobile homes and kitchens across contemporary America.

The currently popular Nazi method was developed in the 1980s by a chemistry student at a Midwest university who discovered that the Birch reduction method could be used to reduce pseudoephedrine to methamphetamine, and *presto, meth-making for dummies.*

This ambitious student wrote the recipe on a sheet of notebook paper, which was copied repeatedly and passed around like

a salacious rumor. Because the original paper happened to have Nazi swastika doodling in the margins, the technique became known as the Nazi method.

The first Nazi lab was busted in California in 1988. Seven years later local police found the first Nazi meth lab site in Pierce County, Washington, though they did not initially realize they had stumbled onto a trend. The cook reportedly taught countless other locals his process and it spread with amazing rapidity because it was simple and all the ingredients were legal and easily available.

Though pseudoephedrine is becoming increasingly difficult to obtain in volume, Howard believes the Nazi method produces the best product. After he has completed the first stage, the extraction of pseudo from the pseudoephedrine, he straps on latex gloves and a white disposable dust mask over his mouth and nose with the theatricality of a mad scientist. He is ready for the reaction stage.

Next to the oatmeal on a kitchen shelf is a jar with lithium strips stored in kerosene, which Amber helped extract from Eveready batteries earlier. Howard, like most tweekers, prefers Eveready because of the Energizer Bunny ads, which he and other tweekers believe to be an inside meth joke. He adds the lithium into the frying pan.

He opens the propane tank and pumps anhydrous ammonia over the pseudo and the lithium. Vapors rise toward his unprotected eyes. He stirs with a spatula, turning the sludge blue and gray. To expedite the evaporation of the ammonia he heats the pan up a touch further, adding water to quench the reaction.

"Mommy, what's that smell?"

"Shut up."

"It's not nice to say shut up."

Continuing to add water, Howard stirs until the concoction turns cloudy white. According to tweeker lore, a penny should be added at this stage, but Howard researched this on the Internet and could not find any justification in chemistry for this, so he assumes it is like throwing a coin into a fountain, *superstitious and futile.*

Into a mason jar Howard pours the paste from the frying pan. Next he adds toluene. Ether is cleaner and more efficient, but Howard passed out the only time he used ether and woke up with a hangover and a burned hand.

He pulls the jar close to his face and stares as a bilayered liquid forms—*molecules of meth*—and he nods along, "*Yesssss.*" He only has one stage to go and he is shaking. He sets down the jar and picks up a turkey baster and begins sucking up the top layer and squirting it into another mason jar.

This is methamphetamine oil, but not yet methamphetamine hydrochloride, *the real stuff that makes you get naked and climb the tree.*

"You stay," he says to Amber, lowering his mask and passing her a walkie-talkie that is the companion to the one on his hip.

"Cook safe, Howard."

"Shut up, don't call me H-o-w-a-r-d in front of the k-i-fucking-d."

"Who's she gonna t-e-l?"

"Why must I live my life surrounded by morons?" he mutters, then picks up the jar containing the siphoned-off oil and carries it outside toward the ramshackle wooden toolshed, which glows blue from a Coleman lamp he left on earlier. He walks quickly through the dark, hunched over to shield the mouth of the jar from the rain.

Howard has thirteen aliases, all backed up by Washington State driver's licenses. Howard A. Schultz is his current and

favorite identity. He paid one of his runners two grams for the date of birth, address, and Social Security number of the Starbucks coffee mogul.

He sometimes worries that he has stuck with this moniker too long. He enjoys being well known—he craves the underground fame, is proud of his place in tweeker lore—but he also recognizes the hazards of being the top cook in Pierce County or, as Howard likes to call the county that leads the western United States in methamphetamine production, *Methlehem* County.

If you want to make movies, you go to Hollywood. If you want to play poker professionally, you go to Las Vegas. And if you want to be the meth king, you go to Pierce County, Washington, Howard is fond of proclaiming. He grew up in Woodinville, a town north of Seattle, but after his first stay in prison, a short one for burglary, he was released to a halfway house in Tacoma, which proved to be an excellent networking opportunity. He quickly befriended addicts and cooks from around the county and recognized the "high-growth" market for methamphetamine.

Entering the shed, he sets the meth oil down on top of a broken freezer that serves as a storage container. Stocked alongside the tools on rickety shelves is muriatic acid, aluminum foil, a Dr Pepper bottle, rubber tubing, and gaffer's tape—everything he needs to create an HCL generator for the gassing stage.

Under the spooky glow of the lamp hanging from the low roof, he mixes muriatic acid and balls of aluminum foil in the Dr Pepper bottle. Usually he uses rock salt and drain opener, which makes for a cleaner and whiter final product, but Amber used up the drain opener on *a goddamned clogged drain,* so Howard must improvise.

He pokes a tube into the plastic bottle, wraps gaffer's tape around the opening, and the gas generated by the acid and foil,

hydrogen chloride, bubbles through the hose and into the methamphetamine oil.

"Time to snow," he whispers, kneeling ceremoniously.

Sparkles form in the haze as the methamphetamine crystals begin forming—white and dirty beige—clouding the mason jar like a snowstorm.

Because the muriatic acid dirties up the product with tan patches, he will have to clean it with acetone before putting it on the market.

Ice, crank, speed, zoom, it all means money.

Howard gets high just watching this, the tingle spiking through his body. He is reminded of snow globes he shook incessantly as an ADHD child. Enraptured, he does not hear the walkie-talkie at the first crackle.

"Howard," Amber repeats.

He is about to tell her not to call him that, not to call him at all unless it is an absolute emergency, *don't bother me, I'm working,* when the walkie-talkie crackles again.

"Howard, cops!"

"You sure this is the right damn place?" Wyatt asks, stopping the gray Ford Taurus with its low nose pointed up the narrow muddy driveway surrounded by blackberry bushes.

"Pretty sure," Marvin says from the back seat.

"*Pretty* sure?"

"Sorry, every goddamn road out here looks the same. Doesn't it? Don't you think?" Marvin's shaking and babbling. "But this is it. I'm pretty sure. We're like out between Bonney Lake and Sumner, sort of?"

"We're where you told me to go."

"Okay, well, a trailer should be at the top of the driveway."

Headlights shine into the streaky drizzle and darkness as they bounce up the driveway, and then Wyatt clicks on the high beams and there's the trailer, an old silver double-wide with a blue tarp hanging off one end.

Trailer, blue tarp, looks like a meth lab.

Leaving Marvin locked in the back seat, engine running, headlights on, Wyatt steps out and walks up to the front door. His senses are attuned to his surroundings as the drizzle falls quietly. He can hear scurrying inside, the micelike noises he usually hears when tweekers are home.

"Hello," Amber says, opening the front door about six inches, just enough so the child can look out past Amber's skinny thighs.

Immediately Wyatt can smell the ammonia. "Hello, ma'am. I'm Detective Wyatt James." He smiles amiably as he opens his blue blazer enough to display his badge and gun. "Is anyone else inside?"

"Just my child," Amber says, switching unconsciously into a pathetic whine.

"You mind if I come in out of the rain and talk to you?" he says. "You have the right to say no," he adds, "but I'd like to come in if I could." Police officers must, under the law, inform residents they can refuse them entry, but experienced criminals already know this, so it is only the amateurs who allow police inside without a warrant. "I'd like to talk to you about someone," Wyatt says casually, "if you don't mind."

Amber has been in jail before and does not want to return and, in her experience, pissing off police officers often results in a trip downtown, while giving information can lead to a free pass.

"Okay."

"Thanks," Wyatt says. From his inside pocket he pulls out a "Ferrier warnings" form, which reiterates that Amber has the right to refuse him entry, limit his search, or revoke her consent at any time, and he has her sign the sheet acknowledging these rights, *blah, blah, blah.*

As he steps inside, blister packs crush under his shoes. He scans the filthy interior and amid the sundry trash he picks out the blender, the coffee filters, the propane tank, mason jars, porn magazines, and a black cylindrical object that could be either a butt plug or a chew toy.

And this is after *she had time to clean up.*

"How long ago did he leave?"

"Who?"

"Howard."

"Howard?"

Amber fumbles long enough for Wyatt to know that Marvin gave them good intel, albeit too late.

"Yes, *Howard.*"

"Howard," she repeats again, jittery and on the down slide. Wyatt figures she was left without any product, a hasty exit, no doubt.

"Howard Schultz," he says impatiently, eyes watering from the ammonia remnants. "The cook." He puts his palm over the frying pan with white crust, *still warm*. "Where did he go?"

"He left."

"Yes, we've established that. Where did he go?"

"I don't know."

Amber's child is on the floor watching the road and driveway on the television monitor. Wyatt studies the screen for a moment, realizes that his approach was observed. "Let's get out of here," he says when his throat starts to itch. "Your child, too."

Wyatt herds them outside. A cat scampers out with them, disappearing quickly. Between the trailer and his car, Wyatt steps in front of Amber and her child so that he is backlit, partially blocking out the glare of the headlamps. Mist has replaced the drizzle.

"So what's your name?" he asks.

"Amber."

"Of course. Last name?"

After a long pause she says, "Johnson."

Wyatt assumes this as a lie but is not inclined to bother with calling her on it yet.

"Were you helping him cook?"

"Who?"

"Or did he do all the cooking and promise you some product in exchange?"

"That."

"What?"

"He promised me some."

Always works: give them two choices and they will pick what they think is the lesser crime.

"So you let him use your place to cook meth?"

"Yeah."

"Okay. Where did he go?"

"I don't know."

"You don't know if you're going to tell me?"

"I don't know."

"How much do you know about him?"

"Nothing. I just met him today, at this party, at this, like, apartment, more like a motel. . . ."

She's so obviously lying, so obviously tweaking, so obviously useless, Wyatt cuts her off by holding a hand up like a traffic cop. Sometimes he just cannot take another damn lie.

"Stop."

"No, no, I swear—"

"Stop."

"Okay, okay."

Wyatt looks down at the child standing behind Amber's legs. His own eyes are still watering, but she stares back at him with clear pupils, apparently immune to the ammonia. He expects meth will show up in her urine test from secondhand smoke and dermal exposure.

"Have you had dinner?" he asks the child, bending down, hands on knees.

She shakes her head.

"You hungry?"

She nods.

"There's a Denny's down the road. Have you been there?"

She nods, almost smiles.

"We're going to meet a nice woman from the government there, and you can get something to eat, okay?"

The child nods agreeably, either uncomprehending or unfazed.

Flipping open his cell phone, Wyatt rings the on-duty supervisor and gives him a situation update and asks for Child Protective Services and the meth lab team.

"You're calling in CPS?" Amber says when he's finished with the call. "Why?"

"Because you're going downtown."

"To jail?"

He reads Amber her Miranda rights by memory and the child mouths along, as though to a nursery rhyme she has heard many times before.

"Tell Grandma I need bail money," Amber says.

"Turn around." Wyatt clicks on the cuffs. "If you decide you want to talk about Howard, let me know." He turns her around by her shoulders and slides his card in the front pocket of her jeans. She is not ready to pull her hand out of the coconut yet, but tweekers generally detox after about twelve weeks. "I'm Detective Wyatt James. Your public defender will know who I am."

BRANDY, YOU'RE A FINE GIRL

I am, I am Superman, and I know what's happening. . . . This snippet of a song lyric plays over and over in Howard's head as he runs for what seems like miles, tromping in his black cowboy boots, through the woods, across grassy fields, over wooden fences, until he arrives at an intersection, where he stops to finally catch his ragged breath. He sounds like Darth Vader.

To the outside eye Howard looks depleted and decrepit, wheezing like a man dying from the plague, but inside he feels dynamic and destined for greatness, ruling the world like a man holding the hammer of the gods. As dopamine surges through his brain cells he is proud that he is zooming on his own homemade fuel, euphoric that he is wildly free, confident that he can outsmart the cops every time, and these sensations flood together in a kaleidoscope of sweaty, teeth-grinding, finger-twitching, head-bobbing, crazy ecstasy.

I am, I am Superman. . . .

Above him a nearly full moon emerges between dark clouds. He steps into the shadows behind the stop sign, clumsily sits in the tall and wet grass. The closest streetlight is a hundred yards away and there are no cars coming. He pulls out a cell phone, calls a taxi service.

Despite all his licenses, Howard does not drive. He does not own anything that can be traced back to him. The cell phone is registered to Ted Nugent, with a PO box in University Place. When the wireless company eventually shuts down the service for lack of payment, as they invariably do, he will get another phone with one of his other identities.

He collects SSI, Social Security Insurance payments, because he is "disabled" and "unable to maintain employment" after his stroke-resembling collapse in the county jail that followed a week-long meth binge. The disability payments are enough for him to live on even when he is not supplementing his income with meth sales. He relies on the kindness of tweekers for shelter and his only expenses are for manufacturing supplies, Kools, taxis, alcohol, and fast food.

I am, I am Superman. . . .

This song keeps playing in his brain, and he does not know it is an R.E.M. song and if he did he would be amused by the band's name.

When the cab approaches, Howard stands up and waves it down, trying to appear normal and amiable, but he is grinning and fidgeting like a fiend.

Still, the cabbie stops. Howard gives directions to Brandy's house on the outskirts of Eatonville. Amber was fun, but Howard was tired of her squalid little trailer and mouthy four-year-old child. "Bag 'ho" is his phrase for addicts like Amber, women who will have sex for whatever meth residue is left at the bottom of a baggie.

Brandy actually owns a house, not a trailer. She inherited it from her parents when they died. Though she used to share it with her white supremacist boyfriend, word on the street is that he went to prison for domestic violence. Howard stayed with Brandy for a few weeks before she hooked up with the wife-beater and he expects her door is always open for him.

Though he thinks she has sad eyes, which he calls cow eyes, Brandy can be attractive sometimes. Better yet, she has a daughter she saddled with the name Porsche who wore hip huggers and chokers at eleven and *must be twelve by now.*

I am, I am Superman, and I can do anything. . . .

Tacoma is famous for its crime.

Serial killer and rapist Ted Bundy lived in Tacoma, as did serial killer and rapist Robert Yates. Gary Ridgeway, the Green River Killer, is said to have buried bodies in Pierce County. Serial child rapist and murderer Joseph Edward Duncan is from Tacoma. John Lee Malvo and John Allen Muhammad, the D.C. snipers, used a Bushmaster rifle from Bull's Eye Shooter Supply in their former hometown of Tacoma.

David Brame, the Tacoma police chief, murdered his wife and shot himself in a Pierce County strip mall parking lot in 2003. This seemed like a high point, or a low point, until two years later when a disgruntled twenty-year-old meth user carried two semi-automatic weapons to the Tacoma Mall and cut down seven shoppers, prompting Charles Mudede, a reporter with *The Stranger,* a Seattle alternative weekly, to write, "The only time Tacoma makes national news is when one of its citizens opens fire on innocent people."

Mr. Mudede is not entirely correct. Tacoma and Pierce County also make national news for leading the country in methamphetamine labs, and it was national news in 2004 when Sperling's Best Places, a research firm, rated Tacoma "America's Most Stressed-Out City," topping such high-tension contenders as Miami, New Orleans, and New York, and it was national news in 2005 when Stacy Fuson, a *Playboy* Playmate and Tacoma native, became the St. Pauli beer girl. Celebrated in the local *News Tribune* as a Tacoma girl "through and through," she moved to Los Angeles.

Downtown, in the most stressed-out city in the country, is quiet at nine o'clock on a Tuesday, when Wyatt exits the freeway. He returns his unmarked squad car to the parking lot of the County-City Building, a plain eleven-story box containing courtrooms, the County Council chambers, the sheriff's department, and the cramped offices of the Pierce County Prosecuting Attorney.

This classically drab example of functional fifties architecture replaced an ominous gothic courthouse, and Wyatt continually laments the lack of grandeur and gravitas the larger replacement presents to its visitors.

Wyatt could drive the county car to his apartment, but he lives less than a mile away and parking is difficult there and he likes the exercise of walking and the meditative aspect as well. He needs wind-down time before he can sleep.

Though it is not raining, he removes a black umbrella from the trunk. The trek ahead is only about twenty minutes, but he does not want to bet on the rain letting up for long. A light wind blows from the north and the horizon is dark.

He walks briskly south on Tacoma Avenue, stepping through the fallen leaves from the Flowering Cherry trees, enjoying the crisp fall air. Earlier in the day the sidewalk was filled with animal rights protesters passing out leaflets demanding the death penalty for a defendant who poisoned a dog. Child molesters, rapists, and murderers are on trial every day and nobody seems to notice, but when an animal suffers, outrage follows.

At the corner of Eleventh and Tacoma Avenue, Wyatt takes a left, enjoys the postcard view of the steel girders of the Murray Morgan Bridge lit up ahead. On his right are office fronts for bail-bonding companies, the dominant business around the County-City Building, and tweeker alley, a dead-end street near a homeless

shelter where riffraff gather to do drugs, make connections, urinate and defecate, and generally keep the area off-limits to anyone but criminals and police.

Overlooking tweeker alley is the wooden deck of a new nightclub, Syren, trying to make a go of it where many have failed. In the summer hipsters congregate near the railing, smoking cigarettes and drinking microbrews while observing the peccancy below. Tonight there is only one couple outside and they are staring out across the alley as if it does not exist.

Wyatt figures he could, if he wanted to take a stroll, observe half a dozen crimes without even trying. The city has conceded tweeker alley to the ne'er-do-wells. Wyatt sometimes wonders why the homeless folks dragging ratty sleeping bags over their shoulders do not leave the cold and wet Northwest for warm and dry Southern California.

Maybe they, like he, prefer the gloom and the gray?

A couple blocks south of this Wyatt takes a right on Broadway, passing a fountain of concrete blocks and cascading water with an enormous sculpture of pink and tan fiberglass salmon poking out of the water on a metal pipe. *Northwest art: fish and water.* He considers stopping by Fujiya, a sushi restaurant and downtown landmark, but it is closing up on schedule with the other civilized portions of the city.

A block behind him is the Winthrop, a former grand hotel that currently functions as federally subsidized housing for addicts, dealers, and their unfortunate low-income neighbors. Ahead of him, just beyond the Sea Grill, is the new $65 million convention center, lights on as always, an astonishing four-hundred-foot-tall trapezoid, a brightly lit vision of the future with a slanted wall of stainless steel mesh and green-tinted windows looking out over the city toward Commencement Bay.

Just past the convention center he crosses a triangular concrete park toward Pacific Avenue, strolling past five stepped infinity pools that slowly spill into each other. Reflecting off the dark water is the sleek new Tacoma Art Museum, which is constructed with steel and glass much like the convention center, another testament to urban renewal.

He recalls twenty years ago when all of downtown Tacoma was like tweeker alley: prostitutes, drug dealers, bums, and thugs. Customers came from all over the county, including from the two military posts, Fort Lewis and McChord Air Force Base. You would not walk around in soft-soled shoes because of the syringes that popped up more numerous than weeds on an abandoned playground. In some ways it was a cop's dream city: real life that resembled the caricatures of crime meccas in graphic novels.

However, the dotcom wave of prosperity that swept through Tacoma's northern neighbor Seattle flooded into Tacoma as well. Pulp mills, which accounted for the infamous Tacoma aroma, began modernizing or shutting down. In 1993 the transition was symbolically sealed when the Asarco copper smelter tower, one of the city's chief polluters, tumbled in a staged implosion. The Environmental Protection Agency is still appraising the damage to the waterfront.

Tacoma and Seattle, like their California cousin San Francisco, are port towns. Ports are the most vital cities. Ideas, trends, and adventurous spirits drift in by land and sea. Seattle's cool peaked in 1992 when Nirvana became a phenomenon and Microsoft, uninhibited by the Justice Department, was taking over the world.

Coolness, though, like freshness, fades, and as it ebbed from Seattle it flowed into Tacoma. People who would shudder at the thought of crossing the Pierce County border in the 1980s were

shopping for Tacoma houses and lofts by the late 1990s. For years the underdog to Seattle, Tacoma emerged in the new millennium as the hip and gritty alternative, humming with possibilities.

"Tacoma is on a roll," Mayor Bill Baarsma continually announces at the rising number of civic events filling local calendars.

Still, the crime continues in this frontier town.

Criminal subcultures took root in the 1970s when the Department of Corrections, which administers the prison system, began dumping hundreds of violent felons, sex offenders, and drug addicts into Pierce County every year through work release and halfway house programs. Pierce County Prosecutor Gerry Horne calls it the crime warp.

Power brokers in Seattle, heavily invested in the state's economic capital and its world-famous image, successfully keep their fair share of felons out of King County. Seattleites find it much easier to be understanding of criminals and their unfortunate childhoods if the crime stays south.

Drawn to underdogs, challenges, and adrenaline, Wyatt moved to Tacoma—or T-Town, as he calls it—when he graduated from law school. He had already decided to be a cop rather than a lawyer. This was done partly because law school bored him nearly to tears, and partly to aggravate his father, but proved to be a fitting choice despite his motives. He does not discuss his law degree with fellow cops, just as he does not discuss his colonoscopy.

Sometimes he wishes he had a more colorful backstory, such as the detective in one of his favorite books who had a hooker mom who was mysteriously murdered because of her scandalous involvement with powerful and corrupt people. Scandal and mystery intrigue Wyatt. The biggest mystery at his own house was when his father broke some china without telling his mother.

Wyatt tried marriage after his first few years on the force. In retrospect, he is not sure what the attraction to his ex-wife was. She was pretty, primarily by virtue of her youth, and he believed their mutual affection, bouncy in the beginning, would evolve into a romantic, mellow, mutually understanding harmony, the two of them chuckling together over the Sunday paper. Instead they became indifferent roommates.

Nearly a year after the relationship died, she initiated a divorce. He surrendered the house, started renting downtown, and soon decided it was a good thing that he had lost the house and the wife. He is forty years old and loves his job and does not mind his age or the detours he took getting here.

The last stretch of his walk home takes him across a corner of the University of Washington Tacoma campus with its meticulously restored brick buildings and well-lit walkways. The shell of a transformer house for the Snoqualmie Falls Power Company still stands, but the interior has been converted to a library and a twenty-foot glass chandelier by Tacoma native Dale Chihuly hangs in the lobby glowing red, putting Wyatt in mind of a giant squid.

Just as sporadic raindrops start to fall, blown by the north wind, he arrives at his building's security door under a green awning. After entering and checking his empty mailbox, he climbs the wide wooden steps to the second floor. Paintings from residents line the hallways. His building is occupied by artists, students, musicians, writers, and one cop, him.

At an open-house party a neighbor told Wyatt that he was the only resident with a normal job and Wyatt explained that detective work is not a normal job, that it consumes and changes people in much the way he imagined artistic pursuits can, sometimes in good ways, sometimes not. He was surprised to hear himself vocalize this and vowed not to get drunk with civilians again.

He turns the key in the lock of his door and quickly realizes it is not locked.

"Hello," he says, entering, wary.

His voice echoes through the long rectangular loft because of the concrete floors, the whitewashed brick walls, and the minimal furniture in the open space. He has lived here ten years and never bothered to furnish it with more than the essentials. A good friend of his, Mike Lawson, thinks that this is Zen, but Wyatt just calls it a low priority.

The hallway leads into one main room with four arched windows facing east over the bay and the industrialized tide flats and the dim orange lights of the port. Against the north wall is a desk with a laptop computer, steel bookshelves, a futon couch, and a stainless steel table where there is a paperback copy of Haruki Murakami's *Norwegian Wood*.

Nobody is home. His girlfriend, Suki, must have forgotten to lock the door again. The paperback and the futon are hers, along with the empty coffee cup. She has been living with him for more than a month and sometimes he wishes he still had his solitary space, but as he stands here alone now he unexpectedly misses her.

They have been together almost a year and he was on the verge of proposing at the nine-month mark. Instead he proposed that they move in together, buying time. Meanwhile, Howard has become the object of his attention.

For years Wyatt has lived by a simple code: work hard and pursue the truth and the center will hold and everything else will fall into place. Instead, things appear to be tearing apart in a storm of gray, and not quite fast enough to be fun.

He crosses over to his bookshelves and picks up a copy of *Moby-Dick*, brings it over to the futon. Sitting down, he opens the book, and inside the 1,011-page paperback is a carved-out com-

partment holding four artfully rolled joints. He places one in his mouth.

Preferring matches to lighters, he strikes one from a C.J.'s Bail Bonds pack and watches the flame for a moment before he touches it to the tip of the joint. After the excess paper burns off, he breathes in and fills his lungs.

The prickly sensation in his head from being on alert all day starts to subside into a low hum as he enjoys the sweet smell of a respite.

CRIME, KAUAI, AND THE HOLY GHOST

Though he is listening to one of Suki's CDs and reading *The Stranger* and thinking of Howard, he still hears the door open when she enters near midnight.

"Hi," he says from the futon, turning down the music with the remote.

"I'm glad you're still awake," she says, coming over and crawling onto the couch and kissing him.

"Me, too," he says after their lips separate.

"Listening to the Raveonettes?"

He nods. One of the advantages of having a girlfriend who is fourteen years younger is that she keeps him up to speed on new music, which happens to sound a lot like the old music, though the names have changed.

Half Japanese, half Scandinavian, with pale skin and large round eyes, Suki is always a welcome sight for him. She is wearing a red skirt and black tights and a white Strokes T-shirt.

Since his divorce he carried the hope that he would someday meet a girl like Suki, but then he found her and that was the end of the hope and it confused him that he missed having the hope. This made him wonder if the hoping wasn't better than the having.

He does not want to blow it this time.

"Did you notice anything about the door?" he asks.

"No."

"It was locked."

Suki starts laughing. "Oops, I guess you're telling me I *didn't* lock it?"

"Yes, we were robbed."

"That's unfortunate." She smiles slyly. "I'll just have to get a third job and pay you back."

They met at Cutter's Point, a coffee shop on the bottom floor of the building where Suki, a caffeine junkie, works as a barista. He dropped by to chat up a pretty barista named Erika, but one night Suki was working Erika's shift and Wyatt asked Suki out and forgot about Erika.

Suki, Wyatt was surprised to learn on their third date, also works at Foxes, one of Pierce County's several strip clubs. Because he formed his opinion of her before he knew she danced, he cannot picture her in this role. Suki is nothing like the strippers he has met who date other officers. She reads and is upbeat and does not do drugs.

An Army brat, Suki has lived all over the world, settling in Tacoma eleven years ago when she was thirteen. This was when she decided to be an actress. As an only child she was a prodigious reader: Anton Chekhov, Jane Austen, F. Scott Fitzgerald, Jack Kerouac, and later Mary Gaitskill. She wanted to be many things when she grew up—a journalist, a dancer, a veterinarian, a psychiatrist—and she realized she could be all these things and more as an actress, and also avoid a nine-to-five job.

She moved to Venice Beach after she graduated from high school and at first she loved it, the palm tress, the salt air, the smoggy orange chemical sunsets. *Just like in the movies,* she thought as many before her have. She took acting classes, met people, signed with an agent, appeared in three television commercials, and endured four and a half years of rejection, compromising proposals, and general soul-numbing nonsense until she decided to move back home to Tacoma.

Stripping seemed to her a natural progression. She is still acting, she tells herself, some nights playing a jaded tramp, other

nights playing a wide-eyed innocent, and almost every night play-ing a psychiatrist to the men who pay her more to sit with them than to dance. She understands why they say she's an excellent conversationalist: she listens.

Each month she puts at least two hundred dollars into her col-lege savings fund, often more. Initially she wanted to attend Ever-green, but changed her mind when the small liberal arts college in Olympia ignominiously invited a con-artist cop-killer to give a taped commencement speech and Suki's Japanese-American father, a staff sergeant in the U.S. Army, told her that Evergreen was a school for "sheltered, spoiled fools." Suki knew this was an overly broad condemnation, but still she turned her ambition to the UW, Tacoma branch.

"Looks like you have the big book out," she says, eyeing Melville's epic.

"Had a couple hits earlier."

"Long day?"

"And a long night, too. How was yours?"

"Some guy wanted me to talk pornglish to him," she says, shrugging. "And I definitely couldn't get into it."

"You left early?"

"Yeah, bunch of kids without money tonight. Arriving in packs. All saving their twenty dollars for a dance at the end of the night. I didn't want to stick around for that grim finale. And, of course, I missed you."

"Nice afterthought," he says, smiling.

They are both still adjusting to the pluses and minuses of liv-ing together and testing out new forms of communication that accompany the change.

He tells her the story of the night and she is into it, laughing at

his descriptions of Marvin's idiocy, but she turns serious when he gets to the part about Amber and her child.

"That's fucked up," she says. "I don't care if the tweekers want to ruin their lives, but why drag a child into that crap? Why have a child if that's how you're going to act? I don't get it."

Wyatt nods. "There's a lot of tweeker moms out there."

"That's fucked up." She slips off her ballet flats and stretches her legs out onto the coffee table. "I have a question."

"Of course."

"Who the hell is the Holy Ghost? We've got the Father, the Son, and the Holy Ghost, right? And the Father is God, and Jesus is the Son, but who the *hell* is the Holy Ghost?"

This is just the sort of question Suki, an inquisitive soul, occasionally comes up with and that he, as the almost omniscient detective, is supposed to answer.

"Internet?" he suggests, not sure about this one.

They pull office chairs on wheels around the flat computer screen and Wyatt surfs to the *Catholic Encyclopedia*. He and Suki were both raised Catholic under the influence of their mothers, though they are similarly casual about it and out of practice.

"'The Holy Ghost,'" Wyatt reads, 'is the spirit of God and at the same time the spirit of Christ.'"

"Okay," Suki says. "Is that it?"

Wyatt clicks to Bible.com for a second opinion. "The Holy Ghost is 'the comforter,'" he reads, "'the spirit God sends to earth.'"

"The comforter." Suki nods. "Okay, I like that." She pulls an Almond Joy from her purse. "I skipped dinner," she says, offering Wyatt a bite of the chocolate-covered almond and coconut candy.

He shakes his head. "How do you eat stuff like that and stay thin?"

"I don't believe a little piece like this can really be that many calories," she says, munching. "It's just a *little* piece."

This makes sense to Wyatt, though he suspects it should not.

"I have an idea," Suki says, "as long as we're here at the computer."

"Yes?"

"Vacation rentals in Kauai."

"Kauai? Why Kauai?"

"I saw it in that movie with you, *Honeymoon in Vegas*, and I've been picturing it a lot and I want to go there."

Wyatt thinks this a waste of time, as he has no idea when he would have enough time for vacation to justify a long and expensive trip, but Suki seems so excited at the prospect that he agrees and types search terms into Google.

Images of lush greenery, palm trees, deserted sandy beaches, and azure surf fill the screen and mesmerize them into a serene contemplation of paradise. A Corona commercial comes to mind for Wyatt.

"Heaven," Suki says.

"Yes," Wyatt agrees.

Many of the houses are inviting, but one stands out for Suki: Keahwaihi Hale, a glass-walled and green-tile-roofed home on Anini Beach with landscaped gardens. The interior is off-white and sea-foam green with fans hanging from the tan wood-beamed ceiling.

"Let's go!"

"Sure," he says.

"I'm serious. Ever since I met you, you've been talking about taking a vacation, but you never do it."

"I've taken some weekends off."

"And stayed here. You need to get away from this crime-is-everywhere mentality."

"Crime *is* everywhere, but especially here."

"Wyatt."

"Yes?"

"We've never taken a vacation together, even though you keep talking about it. What's up with that?"

Wyatt looks back at the screen. "You really want to go here?" he asks, clicking on more of the images.

"Yes!"

"That sounded . . . definite."

"I have two jobs. I want a vacation. I want to spend time with you."

"Okay, okay, I'll look into it tomorrow," he says, recognizing that he needs to be better about delivering on promises. "After I see when the house is available, and check my schedule at the office, and check my bank account. Cool?"

"Mahalo." She pauses. "What exactly does mahalo mean?"

Wyatt googles mahalo. "'Aloha and mahalo,'" he reads aloud. "'If you learn only two words in Hawaiian, learn these. Aloha is an invocation of the Divine and mahalo is a Divine blessing. Both are acknowledgments of the Divinity that dwells within and without.'"

"'Say them often, as they can be life-transforming and life-enhancing.'" Suki reads on. "'Be careful to use them only if you truly feel mahalo or aloha within. . . .'" Suki smiles at him. "I'll truly feel mahalo if we go there."

"Okay, it's a plan."

"Let's check Exit 133 or Creative Tacoma before we go to bed?"

Suki follows numerous blogs, and www.exit133.com and www.creativetacoma.com track what's happening in Tacoma and prove, she likes to tell Wyatt, that there are noncriminal activities.

"No, let's watch a movie," he says, turning off the computer, as her curiosity can keep them up for hours if unchecked. After watching Steven Spielberg's *Munich,* set in an era before she was born, they researched all night until it became too depressing. If Suki is intrigued by a movie, she likes to look up the writer and director on the Internet, seeking clues to the life experiences and history behind the screen story.

Both Wyatt and Suki are movie aficionados and their relationship, built on sensational sex in the beginning, has evolved into a cinema appreciation club. Stadium Video is a frequent date destination. Wyatt, to his surprise, does not mind.

"What do you want to watch?" he asks.

Suki expected a transition like this, as she has been through it before, sensing and studying the reaction of the man as she morphed from a fantasy who craves sex to a homebody who craves a vacation, her public self versus her truer self.

"*Blue Velvet*?" she suggests.

Set in Lumberton, a town that could be in rural Pierce County, the movie includes one of Wyatt's favorite lines, one that Suki immediately started quoting to him, "I can't figure out if you're a detective or a pervert."

Howard wonders if he should just walk right in and establish himself as the man of the house. Knocking, he fears, feels like the act of a stranger or a salesman.

As he steps up a gravel path through the overgrown grass of the front yard of the dilapidated rambler, he sees no lights. He recalls that Brandy's husband was usually armed, considers that he may have left guns behind.

Opening the broken screen door, he raps it quietly, then loudly. Water drips around him from the broken drainpipe on the porch.

"It's me," he yells. "Howard. Howard Schultz." However, he cannot remember if he was using that alias when he last saw Brandy, so he adds, "The King of Methlehem." If you say something often enough people will repeat it and it will thereby become so, Howard believes. The closest neighbor in this rural corner of the county is almost a football field away and so he yells it again, louder. *"The King of Methlehem!"*

After hearing nothing from inside the house, he walks around to the side where he thinks he remembers Brandy's bedroom was. He raps on the window, *tap, tap-tap-tap.*

"Who the goddamn fuck shit is it?" Brandy screeches. "I've got a gun."

"Me, it's just me, Howard, the king."

Moments later the curtain swings open and Brandy does indeed have a gun, a large handgun, which is pointing in his direction, and should, but does not, fully distract him from her

breasts poking through a T-shirt. She lowers the gun as she slowly recognizes him.

He jabs his finger in the direction of the front door.

A few minutes later he is ranting in her living room about his escape from the cops, exaggerating and fictionalizing and making little sense.

"Could you keep your crazy-ass voice down? Kids are sleeping!"

He lowers his voice, but continues at the same babbling pace, sweating and burning off the last of the meth in his amped system, his feet tapping on the brown and orange shag rug, which is peppered with black cat hairs. When she gets a chance to speak she looks in his dilated eyes and asks the only thing she truly wants to know.

"Are you holding?"

"I did it all, had to. Maybe lost some, too."

"*All* of it?"

"You don't have any?"

"*Me?* I'm broke!"

"I'll cook again tomorrow," he says, assuring Brandy that he is of value to her. "Soon as the stores open."

"Okay." She brightens. "After the kids go to school."

"Does the car in the driveway run?"

"Not very well, but yes."

"What's wrong?"

"Carburetor or something, I don't know."

"Is the car yours?"

"It is now, I guess."

"How long is your boyfriend in jail for?"

"How did you know about that?"

"I keep up on the local news."

"He's got about two years left, including good time."

"He beat on you?"

"Yeah, and my boy Joe, too. Porsche called 911. He took a plea when he found out I was going to testify. If he hadn't kicked Joe around, I would have let it drop."

"He was a fuck," Howard says, finishing off a beer. "You deserve better."

"Yeah."

Her ex is a small-time dealer. One of the secrets of the drug trade is that when you add up the hours, dealing drugs pays below minimum wage—only the players at the top make real money. Still, there are plenty of applicants for entry-level positions. Not many other minimum-wage jobs are glorified in song and cinema.

"Did he leave you any money?" Howard asks.

"Are you fucking joking?"

"Guess not. How's your daughter doing? Porsche?"

"Who knows. She's a brat, screwing up in school. Kids today, they're a mess."

Howard nods in solemn agreement.

"And I haven't heard from her dad in years. He's in prison in California, I think."

Good. Howard nods.

"I should go back to bed," Brandy says, rising from the couch and setting down her beer with the other empties on the stained and cigarette-singed coffee table. "I have to go to work tomorrow."

"You have a *job?*"

"Waitressing," she says, coughing.

"You don't strip anymore?" he asks, disappointment in his voice.

"No, I quit Déjà Vu. That's a young girl's job." She stands. "I'm going back to bed. You can sleep on the couch."

"I'm going to stay up awhile, maybe work on the car."

Almost every tweeker house is accessorized by an old American automobile to tinker with. Howard attends to Brandy's, a 1972 black Camaro Z28 with rust spots. Reliable transportation is necessary for his future schemes and, more immediately, he feels the need to tweak with something, to stay outside his head, *to focus.*

Brandy's garage is filled with sundry junk, so the car is parked in the driveway. Ignoring the light rain, Howard begins disassembling various parts of the engine in the dim glow of the garage lights while vaguely imagining how Brandy's home makes a major meth operation possible.

By dawn he has the carburetor, air filter, fuel filter, and spark plugs lying in the driveway. He sits in the midst of the parts and fastidiously cleans them with gas siphoned from the tank.

Birds are chirping as Howard begins reassembling the carburetor and this proves fatally distracting. He cannot seem to remember what goes where and he blames this on the birds and when he throws a nut down in anger it bounces away into the tall grass, disappearing.

He is crawling around the yard, brushing open the grass with his grease-stained hands, when Porsche and her younger brother Joe walk out of the house and notice him.

Neither of the children seems particularly surprised to see a wild-eyed adult on all fours in the yard.

"Hi, Porsche," Howard says, standing, wiping his hands on his pants and leaving long black finger marks.

"Do I know you?"

Wearing jeans and a sweater, skinny and slouching, Porsche looks just as she did last year except taller, blonder, and with

makeup. Ten is too young for Howard, but twelve, he quickly decides, is not. This is an aesthetic, rather than moral, choice.

Her little brother Joe is wearing black Dickies, a flannel shirt, and red shoelaces, which Howard recognizes as white supremacist garb.

"I'm Howard. I was staying with you for a while last time your dad was in prison."

"He's not my dad," she says.

"Your brother's dad." This exchange does not seem to spark a memory, so he adds, "I bought you clothes and . . . stuff."

"Oh, yeah," she says, nodding slowly. "Well, we gotta catch the bus."

"Your mom still asleep?"

"Probably."

Sleep, Howard suddenly realizes, is in his immediate future and he needs to prepare, needs to take the edge off before he comes down, before he *squishes*. He opens his wallet and pulls out a Klonopin, which he washes down with the backwash from a beer bottle. He prefers Klonopin to Xanax because Klonopin has a greater half-life and therefore keeps you under longer.

Twenty minutes later Howard is mildly nauseous, his twitches are less frequent, and his vision is blurring. He recognizes the Klonopin kicking in and gives up on reconstructing the engine parts he disassembled. All his schemes are temporarily forgotten.

Abandoning the mayhem of the driveway, he robotically marches into the house and finds Brandy's room. He tears off all his clothes, which are wet with rain and sweat, and crawls in beside her for a long dreamless crash.

WELCOME TO THE MONKEY HOUSE

"How many in-custodies?" Mike Lawson asks as he steps through the security door into the domain of the drug trial unit, arriving a few minutes before eight a.m. His workday officially runs from eight-thirty until four-thirty, but in practice is usually eight until six or seven or later, and he is never caught up.

The unit's six legal assistants are grouped together in cubicles near the entrance, surrounded by file cabinets and stacks of manila case files on the cabinets and floors and desks. His LAs process over two hundred cases a month, about ninety-eight percent of which will result in guilty pleas that involve over twenty pages of paperwork in triplicate.

"Twenty-seven," Kati says. "First eleven are on your desk."

"Thanks."

Twenty-seven defendants in Pierce County were arrested on drug charges yesterday, and today they must be charged or released. Reports will be skimmed, decisions will be quick. Mike walks down a cluttered hallway jammed with boxes of Xerox paper, file carts, recycling bins, and printers. He often thinks everyone will die if there is a fire.

The thirteen attorneys in the unit are housed in offices slightly smaller than jail cells, mostly two attorneys to an office, their desks side to side butting up against each other, files spilling over between them. At the end of the hallway is a poster of Martin Luther King with a quote: *Unarmed Truth Is the Most Powerful Thing in the Universe.*

But bet on armed truth, Wyatt once told Mike.

Mike's office, which is dominated by his oversized desk, has a

view of downtown Tacoma and a black and white signed poster of Kurt Cobain with an acoustic guitar, *a cautionary tale*. Mike played bass guitar in a band before he went to law school.

When Mike walks in, Wyatt James is already sitting in one of the guest chairs, knees almost banging up against the desk. To Wyatt's left is a badly scarred metal file cabinet, standard government-issue.

"You still have a leak," Wyatt says, pointing to a brown-stained corner of the white acoustic tile.

"It's a slow one." Mike hangs up his raincoat and suit jacket behind the door. "You look like you haven't slept for a while."

"Business is brisk. What happened with the lab they found last week at that trailer in South Prairie?"

"Couldn't charge it."

"Problematic search," Wyatt guesses.

"No warrant, no exigent circumstances."

"How bad?"

"The Gestapo would blush."

"Marcello?"

"Yeah."

"Marcello's a good cop, just a little overeager. I'll talk to him. He felt bad about that lawsuit."

"Which one?"

"Both, but especially the one where he got the lab address wrong, and the elderly neighbor freaked out when his door was kicked down."

"You mean the heart attack?"

"Come on, it wasn't an actual heart attack. The guy just fainted is all. He was fine."

"After receiving his out-of-court settlement."

"Living near tweekers is hazardous."

Mike logs in to his computer. The windows are streaked with rain and you cannot see anything outside but fuzzy outlines of buildings that look like they are melting.

Death has been on Mike's mind of late, his own in particular, but also in general, and it does not take much to trigger the morbidity. Clouds, for example, bring it on, which is problematic when you live in the Pacific Northwest, the cloudiest corner of the country.

"Couldn't sleep last night," Mike says, "so I watched *Cool Hand Luke* again."

"Excellent."

"Best line besides 'What we've got here is a failure to communicate'?"

"'You're going to get your head right, Luke.'"

This is one of their rituals. Sometimes they will riff on and on, until they agree on the best line, but Mike cannot think of another quotable line this morning. His mind is already calculating the miscellaneous tasks ahead.

"So what's up?" he asks as he continues to wait for the outdated government computer to power up.

"I want to try to turn a couple defendants into informants, including a woman from a recent trailer lab. Tweekers who probably don't meet your criteria."

"Probably don't?"

"Okay. Definitely don't."

Mike nods, indicating a willingness to at least listen to Wyatt's pitch, despite the din outside his open door as support staff looking for files and attorneys prepping for court pass back and forth chattering. Someone is always looking for something lost.

Wyatt has known Mike for almost twelve years, going back to when Mike was an aggressive twenty-eight-year-old just out of

law school. Many rookie prosecutors annoy Wyatt with their self-importance and power trips, but he liked Mike, found him to be a kindred spirit. Mike was older than most freshmen and he looked and acted like Wyatt believes a prosecutor should: blue suit, white shirt, passionate about the cause but not psychotically so.

However, Wyatt laments Mike's promotion to team chief. Becoming a supervisor is the worst thing that can happen to a detective or a trial attorney, in Wyatt's opinion. They suddenly have to consider how the herd will react to their every move.

Kati enters and drops a few more files in the bin. "Bail returns," she explains apologetically. "We're up to thirty-one. Looks like about six are labs." On her way out she adds, "Oh, and the Xerox machine is broken again."

"This is about Howard," Wyatt explains after she leaves.

"Your white whale."

"In the last week we've taken down a couple people who can get us close to him."

"You figured out his real name yet?"

"We're sticking with Beelzebub for now."

One of the trial attorneys pokes his head into the office. "Twenty-seven in-custodies?"

"I thought you were in trial."

"Defendant didn't show."

"Grab one, thanks."

He nods to Wyatt, takes a couple files out of the tall stack in the bin on Mike's desk, and disappears.

"Thanks," Mike says, grabbing one himself.

"You want me to come back later," Wyatt asks, "when it's less crazy?"

"I'm not going to be here at midnight."

"Okay, I'll try to keep this quick. Both of these characters could

be good informants, but the guy has an Assault One pending, as well as some domestic violence convictions, and the woman is charged with Endangerment of a Minor with a Controlled Substance."

Wyatt holds up his hand as Mike is about to speak. "I know you wouldn't want to normally work either of these two, but they're high-value, potentially at least. The guy led us to one of Howard's guerrilla trailer labs, we only missed him by a few minutes. And the girl, we found her there, with her kid."

Mike's head fills with headlines from the *News Tribune: Prosecutor Gives Violent Criminal a Free Pass, Prosecutor Says No Jail for Meth Mom*, and then suddenly he's standing in front of a news camera stammering out a mea culpa.

"If you could," the reporter asks, *"would you take back this horrific fuckup?"*

"Can't do it, Wyatt. We have guidelines for informants."

"Rules are made to be bent, Counselor."

"That's fine talk for an officer of the law."

"If you're investigating the devil, you don't go to heaven for witnesses."

"Nice line, but I'm not going to give meth mom a free pass right back to where she was. Maybe we can discuss it again after she's been clean for a few weeks."

Wyatt takes a pause, considers angles. "Let me tell you about the guy, Marvin."

Cort, the assistant supervisor, enters, still wearing his blue raincoat, his short hair wet. "Did you watch TV last night?" he asks, apparently outraged. "There's a new show on called *UnJustice* or something, and it's based on *The Innocence Project*, that whore Barry Scheck's self-promotion project."

"Barry Scheck?" Wyatt says. "The O.J. guy?"

"The very one," Cort says. "This show nearly made me vomit. It takes the ten- to twenty-year appeal process, reduces it to nine days so there's a 'ticking clock' "—he makes quotes in the air with his fingers—"and they actually rip pages off a calendar as each day passes. There are too many clichés to list, the acting is worse than the Shopping Channel, and the writers know nothing about the criminal justice system. They think sua sponte is an Italian ice cream."

Wyatt and Mike laugh as Cort continues his rant.

"Kyle McLachlan is the star, and he totally debases himself, playing a corporate lawyer with political ambitions who thinks he can become the attorney general or something by . . . freeing 'innocent convicted people'—he makes quotes in the air again—and so the show takes the most contrived, ridiculous, laughable conspiracy theories you've ever heard desperate defense attorneys make up, and then alters reality so the ridiculous conspiracy theory turns out to be . . . *true!*" He shakes his head. "It's going to totally poison our jury panels."

"Don't worry," Mike says. "I'm going to start my own TV show. It will focus on the victims of the hundreds of child molesters, rapists, meth cooks, and murderers who walk free on technicalities. We'll call it *The Guilt Project.*"

"How about if a detective," Wyatt suggests, getting into it, "say . . . me, hunts them down and shoots them?"

"All true stories end in death."

"I like it," Cort says, picking up half a dozen files from the bin before leaving for his own office directly across the hall.

"Life in a MASH unit," Mike says. "Tell me about Marvin."

"Assault case pending. Public service shooting. Shot another tweeker with the guy's own gun when they were playing with it. It was a total accident."

"Accident?"

"Yeah, I know it sounds like bullshit, but I looked into it and Marvin's too wimpy to shoot anyone intentionally."

"And the DV?"

"Misdemeanors."

"I hate putting wife-beaters on contract. You never know when they'll go ballistic and kill some woman."

"This guy is a twerp."

"They usually are."

"If you want a tweeker informant, you're going to have to work with wife-beaters, because meth and DV go together like rum and Coke at a high school prom."

Mike leans back in his chair, breathes in deeply.

A drop of water falls from the ceiling onto the rug near Wyatt's feet. He can feel the no coming, but he does not want Mike to say it, so he changes the subject.

"The leak doesn't bother you?"

"I'm used to it."

"I think it would get to me."

"Listen, I appreciate where you're coming from on this," Mike finally says, and Wyatt immediately pegs this as supervisor-speak, and again cuts him off before he can say no.

"I like the straight-arrow thing you've got going for you now, Mike, I really do," Wyatt says. "But you're not prosecuting sex crimes anymore. You're working in the drug world, and it's all about informants, and they're all unpredictable, they're all risky. They're all fucking *criminals*."

Mike nods, missing the days when he was simply a trial lawyer without supervisory responsibility.

"Don't answer now," Wyatt says. "Just think about it. Okay?"

"But we don't know enough about this character. He sounds

like just another garden-variety meth maggot. Nobody worth risking our reputations on."

"*What* reputations? I'm known as a troublemaker."

"Okay, he's not important enough to risk *my* reputation."

"Which I understand is the important thing here."

"Exactly."

"Need help with charging?"

Another deputy prosecutor quickly grabs a couple files from the in-box and goes back to her office across the hall before Mike can even answer.

"What happened to your trial?" he calls out to her.

"Defense attorney didn't show," she yells back.

Mike shrugs to Wyatt: *If it's not one thing, it's another.*

"You believe in signs," Wyatt says.

"Yes, sometimes."

"Communication from the nonmaterial world?"

"Yes?"

"Well, I got a sign on this case, Mike. I swear to fucking God."

"A sign?"

"A Starbucks cup."

Mike stares, trying to gauge his seriousness.

"I mean it," Wyatt says, knowing Mike's look.

"The thing about signs is this," Mike says. "You have to be careful not to misinterpret them."

"You're always worried that using informants is going to blow up, I know."

"I'll just explain to the media that you had a sign. A Starbucks cup. They'll understand."

"I'll take the hit if something goes sideways. You know I'm one of the king's men and I don't want to do anything to hurt your election chances."

"My boss is elected," Mike says. "Not me."

"Just thinking ahead, chief. Like you do."

Politically, the prosecutor's office is a napping giant, but Wyatt recognizes that there are unspoken plans for a wake-up. Politics, as far as Wyatt can tell, is just a matter of understanding and liking people. However, unlike Mike, Wyatt believes these qualities are mutually exclusive.

Another deputy prosecutor steps into the office, breathing heavy, one hand holding multiple files, one hand on his chest.

"You look like you've been shot," Wyatt says.

"Two of the elevators are out," he explains between breaths. "I took the stairs from five, where I saw that reporter from the *News Tribune*. She's looking for you, Mike. She wants a quote on the Bush administration's latest."

"Her name's Karen. What latest?"

"They're taking money from meth prosecution and putting it into marijuana." He removes the hand from his chest and grabs a file for charging on his way out. "Just wanted to give you a heads-up."

"Ignoring cancer," Mike says, "fighting the head cold."

"Follow the money," Wyatt says. "We raid a marijuana grower, we find SUVs and loads of cash. We raid a meth lab, we find blue tarps and porn."

Another deputy prosecutor steps in, frazzled. "When you have a second, Mike, I have to talk to you about this issue that came up in trial. I want to kill the judge."

"Bad idea," Mike says.

"I have definitely *not* reached a state of Zen on this case."

"Give me half a minute here."

"Thanks," he says, picking up a file for charging.

"No," Mike says, "you're still in trial, right?"

"Right," he says, setting the file back. He walks out muttering, exhibiting symptoms of shell-shock, a common sight in a trial unit.

"Okay, I'll let you get back to work," Wyatt says, standing and looking over Mike's head at the poster. "But you know what Cobain said about this sort of situation?"

"'A mosquito, my libido'?"

"'The worst crime is faking it.' We need to go after Howard and those guys, really try to put the stake through their hearts. Either that or quit pretending like we're doing something."

A gust of wind whistles across the window, smearing the rain in streaks. Another drop falls from the ceiling.

"We've got two choices here," Mike says. "Find a semi-clean informant, or find evidence that this Howard Schultz character is worth the risk. What makes him different from the hundreds of other cooks?"

"Well, he's ambitious. He's like you in that way."

Home around eight p.m., Mike has a handful of peanuts and scotch straight up for dinner while he reads the *News Tribune*. He lives a long walk from the courthouse, near Stadium High School, the coolest school building he has ever seen, a gothic castle that was featured in the movie *10 Things I Hate About You.* Mike, who graduated from Bellarmine Prep, believes high school would have been a finer aesthetic experience in such a structure.

Environment matters.

After polishing off the peanuts, still wearing his blue suit, raincoat, and wingtips, he steps out into the backyard of his 1920 Craftsman home. Just off his deck is a long green lawn he uses for drunken croquet in the summer.

At the end of the lawn is a rock garden Mike installed himself, an oval bed of swirling furrows of raked round pebbles, partially surrounded by Japanese maple trees with wet orange and yellow leaves covered with raindrops that glisten in the porch light. There are two boulders on the edges on the rock garden for sitting, and a pedestal birdbath in the middle. Carrying a scotch, smoking an unfiltered Camel, Mike walks across the wet grass and stops at the edge and focuses on the birdbath.

Tiny sporadic raindrops plop into the dark water.

Though he does not particularly like birds, Mike bought the birdbath because of an experience he had at a girlfriend's house in college. One morning, hungover, hoping to clear his head, he was sipping coffee in the backyard and blankly gazing at a birdbath when an epiphany swept over him.

There was sunshine on the horizon but a light rain falling,

and he was watching the concentric circles from the falling drops when suddenly he had a flowing sensation that rose from his feet and possessed his body and then his mind. Suddenly the chaos that had been perplexing him melted and was replaced by a calm understanding that everything was ordered, everything was connected, everything was cool. For the seconds it lasted it was bliss.

He did not know what to make of this.

After college, when he was in the band and had extra time on his hands, Mike studied Shotokan karate and his sensei encouraged him to begin meditating. He considered several mantras, including Rama, which unfortunately put him in mind of Top Ramen noodles. He decided to skip the mantra and concentrate on breathing, and this was relaxing and centered him but never brought him to the bliss he had experienced staring into the ex-girlfriend's birdbath.

Lack of commitment is what doomed his band, in Mike's estimation, and since the failure of the band Mike decided he would not do anything without total commitment. Thus he pursued his interest in the spiritual world as a devoted student, something he had never been in college.

In his search to find a code to live by he bought numerous books, including Zen books, *The Way of Zen* by Alan Watts, *Zen for Americans* by Soyen Shaku, translated by D. T. Suzuki, *Zen and the Art of Archery* by Eugen Herrigel, *Zen and the Art of Motorcycle Maintenance* by Robert Pirsig, *Zen and the Art of Poker* by Larry W. Phillips, and his favorite title, *"Don't Just Do Something, Sit There* by Sylvia Boorstein.

After the Zen binge, he turned to *The Varieties of Religious Experience* by William James, a Kierkegaard anthology and some Schopenhauer, all of Hemingway, which he enjoyed, and Dostoyevsky, which he did not realize he enjoyed until years later.

These books led him to law school and then the Prosecuting Attorney's office because there are not many occupations where the job description is a search for the truth and the paycheck is regular. As novelist Tom Robbins wrote, there is "a certain Buddhistic calm" that comes with having a job and money in the bank.

As far as Mike could determine, the goal of Zen is enlightenment, or satori, and ultimately Nirvana, which, according to Merriam-Webster online, is "the cessation of desire." This perplexed Mike for months. He played the following cross-examination out in his head repeatedly.

Me: The goal of Zen is Nirvana?

Buddha: Yes.

Me: Nirvana includes the cessation of desire?

Buddha: Yes.

Me: Reaching Zen means no longer wanting anything.

Buddha: Yes.

Me: So if you have reached Zen, you don't even want to be Zen?

Buddha stares back, smiling beatifically, cryptic and fat and infuriating.

Mike gave up meditating for a while, *never mind Nirvana*, though he still recommended Zen to his colleagues as a way to temper the maddening absurdities of the criminal justice system.

Hard work became his religion, and it occupied more hours than any church. He gave up activities that took time away from work, most of which, such as television and golf, he did not miss,

and some, such as reading and dating, he did. He attributed his courtroom successes to relentless work, though it came to him naturally.

When the stress of a prosecutor's endless caseload began causing him to lose sleep and grind his teeth and was threatening to take over his life, he returned to meditation and added another title to his shelf, *Meditation for Dummies* by Stephan Bodian.

Bodian posits the idea that there are four popular ways to deal with the noise of the modern world: addiction, consumerism, fundamentalism, and entertainment, all of which are flawed because they are one-dimensional, increase alienation, and do not enrich one's soul.

Based on his experience observing addicts in the criminal justice system, fundamentalists in politics, and consumerists in the legal and civilian communities, all of whom seem remarkably similar, Mike mostly agrees.

Entertainment he can not join Bodian in condemning because Mike loves movies and music and literature and he is convinced these things are good and help him face death.

Accepting death is on his to-do list.

His cupped cigarette becomes soggy in the drizzle, and he drops it, grinds it out with his wingtip. *Advantage of unfiltered smokes: biodegradable and good for the lawn.*

He stares at the birdbath and sips his scotch until the glass is empty and his head is dripping wet, bliss eluding him once again.

Stiff and sore, Howard struggles out of bed after being down for nearly thirty hours, an entire day lost. Though the jittery anxiety of the day before yesterday is gone, it is replaced by a numb depression Howard likes even less. His mind feels like mud.

Taking heavy and awkward steps, he staggers into the kitchen and he is relieved to see Brandy at the kitchen table eating cereal. Rotting apples and bananas sit in a Tupperware bowl in the center of the table.

"Eating . . ." he says, voice hoarse, the rest of the sentence fading away.

"Good morning."

"Do you . . . like . . . have . . . baby food?"

"Baby food?" She frowns. "No."

"Gate . . . Gatorade?"

"No."

"Mountain Dew?"

"No."

"We *need* Mountain Dew."

He sits down across from her, arms on the table, shoulders slumped. Outside it is another gray fall day. Through dirty sliding glass doors he can see an unkempt backyard of dirt and crabgrass that stretches out to a dilapidated barn with faded and cracked red paint.

"What time is it?" he asks.

"A little after one."

"I need some food."

"What do you want?"

"A banana that's not . . . brown?"

"Don't have any. I'd go get you something, but you took the fucking car apart yesterday."

"I can fix it . . . better."

"I missed work because of you."

"Because of me. Who?"

"Because my fucking car isn't running."

"I told you, I'll fix the . . . car."

"You going to cook today? I need to zoom."

Brandy has been off meth for months, but with Howard around it is all she can think about, that rush. His presence makes meth seem imminent, like the dark clouds that portend rain.

Howard wipes his nose, looks around the kitchen. On the wall near the stove is a land line. He shoves back his chair, groaning, and crosses over and picks up the phone to call a client.

"Requisition mission," he says, giving the client instructions on where to pick him up—an intersection about a mile from the house because he does not want a loose-lipped tweeker to know where he is staying.

Brandy and Howard wait by the side of the road, tapping their feet and rubbing their hands. The client, a long-haired pimply-faced teenager whose name Howard cannot remember, drives up in an early seventies black Firebird with a hood that is half gray primer paint and half fire-breathing bird. Tweeker cars are always a work in progress.

First they stop at Schuck's, park in back. Howard purchases Heet and automobile starter fluid, and the clerk looks uneasy as he rings up the purchases, possibly because Howard is shaking and sweating on a cold morning.

"Car issues," Howard says, sensing suspicion, but it comes out sounding like "Carissa."

"What?"

"What? Nothing."

He's going to call the cops, Howard thinks as he walks out the door, and he looks over his shoulder from the parking lot, and sure enough the clerk is on the phone.

Suspicious prick.

Taking the keys from his teenage driver, making sure nobody sees him, Howard stashes his purchases in the trunk because cops cannot open it without a warrant. When he was just starting in the business he had a meth lab case dismissed because the officer opened his unlocked trunk.

Though in the good old days it would be extremely unlikely that the sheriff's department would have the time or inclination to respond to a clerk's suspicions, it seems to Howard that lately *everyone* is on the lookout for meth labs, *it's a clampdown.*

Next stop, Home Depot, and Howard picks up lithium batteries, drain cleaner, and rock salt, again tossing the goods into the trunk. Rarely does he pick up three items in one store, but he's jonesing and so is Brandy and so is his driver and Howard wants to deliver soon, wants to be *the man.*

At Rite-Aid, Howard sends the teenage driver inside for two boxes of Sudafed, the legal limit. Howard and Brandy wait in the car because of the logbook customers must sign to purchase pseudoephedrine. On the Internet Howard followed the legislative battle that accompanied the law that created these restrictions and was surprised to see the retailers, who had billions of dollars at stake, lose the battle.

Pfizer, the company best known for Viagra, also manufactures Sudafed. Sales of Sudafed and other pseudoephedrine products began climbing at an astronomical rate as Nazi labs proliferated across the country in the eighties and nineties. Pfizer

and other pharmaceutical companies are more profitable than the drug cartels and they do not have to pay off or kill police to stay in business.

Howard trusts the pharmaceuticals will find a way to keep the supply lines open.

What's good for business is good for America.

About a mile down the road they stop at a Safeway and once again Howard instructs the teenager to purchase two boxes of Sudafed.

"You have to show ID," he says. "They made me show my license at the Rite-Aid."

"Don't you think I fucking know that?" Howard reaches into a pocket of his jeans and hands the kid a Washington driver's license for Peter Farrelly, the director of *Dumb and Dumber,* one of Howard's favorite movies. Farrelly has salt-and-pepper hair and a goatee.

"That doesn't look like me," the driver says.

"Do you think the minimum-wage slave working here cares?"

"I dunno."

"Well, they don't. I've used that ID plenty."

"Maybe we should go to the chink store instead?"

"Cops shut it down."

"You'll do fine," Brandy says. "You have an innocent face."

An innocent zit-face, Howard almost adds.

Bolstered by Brandy's confidence, the driver completes his assignment in Safeway, skipping out of the store with the boxes held high like a trophy.

A few minutes later they are on their way to one more store, mission almost accomplished, but they are lit up from behind: flashing lights and a siren burst.

"Fuck."

"Fuck!"

"Fucking *shit*," Howard says. "Don't panic. Did you forget to signal your turn?"

"I don't know, maybe. Fuck."

"Turn on your windshield wipers."

"It's not raining."

"Yes, it is."

"No, it's not!"

"Maintain! Everyone just *maintain*."

All three light up Kools, and the car quickly fills with smoke like a scene from a Cheech and Chong movie.

"What should I do?" the driver asks, speed unchanged.

"What should you do? What do you think? Pull over, you idiot."

"Right, sure, that's a good idea, I guess."

"Fucking maintain."

"Maintain?"

"Act like you haven't done anything wrong," Howard says. "And shove the bags under your seat."

"Right," the driver says, hands shaking as one foot presses the brake and the other foot clumsily kicks the bags from Rite-Aid and Safeway under his bucket seat.

Deputy Newton, a twenty-one-year-old rookie, approaches the driver's-side window. "Are you aware that your left taillight is broken?" the deputy asks. He has freckles and looks as though he just started shaving.

"No, Officer," the driver says between nervous puffs.

"Please put out the cigarette."

After the driver does so, the deputy asks him for his driver's license, registration, and proof of insurance. Providing one out of three, his license, the driver apologizes profusely.

"I think my license might be suspended."

"You don't know?"

"I'm pretty sure it is."

"Been shopping?" the deputy asks as he scans the interior the cluttered car, *the usual meth mess.*

"No."

"No?" The deputy points to the bags on the floorboard poking out from under the driver's seat, the Sudafed packages visible through the plastic. "You sure?"

"Oh, yeah."

"Rite-Aid?"

"Yes."

"Anyplace else?"

"No."

"You were coming from the Safeway parking lot."

"Oh, yeah, well, that's right. Rite-Aid and then Safeway because . . . they didn't have everything I needed."

"What didn't they have?"

The driver stares back at the deputy while Howard is thinking *moron* so loud he's surprised he cannot be heard.

"Let me guess," the deputy finally says when no answer is forthcoming. "Cold medicine?"

"I'm not feeling well." The driver coughs, wipes the sweat off his forehead.

"How many boxes?" the deputy asks.

"Just two."

"At each store?"

"Right. I mean, no. Two total. I was looking for Sudafed and they only had one box at Rite-Aid and so we went to Safeway for more."

"More?"

"Just two more."

"That would make three."

"I mean one more, two total."

As the deputy looks over at him, Howard sits silent, controlling his twitching as much as he can, thinking over and over, *Why must I live my life surrounded by morons?*

"You want to show me there's only one box in the bag?" the deputy says, turning his attention back to the driver.

"I think it's only one."

"So it might be two in each bag?"

"I don't know. I don't remember."

"Sounds like there might be two in each bag."

"Okay, yeah, maybe."

"Who bought them?"

Howard, for the first time, moves his head and speaks up. "We're just hitchhikers," he says. "This kid offered us a ride in the parking lot, out to. . . Orting. We don't really know him."

"That's true," the driver says on cue.

That's bullshit, the deputy thinks. "So who bought the boxes?" he asks the driver.

"I did."

"Four boxes for yourself?"

"I guess so, yeah."

"Today?"

"Yeah."

"Do you know it's against the law to buy more than two packages of pseudoephedrine in a twenty-four-hour period?"

"Yeah, I mean, no."

After arresting the driver for the misdemeanor and placing him in the patrol car, he clears the passengers out to the side of the road and commences a search of the car. He finds withered french

fries, coffee cups, cigarette butts, candy bar wrappers, and endless junk, but no evidence beyond the four full packages of Sudafed and several empty pseudo packages, presumably from previous smurfing, as the purchasing of large numbers of pseudo packages is known in the trade.

As strings of rain begin falling, he walks back to the patrol car and asks the driver if anything is in the trunk.

"A spare tire, I think."

"Anything illegal?"

"Not that I know of."

"So there might be?"

Not wanting to fall down that slippery slope again, the driver quickly says, "No, sir."

"Whose car is it?"

"A friend's."

"What's your friend's name?"

After a long pause the driver says, "Hugh."

"Hugh."

"Yeah, Hugh." His head nods rapidly. "That's his name."

"Hugh what?"

"Hugh . . . don't know."

"Of course."

For a moment there's a silent standoff. The deputy lacks probable cause for a warrant to get into the trunk, and the driver has gone into denial mode.

"Can we go now?" Howard asks, still standing on the side of the road with Brandy, pulling out his cell phone to call a taxi, knowing the deputy cannot even ask for ID from a passenger.

I know my rights, he gloats silently.

Holed up at a Lakewood motel that Howard paid for with a stolen credit card, he and Brandy sit on the bed hunched over a mirror he tore off the bathroom wall, clothes wet, heat on high, sweating. Their sinuses are sufficiently damaged that they cannot smell each other.

Howard methodically cuts the off-white lines with a Swiss Army knife as Brandy stares, her eyes jerking back and forth as she watches.

"Would you fucking hurry up?"

"Would you fucking shut up?"

"I'm sorry, I just don't wanna squish."

"Don't act like a bag 'ho."

Delaying consciously now, he chops the powder up for another thirty seconds, meticulously shaping two lines to the side of the pile. Moving slowly, he snorts up one of the lines with a dollar bill.

"*Please*," Brandy says. "I'm *really* sorry."

He hands her the bill and she quickly hoovers up the other line. "Holy Mother of fucking Christ," she says, reeling her head back. "That's *harsh*."

"It's been stepped on, fucking Mexican crank."

Howard hates buying from competitors, but he needed a boost after the kid was busted, and so he tracked down an identity thief who sometimes deals from the motel. Their room is dirty beige and orange and on the wall above the bed is an amateurish painting of a cowboy sitting on a horse in a field looking out at a sun setting over a distant mountain.

As Howard loses his high, he starts to get into his head and this is the last place in the world he wants to be, *can't go there, can't go there.*

"Here's the plan," he says, looking up, wiping his nose. "Like what's-his-name said, the 'times are a-changing.' They're keeping logbooks on pseudo purchases, following the runners, busting people, turning them into snitches. Smurfing has become too dangerous."

Brandy has no idea what Howard is babbling about, but she can sense it is important to him and so she nods encouragingly.

"Yeah?"

"Absolutely."

"Are you going to cut more lines?"

"I have to do something to deal with the changes," he says, bending over, slicing up a new set of lines. "Here's what I do. I got the know-how, I got the clients, I got the distribution network. I just need to start a major cook operation. No more of these little guerrilla labs, but a big-time lab."

"Where?" Brandy asks, thinking a response is required.

"Your place."

"My place?"

"The barn." He lifts the knife off the mirror and points at the line nearest Brandy. "All I need is a pseudo supplier, someone with serious access, so I can do some serious cooking. I mean, I'm almost thirty-three, it's time for me to do something with my life."

Brandy leans forward with the dollar bill and snorts up the line and it is less painful this time but she still makes a face and shakes her head.

"So what do you think?" he asks.

"Fucking harsh."

"About the plan."

"The plan?"

"Big labs are the next wave. And I'm going to be riding it." He juts his arms out as though he's up on a surfboard. "What do you fuckin' think?"

Brandy wipes her nose, breathes in raggedly, her white-crusted nostrils flaring.

"You think a lot," she finally says.

He nods. "Yep."

"More people should," she adds. "Thinking's good. I've always liked that about you."

"That's why I'm the King of Methlehem. And now you're going to be the queen."

The future queen greedily leans down for the other line and it all sounds good in the moment.

FOOD FOR THOUGHT

Over two hundred people line up under the freeway overpass near the Tacoma Dome every Friday night, some homeless, some low-income, some in wheelchairs or on crutches, many with their children.

Volunteers in orange safety vests hold them in a semi-orderly line on the north side of Twenty-fourth Street while a diverse group of do-gooders set up tables in a parking lot on the other side of the street and load the tables with blankets, clothes, sandwiches in plastic baggies, boxes of cereal, apples, and Bibles.

Diesel generators provide the electricity for the bright construction-site lights that flood the area with a warm glow, and for the amplifiers of the surprisingly tight band that plays everything from folk tunes to Christian rock to Bruce Springsteen.

Pastor Ed and Pastor Jack are the chief organizers of this event, though they deny the organization is by design. People show up to give out food and clothes, and other people show up to receive food and clothes. That's all there is to it, they say, along with the most important thing: *God's will.*

On his way to reconnoiter the Friday Night Feed, Wyatt stops at the Tacoma Book Center two blocks away, a used book store in a one-story brick building. The windows are boarded up. Out front on a cart, when it is not raining, there are books offered up for twenty-five cents, including some good ones.

Inside, the air is musty and stale and the lighting dim, but Wyatt can spend hours browsing. He keeps a close eye on his

watch so this does not happen. After a few minutes he finds a Murakami novel he thinks Suki has not yet read, *A Wild Sheep Chase*, and buys it for four dollars.

Wyatt has blown countless relationships in his life and wants this one to be different. He does not quite know yet what makes a relationship work, but he knows that little gestures help, and indifference is death.

Placing the paperback in his blazer pocket, protecting it from the light drizzle, he walks down Dome Street across the railroad tracks. At Twenty-fourth he takes a left toward the Feed.

Tweekers do not usually attend the Feed, as food is not a priority, but when Marvin is out of money he withdraws from meth and develops an appetite. As Wyatt circles the parking lot he spots Marvin on the fringe with a fidgety group, not quite in line, wearing a ragged overcoat. The men around him scatter like a covey of quail as Wyatt approaches.

Marvin is about to bolt, too, but Wyatt freezes him in place with eye contact. "Hi, Marvin."

"What's up?"

"I have to arrest you on a warrant."

"Oh, man. No, you said . . . no, *man*."

Wyatt snaps the cuffs on as bystanders watch, accustomed to the sight. A preteen girl in a jean jacket scrutinizes the process with particular attention. Wyatt smiles at her reassuringly, but all he gets back from her is a cold stare. He suspects her parents have not told her good things about the police.

"Man," Marvin says, "you told me—"

"Shut up."

When they have walked far enough away from the crowd Wyatt explains that he just wants to talk, but had to arrest Marvin so his friends would not suspect he is a snitch.

"Oh. Thanks, man."

"You're welcome."

"So the warrant is squashed?"

"No, the warrant's still outstanding."

They continue to walk toward the Taurus so that Wyatt can drive him away and minimize suspicion. Marvin would otherwise just return to the Feed and gab.

"I thought you were going to squash the warrant on that assault case," he says.

"The prosecutor wasn't willing to put you on contract. Not yet."

"Why not?"

"Because you have a shitty criminal history."

"Doesn't everybody?"

"Yeah, well, not quite as bad as yours. You've got that Assault One."

"It was an accident!"

"Yeah, you've told me, but we're going to have to promise the prosecutor something big you can deliver."

Wyatt is so used to lying to defendants about this sort of thing—playing the good cop to the prosecutor's bad cop—he worries that he might sound different telling the truth.

"Like what?" Marvin asks.

"I want to know what Howard has his hands in, besides cooking."

"Everything."

"What do you mean, 'everything'?"

"Like cooking and identity theft and stolen property and stuff?"

"Was that a statement or a question?"

Marvin pauses. "What do you mean?"

"Tell me about his involvement in identity theft."

"Well, he knows dozens of tweekers and he sometimes trades meth to them for stolen identities, and sometimes he hires people."

"Hires people to do what?"

"Steal shit, steal identities. They usually go bad quick, the identities, people report it, so there's like a constant demand for new ones."

"Can I prove it?"

"Prove what?"

"That he's an identity theft ringleader."

"Everybody knows he's into identity theft."

"What do you think would happen if a prosecutor called me to give evidence in a trial and all I said was, 'Everybody knows he's into identity theft?' "

Marvin thinks hard about this. "The guy would go to jail?" he finally answers.

"True, but that's not my point." Wyatt wonders if Marvin's brain will ever return to full functionality. "My point is that the prosecutor wants proof, something more than hearsay."

"And you'll squash the warrant if I give you something? Proof?"

"Yes, and the word is *quash*. You quash a warrant."

Soft daylight streams into the barn through cracks, knotholes, and missing side planks, illuminating ragged spiderwebs throughout. The space is slightly larger than a two-car garage, and the tall double doors open wide. Against the far side is a rusting refrigerator, a wheelbarrow, an ancient lawn mower, and a long and worn wooden workbench.

Kicking the dirt with the heel of his cowboy boot he announces, "This is it, this is where Pierce County history is going to be made."

Howard is confident that this is one of the qualities that lift him above his loser peers: foresight.

Brandy, standing beside him, looks around. They have been zooming for a couple days and she is shaking and feels the squish coming on.

"There's no electricity," she points out. "Or anything, really."

"That's why it's perfect."

He is so pumped up, Brandy's suspicious.

"If you had any more now you would share it, right?"

"Baby, of course. We did it all. And I'm not high anymore," he lies. "I'm just . . . *into* this."

"You'll have to get rid of the fucking spiderwebs or I'm never coming out here again."

"Let's get the kids."

"For what?"

"To help us push the car."

Porsche steers the Camaro up the muddy dirt driveway to the barn while Howard, Brandy, and Joe shove on the rear, slipping

occasionally as they try to keep their momentum going through the shallow puddles along the way. Joe, wearing surplus military boots, has the best traction.

"Don't stop," Howard warns, "don't stop or we'll be stuck."

"Why are we doing this?" Joe asks.

"This is going to be my work area," Howard explains. "My private work area. For fixing the car and other stuff."

"Why didn't you fix the car where it was," Joe asks, "and then you could *drive* it here?"

"Nobody likes a smart-ass, Joe," Brandy says.

"Fuck you," he mutters.

"Fuck *you*," Howard says, slapping the top of his head.

"Hey," Joe says, "you can't do that."

"Yes, I can." Howard whaps Joe's head again. "We're like a family now!" Family is a remote concept to Howard. His only memory of his father is some domestic violence before he left, and shortly thereafter his sister was taken by Child Protective Services—*the goddamn government*—for reasons that were never explained to him, and his mother, he once heard as a child, was the "the whore of Tate Estates." Tate Estates was the trailer park where he grew up. "So," Howard says, smiling awkwardly at Joe, who is rubbing his head, "you're going to listen to me."

"Whatever," Joe mutters.

Rain starts to fall as they resume pushing for the final few feet. Once inside, as the Camaro coasts toward the wall, Porsche slams on the brake pedal and all three of them careen chest first into the back of the car.

Porsche hears the banging and glances up to see the aftermath in the rearview mirror and laughs.

"Very fucking funny," Brandy yells, standing up, shaking her jammed wrists.

"It's okay," Howard says. "Thanks for driving."

"Yeah, 'cause driving was, like, really the hard part," Joe says.

"What did I say about being a smart-ass, Joe?" Brandy says, wagging a finger.

"You couldn't do it," Porsche says to Joe, stepping out of the car, wearing tight jeans, Roxy boots, and a red sweater.

"Yeah, I could."

"Shut up, you're ten."

"You shut up. You're only twelve."

"Shut up all of you," Howard says.

He takes a long breath, surveys the space. Now that it is raining he notices that thin streams of rainwater are squeezing through and gathering on the rafters, pooling into drops that gravity tugs down.

"It's leaking in here," Porsche says.

"Yes," Howard says to Porsche, as if she just illuminated the situation. "You're right."

"Yes," Brandy echoes. "I forgot about that."

"Joe," Howard says.

"Yeah?"

"I'm going to have a project for you."

Brandy stares at Howard until it dawns on her. "You're not putting him on the roof?"

"It's safest. He's the lightest."

"I can do it, Mom."

"This should be funny," Porsche says.

Rain increasing, Joe climbs up the ladder and then crawls onto the roof. As he stands he realizes he likes being up here, likes the view, likes being away from everyone. Just beyond the barn is a creek that separates their property from the family who live south of them, and he has never seen the creek from this angle. The

water is dark except in patches where it narrows and froths over rocks. On the other side of the creek are a few houses spaced far apart and long strips of pastures, mostly undeveloped land. Beyond that, snowcapped Mount Rainier, shrouded in clouds, dominates the horizon.

"What are you doing?" Howard yells up. "How many?"

Joe's assignment is to identify and estimate the number of roof shingles that are missing or broken.

"There's a lot," is the first thing he reports back.

He steps toward a particularly damaged area and his boot slips on a patch of moss and *whoooosh,* he's on his back and sliding down the roof fast and suddenly he's airborne, feet first, and headed toward the ground, as though launched from a very long and high slide. He lands on his feet and then his butt and hands, mud kicking up into the air.

"Fucccccccck." He grabs his ankle and begins rolling around on the ground swearing.

Brandy and Howard are quickly upon him, trying to help without much effect, while Porsche stands there impressed.

"Wow," she says to nobody in particular. "Awesome."

"You okay, honey?" Brandy keeps asking in a rapid-fire voice. "You okay, honey, you okay?"

Joe just keeps swearing and rolling around, caking himself with mud. "Fuck, fuck, fuck, stupid fucking barn." His yelling sets a dog off in the distance.

"Can you walk it off?"

Joe continues to carry on, not hearing this.

"We have to take him to the hospital," Brandy says, kneeling helplessly.

"No." Howard grabs Joe's leg, runs a hand over the calf and ankle. "He's fine. Nothing's broken."

"How do you know? You don't know."

Howard stands, and lifts Brandy up to her feet while Joe continues to moan. "Here's the thing," he explains. "You take him to a hospital, and they're going to ask questions, get CPS involved, call you a shitty mother."

"Why, what did I do?"

"It's going to be a whole fucking horrible scene. You want to lose your kids?"

"I didn't do anything wrong!"

"They don't care. Kid comes in injured, there's a whole investigation. You still scamming welfare?"

"Yeah, but—"

"They'll look into everything. We can't take him to a hospital. A private doctor would be okay, a local doctor. Who won't call fucking CPS."

"Doctors don't work on weekends."

"So you can take him in later, if necessary."

"What's he do until then?" Brandy goes back to her knees, leans over her child helplessly. He has curled up and his profanity has subsided into quiet tears. "He's really hurt," she says, a long-dormant maternal instinct stirring slightly.

"I have plenty of Vicodin," Howard says. "Mostly in my storage unit. He can have some. Like I said, we're a family now."

"You have Vicodin? Any OxyContin?"

TWELVE

Using Porsche as his mechanic's assistant, focused from the remaining meth he does not share with Brandy, Howard spends almost an hour in the barn reconstructing and reinstalling the carburetor, fully engaged with the task at hand, his universe reduced to a simple, solvable puzzle.

"Start it up," he says to Porsche.

He stands by the open hood while she slides into the driver's seat.

"Now?"

"Now."

She turns the key and the old Camaro's 305-cubic-inch V-8 cranks up with an unsteady rumble.

"Wow!" Howard yells, surprised. "Okay. Go ahead and turn it off."

"Sounds better," she says after shutting it down. Though she affects a bored attitude, she enjoys the fact that they accomplished something. "It really does."

"Yep. Now go check on your mom and Joe, then clean up and change. I'll pick you up in the driveway."

"Yeah?"

"We've got errands to run."

After Porsche rushes off, Howard turns his last baggie of meth inside out and snorts the residue, running his nose across the plastic, sucking back and forth until there is absolutely nothing more to be consumed. He then washes his hands in the gasoline he used to clean the carburetor, takes off his dirty sweatshirt from over his Wells Fargo Bank T-shirt. He likes the stagecoach logo.

Backing the Camaro out of the barn, he pulls a Y turn in the dirt and grass, then drives through the open gate and idles in front of the house, proud to be mobile.

Porsche emerges from the front door wearing the same tight jeans, a thigh-length faux-fur coat that hangs open, a black studded choker, lipstick, and a short white shirt that leaves her midriff exposed. Howard is not sure exactly when twelve-year-old girls started dressing like hookers, but he likes the trend.

"Where are we going?" she asks as she climbs into the passenger's seat.

"We have to get Joe some medicine."

"Mom's giving him beer, so he likes that."

"Places to go," Howard says, tapping his hands on the steering wheel, "things to do."

Porsche senses that he wants her to be all curious and beg for information, and so she just shrugs indifferently.

"So, you're twelve now?" he asks, staying within the speed limit.

"Thirteen in January."

"What do you want to be when you're older?"

"Famous."

"Okay. How?"

"I was kidding. *Jesus.*" She slouches farther back, stomach exposed. "I don't know what I want to do."

"Most people lack ambition."

"Including me, I guess."

"It's never too early to have goals."

Porsche shrugs and holds up her thumbs and forefingers in a W and says, "What*ever.*"

Howard is both annoyed and aroused by her immaturity.

Almost missing a red light, he stops at the last second, slamming the brakes.

"Whoa, speed racer," she says.

"You can always walk."

"What. Ever."

"So . . . what do you and your girlfriends do for fun?" he asks, ignoring her petulance, taking a free right turn because he does not like waiting for lights.

"Party."

"Yeah? Who with?"

"Guys from the high school mostly."

Jealousy seizes Howard as he thinks of the pimply-faced adolescent boys who no doubt do not appreciate their time of good opportunity.

"You drink?"

"Of course. Everybody does. Well, not everybody, but everybody I hang out with."

"Drugs?"

"Yeah."

"Like?"

"Mushrooms, when we can find 'em. Weed, of course. Ecstasy. Some girls like meth."

"You?"

"What?"

"You like meth?"

"Of course."

"You're a little young for meth," he says, testing.

"I know plenty of girls my age who use it."

"Yeah?"

"It helps you stay skinny and stuff."

"Yeah, that's true."

"And Vicodin," she adds, putting the hint out there. "Sometimes that's going around. I like it."

Sitting up and bringing the jacket in around herself, Porsche pulls a pack of Marlboro Lights from her pocket. She glances at Howard as she pushes in the car lighter.

"Your mom lets you smoke?"

"Just not in the house."

She turns on the radio, dials in KNDD at the far right of the dial, cranks it up.

"Who's this?" Howard asks.

"The Strokes. Preppy East Coast guys, but I like them anyway."

"*I wanna steal your innocence, to me my life doesn't make no sense . . .*"

"Catchy tune," he says.

"'Barely Legal.'"

"What?"

"That's the song title."

Howard catches her coy smile out of the corner of his eye and wonders if she is teasing him or if he is imagining this.

After a couple more songs—tunes Porsche knows and he does not—they pull into a Shurgard storage facility in Lakewood. They drive past several orange and white garage-sized units and stop at the back.

Howard hops out of the car and crosses to the combination lock hanging on the door latch. He pulls a piece of paper from his wallet and reads the combination, lips moving. Twice before he used a hacksaw on the locks because he could not remember the combination, but he does not want to switch to a standard padlock because of the fear of being caught with the key.

Porsche steps up behind him and watches as he opens the door. Stacks of junk come into view: cardboard boxes, plastic milk crates, porno magazines, blue tarps, full green garbage bags, propane tanks, a pinball machine, and an ATM machine with a

gold and red logo and lettering that matches Howard's Wells Fargo Bank T-shirt.

Her nose crinkles as she smells ammonia. "Yuck."

"What?"

"That smell."

"Cleaning fluids," he says automatically, though there is no reason to lie other than habit.

He tries to open the trunk of the car with the ignition key, but it will not turn. He keeps trying until the key starts to bend.

"Mom lost the trunk key a long time ago."

"How do you get into the trunk?"

"We don't."

"You don't?" He shakes his head. "Okay, open the passenger door and slide the seat forward."

Porsche does and he wheels the ATM machine over from the storage unit and lifts it up and shoves it onto the back seat of the car, the top edge of the machine catching on the aging vinyl and ripping a gash, which stops their progress. Howard then manhandles the machine into place.

"You ever work as a baggage handler?" Porsche asks.

Howard ignores her and returns into the unit, rummages through a cardboard box.

"Bingo," he says.

Porsche observes closely as he shoves two prescription pill bottles into his pocket, then holds a third bottle up. He walks toward her until the label is inches from her face.

VICODIN, it says, prescribed to Bret E. Ellis.

"Who's Bret Ellis?" Porsche asks.

"Me, for about a year." This was after he read *American Pyscho*, his all-time favorite novel, and one of the very few he has read to the end.

He taps one pill out and holds it up with two fingers like a jewel. Porsche wants to grab for it, but resists the temptation.

"Want one?" he asks.

She shrugs, then nods and holds out her hand. He starts to hand it to her, then pulls it back, grinning.

"Hey!"

"We'll get something to wash it down with," he says. "Vicodin doesn't really work without booze."

Howard closes up the unit, and they drive away, the ATM machine rattling in the back seat. They stop at a 7-Eleven and pull into the corner of the lot. He leaves the engine running.

"Do you have fake ID?"

"No."

"Well," he says, handing her a twenty, "go in and try to buy cigarettes and beer and see what happens."

"I'll tell you what will happen. Nothing."

"Try it."

As she enters the store, the middle-aged male clerk's eyes follow her. Howard meanwhile unloads the ATM machine, which he wheels up against a wall near the front entrance, just out of the sight line of the clerk. He flips a switch in back and activates the modified computer, which lights up like the real thing.

Shortly after he finishes, Porsche emerges from the store empty-handed. She joins Howard who is waiting in the car with the engine still running.

"You're not as hot as you thought, are you?"

"I'm twelve."

"Give me back the money."

Porsche hands him back the twenty, notices the ATM machine on the sidewalk against the store wall.

"Hey," she says. "What's up with that?"

"Stay here and watch."

Howard buys a pack of Kools, a six-pack of Mike's Hard Lemonade, a can of Mountain Dew, and copies of *People* and *Penthouse* magazines. He returns to the car and hands the lemonade to Porsche. They wash down Vicodins with the malt liquor and light cigarettes and wait.

"Nothing's happening," she says.

"Patience, hon."

Howard picks up the *Penthouse* magazine, quickly finds the centerfold.

Porsche turns the radio back on, tunes in KEXP, "member-supported radio," which plays everything from alternative rock to country. She nods along to the Killers.

After a few minutes a man pulls up in a massive new pickup truck and steps up to the machine and puts his card into the intake slot. *English or Spanish* flashes up on the screen, followed by a command to enter his PIN number.

After he puts in his PIN number, the screen flashes, *Sorry, unable to process at this time. Please contact your financial institution.*

"Now we have his ATM card and his PIN number," Howard explains to Porsche as the man futilely continues to push buttons.

"Where did you get it, the machine?"

"I got it in trade for some stuff. It's paid for itself many times over."

"Can you get them on, like, eBay?"

"I don't think so. You need to know people."

"You know people?"

"I know people."

They continue waiting and watching, turning on the windshield wipers when sheets of rain begin falling across the parking lot. A second victim, a woman driving an old Honda, follows the

same steps to disappointment as the previous mark. Porsche shakes her head and laughs.

"This is awesome."

"Sometimes it's a good thing that I live my life surrounded by morons."

Two more victims later, too jittery to sit any longer, Howard wheels the machine back to the car and loads it into the back seat after removing the ATM cards and the PIN log.

They drive to various ATMs and Howard makes the maximum withdrawal from each, one card per ATM. There is no reason he cannot use all four cards in one machine, but he habitually spreads out his hits on the theory that he wants his trail to be as difficult as possible to follow. Cops, he believes, are mostly lazy and overwhelmed and chase the incompetent criminals, the ones who are easiest to catch.

As he is heading south on Pacific Avenue, counting the loot in his head, he becomes careless and exceeds the speed limit. Suddenly a Tacoma Police car lights up its wig-wags behind them.

"Fuck me," Howard says, startling Porsche.

"What?"

There's a single burst from the siren as the patrol car pulls closer.

"Hold on."

His foot presses down on the pedal and he swings out into the left lane. He accelerates and cuts between traffic, putting distance between himself and the patrol car. One of the things Howard likes about Tacoma, and the reason he executes most of his scams in the city, is that the police department has a no-pursuit policy.

At the first intersection he makes a crazily dangerous left turn through oncoming traffic, laughing at the honks, knowing

the patrol car cannot follow. Two reckless turns later, he loses the officer.

"Bonnie and Clyde without killing anyone," he says to Porsche, reaching into his pocket and removing five twenties, which he drops onto her lap.

"Thanks."

"Let's keep this adventure to ourselves."

Porsche nods and pockets the money with no hesitation, buzzed from the Hard Lemonade and the Vicodin and the adrenaline of it all.

"I'm going to let you hold some of goodies here." He hands her three Vicodins as they pull up in front of her mother's house. "Give a couple to your brother if he needs them. One-half at a time. And it's okay if you have one yourself, but not more than one."

Howard feels confident he can parlay the day's activities into sex, a plan much like when he used to take girls to the Puyallup Fair and the thrill of the rides operated as foreplay, but he does not sense that the time is right yet.

"I'll be back later," he says.

"Where are you going?" Porsche asks, her affectation of indifference completely dropped.

"I need money for my project. It takes money to make money."

In Howard's experience girls like ambition, even in their bad boys. Though he did not graduate from high school, has never held down a job, and treats women shoddily, he has always, as he likes to put it, *done well with the ladies.*

Inside a motel room just off the freeway, four tweekers make their way in the world by sifting through trash and mail. Their dingy nicotine-stained room with closed curtains is filled with garbage bags, meth pipes, mirrors and razors, butts on the floor, empty baggies with white residue, Scotch tape, an X-acto knife, a Dell computer, a Hewlett-Packard 620C printer, and a GBC 40 laminator, the high-tech tool of choice for identity thieves.

One stunningly thin blond woman, who usually works as a prostitute, sits cross-legged and methodically tapes together shredded credit card bills from out of a garbage bag. She finds the matching puzzle pieces of the long strips next to each other usually, often tangled together.

Beside her is a midget rummaging through a vinyl gym bag of stolen mail, separating out the potentially useful items into a cardboard box, his speedy little hands moving like a squirrel's. He is wearing a University of Puget Sound T-shirt that says LOGGERS across the front.

Both of them only vaguely know the man who is paying them, but they know what they need to know: Howard pays in high quality Nazi meth and he has been delivering regularly. He takes the information, prints out licenses and checks, lays out the lines, fills the pipes, and leaves. High as they are, it still occurs to them that if there is a bust, they will likely take the rap. However, they care only in the most abstract sense of the word.

People will stress endlessly and lose hundreds of hours of their lives trying to clean up the damage from the theft of their identity, but the only consequences the tweekers consider are the minimal

sentences they will face if caught. They know their plea bargains will probably not require jail time, the fines will go unpaid, and the government will pay for their attorneys. Identity thieves come to Pierce County from all over the state because it is well known that the prosecutors and the cops are snowed under with cases.

When there is a knock on the door followed by, "Police, warrant," and seconds later the door is kicked in and four Fife police officers enter in a clattering rush and take positions with their weapons drawn, it is not a big shock or upset for the tweekers.

"Hands the fuck up!"

"Police!"

The midget and the blond prostitute both raise their hands, and though they are shaking it is from the meth rather than fear. They are not quite grasping the situation. Still, they remember their patron's advice—don't talk except to say you want a lawyer.

Wyatt arrives in the parking lot, called out by the Fife detective he tipped off based on Marvin's information. The blonde and the midget sit in the backs of separate patrol cars as the scene is processed.

Barely peeking up over the bottom of the window are the midget's eyes, staring at Wyatt, who is standing in the parking lot with the detective. The riffraff has temporarily cleared out of the area.

"The midget keeps looking over here," Wyatt says.

"He lawyered up."

"No sign of Howard?"

"Well, there are signs of somebody; these tweekers weren't working alone."

"Any latents?"

"Unlikely."

"Any cigarette butts, anything we can pull DNA from?"

"You fucking kidding? This ain't *CSI*."

Wyatt nods, understanding. DNA testing is expensive and time-consuming and only used on homicide cases, rapes, and television.

"I should talk to the midget," he says.

"I told you, he lawyered up."

"Guess it won't be admissible, then."

Wyatt turns and approaches the patrol car where the midget sits in back. "Hello," Wyatt says, opening the door of the car and lowering himself onto his haunches next to a rain puddle in the uneven concrete.

"You busted me before." The midget's voice is deep.

"Yeah, a lab in Buckley."

"You let me go."

"Yep." Wyatt cannot remember why exactly, except that he probably did not make the midget to be one of the ringleaders, or maybe the midget gave him information. "I see you haven't been staying out of trouble."

"It's harder than it sounds."

"Whose operation was this?"

"Not mine."

"Not hers, either?"

"No. She's brain-dead."

The midget keeps jerking around, his stubby legs kicking up involuntarily, head bobbing, face twitching, and though Wyatt has seen all these meth tics before, they are especially disconcerting in a midget.

"So this was Howard's operation," he says.

"Is that his name? He never told us his name."

"Did the woman with you know him at all?"

"No."

"How did you end up in business with him?"

"A friend of mine."

"Who's your friend?"

"I don't know his name."

Wyatt knows that the midget, like most suspects, has talking parameters he will have to work around. Still, the midget strikes Wyatt as a survivor, someone who might know enough to pull his hand out of the coconut.

"What did Howard look like?"

"Short, skinny, muscular."

Wyatt is not sure what short means in the eyes of a midget. "How short?"

"Five-foot-five, I guess."

"White?"

"Yeah."

"What kind of complexion?"

"Bad."

"Hair?"

"Long, blond. Goatee kinda."

"Tats?"

"Swastika on his forearm, I think."

"Which arm?"

"I don't remember."

"Anything else about him you remember?"

"He had good meth."

"Nazi or Red P?"

While there really is no discernible difference in the final product, tweekers generally think otherwise, and cooks often boast of their particular technique.

"Nazi," the midget says. "Pretty pure."

"Do you remember what kind of shoes he wore?"

"Boots. Cowboy boots."

"Color?"

"Black."

"Thanks." Wyatt rises, starts to close the car door.

"Can you get me out of this?"

"Sorry."

"Next time, maybe."

"Maybe."

Back in the motel room, the gloved detective is bagging up items that might have latent fingerprints—Mountain Dew cans, an ashtray, a meth pipe—when Wyatt enters. This is not something the small-town detective would normally bother with on a minor case, but he knows about Wyatt's obsession with Howard and can relate. Almost all officers have come across the one bad guy who crawls under their skin.

"Thanks," Wyatt says.

"Is this Howard's work?"

"Not absolutely sure." Just then Wyatt notices a crumpled Starbucks cup lying on its side next to the computer, logo up. "But sure enough."

THE PERSONAL LIFE

Two of the wooden booths at the downtown Swiss Pub are marked with plaques reserving them for local congressmen Adam Smith and Norm Dicks. The reserved status is honorary and not taken literally by anyone and the booths are often filled with drinkers who have no idea who their congressmen are and do not care, except to believe strongly that they should be doing more for Pierce County and Tacoma.

In 1993 the Swiss Hall was just another boarded-up downtown building in an area populated by drug dealers, addicts, vagrants, and the occasional hooker. Gayle, a chef, and Bob, and Jack, bartenders from Engine House #9, leased the building from the University of Washington. They tore the faux-wood paneling off the brick walls, opened up the pressed-tin ceiling, cleaned the concrete floors, polished the mahogany bar, and opened for business.

Quickly the Swiss became a beacon amid downtown dilapidation, a casual hangout for politicians, prosecutors, defense lawyers, and a diverse crowd of young and old locals that vary with the bands. Tacoman Dale Chihuly, jazzed by the idea of a cool bar in his 'hood, donated half a million dollars' worth of glass art: eight spindly and shiny pieces that sit on a brightly lit ridge behind the bar just above the beer taps and bottles.

Mike and his date, June, a teacher and English lit PhD candidate with short hair, cat-eye glasses, and excellent cheekbones, are here early to have dinner before the cover band, the Retros, fills the club with songs by the Cure, Depeche Mode, Psychedelic Furs, the Bangles, the Smiths, and all the rest that send Mike into nostalgic reverie.

When he is on a date that is going well, he feels he might live a long time and does not worry about accepting death. June and he have been going out for two months and she usually has that effect on him.

He is enjoying a house specialty, pan-fried oysters, in the Adam Smith booth, listening to June talk about her comparative literature paper on Kurt Vonnegut and Jacqueline Susann and their concurrently best-selling novels, when his cell phone rings.

Wyatt James comes up on the LCD screen.

"Business," Mike says to June. "Excuse me."

"No problem," June says good-naturedly, setting down her salad fork and reaching for her scotch on the rocks.

"What's up, Wyatt?"

"Marvin's tip was good. Busted some of Howard's tweeker thieves in a motel room with lots of stolen mail."

"And Howard?"

"Missed him."

"Anyone talk?"

"Midget talked, gave me a description of the ringleader that pretty much matched Howard."

"Midget, did you say?"

Mike looks over at his date, who is holding up her glass and wiping off a smudge.

"Yeah," Wyatt continues, "he was working for Howard, though he didn't know he was working for Howard."

"Sounds like we should discuss this next week?"

"What are you doing?"

"Trying to have a life."

"Are you on a date?"

"Yes."

"So why did you pick it up?"

"I thought it might be important."

"You made a mistake."

"Clearly."

"I want the go-ahead to put Marvin on contract. He's proven his reliability, chief."

"Let's talk about this later, okay?"

"How's your date going?"

"Very well," Mike says, smiling at her, "if I don't continue this conversation much longer."

"Best line from *Doctor Zhivago*?"

"'The personal life is dead.'"

June looks up. "*Doctor Zhivago*," she mouths to him.

"Yes," Mike says to June, impressed.

"Who are you with," Wyatt asks. "June?"

"It's Wyatt," Mike says to her. "Good night, Wyatt."

June's cell phone rings with a chime similar to Mike's phone and she answers it, shrugging apologetically.

"I can't decide if I miss dating or not," Wyatt says. "Is it cool? Not knowing whether or not she is going to sleep with you tonight, wondering what comes next?"

"Say hi to Suki for me."

"I'm serious about putting Marvin on contract."

"Good night."

Mike hangs up. June follows suit a moment later.

"My friend lost her Prozac," she explains.

"Prozac, very old-school."

"Are you on Prozac, or lithium, or Klonopin, or . . . *anything?*"

"No."

"Me neither." She smiles. "Wow."

Sound checks float in from the other room, including the

opening riff from "Don't You (Forget About Me)," which causes them both to smile in recognition.

"Which version of 'Pretty in Pink' do you prefer?" June asks, hand moving lightly to her cheek. "The *Talk, Talk, Talk* recording, or the movie soundtrack?"

"*Talk, Talk, Talk*. You?"

"The same." June nods. "Do you own the CD?"

"Yes. You?"

"I have both, even though soundtracks disrupt my CD organization. Have you heard of Wreckless Eric?"

"'Whole Wide World.'"

"Right." She smiles. "Do you have any of his CDs?"

"*Bungalow Hi* and *Greatest Stiffs*."

"Do you put him under W or E? He's a person, not a band, so he should be listed by his last name, but what's his last name? Eric's his first name, right? And Wreckless isn't a name at all, it's an adjective."

"That's a good point," Mike says after a pause. "I wrestled with that, too, and I decided to treat him like a band and put him under W."

"That's a reasonable solution," June says. "But I think I might just say fuck it and switch to an iPod."

"iPods are a relatively safe addiction."

Mike's cell phone rings again and they look at each other for a beat, then simultaneously turn off their phones.

Frustrated with Howard's elusiveness, frustrated with Mike's nonchalance, frustrated that he comes home alone on a Saturday though he has a girlfriend, Wyatt resorts to a reliable tonic: *The Godfather* on DVD. He has all three parts, but the first remains his favorite.

He sips a Cabernet on the couch as the movie begins with Bonasera, the mortician, in the Godfather's dark study, reporting that his daughter was beaten in an attempted rape.

"I went to the police, like a good American. These two boys were brought to trial. The judge sentenced them to three years in prison— suspended sentence. Suspended sentence! They went free that very day! I stood in the courtroom like a fool. And those two bastards, they smiled at me. Then I said to my wife, for justice, we must go to Don Corleone."

Before Marlon Brando can make things right, Wyatt's cell phone rings. He picks up only because it is Suki.

"Can you come get me?" she asks, her voice unusually pleading, music pounding in the background. "I'm at the club and I didn't drive."

"You okay?"

"Just please come get me."

Wyatt drives his own vehicle, a navy-blue Jeep Wrangler with a removable hardtop, to Foxes in Parkland, just north of Pacific Lutheran University. He parks beneath a tall pole with a weathered marquee advertising FULL NUDE DANCING, OPEN UNTIL 3:00 A.M.

Outside the unmarked front door of a one-story building

stands a bulky man in a white jumpsuit. He acts as a bouncer and an escort for the girls—walking them to their cars when their shifts are over. Suki always tips him, ending her night "as a tipper rather than a tippee."

Wyatt nods at the doorman and steps into the noise and darkness of the club, pausing to let his eyes adjust. At the front cash register he tells the assistant manager why he is here.

"Your name?"

"Wyatt James."

Quickly the assistant manager registers that Wyatt is probably a cop—it is part of his job to know these things. More than once the Pierce County Sheriff's Department has visited Foxes with vice operations, citing dancers for violations of the generally ignored ten-foot rule.

Lynnwood police, in Snohomish County, more hands-on, bought "happy endings" for officers in a recent massage parlor sting. The prosecutor on the case, Mark Roe, dismissed the prostitution charges because of the investigative tactics and the media attention.

Strip clubs and massage parlors, meanwhile, meet the challenge by employing people with an eye for law enforcement.

"I'll get her right away, Detective," the assistant manager says to Wyatt with an obsequious smile.

Wyatt does not appreciate the familiarity.

Velvet Revolver plays through a sound system heavily laced with bass, and the thumping music and the darkness broken up by flashing lights disorient Wyatt as he scans the room.

There are three half-circle stages, each stage stretching out from a different wall. All the stages are lit with black lights and Fresnel gels. Two of the dancers are totally naked, their outfits

strewn across the stages. The third one is on her back, legs together in the air, her bottoms momentarily tangling on her stiletto heels as she attempts to slide them off.

Closest to the stages are tables and chairs filled by young men who are there to watch the stage show. Beyond the tables are long couches where the men who want dances lurk. These are the men, generally older, who want to talk to the girls. They use the dancers as therapists and relationship counselors. Sometimes the men ask them out, offer to take them away from all this.

Leaning against the deejay booth is a pretty Filipina girl in pink lingerie, smoking. She wears a white orchid in her hair and Wyatt recognizes her as Suki's friend "Duchess," real name: Alexis. She and Suki belong to the same book club.

Beyond the deejay booth is the backstage door and a few moments after the assistant manager goes in, Suki comes out. She quickly crosses the club, carrying a black gym bag and wearing a tan cardigan over a white blouse and dark thrift-store skirt.

"Thanks," she says, taking his hand and not slowing down a step in her march out.

Not until they are in his Jeep and driving on the freeway does she ask a question. "When does someone become famous enough so that a murder is an assassination?"

"I don't think there's a bright-line standard."

"I can't take it there anymore," she says, putting on her seat-belt. "No more pornglish for me. *Je ne parle pas pornglish.*"

"Good."

"I quit."

"I figured."

"And I didn't want to wait around for Alexis."

"Since you quit midshift?"

"Right."

He wants to know why, but knows she will not talk about the details until she has mulled it over for a while. Like him, she does not easily give things up about herself.

She turns to him. "Are you glad?"

"Yes."

"I'll just work more hours at the coffee shop, at least until I go back to school."

"Good plan."

Wyatt turns the wipers on and the defroster up as pellets of rain start to smack against the windshield.

"I would have just taken a taxi," Suki says, "but I didn't do a single dance tonight. Sometimes you just hit a breaking point, you know?"

"I know."

"I was reading an interview with David Lynch, and he said there comes a time in most people's lives when they quit banging their head against the walls and become a seeker."

"That guy's a freak. He makes a good living at it, though."

"I'm going to be broke now."

Wyatt shrugs. "Money's not that important."

"People who grew up with plenty of it always say that. I didn't grow up with any, so it's important to me."

"It's not that important as long as you have a roof and food."

"Yeah, well, I'll have your roof." She smiles. "And I guess you'll be buying dinner more often."

Wyatt nods. "Subway will be getting lots of our business."

"You wanted me to quit, didn't you?"

"Of course."

"Why didn't you just say so?"

"It's better this way."

"That's not why, not because it's 'better.' You didn't say so because you thought that if you asked me to quit it would mean something, like asking me to quit would mean you were making a commitment or something."

Wyatt recognizes this as true, so he does not reply.

"We'll see how you adjust to having me around more," Suki says, lightening up as they put more distance between themselves and Foxes. "Let's do something now, like go to a movie, stop at a Starbucks, something normal people do on Saturdays."

COLORS

Joe's ankle, purple and yellow, is swollen to almost twice its normal size. His foot is propped up on a pillow and bread bags full of melting ice are wrapped around the contusion.

"The swelling's gone down some," Howard says, feeling good from a meth recharge.

"Not fucking much," Joe says, staring at the freakish abnormality his ankle has become.

"The pain better?"

At this the boy nods gratefully.

"Your sister took care of you?"

"Yeah."

"Good girl."

Howard reaches into his pocket and pulls out a Vicodin and sets the pill between a CD player and an empty Mountain Dew can on the nightstand.

"Take that when you need it. But not before."

"Thanks."

"You know where I've been?"

"No."

"Porsche didn't tell you?"

"No."

She's a good one.

Joe is anxious for Howard to leave so he can pop the Vicodin. He is not sure why he is waiting, but thinks he should.

"Don't go out in the barn," Howard says, out of nowhere.

"The barn?"

"Yeah, it's my private workshop."

Suddenly it occurs to Howard that telling a boy not to do something is tantamount to daring him.

"Never mind," Howard adds, as though this will negate the dare.

"What?"

"Nothing." Howard is confusing himself. "I'll see you in a day or two."

"Should you leave more pills with me?"

"I'll leave them with Porsche."

"Okay. Thanks."

"No prob. We're a family now."

As Howard exits, stepping over the clothes, the shoes, and the CDs by rappers named 2Pac, 50cent, Eminem, Snoop Dogg, and Ludacris—not a properly spelled word in sight—he notices red shoelaces on a pair of Doc Martens.

"Joe?"

"Yeah?"

"Do you know what red shoelaces mean?"

"Yeah."

"What?"

"It means you've beat up someone of an inferior race. Enough to make them bleed."

This, Howard knows, is correct.

"How old are you?"

"Almost eleven."

"Ten."

"Don't worry, I earned them."

"Yeah? Who did you beat up?"

"Mexican kid."

"That's fucking stupid."

"Why?"

"Because Mexicans have big brothers and cousins and they could kick your ass bad."

These words do not seem strong enough to Howard, and he cannot seem to find words that do, so he walks back to Joe and punches him in the side of his head at half speed, leaving no mark but what he hopes will be a lasting impression.

Joe's mouth flops open from the impact and surprise.

"You're a tough kid, I like that. But I don't want to see you get your ass killed. So watch it, okay?"

Joe is confused because Howard seems to actually care.

"Are the white kids at school listening to that rap crap?"

"Yeah."

"What's up with that?"

"I dunno."

"Joe, you seem a little confused. You can't wear red shoelaces and listen to Negroes."

"Eminem is white."

"You're missing the fucking . . . point." Howard, however, has not slept in almost three days and he has lost the point himself and so cannot share it with Joe. "Just fucking . . . be tough, use your head, don't take any wooden nickels, okay?" Howard turns and heads into the hallway, muttering.

BUY AMERICAN

Shortening the amount of time between doses, Howard stays focused enough to go on a shopping spree, leaving shredded credit histories in his wake. In seventy sleepless hours he prepares the barn for business.

Each corner of the barn has a video camera, and two more cameras are mounted on the fence where the dirt driveway meets the road. All the cameras are wireless, and there are two television monitors in the house, another in the barn.

Electronics in the barn are powered by thick extension cords running over a hundred feet back to the house. Several lighter-duty extension cords snake out from surge protectors, supplying electricity to two blenders, two extra-large pancake griddles, a refrigerator, and four sets of double fluorescent lights in white metal shields nailed crudely to the walls of the barn.

The blenders and the griddles are on top of the workbench, along with multiple cans of HEET, Coleman fuel, liquid drain opener, coffee filters, funnels, a bag of rock salt, two propane tanks full of anhydrous ammonia, and numerous mason jars. In the drawers of the workbench are dozens of lithium batteries.

On the floor between the car and the bench are two crude HCL generators, gas cans with rubber stoppers in place of the cap and tubes hanging out. Next to these is a freezer for converting the meth powder to crystal for the ice freaks. Howard recognizes there is no chemical difference—ice is just a crystallized form of methamphetamine—but some users believe devoutly in the purity of ice and Howard, like Nordstrom's, recognizes that the customer is always right.

With this lab Howard plans to make two batches at a time, working on a phase of batch two while he waits for a phase of batch one to complete, thereby staying in motion constantly and producing significant quantities. No more dealing in penny-ante teeners, he will market $600 ounces cut with MSM, a dietary supplement for horses, pounds of powder for around $5,000, and pounds of ice in the $9,000 neighborhood, depending on market fluctuations. He is ready to go head-to-head with the Mexicans who have to hustle their product across the border.

"Be patriotic," he tells customers, "buy American."

All he needs to kick-start his meth factory is pseudo-ephedrine, which is becoming increasingly difficult to obtain with local runners.

Adapting, Howard sets up a six-pound pseudo purchase with a Canadian who lives in Bellingham. He has heard that terrorists are moving into the pseudo business, supplementing their oil and poppy field profits, but business is business.

Howard and the Canadian agree to meet in Seattle in the parking lot of the downtown Déjà Vu, the only landmark business that comes to mind. Because it is outside of Pierce County, Howard expects it is less likely to be a setup. Local agencies generally do not like to reach outside their jurisdictions.

Or so he tries to persuade himself as the paranoia kicks in and he smokes a quick bowl to take the edge off the wait, parked with the trunk against the brick wall of Déjà Vu. He inhales deeply as he studies the parking lot and First Avenue through the drizzle-spotted windows. On his right is a large gray van with no windows, *a rape van*, as they are known in Pierce County.

Howard is using a client's car, the Firebird of the kid who was arrested. Howard gave the kid's girlfriend the money to get the car out of impound. He did not want to use Brandy's, as it could be

tracked back to her. The level of his paranoia, and therefore the extent of his security precautions, varies drastically from day to day, hour to hour, minute to minute.

Just as the smoky rush of invincibility kicks in from his lungs to his brain and down to his wiggling feet, Howard sees the Canadian's silver Lincoln Navigator pull into the lot. Surprisingly quick, the monster SUV maneuvers over and pulls into the spot on Howard's left. Howard and the Canadian have only met once, in the Pierce County Jail where the Canadian had a short stay, but they have mutual acquaintances in the drug world.

They step out of their vehicles and shake hands and they are remarkably similar physically: two wiry guys with goatees and long unwashed hair. The Canadian is shorter.

"Nice sled," Howard says.

"Too bad business isn't better."

"Yeah, they've clamped down on Sudafed and all the over-the-counter pseudo."

"Fuckin' politicians."

"Goddamn government."

They are chattering rapidly, twitching and grinding teeth and looking all around, their heads rotating like geese.

"So let's do it," Howard says, anxious to get back to the barn for cooking.

The Canadian swings the heavy passenger door of the Navigator open and he reaches behind the front seat and pulls out a black duffel bag with a white Nike swoosh across both sides.

"Six American pounds," he says.

Howard nods and hands him a Stadium Thriftway grocery bag with thirty-five hundred dollars. This takes a while for the Canadian to count out, as it is mostly in twenties from ATM machines.

"It's all there," Howard says.

The Canadian quits counting and stashes the money in the SUV, not because he trusts Howard, but because he already lost count twice and does not feel like trying a third time. He expects he will see Howard again.

"I'll call you," Howard says as he climbs into his car, setting the duffel bag on the passenger's seat.

As the Canadian walks into Déjà Vu, Howard pulls out onto First Avenue and drives south past the Pike Place Market and the ShowBox Theater, oblivious to the numerous pedestrians and the neon of the city reflecting off the wet cement, tunnel vision taking hold. He is grateful the rain has let up because windshield wipers can sometimes drive him batty.

On the freeway he drives at exactly fifty-five miles per hour until he's past Tacoma and off 512 and onto Pacific Avenue and the Mountain Highway. Clenching his sweaty hands on the wheel, he rolls down the window and enjoys the air as he starts to speed up.

He is only a few miles from home, tailgating a pickup truck, when suddenly an old Dodge Dart comes fishtailing around a corner of the wet road and the pickup's red brake lights flash and he locks his brakes just as he hears the smoking screech of brakes from the other vehicles.

Seconds later the Dart and the pickup truck clip head-on into each other and the Dart spins off into the ditch, radiator steam jetting out from under the hood. The pickup spins and ends up sideways across the road. Howard's foot is frozen on the floor and his eyes close as the Firebird is about to slam into the side of the pickup, but the impact is not as severe as he expects.

Opening his eyes, heart pounding madly, Howard appraises the scene. First he notices an overpowering odor of ammonia, the odor of a mobile meth lab. In a shallow ditch the Dart sits crip-

pled, hood bent, steaming. The pickup, completely blocking the road, has a badly damaged front corner, a quarter panel bent back onto a flat tire. On the side of the road are green garbage bags, broken mason jars, and a propane tank.

He steps out and checks the front of his car. Damage appears minimal—one broken headlight with wires hanging down helplessly.

The driver of the pickup stumbles out of the cab and Howard immediately recognizes him, a local tweeker.

"Wow," the tweeker says.

"Shit," says the driver of the Dart, who squeezes out of the passenger door, which opens only partially. Howard recognizes him as well, another local tweeker.

This is not a reunion Howard wants to be party to, especially when the police and the fire department make their appearance. He climbs back into the Firebird, backs up, and drives around the pickup on the open side of the road, trying to avoid the jars and broken glass.

Once clear, he speeds away from the scene as fast as he can, vaguely appreciating the poetic justice of almost being undone by tweekers he may have supplied. Only a couple miles from where he is about to turn onto Brandy's street, a Pierce County Sheriff's Jeep Cherokee drives past him toward the accident.

Maintain, maintain.

Deputy Newton remembers the Firebird with the gray primer hood from the previous encounter, and the broken headlight is an invitation for a stop even though his shift is done. He executes a quick U-turn and speeds up behind Howard and lights him up with the wig-wags.

"Fuck, fuck, shit." Howard pounds the wheel.

Flight, fight, or surrender thoughts ping-pong around his brain, but his first instinct is to push the gas pedal down. The Firebird jerks forward with a horrible rattle.

Deputy Newton sees the Firebird speed up and follows suit— *if they run, they're guilty.* Pierce County cops, unlike Tacoma's, still give chase. Adrenaline surges as he gains ground, closing fast.

Howard reaches over with his right hand and stuffs the duffel bag under the passenger seat as his left hand grips the steering wheel, the car shaking and swerving. Once the duffel bag is mostly out of sight, he slows down and pulls over, muttering to himself, "*Maintain, maintain.*"

Because the chase was only a short burst, the deputy does not draw his weapon when he pulls up behind Howard. However, he does keep one hand on the butt of his Glock .40 as he approaches the driver's side of the car.

Howard pulls out a driver's license from his wallet—Lars Ulrich—and then rolls down his window.

"License, registration, and insurance, please."

"I'm just borrowing the car," Howard says as he hands over the license.

Deputy Newton looks back and forth from the license to Howard, and recognizes him as the passenger he had to release after their previous encounter. Howard makes the same connection a few seconds later.

Lars Ulrich sounds dimly familiar, but the deputy is twenty-one and not a Metallica fan and so the name is lost on him.

"Does the owner have registration or insurance, Mr. Ulrich?"

"Probably not." Howard smiles, hoping to impress the deputy with his honesty.

"I pulled you over because you have a headlight out."

"Sorry about that. I've been meaning to change it, or replace it. Put in a new one."

"Why did you try to elude me when I activated my lights?"

"I didn't, it wasn't a Felony Elude."

This use of the proper legal term arouses the deputy's suspicions, and the swastika tattoo on Howard's forearm does not help to dispel his misgivings.

"You sped up," the deputy says.

"It was an accident."

"An accident?"

"I accidentally pushed down on the gas pedal. I meant to push down on the brake."

"You sped up for nearly half a minute."

"I don't think it was that long."

"And you were swerving."

"I was swerving? You sure?"

"Yep."

"But I pulled over, though. When I saw you. As soon as I saw you. Here I am, see? Pulled over."

Deputy Newton recognizes that Howard is tweaking, but he has seen far worse and he doubts Howard would flunk field sobriety tests. Eyeing the interior, the deputy notices a Nike bag poking out from under the passenger's seat, and he figures this is what Howard was reaching for when he was leaning over during the pursuit.

"Are there any weapons in the bag?"

"Where?" Howard's head pivots back and forth quickly, sweat glistening.

Bingo, there's something in the bag.

"On the passenger floorboard."

"I don't know whose it is. Must be the guy whose car this is, I guess."

Howard compliments himself for using the kid's car.

"I saw you reaching over there when I was pulling you over."

"I was just adjusting things."

"What were you adjusting?"

Howard knows he should probably shut up, but he also thinks he can still talk himself out of this, and these thoughts collide and confuse him.

"Adjusting? What?"

"You were adjusting the bag?"

"I was, yeah, it was slipping around, so I pushed it back."

"Are there any weapons in the bag?"

"It was slipping out," Howard rambles on, "like onto my feet, causing problems, driving problems, and so I pushed it."

"It was under your seat?"

"Under my *feet*. It was . . ." Howard realizes he's losing it here. He licks his dry lips and can taste the sour drops of sweat. "Oh, fuck it. Am I under arrest? If I am, I want to talk to a lawyer."

This is the moment of decision for the deputy.

His training says his probable cause is dicey, but his instinct says he would regret letting this one go. Furthermore, he does not like that the suspect made the experienced move of forcing the issue of arrest while simultaneously invoking his right to a lawyer.

What the hell, he decides, *let the prosecutor sort out the legal crap*.

PLAY IT AS IT LAYS

An ace, king, and a seven come out on the flop, a rainbow. Wyatt regrets for a moment mucking his ace-deuce off suit, even while knowing this is the right move, particularly in early position.

Wyatt folded not just because he did not like his hand, but because he is not mentally in the game. The other players are jawing as usual, mostly about crime and politics and office gossip, random riffs, but Wyatt's mind is skipping from Howard to Suki, who has been making it clear that children are part of her vision of the future. This ups the stakes.

Graham, just to the left of Wyatt, cannot remember if this is a one-dollar betting round or a two-dollar round, so he checks and sips his water. He is a sober alcoholic who played college football and has a master's degree in philosophy.

Jay, just out of a robbery trial, a stout poker aficionado who plays more than anyone else at the table, has queen-jack, and he bets out though he knows he should check.

"I'm here to gamble."

Liza, the supervisor from the identity theft unit, arguably the most grossly understaffed trial unit in a chronically understaffed office, calls with her pocket eights, too tired to think through all the good reasons to fold.

"Why am I doing this?" she asks, splashing the pot.

Mike has a pocket pair of kings and the one on the table gives him a set. He pauses, considering whether to raise or slow play. He raised before the flop and nobody reraised, so he rules out pocket aces as likely competition.

Their monthly game takes place at Mike's house in the dining

room he converted to a poker room. The ceilings are coved and the walls are green and hanging behind Mike is a framed movie poster from *Pulp Fiction*. Uma Thurman lies on an unmade bed with a cigarette, a gun, and a paperback in the foreground. Small speakers in the corners carry music from a stereo in the main room and a compilation CD Mike made is playing, currently Tears for Fears' "Everybody Wants to Rule the World."

Mike sets two blue chips out in front of him, a raise. He forgoes the slow play opportunity because he is going to have plenty of callers and his raise will likely be misread anyway.

Mix it up.

"Fuck," Liza says, shaking her head, "I knew I should have folded."

Tears for Fears segues into a Sid Vicious cover of "My Way" on the CD and Josh, a prosecutor who just finished trying a murder case for the third time—it was reversed twice on technicalities—looks over in mock horror.

"Who in the hell is this?"

"Sid Vicious doing Frank Sinatra."

"Sounds like he's doing him in the ass."

Julian, a drug unit trial prosecutor, laughs and calls with his ace-eight suited. Though his eight is a weak kicker, hope springs eternal.

After thinking about it, Bennet says, "Raise, huh?"

"Put two blue chips in," Josh says.

"Relax, Rumpelstiltskin."

"Rumpelstiltskin?"

Bennet, a homicide detective Wyatt used to work with, is unflappable. He pays no mind to Josh, makes Mike for an ace, maybe ace-king, figuring he would slow play if he had a set, and decides to stick around for the action with his king-ten.

"Call," Bennet says, putting his two chips out.

"Fucking Jay," Josh mutters, angry that Jay bet into Mike when he should have expected the raise. He calls, bitterly.

Wyatt and Mike exchange a look, as they have the same thought: *Josh is likely on a gutshot draw.*

Adam, a former prosecutor turned politician, also catches Mike's look and has the same thought, though it does not affect his play. The flop missed him and so he folds.

"It's just a couple dollars," Jay says.

"Wouldn't be prudent."

Graham likes his hand, but calls instead of suffering the abuse that follows a check-raise.

"Fat pot," Jay says, also calling.

"What am I doing?" Liza repeats as she calls.

Adam burns a card, then lays out the turn card, a queen of diamonds.

"'Don't you draw the queen of diamonds, boy.'"

"'She'll beat you if she's able.'"

"'The queen of hearts is always your best bet.'"

For the approximately one millionth time, the Eagles are quoted at a poker game, and Mike decides he'll follow his compilation CD with *Hotel California,* the title song being one of his longtime favorite addiction tunes.

"Do you think I should marry Suki?" Wyatt asks Mike.

"Sure," Mike says, watching reactions to the queen.

"I'm serious, Counselor."

"You're forty. You should get married."

"You're almost forty. You're not married."

"But you've already got your money in the pot, so to speak, with Suki, and I'm not there yet with June."

"Almost everything in life," Adam says, "can be analogized to poker."

"Graham," Josh says, "the action's on you. Check?"

"I like marriage," Jay says.

"Jay, what the fuck world do you go back and forth from?" Josh asks.

Graham bets one dollar.

"Nice bet," Josh says. "Except it's one dollar on the flop and before the flop. Two dollars on the turn and river, as it's been for the last four years. I know it's complicated."

Graham shrugs and pushes out another blue chip. "I wish kids hadn't been so mean to you on the playground."

Jay nods in drunken agreement, "Yeah," and then calls.

"What am I doing to myself?" Liza asks, also calling.

Based on table observation, Mike believes the queen did not make anyone's hand, and so he thinks he still has the best hand. There are a lot of river cards that could potentially beat him, but he wants to make the draws pay, so he raises.

Force your opponents into difficult decisions.

Julian grimaces. He hates to fold aces, but he runs through a quick list of some of the better hands possibly out there: *ace with a better kicker, two pair, a set, a straight,* and he lets go.

Bennet calculates his pot odds. He figures he has about a one-in-twelve chance of drawing a jack on the river, which would give him a straight. Calling will cost him four dollars and there is about forty dollars in the pot, so he is getting ten-to-one on his money, but he would need better than twelve-to-one odds to justify a call and should, mathematically speaking, fold. *Except,* the pot is likely going to grow and improve his odds, and so he can justify calling.

"Call."

Josh, needing a ten for a straight, goes through the same math, and comes to the same conclusion, *long shot, but fat pot.*

"Call."

Graham considers reraising, but by now he sees the straight possibilities and just calls Mike's raise, as do Jay and Liza.

"Let's see the river."

Adam, with a dramatic flourish, burns a card and then slowly turns the river card up from the deck, looks at it himself, laughs, then lays the queen beside its sister for all to see.

"Siegfried and Roy on the board."

Graham bets a dollar, and then notices that he has a full house.

"Two dollars on this round," Mike reminds him.

"My bad."

"You better not fucking win this pot," Josh says to Graham. "You just better fucking not."

Jay has trip queens and though he recognizes it is probably a losing hand he calls because it *could* be a winning hand.

"Cards were just good enough to get me in trouble," Liza says, folding.

Graham laughs at this, which turns heads.

"You better fucking *not* win this pot," Josh repeats.

Graham's laughter worries Mike. Giddy players usually have good cards. Mike looks at Wyatt and again they can tell they have the same thought: *goddamn Graham.* Anytime they think poker, or life, is something that can be controlled or predicted, there's Graham.

"Raise," Mike says, unwilling to slow down, as Graham would have to hold pocket aces or pocket queens to beat him. Though this is possible, it is inconsistent with the betting, even taking into

account Graham's randomness. He puts Graham on king-queen at best. "So," he says, turning to Wyatt, "are you going to marry her?"

"I should."

"You got that right at least."

Grateful for Mike's raise because it gives him an additional reason to fold, Bennet mucks his cards.

"Trouble waiting to happen," he says.

"Like life," Adam says.

Though the queen improved Josh's hand, he suspects it is just good enough that he cannot get away from it when he should. He weighs the possibility that Mike is now stuck with three pair to choose from, known as a Selby, and that Graham and Jay are completely out to lunch. He thinks the latter is a good bet, but the former *unfuckinglikely*. *Mike's not going to raise with a Selby, he's probably got pocket aces or kings.* He decides to hold on to the few chips he has left, regrets playing to see the turn card.

"I fucking hate poker," he says, folding, disgusted with himself, the game, and the world.

"Call," Graham says.

Mike is expressionlessly pleased. The pot is rich by their standards and it is his—if Graham had him beat he would have raised. Mike does not care about the money or the results of any given night because he believes poker is a single lifelong game with breaks and changing players and it is not over until you give it up permanently or you die, but nonetheless he wants this pot.

"You really think I should marry her," Wyatt says.

"Sure," Mike says, "what's life without risk?"

"You planning to call the raise?" Josh asks Jay.

"I don't know," Jay says, stalling to annoy Josh. "Right now I need a scotch, though."

"Yeah," Josh says, "that's just what you need."

Julian hands him the green bottle of Laphroaig, and Jay smiles as he half fills his lowball glass.

"Side bet," Wyatt proposes to Mike. "If you win the pot, I'll quit pestering you about signing up Marvin as a CI. If you lose, you sign up Marvin or the midget."

"The midget?"

"Yeah, I think he's got a little info."

"Just a *little?*" Josh says, grinning.

"How about if I win you marry Suki?" Mike says.

"How about if we finish this hand?" Liza says.

"Are you going to win?" Wyatt asks Mike.

"Probably."

Jay, mistaking candidness for weakness, and simply unable to fold this late in the game, calls.

Mike flips over the pocket kings, an apparent winner.

"Well played, Jay," Josh says as Jay mucks his cards.

Jay shrugs. "I'm an addict."

Eyes turn to Graham, who slow-rolls his pocket aces. Astonishment, groans, laughter, and facetious applause erupt around the table.

Be Zen, Mike reminds himself. *Put on the Eagles.*

"Did we have a side bet?" Wyatt says. "I think I just won. Gotta love this game."

"You didn't *raise* with that hand?" Josh says, staring at Graham, shaking his head.

Graham smiles as he spreads his hands out in a circle around the chips and drags them in, the large pile clacking and shifting, so many chips that some slip out of his grip. He tries not to laugh, but fails.

"Play Sid Vicious doing Sinatra again."

The barred door is electronically clanked open and Ted Haller enters the jail and walks alone down the empty hallway under flickering fluorescent lights. Ted has a slight post-lunch buzz going, just enough so that he is indifferent to the dank air and bad vibes.

One of the many advantages of being a prosecutor is that you do not have to visit clients in jail. Ted, a public defender for twenty-three years, feels he is serving a penance every time he enters what he calls the Gray Bar Hotel. He is known by other lawyers and some of his clients as "Cocktail Ted" because of his penchant for bourbon lunches that precede afternoon visits.

The guard at the next check stop knows Ted—the guards and the lawyers are all well acquainted in Pierce County—and opens Visitors' Room F for him. A few minutes later his client, Howard, is brought in and they are left alone in the small drab space with no windows and two wooden chairs. Between them is a green metal desk.

"Hello, Lars," Ted says, setting his manila folder on the desk. "I'm Ted Haller. I'm your lawyer."

I'm fucked, Howard thinks as he checks out this pudgy balding middle-aged man wearing worn khakis and an old tweed coat.

"Do you prefer Lars, or Howard? There seems to be some confusion about your name on the charging documents."

"My name is Howard. Friends call me Lars."

Ted recognizes all the symptoms of a tweeker: pasty skin, twitchy limbs, a hollow stare, and the scabs on his hands and forearms from meth bugs—imaginary creatures tweekers

scratch incessantly. In Ted's experience it takes eight to twelve weeks of cold turkey before tweekers can communicate. Even then, though, a dialogue with a tweeker is roughly akin to one with a snotty ten-year-old.

Because of seniority, Ted is one of the attorneys at the Department of Assigned Counsel who assign cases, and he awarded himself this one because it was solid and he expected it would be a quick guilty plea. The strung-out defendant left him a voice-mail message implying that he just wanted to take a deal and get it over with.

Once, ten years ago, Ted defended a man he actually thought was innocent and this was so stressful, so outside his comfort zone, he swore he would never to it again. He is grateful the situation has not arisen since.

"I understand you just got back from Western State," Ted says, "and the docs declared you competent."

"Yeah, I'm not crazy, I was just squishing."

"Right, okay."

"Should I have pretended I was mental?"

"No, no, no sense in that, Lars. Sometimes it's good for the soul to just take responsibility. And it can reduce your prison term, too." Receiving no reaction, Ted continues. "Looks like they caught you cold with a very large amount of pseudoephedrine. No pun intended."

"What?"

"Caught you *cold* with pseudoephedrine."

Howard stares back, eyes blinking.

"Never mind," Ted continues. "You had six pounds of pseudo. That's a boatload, Lars. The prosecutor is likely going to take this case pretty seriously."

"It's just one case, they have thousands."

"You can't slip under the radar screen with a quantity like that."

"It wasn't mine."

Let the lying begin.

"You said in your message that you just wanted to get this over with," Ted continues, ignoring the customary mendacity. "Get the best deal you can?"

"I was out of my mind when I left that message."

Ted nods, though Howard did not sound any worse than any other tweeker in any other voice mail.

"I've been talking to some of the guys," Howard continues, "and I'm pretty confident I can beat this."

Shit, the jailhouse lawyers have gotten to him.

"So you've been taking advice from fellow inmates?"

"Some of the guys know a lot."

"If they know so fucking much," Ted says, shifting from his empathetic voice to his authoritative voice, "why are they in jail?"

Any defense lawyer has seen this cycle before: the defendant initially wants to unburden himself through confession, but then the consequences of confession begin to occur to him, and he decides that everyone else is getting away with murder, figuratively or literally, and so why shouldn't he?

Is it not his right as an American—nay, his obligation—to get a lawyer, to deny responsibility, to squeeze through the technical cracks, to beat the system?

"First thing we need to do is set up a bail hearing," Howard advises Ted.

"You're looking at fifty-one to sixty-eight months if you're convicted at trial, Lars." Ted mistakenly thinks Howard has no criminal history, because none comes up under his current moniker. "High end for sure if you go to trial."

"I can't do that much time."

"What if I could get a plea for something less?" Ted tries. "Maybe a DOSA. You're familiar with the DOSA program, right?"

"It cuts your prison time in, like, half?"

"That's the general idea. Let's say you receive a sixty-month DOSA. You only have to serve the first thirty months in prison, and you get half off for good behavior, so that cuts the thirty to fifteen, and the Department of Corrections will release you to a halfway house about six months before the fifteen months are up." Ted smiles, always eager to deliver the money line. "So you serve about *nine months* on a sixty-month sentence!"

"No bullshit?"

"No bullshit, Lars. In theory you're supposed to do drug treatment for a couple years after you're out, but it's not really enforced."

"What if you screw up the treatment?"

"Everybody does. Once you're out it's almost impossible to get thrown back in jail."

"DOSA?"

"Right. Drug Offender Sentencing Alternative."

"Sounds okay, but I think we can get the evidence suppressed."

"What?"

"I don't want to plea," he says, increasingly twitchy. "I want to get the evidence suppressed. Then the case gets dismissed."

"Yes, I know how it works."

"So we'll do a bail hearing, then a hearing to get the evidence suppressed?"

The only thing I'm suppressing is an urge to bitch-slap your head.

"The cop was out to get me," Howard continues. "It was a pretentious stop."

"A *what?*"

"A pretentious stop. Judge Sanders says you can't do that in Washington. Some of the guys in here are friends with him. He's on the Washington Supreme Court."

"Yes, I know who the fuck *Justice* Sanders is," Ted says, surprising Howard with the f-bomb, "and I'm sure everyone in gray pajamas claims to be his friend."

"Sanders made pretentious stops illegal."

"It's called a 'pretextual stop.' " *Idiot jailhouse lawyers.* "Not a *pretentious* stop."

"Oh."

Ted sighs in a long exhalation, not caring if his bourbon breath envelops his client. Sometimes Ted hates his job—most of the time, in fact.

"I can pursue the suppression motions if you want," Ted finally says, "but the prosecutor will withdraw the DOSA offer if I do."

"Can they do that?"

"Yes."

"Bastards."

"Actually, many of them are women."

PEOPLE WANT THE TRUTH

"Are we winning the war on drugs?" Mike repeats the question back to the interviewer from MSNBC, a standard gambit to clarify and buy time to think. Working late, he had to cancel his date with June. Sometimes he wishes he could go back to grad school and just read piles of books.

"You're in the trenches," the reporter says. "Is victory in sight from your perspective?"

People want the truth?

A cousin of his, a politician, told him this once—people want the truth and will not hold it against you for telling them. He would like to believe this.

"War is not really a useful metaphor," he says, starting off with his stock answer. "Drug use has been with us forever, always will be."

"Why do you think that is?"

"People like to feel good."

"So you're saying we're never going to win this war?"

"Again, war is not a useful metaphor."

"So if war isn't a useful metaphor, what is?"

"Realism is useful."

"And by that you mean?"

He stares up past the Cobain poster at a small ball of water slowly forming on his ceiling, not yet heavy enough to drop.

"People like their drugs," he says. "People like caffeine, alcohol, nicotine, painkillers, antidepressants. People like to alter their consciousness."

"Okay, but what about methamphetamine? Can we eliminate meth use?"

Mike listens to reporters carefully to gauge their angle, Googles them when he can, but he did not have time with this one.

"Not until the next drug *du jour* comes around."

"So what do we do in the meantime?"

Kill all the meth cooks?

"Two-prong approach to stop the bleeding," he says. "Cut supply, and cut demand. Right now, however, we don't have sufficient resources to do either, so we need to be more innovative."

"How do you cut supply?"

"Shut down sales of ephedrine or pseudoephedrine for starters, but the pharmaceutical companies have been blocking that for years. Billions of dollars are at stake. The corporate profit margin on pseudoephedrine would embarrass most drug dealers."

"Isn't Congress considering a bill this session?"

"Yes, Senator Cantwell is working on it, it's called the Combat Meth Act, and it's been tacked onto the Patriot Act, but even if we could cut off the legal sources for pseudo, there's still the black market, which will expand to meet the demand."

"Okay, so how do you cut demand, then?"

"We need to work with the addicts, get innovative in that area as well."

"What drives people to damaging drugs?"

People want the truth.

"You got me."

"What?"

"I don't know why people want to screw up their lives chasing drugs or money or sex or their obsession of choice. I don't know why politicians destroy their careers and reputations over petty

bribes or sex with an intern. I don't get compulsive behavior. Of course, I don't even know how to work a microwave."

"Good night," one of his attorneys says on her way out, waving her umbrella.

"I'm leaving, too," Cort announces, stepping out into the hallway in his blue raincoat. "The Xerox machine is broken again, by the way. I've alerted *the others.*"

Taken from the television series, *Lost,* "the others" is Cort's reference to office administration.

"Good night."

"What?"

"Nothing, I was just saying good night to the attorneys."

"Oh, late night for you there."

"Yeah."

"So do you feel like your trial unit, right there on the front lines, can see any progress?"

"As much progress as possible when you have thirteen attorneys handling about twenty-five hundred cases a year. And most of the attorneys in the unit, including me, are also handling homicide cases. We have over seventy defendants in the jail with pending homicides. There are more murderers in our jail than there are felony attorneys in our office."

"You're swamped."

"We're drowning. And the meth tsunami is rolling east."

Sensing that the interview is detouring, the reporter regroups. "You said earlier that people will always want to alter their consciousness?"

"One way or another, not necessarily in a destructive way."

"So why do people choose methamphetamine?"

"It's cheap, fast, and easy to make. Meth is the lazy way to alter consciousness."

He can hear the reporter typing again.

"The problem," Mike continues, "one of the problems, is that we've cried wolf too many times—about pot and heroin, for example—and now people are understandably slow to accept that we really do have a drug that's like putting your brain in a frying pan."

"You know who Norm Stamper is?"

"Former Seattle police chief."

"He's been doing op-ed pieces advocating for the legalization of all drugs, including meth."

"I think it's a good dialogue to open up."

"So you think legalization is a good idea?"

"No, I think a *dialogue* is a good idea."

"Stamper argues that drug use and abuse would not increase with legalization."

"I don't think that's realistic."

"Stamper believes legalization will dramatically reduce the public expenses of incarceration and law enforcement, and that it will put violent drug dealers and home meth labs out of business. He argues for letting the government sell it and tax it and regulate it."

And there's the reporter's angle.

Though exhausted, Mike has managed to maneuver his way through this interview mostly on message—*need resources and innovation*—and he knows he should end this interview now.

"Do you think keeping drugs illegal is reducing the number of addicts or crime?" the reporter asks when Mike does not respond to the Stamper argument.

"Or wasted lives?"

"Right, is keeping drugs illegal, is the drug war ... *working?*"

Bone-tired, Mike can no more answer this than he could tell

the reporter the meaning of life or whether God exists—though he believes there is a meaning to life and God does exist. He stares up at the drop of water, still clinging to the ceiling.

"You want my personal opinion on this? Not the position of the office, but my personal opinion?"

"Absolutely."

This, Mike knows, is the moment journalists seek—the breaking point where the interviewee tires of rhetoric and lets his guard down, puts himself at the mercy of the interviewer.

"I don't think you can do a comprehensive piece on drug abuse without discussing three other subjects: spirituality, consumerism, and stupidity."

"No?" *Tap, tap, tap*, the typing begins again.

"I'm going to have to quote P. J. O'Rourke here: 'No drug causes the fundamental ills of society. If we're looking for the source of our troubles, we shouldn't test people for drugs, we should test them for stupidity, ignorance, greed, and love of power.' "

"So where does what leave us?"

It leaves me wanting a drink.

"I think," Mike says, "that O'Rourke's point is that drugs are a symptom of bigger problems. And he should know, he's done a lot of drugs."

After pulling out of the conversation, Mike stares at the drop of water until it falls, disappearing into the rug. Then he rummages through a stack of correspondence and court orders overflowing from his in-box. He wonders if he should have blown off the interview and everything else and gone out with June, but right now he needs the satisfaction of checking things off his list, cleaning tasks off his desk.

On top is a letter he opens despite the prison return address:

DEAR SIR MR LAWSON,

IM CORRENTLY IN DEPARTMENT OF CORECTOINS. IM WANTING TO NOWE IF YOU WILL MAKE A DEAL FORE MY TEST TOMONY AGANST METH COOKS. I NOWE A LOT OF METH COOKS AND THEY DISTOYD MY LIFE AND MENY MORE. WHUT IM ASKIN IS A REDUTION IN MY SENTIC FOR MY TEST TOMONY. I DO NOWE THAT PRISON IS AND ISNOT THE ANSER FOR ME PLEAS CON CIDER THIS THANK YOU.

The aspiring informant signs above his inmate number with his real name, Garth Ericksen, and his proposed alias, "Rocky Sly," and Mike shakes his head, thinking what he often thinks in his job.

Nobody could make this crap up.

Beneath the tweeker letter is a scheduling order from Ted Haller setting motion dates and a bail hearing, which triggers Mike's curiosity because Cocktail Ted almost never notes up motions, almost never goes to trial.

Ted is famous for cajoling, coercing, and begging his clients to plead and thereby avoid the extra prison time that follows a trial. Celebrities may be acquitted, but for garden-variety defendants it is usually merely a question of "guilty" or "incredibly guilty."

The defendant's name on Ted's scheduling order is Lars Ulrich, a.k.a. Howard Schultz, and he is currently in custody.

Mike smiles as he picks up the phone, *the job does have many moments of joy.*

THE CITY OF DESTINY

"If you had to arrest a mime," Suki asks Wyatt, "would you tell him he had a right to remain silent?"

"You're a nut, you know."

He is the nut, in her eyes, but she believes she can crack him, open him up and solve the puzzle inside as she likes to do.

They stroll the wide and wet pedestrian boulevard on the shore of the Foss Waterway, wearing dark sweaters and holding hands, a routine image on the new walkway. Seagulls hover and swoop above, occasionally perching on the metal rails separating the boats from the boulevard, eyes alert for food. A light breeze ruffles the water and rattles the halyards, which clank against sailboat masts with a hollow knocking. The red neon sign of Johnny's Dock, an old-school restaurant on the east side of the waterway, reflects off the rippled surface.

Just a few years ago there was nothing on the west side of this polluted waterway into Commencement Bay but dirt, garbage, puddles of toxic mud, and the occasional drug addict skulking in the dark. Now graceful boats rest in a well-maintained marina on the right of the walkway and modern condominiums rise on the left just south of the Tacoma Museum of Glass, all gleaming in the city lights. The sounds of socializing buzz out of the Blue Olive, a cocktail bar on the bottom floor of the condos.

This metamorphosis, known as the Thea Foss Revitalization Project, won the Outstanding Civil Engineering Achievement Award from the American Society of Civil Engineers in 2005, and is part of the basis of Wyatt's faith in Tacoma's future. He loves the city. Tacoma, he believes, is on the verge, a frontier town prepar-

ing for the boom that brings civilization and a sense of pride, held back only by the stubborn idiocy of lawlessness.

Sometimes Wyatt thinks he wants to be a golf course groundskeeper when he retires, maybe work at Ladenburg's links, something like Bill Murray in *Caddyshack,* a job where he would just come out at night to mow the lawn and practice putting and not deal with criminal miscreants.

"So what do you think?" Suki asks as they pass under a bright new street lamp.

"About what?"

"What we were talking about."

"About arresting a mime?"

"Before that."

"What were we talking about before that?"

Suki sighs. "Are you serious?"

Wyatt tries to quickly recall what they were talking about, but his mind has left the subject too far behind. "Yes, I guess I am."

"Why do you seem so ambivalent lately?"

"Oh, right. Well . . . I don't know. Do I seem ambivalent?"

"You even seem ambivalent about your ambivalence."

"What?"

"I'm serious. It started after I moved in, after we started seeing each other all the time, after you started seeing me lying around in sweats."

"Okay."

"Okay?" Suki stops, releases his hand. "That's what you have to say?"

"You're probably right. You are right. But it has nothing to do with your sweatpants."

"What does it have to do with?"

"I don't know." Wyatt shrugs.

"You're infuriating." Suki shakes her head. "Why are you ambivalent about this? You don't seem ambivalent about anything else in your life. You're not an ambivalent person, and yet . . . here we are."

They stand there facing each other in the outer circle of a lamp's glow, able to hear the electricity humming from the pole, and he cannot help but notice that she looks especially pretty in this light.

"I've just been distracted sometimes."

"Not sometimes, pretty constantly."

"Yeah?"

"Yeah."

"Sometimes cases consume me," he says, knowing it sounds lame. "It's just that . . ." He doesn't know where to take this.

"You really think it's this one case?" When he does not answer immediately, she replies for him. "It's not. I don't believe this is all about . . . this Howard guy, or whatever he represents to you."

"Well, I'm not seeing anyone else."

"I didn't say you were. Where did *that* come from?"

"What are you implying, then?"

"Just what I said. It seems like whatever is going on is about more than one case." Suki wipes the hair out of her face as the wind picks up, carrying dark rain clouds from the east. An Air Force cargo plane rumbles overhead on the heavily used flight path over downtown. "Have you scheduled our vacation yet?"

Wyatt grimaces. "Shit, sorry."

"Wyatt . . ."

"I just . . . forgot. Sorry."

"You just forgot?"

"Yes, sorry."

"Wyatt . . . have you checked out of this relationship?"

"No. I don't want to check out."

"So you're checking out without even *choosing* to?"

"I didn't say I was checked out."

"You didn't say you weren't."

"Okay, stop. You're worse than a lawyer."

"I'm just trying to figure out what's going on, to understand."

"I get that."

"So I can make good choices."

After a few seconds of silence, with the quietness bringing a sense of possible reconciliation and shared desire, Wyatt's cell phone rings.

Their eyes meet; Suki purses her lips. Wyatt hesitates, starts to speak, but then reaches for his phone.

"Christ almighty," Suki says.

"It's Mike," Wyatt explains, "calling from the office. It's probably business."

QUAALUDE TO A KISS

Howard wakes up to the sound of robins outside the window. Normally he would go back to sleep, but the adrenaline kicks in when he realizes he is out of the stifling Pierce County Jail. This, at least, is good.

As he lies in bed beside Brandy, who is snoring like a truck driver, disgusting him, he formulates a plan for the day. His options are limited because of the clunky ankle bracelet he wears from the Electronic Home Monitoring agency.

Ted Haller, giving in to Howard, set up a bail hearing and argued halfheartedly that Howard should be released on home monitoring until trial. The judge agreed over the prosecutor's objection. Howard attributed this to fine lawyering by Cocktail Ted, but the judge was only thinking about the county budget.

Because of jail overcrowding and the accompanying lawsuits, criminals in Pierce County are regularly set free before their sentences are completed, and so the judge accepted the opportunity to make a jail bed available. Howard pays ten dollars a day to the EHM agency and he is not costing the county bed space or meals. However, the cost of Howard's continuing criminal activity did not figure into the judge's calculations.

In the kitchen Howard finds Brandy and convinces her that he has no meth, so she might as well go to work and he will see the kids off to school.

"What are you going to do all day?" Brandy asks as he is ushering her out.

"I have to talk to my lawyer."

He likes saying *my lawyer.*

"All day?"

"Legal motions are complicated, you know. We've got a whole pretentious stop issue, like I already told you."

Three years ago when Howard was on EHM after assaulting his girlfriend, he moved back in with her and would not allow her to leave the house until his sentence was completed because, as he told her, it was all her fault. However, Brandy cannot be blamed for his arrest, so he allows her to leave the house and, furthermore, he needs her out.

"Make sure that Porsche and Joe are on their way in time," she says as he opens the front door.

"I think they're up." He saw Porsche walk into the bathroom in a long white T-shirt and, it seemed to him, nothing else. "At least Porsche is."

"Make sure they have some orange juice or something for breakfast."

"Hey, they got to school fine before I moved in here."

"No, they didn't get to school fine. They're both late and absent all the time. Especially when I work mornings. That's the reason I don't work much."

"You sure it's not just because you're lazy?"

"You're one to talk."

"I may be many shitty things, but I'm not lazy." He tugs up his pants, scratches his crotch. "I'm the freakin' king."

"Well, then prove it. Get cooking."

"Keep nagging me," he says, "and see where that gets you, bitch."

"I'm sorry, honey," she says, staying in the doorway, switching into a little-girl voice. "I just want to get highhhhhhh."

They kiss and wish each other a good day, imitating a normal couple, and Howard closes the door behind her with relief and excitement.

Half an hour later he has Joe out the door, dressed in his quasi-gang attire, limping only slightly on his sprained ankle.

Porsche stays back. She is half dressed for school in "winter pink" lipstick, eyeliner, her black choker, tight hip-hugging jeans, and, to his disappointment, a bra under a black and red band T-shirt emblazoned with stencils of the three members of the Yeah Yeah Yeahs. Her dirty blond hair is up in a ponytail.

"Mom will be pissed if she knows," Porsche says.

"'Cause she's usually so good about caring if you go to school?"

"She cares. She's just . . . you know, a tweeker. That's why this house is, like, a disgusting double-wide trailer or something."

Howard nods, glancing around the living room. The brown and orange shag rug looks like it hasn't been vacuumed since the 1970s, the black vinyl couch has a dirty plate on a crooked cushion, the coffee table has two empty Olde English "800" cans and a half-full glass of what appears to be orange juice and an overflowing ashtray, the beige walls are stained in patches, and there is cat hair everywhere even though Howard has never seen a cat. Some tweekers will vacuum endlessly, but apparently not Brandy.

Howard opens the mini blinds over the front window, just a slit in the middle. He hunches over, peeks out, closes them back up.

That's why they're called tweeker blinds, Porsche says to herself.

"Okay," he says, rubbing his hands together. "Let's break out the good shit." He shamelessly leers at Porsche. "Sound good? Yeah?"

She shrugs. "What do you have?"

"What do you think I have?"

"Mom said you didn't have any meth."

"Since when do you listen to your mom?"

Though Porsche refuses to beg, she flashes just enough enthusiasm to show a smile.

Howard hustles off into the bedroom and a few moments later he comes back out with a purple Crown Royal bag. He sits on the couch and out of the bag pulls an amber glass vial with crystals, a baggie with white powder, and a glass pipe. The baggie is stamped with a Superman logo.

Porsche sits beside him, crossing her legs, intently watching his actions.

"This is from one of my personal cooks," he says, holding up the baggie. "You can tell by the logo." He sets down the baggie on the coffee table, holds up the vial. "And this is ice, from the same cook."

"Yeah?"

"Home-cooked means better than ninety percent purity. The shit you kids get at school is probably thirty percent pure, at best."

Porsche nods, though numbers generally bore her.

"I picked up this shit when we were at the storage unit and hid it from your mom." He sets down the vial next to the baggie and pulls a razor blade, butane lighter, short wire rod, and mirror out of the purple bag. "It ain't easy hiding shit from your mom."

She nods knowingly and watches Howard shake the powder into a corner of the baggie and then tear off that piece of the baggie and pour the powder onto the mirror.

"Since you helped out that day," he says, chopping the lines up with practiced strokes, "I might not charge you for the drugs here."

"*Charge me?* Girls don't *pay* for drugs."

"Oh, yeah, they do."

"Well, *I* don't."

"You've never paid for drugs?"

"I have, but with, like, other girls. The guys always pay if we're partying with them. Everybody knows *that*."

"You have a boyfriend?" he asks, looking up from his chopping.

"No."

"Why not? You prefer girls?"

"Nooooo. Why do guys always say that, like they hope it's true?"

"It's sexy."

"*What's* sexy?"

"A pretty young girl with another pretty young girl."

"If the girls are into girls, how is it sexy for a guy?"

"It just is, hon, it just is."

"Guys are weird."

"Here's everything you need to know about guys." Howard enjoys sharing his wisdom. "Guys do everything for sex. All guys, from Bill Clinton to George Bush to everybody."

"*George Bush?* Does everything for sex?" She holds up her thumbs and forefingers in the W, not knowing this is the president's middle initial. "What*ever*."

"Why do you think he did cocaine? Just 'cause he liked to get high? No. Because girls are into guys with cocaine." He returns to chopping the lines, straightening them and lengthening them. "And you gotta figure George Bush had good coke. Like, straight from a Colombian drug lord."

Porsche, tuning in to the sexual drift, shrugs.

"You prefer snorting or smoking?" he asks.

Porsche shrugs again. "Whatever."

"Well, we're gonna do both. Best of both worlds."

Porsche has never smoked meth, thinking that smoking it was somehow stepping past a line she should not cross. When she snorted, she did not feel much, and decided the chunky tan powder was hardly meth at all, but the sort of bogus dope that dealers sold to those who did not know better. The high school junior who provided it to her dropped considerably in her estimation.

"The rush of smoking, plus the longer and smoother high of snorting," Howard continues, picking up the vial and tapping a couple of crystals into the pipe through a hole in the top of the bowl.

Howard has numerous theories about meth and its production and consumption, as people fully involved in an occupation or hobby do. He thinks he should start a meth blog with MySpace because there is so much erroneous tweeker lore.

He wants to title the blog, "Don't Meth with Me!"

Delicately holding the glass pipe to his lips, he flicks the lighter on, directs the flame under the bowl until the crystal starts to boil, and then quickly sucks in the white vapors with a raspy desperate breath.

Porsche watches, fascinated with the process.

His eyes close as he sucks out the last ember of light in the bowl, and he holds the hit for several seconds and then finally exhales, his whole body slumping forward in surrender as he does.

After a few seconds of silence, which Porsche senses she should not break the sanctity of, Howard sets down the pipe, picks up the wire rod, and cleans out the residue with the fastidiousness of an artist tending to his tools.

As the meth enters his bloodstream through his lungs and then pumps into his brain, his synapses start to fire and burn— *snap, crackle, and pop*—as the meth kicks on the dopamine neurotransmitters and he starts to feel like Superman again.

I, I, I am Superman and I can do anything. . . .

He loads a jagged crystal of ice into the pipe and hands it to Porsche, who receives it carefully with both hands. She notes that her crystal is smaller than the one he smoked and she wonders if he is looking out for her or just being stingy.

"Put it in your mouth."

Closing her lips lightly around the end of the glass, Porsche watches as Howard moves the lighter flame under the bowl and the crystal starts to melt.

"Suck."

Ignoring what sounds like a sexual edge to the word, she breathes in the vapors. At first she does not feel anything and so she looks at Howard.

"Hold it in."

Her eyes grow big and wide as she does, and then she opens her mouth in an O and the smoke comes out in a thin stream.

"Good girl."

And then she feels it—a tingle and her heart thumping and she feels the rush sweep her to the edge of euphoria, but not quite there.

"It's hitting you," Howard says, smiling, watching.

"Uh-huh."

"That's just a taste."

She has smoked pot, dropped X, and drunk plenty of alcohol, but the high coming on is different—it fills her with confidence instead of insecurity, something no drug has done for her before.

"Should I have . . . more," she asks.

Porsche wonders if she made a mistake by letting him know what she was thinking, wonders if he can tell just how badly she wants more.

"We're going to play a little game," Howard says.

"Yeah?"

"It's called 'strip and snort.' "

"Strip and snort?"

"Yep. Smoking is a nice instant rush, but snorting prolongs it all goddamn day."

"So you're geeking."

"What?"

"That's what it's called at school—you're geeking if you're stoned."

"Well, you're going to like geeking." Howard starts chopping out the meth on the mirror. "For each item of clothes you remove you get one snort."

Porsche stares at him for a beat, trying to gauge if he is serious. She quickly realizes he is, and that she is possibly in over her head, but she has dealt with older guys before and feels she can hold her own.

"That's sort of juvenile," she says. "Don't you think?"

"I think . . . you just missed your turn."

Howard holds up his leg with the ankle bracelet and makes a show of taking off his sock, which grosses Porsche out. After he removes his other sock, he leans over and puts a snort straw to a short line and quickly huffs it all. Sitting up, sniffling, he smiles at Porsche.

She removes her socks, revealing pink-painted toenails.

"Nice," he says, "but keep going."

"Keep going?"

"Yeah, you skipped your first turn, so you're one behind. Keep going."

"That's . . . dumb."

"You want to play or not?"

"Not."

Howard shrugs. "More for me."

He begins cutting another line out from the pile in the corner of the mirror. Porsche, heart pattering, sees her reflection there, her flushed face, distorted but pretty, *desirable,* as the white line takes shape.

"Okay," she says, "whatever," and she unceremoniously removes her T-shirt. Her bra is white and plain.

"Small tits," Howard comments.

"So? Models have small boobs."

"Only homos like models."

"The singer of the White Stripes married a model."

"Homo."

"And Eddie Vedder dates Jill McCormick, a model."

"Homo."

"No, he's not."

"Yes, he is."

Porsche, surprised by Howard's insistence, decides to drop this course of conversation, though she feels bad about not carrying on a defense of Eddie Vedder, her choice for cutest older man in the world.

Howard bends down and fine-tunes the line on the mirror, which she assumes, hopes, is hers. He hands her the straw. Imitating what she observed, she puts the straw in one nostril, gently closes the other nostril with her index finger, leans down, and clumsily guides the straw toward the line and when it is there she

breathes in deeply and slides the straw over the line, the white powder disappearing, *poof.*

"You don't have to hold your breath."

She exhales as she sits back up and the only thing that hits her right away is the burning in her nose, but she knew there would be some of that and accepts the pain.

"That was just a toddler line," Howard says.

Gulping, Porsche feels the meth drip from her nasal passages into her throat, a dry and tinny taste.

"Nice tat," she says, looking at his forearm as he chops up another line.

"Yeah, one of these days we'll get you one."

"Seriously?" It sounds cool at the moment. "Like what?"

"Something with . . . blood and roses."

"Mom will freak out."

Shifting nostrils, Howard whiffs up a line and turns to Porsche with a maniacal heaven-is-just-around-the-corner grin. "Want to feed the other half of your brain?" he asks, as if inhaling a drug through just one nostril would leave a user only half affected.

Porsche nods, knowing what he will say next.

"Lose the jeans, then."

Shrugging, as indifferently as she can manage, she stands and wiggles down the jeans. She is wearing plain white full-back bikini underwear.

"Step out of the jeans and turn in a circle."

Unsure why, she does so, goose pimples rising.

Howard leans back and unabashedly stares. "Skinny," he says, "but nice ass anyway."

She makes a face over her shoulder and quickly sits back down. A few girls at her school are on what they call the "Jenny Crank" diet, but she is naturally slender.

Howard chops up another small line and hands Porsche the straw. He stares at her ass as she leans over to fill the left nostril and she does not flinch as he slaps the top of her cheeks over the worn cotton.

"You got the hang of it now," he says.

She whips her head back and wipes her nose. "This is so much better than boys have at school," she says, suddenly in an open and generous mood.

Howard smiles, calculating that so far he has only given her about twenty dollars' worth of meth, *a bargain*. He appraises her gangly body, touches a hip bone jutting out over the elastic of the bikini panties.

"Are you the prettiest girl at your school?"

"No," she says, moving his hand away.

"I have to admit something."

"Yeah?"

"You *do* have the body of a model."

"You said only homos like models."

"I mean famous models. You've got the body, without being a famous stuck-up bitch. When you're older, boys are going to be falling all over each other to get to you."

"Thanks." Breathing rapidly, unconsciously grinding her jaw and rolling her tight shoulders, Porsche looks around the room. She can hear the rain pattering on the roof, weirdly loud. "We should clean this fucking ugly-ass house up."

Howard laughs.

"I'm serious. I hate what a fucking pigsty this house is." She stands up in her underwear, making no motion for her clothes. "Let's clean it up."

"That black choker doesn't match your white undies."

"Black and white always match." She tilts her head, puts her hands on her hips. "Are you gonna help?"

Sex is more where Howard would like Porsche's peppiness channeled, but they have plenty of days and nights of Electronic Home Monitoring ahead, and he knows he will have her soon and often, *welcome to my world, princess.*

"If you're good," he says, "I'll give you a 'lude later."

"What?"

"A Quaalude, to come down."

"You have those, too?"

"Just for my very favorite girls."

At 4:20 p.m. Ted's legal assistant faxes Mike the Howard Schultz brief for the suppression motion, which is set the next morning at nine-thirty. Ted left his office after lunch to go play golf, taking advantage of a rare fall day without rain. He told his assistant to fax the brief before she left for the day, *no rush, it's already late.*

The brief was due two weeks ago. However, for most criminal defense attorneys it is customary to deliver their briefs shortly before the motion. Then the prosecutor must either continue the motion, thereby delaying the case, or go forward less than fully prepared. Prosecutors often opt for the latter because continuances invariably work to the advantage of the defense—witnesses disappear, memories fade, other cases take priority. Furthermore, prosecutors often find it is easier to respond orally in court than spend hours they do not have writing a brief.

Sometimes defense attorneys push the prosecutor into this decision by design, sometimes it just works out that way. Though Ted is familiar with the popular obstructionist theory of criminal defense—stall and obfuscate—he will not go out of his way to do either. One thing he has in common with local prosecutors is too many cases and not enough of a life.

Nearly six hours after Ted left his office, Mike is checking his e-mail and in-box, about to call it a day. He finds the fax from Ted and this halts his exit. He spends a few minutes skimming the brief, making notes in the margins. Then he goes online and makes copies of the two cases Ted cites, though he is already familiar with both.

Shockingly to Mike, Ted has spotted the issue. Though the

leading case Ted relies on is absurd, a close five-to-four decision, it is still good law and it appears on its face to apply to the
facts.

Because there is not time to type up a brief, Mike hand-writes
a memo that he will use as a crib sheet for oral argument. By midnight he goes home, hoping for five hours of sleep, about an hour
less than his weekday standard.

His bed is king-sized, and the walls are light blue, *teal,* because
Mary, the team chief of the Special Assault Unit, a fellow night
owl, told him that teal was a soothing color and would help him
sleep. Especially, she added, if he used Ambien. A few people in his
office are on drugs, antidepressants, but Mike has never been
truly depressed and he will not use chemical remedies for sleep,
except for alcohol.

A variety of matters can keep him awake, mostly related to a
constant sense of falling behind in his workload, but this has been
happening less since he resumed meditating. When he was a trial
attorney in the Special Assault Unit, SAU, his bouts of sleepless-
ness were sometimes adrenaline-charged and he did not mind
losing sleep when he was in trial. In this he recognizes that trial
lawyers are like drug addicts, *living for the high.*

Tonight a touch of the adrenaline is back. He is looking forward to court tomorrow and his mind is playing through arguments: what Ted will open with, what he will respond, what Ted
will counter, what the judge will likely ask, and on and on. He
canceled another date with June because he knew he would be
bad company.

Before his alarm goes off he wakes up, instantly alert, which
only happens on trial days. Though a motion is to a trial as a skit
is to a play, a miniature of a drama, he is glad to have some of that
same showtime buzz. He pads into the kitchen in his boxers and

drinks a glass of orange juice mixed with cranberry and munches down a handful of granola from a box of cereal.

Patti Smith's *Wave* is already loaded in the stereo and he turns it on and clicks to track three, an ever-reliable picker-upper. Speakers throughout the house blast out the screeching guitar and then the pounding drums and then the bass line and chords and finally her awesome heroin voice, *"So you wanna be a rock and roll star, then listen now to what I say . . ."*

Showering, shaving, and brushing his teeth takes about fifteen minutes. He plays through all the likely arguments again in his head, making sure he has not missed one, knowing there is always one. Trials are a game that move as you play.

Picking a suit for court is easy, as he owns nothing but blue standards from Brooks Brothers, and the choice of shirt is equally uncomplicated, as he has only white button-down oxfords. Most of his dates have been disconcerted by his monochromatic wardrobe, except for June, who seems strangely pleased.

Just before he exits the house, Mike picks out a watch, a traditional white-dial Timex with black hands and leather strap. Though he consciously minimizes his possessions, he has an uncharacteristic indulgence in his nightstand drawer: twelve watches, four Timex, three L. L. Bean, three Orvis, one Swiss Army, and one Rat Pack–style Rolex from the early sixties.

Sometimes late at night, when it is especially quiet, he can hear ticking from the drawer.

LUCK OF THE DRAW

At nine in the morning the presiding court comes to order with the proverbial rap of the gavel. This triggers a Pavlovian response in the lawyers, their heads turning toward the judge's empty chair, which is flanked by the flags of Washington and the United States.

Here the attorneys and defendants gather before being sent out to trial, and it is heated up with bodies that exceed the fire code limits. Four dozen lawyers stand in shifting groups around the counsel tables and about a dozen more sit in the jury box. Behind them, about fifty people line the bench seats of the gallery, mostly out-of-custody defendants, but also their friends, lovers, and relatives, some of whom are victims or witnesses in their cases. Court can be a family affair.

The in-custody defendants sit in the adjoining jury room, enjoying comfortable seats that are second only to those of the judges. When his or her case is up each defendant is escorted out by two of the six guards standing by.

After the judicial assistant calls the court to order, Judge Sorensen enters, gray-haired and black-robed. He takes the bench with the beleaguered countenance of a twice-bitten lion-tamer working for a low-budget circus.

When the Howard Schultz case is called Mike responds, "Present and ready, Your Honor."

Most drug trials are resolved at the motions stage—if the defense fails to suppress the evidence the next logical step is a plea.

"Thank you, Mr. Lawson. Mr. Haller?"

"What?" Ted says, looking up from a conversation with a young female prosecutor he has a crush on.

"You want to be assigned out for a motion?"

"Sure."

"Is your client present?"

"I don't know." Ted looks in the gallery. "Mr. Ulrich? Or Mr. Schultz?"

Howard raises his hand from the back row. He is sitting with Porsche, who is wearing a lavender camisole top, and the sight of a defendant sitting with a twelve-year-old girl confirms Judge Sorensen's usual despair and he checks the file to make sure it is not a child-molest case. Though the judge cannot tell from his perch fifty feet away, both Howard and Porsche are shaking from their morning bump.

"My client is here," Ted reports.

"Yes, I see."

"But if there aren't any courtrooms available . . ." Ted shrugs. Though he does not complete the sentence, the meaning is clear: there usually are not enough courtrooms to go around, so some of the cases need to be continued and Ted is happy to be one of those continuances.

"How long will the motion take?" the judge asks.

"About an hour," Mike says.

"Or two," Ted says.

"Judge Stuber is available."

Eccentric is the word most often applied to Judge Eva Stuber. She has two dozen cats, writes romance novels under a nom de plume, and is given to wearing colorful hats and making impolitic statements.

As Mike steps out into the hallway with the manila court file, Wyatt joins him.

"I couldn't breathe in there," Wyatt says.

"I think it's the oxygen deprivation that makes everyone in there act half crazy."

"Did you see him?"

"Ted will bring him to Stuber's court."

"She's the cat lady, right?"

"The very one."

They step down the hallway, their footsteps echoing on the granite as they pass the usual cast of characters: suited lawyers, uniformed police officers waiting idly to testify, plainclothes detectives using cell phones, unkempt defendants and their girl-friends, and numerous children with no apparent supervision.

"Have you seen the deputy this morning?" Mike asks.

"Yeah, he went up to the café on eleven. I told him we would call when we were assigned out." Wyatt pulls out his cell phone and pages him, punching in the courtroom number. "The kid looks like Howdy Doody, by the way."

When they enter the courtroom they are warmly greeted by the judicial assistant and the court reporter, everyone taking a moment for personal and professional updates. One of the plea-sures of working in the courthouse are the mostly good-humored people who maintain an upbeat attitude despite the wretchedness they see every day.

Judicial assistants and court reporters have seen up close the damage defendants wreak, they've heard from the victims, and they develop the same style of gallows humor and protective cyn-icism as the lawyers. They tend to silently side with prosecutors because they appreciate veracity, accountability, and availability. The prosecutors are housed in the same asylum.

Wyatt sits in the gallery behind Mike, waiting to see Howard. After a few long minutes the tall doors of the court open. Porsche

enters, and Howard steps in behind her, cocky in his cowboy boots.

Wyatt stares, *shorter than I expected.*

Other than that, Howard fits the descriptions Wyatt has been given: wiry, pale, long blond hair, goatee. He is wearing a long-sleeved sweatshirt with GOD CAN CHANGE HOPELESS DOPE FIENDS INTO DOPELESS HOPE FIENDS in block letters across the front, apparently trying to represent himself as rehabilitated and converted. Tweekers often have slogans on their clothes and Wyatt suspects it is because nobody listens to them.

Howard crosses over toward Ted, but on the way he feels Wyatt's gaze and meets it and it instantly unnerves him. Still, he stares back for a moment before looking away. He has heard on the street that Detective Wyatt James has been hunting for him and now he knows his face.

When Judge Stuber emerges from her chambers, her judicial assistant raps the gavel and everyone rises. Porsche stays in the first row of the gallery directly behind Wyatt.

"Good morning," the judge says, ready for the day's entertainment.

Mike stays on his feet while he calls the case for the record. "This is State versus Howard Schultz. The defendant is present out of custody, represented by counsel Ted Haller, who is also present. We're here on a 3.6 defense motion."

"You ready, Mr. Haller?"

Ted, wearing rumpled corduroy pants and a frayed blue blazer, is listening to Howard whisper when he suddenly hears the judge.

"What?" Ted says.

"Are you ready to proceed, Mr. Haller?"

"Yes, sure. Let's go."

Judges are generally control freaks, and Ted's lack of focus and deference makes some spitting mad, but Judge Stuber likes Ted.

"Call your first witness, Mr. Lawson."

Deputy Newton stands stiff and straight as the judge swears him in, and he practically yells back, "Yes, Your Honor," before sitting down in the wooden chair.

Clean-shaven, hands fixed in lap, the young deputy has never testified before and he is nervous on the stand even as Mike leads him through the easy preliminaries. When they progress to the stop, Mike pauses to let the deputy know it is game time. From here on Mike works off a script.

"What was the first thing you noticed about the defendant's vehicle when you saw it driving toward you?"

"One of the headlamps was out."

"And what time was this?"

"About ten o'clock."

"At night?"

"Yes. Right."

"Are there any streetlights on that road?"

"Only at intersections."

"Were there intersections where you first saw the defendant?"

"No."

"So the road was dark?"

"Yes."

"Was it raining?"

"Yes."

"Which headlight was out?"

"The driver's side."

"Did you consider that dangerous?"

"Yes."

"You weren't on duty at the time?"

"I had just clocked out."

"When you're off duty, do you respond if you witness a crime or an infraction?"

"Yes. I have."

"How many times have you pulled people over when you were off duty?"

"At least two. Once I saw what I thought was a drunk driver ahead of me and so I pulled him over."

"What caused you to pull the defendant's car over in this case?"

"Two things. The broken headlamp, and the fact that I recognized the Firebird from a previous stop."

"When was this previous stop?"

"A couple of weeks before this stop."

"At what point did you realize that the car with the broken driver's headlight was the Firebird you had contacted previously?"

"Not until it drove by me."

"Had you already decided to pull the car over?"

"I was already thinking about it, yes."

"Can you describe your previous contact with this Firebird?"

The deputy looks up at the judge, suddenly conversational. "I stopped the car once before for a broken taillamp. And it turned out the occupants had been buying boxes of pseudoephedrine at different stores, which is common for methamphetamine cooks and their runners."

Ted could object, but does not.

"Was the defendant Howard Schultz the driver during that first contact?" Mike asks.

"No," the deputy says, turning back to Mike. "He was a passenger."

"Was he arrested?"

"No, just the driver was."

"As the Firebird drove by you, could you tell who was driving?"

"No. I just recognized the car."

"What about the car was distinctive?"

"The hood had a half-finished fire-breathing bird painted on it. The rest was gray primer paint."

Mike and Judge Stuber exchange an amused glance, and Mike flips to another page of his script.

"What did you do after the defendant's car passed?"

"I performed a U-turn and followed him."

"Did you activate your wig-wag lights and siren?"

"Yes."

"And what did you intend to pull him over for?"

"The broken headlamp."

"Was the fact that you had a previous contact with him part of the reason you decided to pull him over?"

"Yes."

"Was the previous contact the *only* reason that you decided to pull the defendant over?"

"No."

"Was the previous contact the *main* reason that you decided to pull him over?"

"No."

"There was also the broken headlamp and the danger that potentially posed on the road?"

"Correct."

Mike's questions have become leading, but Ted barely objects during trials, let alone during a motions hearing. He considers objections to be in bad form and mostly ineffective.

"What did the defendant do when you activated your lights and sirens?"

"He sped up."

"What speed were you initially following him at?"

"About forty miles per hour, the legal limit."

"And what did he speed up to?"

"About fifty, maybe a little faster."

"What did you do?"

"Speed up to about sixty."

"And what did he do?"

"Sped up some more, swerved back and forth over the center line."

"And what did you do?"

"I sped up to about eighty."

"For how long did you pursue him?"

"I'm not sure, less than a minute. I started gaining on him, so he pulled over."

"What did you do then?"

"I contacted him at the driver's-side window."

"Did you tell him why you pulled him over?"

"Yes."

"What did you tell him?"

"That one of his headlamps was out and it was dangerous."

This establishes the gist of the record as to the stop, which was the entire focus of Ted's brief. Mike also details the steps of the eventual arrest. He believes the truth nearly always emerges in a courtroom, though sometimes it needs nudging.

After finishing up with a quick description of the bag's contents, which were discovered in the search incident to arrest, he thanks the deputy and sits down.

"Mr. Haller," the judge cues Ted, who is wiping off breakfast cereal stuck on his tie.

Howard, hunched over beside Ted, is scribbling notes at a mad pace. This is a defense attorney strategem to shut up their clients: hand them yellow pads and a pen and tell them to write down their thoughts.

"Yes," Ted says, rising, "okay, thank you."

Howard looks up from his pad and stares at Ted with something between an encouraging smile and a worried glare. Mike can tell that Howard is one of those defendants who would like to do the cross-examination himself, but is smart enough to know he needs a lawyer.

"Now, Deputy," Ted says, ignoring Howard and approaching the witness, "you, uh, recognized the car as it approached you?"

"Yes."

"I just want to be sure I get this right." Ted checks his legal pad. "You recognized the car because of the fire-breathing dragon thing on the hood?"

"Right."

"And you had recently stopped this same car?"

"Yes."

"And you arrested the driver for . . . what, manufacture of meth? After the first stop?"

"Possession of pseudoephedrine with intent to manufacture."

"Right, okay, thanks." Ted scratches his head, reminding Mike of the bumbling yet effective television detective Columbo. "And oftentimes when defendants are arrested they're released on bail, right?"

"Right."

"And in the meth world, the first thing tweekers usually do when they are out on bail is manufacture more meth to help them pay back bail money or hire a lawyer, right?"

Ted smiles up at the deputy, who is shocked to hear something this honest in a courtroom, *and from a criminal defense attorney, to boot.*

"Well, yeah, that's generally true," the deputy admits, hoping it is not a trick question.

"So as soon as you saw the Firebird with the fire-breathing dragon on the hood, you suspected possible criminal activity?"

"Yes, I did."

"You suspected criminal activity because the previous time you stopped this car, there *was* criminal activity."

"Right, yes."

"And that's good police work, to make connections like that, right?"

"I think so, yes."

"And you also noticed that there was a headlight out on the car, right?"

"Yes."

"And you were off duty at the time. You testified to that earlier?"

"Yes."

"And you were on your way home to . . . what?"

"To what?"

"I can see by the ring you're married, right?"

"Right."

"So you were headed home to see your wife."

"Oh, yes. Right."

"You have kids?"

"One girl. She's three."

"That's nice," Ted says, completely sincere. "What's her name?"

"Kendall."

"Nice name. Anyway, so you're on your way home to see your wife and Kendall."

"Right."

"It was almost eight, so you were probably late for dinner?"

"I don't remember, but probably."

"Have you ever pulled anyone over before when you were off duty and heading home?"

"Yes. As I testified earlier."

"Right. Twice before, you said."

"Twice that I can remember."

"And you've been a deputy for how long?"

"Almost a year."

"And in a year as a deputy, you can only think of two other times you've pulled someone over when you were off duty?"

"Right."

"So you would agree it's unusual? For you to pull someone over when you're off duty and on your way home?"

"A little bit, yes."

"So . . . isn't it true you don't always pull people over when you see an infraction?"

"Right. Not always."

"But you pulled my client over because you recognized the car and suspected criminal activity, right?"

Ted asks this nonchalantly, looking down at his pad, not emphasizing that this is the critical question in the case.

Judge Stuber, who has been taking notes even though she has a computer wired to the court reporter's transcription, looks up at the deputy, her pencil poised above her pad for the moment.

"Yes," the deputy answers. "And because of the broken head-lamp."

Mike nods, *that's right*.

"Could you look at your report, please?" Ted says. "Second page, third paragraph?"

"Yes, sir." The deputy looks at the report he is tightly clutching in his lap. Mike had the report marked as an exhibit during his preliminary questions, but the deputy has not yet required it because he did his homework and memorized the contents.

"You wrote in your report that you recognized the car from a previous arrest and you suspected criminal activity, possibly related to methamphetamine manufacture."

"Yes, I wrote that."

"And that passage is above the passage where you wrote about the broken headlamp?"

"Yes."

"So you wrote about the suspected criminal activity *before* you added the paragraph about the broken headlamp."

"Right."

"Because the suspected criminal activity, especially since it related to possible methamphetamine manufacture, was more important to you than the broken headlamp?"

"Both were important."

"Okay." This was not the answer Ted hoped for, but he made his point. "Thank you."

"Mr. Lawson," the judge says as Ted sits back down.

Mike stands at counsel table. "Deputy, please look farther down on page two of your report, to the last sentence of the third paragraph."

"Yes," the deputy says, jumping ahead of Mike's next question, "I wrote there that I pulled the defendant over for a broken head-lamp that posed a danger on the road."

"Would you have pulled a U-turn and followed the defendant if he didn't have a broken headlamp that posed a danger?"

"No."

"Would you have pulled over the defendant that night for the broken headlamp even if you didn't recognize the car from the previous stop?"

"Yes, I believe so."

Mike was expecting something more definite, but he says, "Thank you," and sits. He is bored with the routine hair splitting, ready for oral argument.

The judge looks over at Ted, who leans back in his chair as though he is going to stand, but then he decides it is too much effort.

"Deputy," he calls out. "You can't say for sure whether or not you would have pulled my client over if you didn't recognize him from the previous stop, can you?"

"For sure? No."

"I'm done."

"Mr. Lawson?"

"Nothing further, Your Honor, thank you."

"Deputy, thank you. You can be seated. Are both parties ready to proceed to argument?"

"Yes, Your Honor."

"Mr. Haller, it's your motion."

Ted stands, holding his brief with both hands.

Howard takes a moment from his note-writing to look back over his shoulder at Porsche, nodding at her reassuringly. Wyatt observes this exchange and feels like strangling him.

"How do you think it went?" the deputy asks Wyatt as he sits down next to him.

Wyatt pats him on the shoulder. "We're probably fucked," he whispers, "but it's not your fault."

"Please proceed," the judge says to Ted, who is still standing, reading his brief.

"*Ladson* is right on point," Ted says, letting the brief drop to his side. "Pretextual stops are unlawful. In *Ladson,* the detectives suspected that the defendant and his partner were involved in drug dealing, so they followed them and pulled them over for expired tabs. Everyone agreed that the tabs on the car were expired, and that's probable cause.

"The problem, the Supreme Court said, was that the officers used the expired tabs as a *pretext* for pulling the vehicle over. A *pretextual* stop. Just like we have here. Everyone agrees that my client's headlight was broken and he could be lawfully pulled over. However, the deputy admitted that he recognized my client's vehicle from a previous contact and that he suspected criminal activity and therefore pulled him over. He's off duty, on his way home, and he isn't going to pull my client over except for the fact that he recognized the car as a tweeker car.

"This is a classic pretextual stop, Your Honor. In *Ladson,* the officers used the expired tabs as an excuse, as a pretext, to pull over someone suspected of drug dealing or something like that, while here the officer used a broken headlamp as an excuse, as a pretext. Right? I mean, that's what happened. Some could say it sounds like good police work, but our Supreme Court has said it's unlawful. So this court has to suppress all the evidence as the fruit of the pretextual stop, as fruit of the poisonous tree."

Ted stands there for a moment, unable to think of anything to add. This is a highly unusual situation—the law is on his side. He savors the self-assurance this inspires and notices that you do not need to pontificate and obfuscate when you are not trying to snooker the court.

Mike, simultaneously, gains an appreciation of the creativity defense attorneys must develop as he prepares to suggest to

the court that the law could not or should not mean what it means.

"Mr. Lawson?"

Mike stands and makes eye contact with the judge and he appears confident as he taps into his large capacity for barely justified optimism.

"This case can be distinguished from *Ladson* in three ways, Your Honor. One, in *Ladson* the probable cause for the stop was an expired license. Here, we have a broken headlight that poses a danger on the road in a way that an expired license does not, and therefore cannot be accurately characterized as an excuse, or as a pretext.

"Two, the officers in *Ladson* admitted that their suspicion that one of the occupants was involved in drug dealing was their primary motive for pulling the car over. In fact, they followed the car with the intention of finding a pretext to pull it over. Here, the deputy testified that he noticed the broken headlight even before he recognized the vehicle and suspected possible criminal activity. The broken headlamp, not the suspected criminal activity, was the primary reason for the stop.

"Three, the majority in *Ladson* specifically made note of the fact that the defendants were African-Americans. So either the author of the opinion was making an irrelevant observation, or the court was suggesting that racial profiling was also a factor, a factor that does not exist here."

These distinctions, Mike can tell from the judge's flat demeanor, are not persuading her. She has the expression of imperial disgust trial judges display when they are about to rule in the way they feel they must rather than in the way they would prefer.

"Your Honor," Mike continues, sticking to his scripted argument, despite the unfavorable reception thus far, "on page 843 the court instructs judges to look at the 'totality of the circumstances' in deciding whether or not a stop is pretextual, including, quote, 'the objective reasonableness of the officer's behavior,' unquote. Here the officer's conduct was entirely reasonable, he pulled over a car with a broken headlamp, which posed a danger on a dark and rainy night."

Judge Stuber smiles. "Is objective reasonableness really the test, though, Mr. Lawson? Doesn't *Ladson* require trial courts to consider the subjective intent of the officer? And if the subjective intent is investigation, rather than traffic enforcement, as it was in *Ladson,* and as it appears to be here, doesn't that make for an unlawful stop? Isn't that the opinion of the majority?"

Mike was expecting this, for what it is worth. "In *State v. O'Neill,* 148 Wn.2d 564, a 2003 case, the court backed away from *Ladson,* rejecting a defense argument that the officer's subjective motivation must be considered in weighing reasonableness under article I, section 7. Though *O'Neill* can be distinguished from *Ladson,* it's still significant that the court was unwilling to expand *Ladson* beyond its specific fact pattern."

"I read *O'Neill,*" the judge says, cutting him off, "and in conjunction with *Ladson,* it just confused me. Both were five-four decisions. And Justice Madsen, who wrote the majority opinion in *O'Neill,* wrote the dissent in *Ladson.*" This clearly amuses the judge. "Madsen argued that Justice Sanders, who wrote the majority in *Ladson,* was misstating the issue, misrepresenting legal authority, and basing the majority opinion on false premises."

There is only one answer to this. "Yes, Your Honor."

"That said, I believe *Ladson* is the controlling case here." She puts her hands in the air. "I'm just a trial court judge."

"Yes, but Your Honor, if trial courts follow the reading of *Ladson* that the defense proposes, then it's lawful to pull over a law-abiding citizen for a traffic infraction, but *not* lawful to pull over a suspected criminal for the same infraction. That's so absurd it would make Kafka blush. Therefore, it can't be what the Supreme Court intended. So I'm asking this court to not expand *Ladson* by applying it here. Thank you."

Mike sits, believing more than ever in his position.

"Do you really want to hear anything more from me," Ted asks.

"No."

"I didn't think so."

"Mr. Lawson, you make some good points," the judge says, and Mike knows he has lost. "However, just because something is absurd does not mean it couldn't be what our Supreme Court intended."

Mike has to nod in agreement to this, as does Ted.

"There certainly are some shortcomings in the majority's logic, and some tension between *Ladson* and *O'Neill*, but I believe this raises issues that are more appropriately heard at the appellate level. It is the trial court's duty to follow the law.

"Under our current law if a deputy has a subjective interest in investigating criminal activity, as the deputy here did, but does not have probable cause to pull over a suspect for that criminal activity, but instead pulls the suspect over for a traffic infraction, it's unlawful."

Howard is elbowing Ted excitedly and Ted is whispering back, "*I know, I know.*"

Looking up from her notes, the judge makes eye contact with the young deputy. "Though I may personally think this was good police work, my personal opinions are irrelevant. The Supreme

Court has addressed this issue and I don't have the authority to overturn or ignore the high court. I am therefore granting the defense motion to suppress all the evidence found subsequent to the unlawful stop as fruit of the poisonous tree...."

After a couple of minutes of paperwork formalities, Howard heads back into the gallery, grabs Porsche's hand, and begins quickly stepping out of the courtroom, jumpy from his good fortune, throwing a gloating glance at Wyatt over his shoulder.

"That fuck," Wyatt says as the doors shut behind Howard. "The problem with courtrooms is you can't just shoot people."

Mike gathers his trial notebook and leads Wyatt and the deputy into the hallway.

"Did you guys notice that girl with the defendant," the deputy asks, angry. "She looked like she was about thirteen."

"Of course," Mike says. "The defendant is providing meth to the girl's mother and so she ignores what's going on with her daughter."

"How do you know this?"

"Educated guess after five years in SAU."

"Pretty standard scenario," Wyatt confirms. "Meth," he says, switching into an announcer's voice, "it's not just a drug, it's a lifestyle."

"What are we going to do?" the deputy asks. "This is fucking ... insane. He's just walking."

Mike and Wyatt exchange a knowing glance, sharing their amusement at the rookie's enthusiasm and naïveté, remembering when they, too, had a sense of outrage.

Wyatt's career choice of cop over lawyer is once again affirmed for him. What Mike could not do in the courtroom, he will have to do in the field. Mike, for his part, has seen the appellate courts reverse convictions for child molesters, rapists, and nearly three

hundred murderers with the *Andress* decision, so one meth cook walking is not enough to put him on tilt.

Observing absurdities helps lead to a state of Zen.

"You ready to sign Marvin up?" Wyatt asks. "That was our bet. And now there's this."

Mike nods. "And I'm ready for a drink, too."

"What do you say we push Marvin's assault trial out about four months or so, make Howard his only target, and give him a no-jail deal if he delivers?"

Mike nods again, wondering if he will regret this.

"Who's this Sanders guy you were talking about?" the deputy asks, still baffled and angry.

"That's the problem," Mike says.

"Yep," Wyatt says. "Nobody pays attention to judges."

"Sanders has a power base of right-wing pro-lifers who know nothing about him other than that he's anti-abortion and anti-government," Mike explains to the deputy. "He's like the wacko uncle at the family party, the contrarian who mutters nonsensically and occasionally lashes out, but nobody pays him any attention until he breaks something."

"How did a freak like this get on the Supreme Court?" the deputy asks.

"He was elected."

TRUE GRIT

Mike and Wyatt drive down Sixth Avenue in Mike's eleven-year-old Range Rover, a vehicle that has oddly become the preferred ride for Pacific Northwest drug dealers. They pass House of Records, Shakabrah, Jazzbones, and various new businesses cropping up in the gentrifying neighborhood.

Hell's Kitchen, façade bright red, stands out among the storefronts. They park just beyond the club by Rocket Records, across from the West End Pub and Grill. Smokers linger in front of the bars, relegated outside by the smoking ban and undeterred by the drizzle. Wispy trails of nicotine mix with breath clouds. Mike would join them, but his thirst for alcohol trumps his desire for nicotine.

Mike and Wyatt enter Hell's Kitchen and there is no music and half of the beer-stained pool tables are unused and the crowd is sparse, which surprises them.

"You said Vicci Martinez was playing tonight?"

"I thought it was tonight," Wyatt says. "Suki told me a while back."

A Tacoma singer, guitarist, and *Star Search* finalist, Martinez usually draws large crowds to local venues. Something is therefore amiss.

Wyatt consults the bartender and learns that Martinez is next week and tonight a poetry slam is about to begin.

"Fuck me," Wyatt says to Mike.

"Should we go to the Parkway?" Mike suggests.

"No, I need hard liquor. Now."

Mike orders two scotches and two Budweisers and the scotch arrives promptly and strong. Buds follow, served in plastic cups.

Behind the bartender is a poster of Stacy Fuson, the St. Pauli beer girl from Tacoma, posing in a red skirt and a black and white top that is a cross between traditional Bavarian wear and a Victoria's Secret bustier. Her blond hair flows down to her breasts where the ends curl like fingers, her mouth is slightly open in a come-hither expression, and one hand rests on her bare hip while the other holds out a tray with three green bottles of St. Pauli beer.

"Do you think Stacy ever comes back to Tacoma?"

"You can take the girl out of Tacoma," Wyatt says, "but you can't take Tacoma out of the girl."

"Does Neko Case still live here?"

"The singer? I don't think so."

"Some good musicians come from Tacoma," Mike says, sipping his cheap scotch before he realizes it is better suited for gulping. "Have you ever heard Leonard Cohen's song, 'Tacoma Trailer'?"

"No."

"It's an instrumental. Cool song."

"Too bad he's famous for his lyrics."

"And for being with beautiful women. Including Rebecca DeMornay."

"That's impressive, especially since the guy looks like a basset hound."

"He's an artist." Mike shrugs. "I have to tell you, Suki is the best looking and coolest woman I've ever seen you with."

"Thanks for mentioning that. She moved out last week."

"No shit?"

"No shit."

"How did that happen?"

Wyatt shrugs. "How do these things ever happen?"

"The guy fucks up?"

"She quoted *Annie Hall,* the line about how a relationship is like a shark—if it doesn't keep moving, it dies."

"You should have never turned her on to Woody Allen."

"She loves funny movies. Best line in *Annie Hall*?"

"'I have to go now, Duane, because I'm due back on planet Earth.'"

"'Don't knock masturbation. It's sex with someone I love.'" Wyatt polishes off the house scotch with a grimace. "I can't believe she moved out."

"You blew it," Mike says, then orders another round.

"No argument on that point from me, Counselor."

"We need a new plan."

"For Howard, or my love life?"

"Both."

"I have definitely not reached a state of Zen on this case."

"Neither have I."

"Okay." Wyatt takes a long sip of his beer. "I have a confession to make."

"Yeah?"

"I always kind of liked Bill Clinton."

"That's your idea of a confession?"

"You know what he should have done? When everyone was nipping at his heels he should have just said, 'Yeah, I smoked some pot in college, yeah, I banged a few gals in trailer parks, and yeah, I got a blow job in the Oval Office, but most of the time I was *working my ass off for all of you*. Now, let me get back to work.'"

"Where were you when he needed you?"

Wyatt shrugs. "He should have called."

Fresh drinks in hand, they leave the bar for the dark and small band room on the west side of the club. Onstage, under a single unsteady spotlight, a middle-aged man with thinning hair and tinted wire-rimmed glasses introduces himself as Apple Seattle and begins an adjective-laden poem about a suicidal poet.

He says "famous poets" with no hint of irony and the audience stares up at him as though he is a misshapen zoo animal.

"You suck," a guy in a stocking cap yells.

"Seattle sucks," a woman adds.

As a young teenager Mike often took the bus to Seattle for rock shows, catching national acts as well as Seattle bands like the Fastbacks and Tacoma bands like Girl Trouble, but lately even the staid *Seattle Weekly* has taken to calling its namesake city "Nannytown" because of the clampdown on smokers and strippers and music clubs. Mike used to blame the poseurs who flocked to Seattle in the boom years, though truth be told Seattle was never as grungy as Aberdeen, Olympia, Spanaway, or Tacoma.

As the crowd static rises, Apple Seattle moves his mouth closer to the microphone, carefully enunciating "precious" and "ponder" and other *p* words that pop as the heckling continues.

"That's it," Wyatt says.

"What?"

"We've got to welcome him to Pierce County."

"Who? The clown on the stage?"

"No, Howard. I think it's time to show him some true Pierce County grit. Maybe even turn Marcello loose on him."

"This does not sound good."

"We've been too easygoing, playing nice, playing by the rules."

"We have to play by the rules."

Suddenly a cup of beer is launched from just left of Wyatt. As the projectile enters the glare of the spotlight the poet spots it, but

he freezes and the cup explodes on his chest, cascading beer over his surprised face.

This inspires applause and hearty cheers.

"Welcome to Tacoma!"

"What the hell is wrong with you people?" the contestant asks, wiping beer from his glasses, dripping.

"You're pretentious!"

"You blow!"

"Loser!"

Mike turns to Wyatt. "We're going to have to leave, or you're going to have to arrest someone."

"'Forget it, Jake,'" Wyatt says, slipping into a vaguely recognizable Jack Nicholson imitation, "it's T-Town."

THE INFORMATION AGE

yr free nothin has meaning u will rule
no way
out no way to escape yrself u have
no control
of yr mind u cannot stop yr thoughts
they pour
in from the world they well up inside they whisper
they lie
yr mind will destroy u it produces
uncontrolled urges
to whatever u will rule the known world
rule all
dream of power of money of genius u will be famous
u will
know the gutter the want the the

Howard suddenly stops typing midsentence, his fingertips wet and slippery and momentarily disconnected from his brain, which has suddenly been seized by a need for information.

He minimizes the tweeker blog window, brings up LINX instead, glancing over his shoulder to make sure the other patrons are not watching. Bertolino's, a twenty-four-hour Internet coffee shop near the University of Puget Sound, is a frequent late-night haunt of his. The 77s play on the house stereo and the crowd mostly consists of college and high school kids playing chess, staring at their laptops, and chatting across old wooden tables. Nobody appears to be paying attention to him.

LINX, the Legal Information Network Exchange, available to all at the Pierce County Web site, lists court dates for defendants. Howard, like most other cooks and dealers, tracks tweeker cases and when he sees a court date set out unusually far, as Marvin's Assault One trial has been, it serves as a warning that the defendant might be working the beef off as an informant. Suspicions confirmed, and unable to concentrate on a single task long, he clicks the blog back up and begins typing again, continuing to cut and paste as he riffs on the entries of other tweekers.

> *u will*
> *die in the gutter u will do or be none of it*
> *sweet revenge*
> *demands that u even the scores first and last*
> *betrayal is*
> *the lowest low of the lower lowest lowdown*
> *snitches suck*
> *u long*
> *to stop yr mind but u cannot stop nothin*
> *yr mind*
> *is in constant turmoyle and it rules doesn't rule*
> *it lies*
> *u long to be loved but u hate those u long*
> *to love*
> *u long to destroy those u love u love those u destroy*
> *no control*
> *u know what u are doing but not why u do it*
> *u decide*
> *that u will do one thing and then do the other*
> *u drive*
> *to do what u will never understand u think but*

u remain
outside yr thoughts u act but yr actions
mean nothin
u place yrself in situations that will cause u mental
and physical
harm but u deny the harm it does even tho u know
cannot stop
moving u cannot stop time everything is unbearable
everything is
the empty nothing that is life the known
empty ness
reminds u constantly of the possibility of being
filled up
yet if it existed completely then u would have no need
to exist
u will never change u enjoy it for u need pain like
u need
pleasure they both give u a glimpse of the infinite
they release
u from life by intensity to the extreme so that u
no longer
exist within u scream u beat yr body
u feel
pity for yrself as u hollow in self satisfied
self hatred
in dreams u think are forever u think u are
special different
u are nothing u are human u are worthless u will
never change
porsche is fast as the white lines gone
white skin

*powder and ice u are my life and my wife
tweaking forever
u will never die u will die slowly as the world ends
but death
will not save u there is no way out there is no
hope here*

WHERE AMERICA SHOPLIFTS

Howard strolls through the Sears at the Tacoma Mall looking for the chainsaw section, humming "Kill You," the Eminem song he heard on Joe's boom box that gave him the idea.

He has been up for three days and he is jerking like a marionette and none of the floor people have offered to help him, which he is completely okay with. So far he has stolen lithium batteries, a pocket knife, and pliers, just because he can. His pockets are bulging and he feels invincible.

One of the best ways to increase your cachet as a drug dealer is to beat the System, *beat the Man,* and Howard enjoys his resulting status. In the last few years he has been charged with meth-related crimes three times and three times the charges have been dismissed.

Such news spreads quickly in Methlehem.

"I'm bulletproof," is what he likes to say by way of explanation, sometimes implying that he is so heavily connected the prosecutor made the cases disappear.

While the cops and prosecutors hammer the stupider cooks, sending them away with double-digit sentences, Howard's stature and sales increase proportionally. He believes he is the only major local cook competing successfully with the Mexicans.

This, in his mind, is why the Mexicans have been trying to recruit someone to snitch him out—they want to eliminate the competition because they cannot match his product. He is convinced that the Mexicans were somehow behind his recent arrest. This is how it is done in the drug world: dealers wipe out other

dealers by having one of their clients turn snitch and let the cops do the work.

After several minutes of confused wandering, he spots a yellow chainsaw displayed on top of a stack of boxes. He does not like the yellow, it strikes him as too sissy, but a black and red one nearby appeals to him. Electric, the box says, which conjures up visions of lightning bolts for him.

Though the woman at the checkout counter appears nervous, she accepts his stolen VISA card with no questions and he walks out with a sixteen-inch 3.5-horsepower Craftsman chainsaw with "vibration neutralizing technology" and a twenty-foot extension cord.

"Would you ever live with a cat?" June asks.

Mike has no idea where this question is coming from.

June is sipping a Manhattan on the couch, the martini glass held just below her chin, the red cherry magnified at the bottom of the amber liquid. She is wearing a black evening dress and cat-eye glasses.

"No," he admits, on the couch beside her, scotch in hand.

June's studio apartment is suggestive of a mild obsessive-compulsive disorder: books are alphabetized in a tall Plexiglas bookcase and broken into categories, fiction, nonfiction, hardbacks, mass-market paperbacks, and trade paperbacks; Almond, Bushnell, Coupland, Fitzgerald, Janowitz, McInerney, Minot, Pasternak, Rust, Stein, Susann, Tartt, Vonnegut, and so on. Magazines—*Vogue, Glamour, Pages, The New Yorker*—are laid over each other in a perfect fan shape and there is not a CD, DVD, or knickknack in sight, only a white iPod. Her hardwood floors are polished, the pink and green throw rug appears freshly vacuumed, and the couch and two chairs are perched on the rug at perfect angles to each other.

Mike is put in mind of a showroom.

"I don't want to freak you out," June says, "since we've only been dating three and three-quarter months, but I just want to know where you stand on the cat question."

He nods and sets his scotch on the square coaster on the wooden coffee table, twirling the coaster slightly. June reaches out and moves the coaster so the sides are parallel to the table edges again.

Mike does not remember her doing this at the Swiss, or 21 Commerce, or anywhere else they have been drinking, and he is sure he would remember. As a test, he takes another long pull of his drink and sets it down again, twirling the coaster again.

"I don't know how anyone could live with a cat," June says, eyeing his askew coaster.

"I wouldn't want to," Mike says, "but I can see how someone else might find it . . . possible."

"They defecate in the house."

"I think they use kitty litter boxes."

"Which are inside the house."

"True."

"I was dating this one guy, and he told me he was a cat lover." Unable to take it any longer, June adjusts the coaster again. "What kind of guy is a cat lover?"

"I don't know."

"I told him I couldn't live with a cat unless the cat stayed outside. He said his cat was an indoor cat, so I suggested the cat could live in a cat shed."

"A cat shed?"

"Like a toolshed," June says, tapping a finger with a red-painted nail against her cheekbone, "but you put cats in it instead of tools."

"Of course."

"And he answered that the shed would be outside and so it would be like putting the cat outside and I said it's not outside if the cat is *inside* the cat shed. He repeated that the cat shed itself was outside, and I said, yeah, well, a house is outside, too, but if the cat is inside the house the cat isn't outside, is it?" June smiles like a lawyer who has just made her case. "Don't you agree that if a cat is in a cat shed he's inside, not outside?"

Mike wonders if everyone he knows is nuts.

"Well," June says, "isn't that true?"

Funny how normal she seemed in other environments, Mike thinks. Here, in her natural habitat, disorders he cannot quite identify are freely emerging.

"Absolutely," Mike answers, wanting to get the hell away from this subject. "How did your paper comparing Vonnegut and Jacqueline Susann work out?"

"The professor gave it an A." June shrugs. "He says I'm an 'astonishing' writer. But maybe he says I'm that because he wants to sleep with me?"

"Maybe he wants to sleep with you because he thinks you're an astonishing writer."

This elicits a smile. "Yeah, you think so?"

"I do."

"I hadn't thought of it that way." June finishes her Manhattan, then delicately fishes the cherry out and sucks it off the stem into her mouth. "I was worried you were going to have to cancel again tonight, since you're so busy here in crime city USA, and I'd have to eat alone."

"Well, I'm glad I'm here."

This is true. He is not willing to rule her out as a marital possibility just because of her eccentricities, especially given her tolerance of his own quirks.

"Me, too. And I'm glad you don't mind vegan stuff."

He does, but not too much. Again he takes a sip of his drink and sets his glass down so it twirls the coaster slightly. Again, June squares the angles. He is starting to find this strangely charming.

"You never answered about the cat, though," she says.

"What part?"

"You don't want to live with a cat? Do you?"

"No."

"Good. Everyone has their idiosyncrasies, their carnival desires and so on, but I couldn't have a future with a guy who liked cats. So maybe we have a future."

Mike nods. "I'd like to read one of your stories."

"I just finished one about a girl stalking Robert Downey, Jr."

"Cool."

"Maybe I'll write one about you."

"I've always wanted to be immortal."

"You don't think it would get boring?"

TRUST

Marvin sucks in the white smoke as he holds the lighter under the bulb of the meth pipe and for a brief moment he remembers that he has a urine test scheduled tomorrow as part of the pretrial release conditions, but no matter. Missed urine tests are customarily without consequences.

Though Marvin is still facing potential prison time for "the unfortunate accident," as his attorney calls the shooting, he feels confident he can fulfill his deal with Wyatt and the prosecutor and thereby stay free. While he is working for *the Man*, he is also working for the other man, Howard, delivering one-ounce baggies stamped with Howard's Superman logo.

He is sharing part of a recent delivery with the customers at a double-wide trailer when the door is kicked open, aluminum snapping and glass breaking.

In steps Howard with a chainsaw in one hand and a long extension cord in the other.

"Holy fuck shit," the resident tweeker says.

Marvin stands, while the other tweekers stay seated in front of a television, two playing with Xbox controllers, one disassembling a controller and wearing a Bates Technical College sweatshirt, all craning their necks to stare at Howard as he kicks his way through the trash piled on the floor, the empty cans, ashtrays, clothes, mason jars, stolen car stereos, and porn magazines.

A cat dashes out past the broken door.

"Howard," Marvin says.

"So you're Howard," the resident finally says, pausing the video game, Grand Theft Auto. "What's going on, man?"

"You shut the fuck up," Howard answers.

Finding an outlet, Howard plugs in the chainsaw and turns it on and revs it up into a menacing whine. Nobody moves. Raindrops echo off the metal roof of the trailer and this is the only sound left in the room when Howard eases the trigger back off.

"Hello, Marvin," Howard says. "Sit down on the couch over there."

"I—I was bringing you the money," Marvin stutters, sitting. "I was just having one hit first."

"I know you were bringing me the money."

"Well, then . . . what is the . . ."

"The problem?"

"Right, yes."

"The problem is that there's been a lot of snitching going on. And nobody is going to fucking snitch on me."

"No snitches here," one of the video gamers says.

"*You*," Howard says, "sit down and shut the fuck up."

Already sitting, the gamers decide to stay that way.

"So Marvin," Howard says, turning back to him, stepping closer. "Looks like your case was set out several months."

"LINX?"

Howard nods. "Why, Marvin?"

Marvin, who has been to the paranoid abyss on many meth runs, recognizes exactly where Howard is—the madness, the anger, the voices—and it scares the holy hell out of him. He tries on Howard what people have tried on him when he was out of his mind: calm reasoning.

"You know you can trust me, right, Howard?"

"Can I trust you, Marvin?"

"Yes, yes, of course."

Howard revs the chainsaw back up. "I can trust you?" he yells over the rising whine.

"Yes, you know you can." Sweat is running down Marvin's greasy face as he suddenly remembers that reasoning has never worked on him or any other tweeker at a time like this. "Please, you know you can trust me."

"I know that?"

"You do, yes."

"Question is, though, do you trust me?"

"Yes, yes!"

"Good, Marvin. Good. That's the right answer."

Marvin exhales loudly, and his body sinks back into the couch, but his eyes stay on the chainsaw as it suddenly lashes out—Howard rapidly and crazily sweeps it back and forth over the coffee table, knocking off beer cans, cigarettes, and makeshift ashtrays, and the crashing sounds mix with the screech of the chainsaw.

"Fuck," Marvin yells, his voice weak in the face of the chainsaw's volume.

Howard swings the chainsaw up over his head like a samurai's sword. He lets the engine wind down as he stares at Marvin and after a few seconds the room is utterly quiet again except for the echoing rain.

"Please," Marvin says.

"Have you ever read Nietzsche?" Howard asks.

"Who?"

"Why must I live my life surrounded by morons?" Howard asks the ceiling, then gazes down again at Marvin. "Have you read *Mein Kampf*?"

"No."

"Do you know what it is?"

"No."

"It's probably the greatest book ever written."

"Who wrote it?" Marvin says, desperately trying to participate in the conversation, to act as though everything is normal, to *maintain*. "That guy, Nietzsche?"

"You fucking moron. *Hitler* wrote it."

Howard's eyes bore into his employee with such ferocity it causes Marvin's hands to start shaking in his lap, fingers twitching like he is playing the piano.

"Hitler says a man can't serve two masters," Howard says, still holding the chainsaw steady over his head.

"Hitler says." Marvin nods.

"Will you serve me, Marvin?"

"Yes, yes."

"Do you trust me?"

"Yes."

"You have to trust me to serve me."

"Yes, I do, I do."

"Put a finger out on the coffee table."

"What?"

"Put a fucking finger on the coffee table."

"What . . . finger?"

"What finger? I don't care! Your fucking forefinger!"

"My forefinger?" Marvin examines his hands, trying to remember which finger is his forefinger, trying to avoid thinking about what is happening.

"The one next to your thumb, moron!"

"The one next to my thumb."

"Put it out on the coffee table. Now!"

Marvin complies, moving in slow motion except for the shaking finger. He watches it twitch on the table as though it has no connection to him.

"Close your eyes."

Marvin squeezes them shut, *it's just a test, it's just a test, it's just a test . . .*

Still frozen on the floor in front of the television, open-mouthed, the gamers stare at Howard. The reality of the rattling chainsaw is no more or no less engaging to them than the mondo-violence of the video games, but the sound effect is quite impressive.

Stepping to the side, focusing on the finger, Howard brings the chainsaw down like a guillotine, pulling the trigger as he does. The whishing saw teeth cut through Marvin's finger and the table in a flash, blood and sawdust and bone erupt into the air in a red and yellow mist.

Snapping open his eyes, Marvin quickly brings his hand up to his face. Blood pumps out of his jagged finger nub in rhythm with his rapidly beating heart and pours in bright red streams down his palm from where his knuckle used to be and all he can think is, *How did I get here?*

Flames in the natural gas fireplace flicker over the ceramic logs and only a couple customers remain, both reading on the leather couches near the fire. Suki does not mind working at Cutter's Point on weeknights like this.

She sits on a stool behind the mahogany counter and reads the book Wyatt gave her before they broke up, *A Wild Sheep Chase*. Because the book is a detective novel of sorts, and the lead character is not unlike Wyatt in some ways, she wonders if he gave it to her as something to remind her of him.

If so, it works.

Though she left Foxes on her own, she partially credits Wyatt. He gave her confidence and he helped her to realize that she overvalued money. When she was eighteen and ambitious and new to dancing she could make hundreds of dollars in a night and that seemed important.

Her promise to herself was that she would not get old in the club. Old, however, is a relative term. When she was eighteen she thought twenty-two was old, but now that she's twenty-six she thinks twenty-two was young but twenty-six is not quite old and, therefore, she kept her promise.

Unable to concentrate on her book, she begins cleaning up. As she is wiping cup circles from the polished bar, the front door swings open and cold air rushes in along with a thin blond man wearing jeans and a burgundy Washington State Cougars sweatshirt. He tracks in dead wet maple leaves with his cowboy boots.

Instantly she does not like his vibe, her creep radar going off as it did so many times at Foxes, *tweeker*. Because of their constant

need for stimulation, tweekers often visit strip clubs when they are not busy stocking up on porn videos and sex toys from the Castle Superstore.

"Can I help you?" she asks as he approaches.

"You're Suki, right?"

"Who are you?"

"Duchess told me you were working here now. Duchess from Foxes. The Filipina girl."

"Yes, I know Duchess." And the man before her does not, Suki assumes, or he would not be referring to Alexis by her stage name.

"Do you know who I am?" Howard asks.

"No."

"Your boyfriend does."

"He knows lots of people." She wonders if telling this tweeker creep that Wyatt is no longer her boyfriend would make him go away. "That's his job."

"Yeah, and it's my job, too. I'm Howard Schultz." When Suki keeps her poker face, he adds, "Your boyfriend knows me as the King of Methlehem."

"What would you like to order, Mr. Schultz?"

"I just want you to tell your boyfriend that I know he's looking for me, and I'm waiting for him to figure it out. Can you handle that message?"

"I'm going to have to ask you to leave now."

He laughs, flashing tweeker teeth. "I'm already gone, hon, already gone."

Before he is even out of the door Suki is on her cell phone, calling Wyatt, hoping he is home in his loft just above the shop. She hangs up when he does not answer.

EVERYBODY WORE KEVLAR

Into the back of the former milk van thirteen Pierce County officers file in order, taking bench seats in the cargo section, facing each other. Each of them is dressed in black boots, dark canvas jumpsuits, and Kevlar vests. SHERIFF is written across their chests in large yellow letters. Assault rifles are in hand or slung over their shoulders, Glocks hang in hip holsters.

As the unmarked van drives at the pace of traffic from their headquarters toward the area between Roy and Eatonville where Howard is reportedly operating a lab, enough testosterone runs through the men to field a professional sports team.

Wyatt reviews a map of the area while he talks on a headset to a deputy who is positioned on a hill above the property, reconnoitering through a light morning haze that glows in the low sun. When the clouds part and the sun brightens the landscape, the beauty of the Northwest is stunning.

"It's a good day," the deputy reports, "clear view, but the only action I've seen is one man moving something from a shed or barn to the main house."

A good day—the line calls to Wyatt's mind a quote from "Little Big Man" where Chief Dan George says, "It's a good day to die."

"Was he armed?" Wyatt asks.

"Not that I could see."

"Blue tarps?"

"Roger that."

A few minutes later the word is given to suit up and the officers don breathing masks with glass visors and dark metal helmets, prepared as always for the worst.

The van turns up the dirt driveway, passing piles of garbage and hulks of rusted cars. Three Harleys rest on kickstands near the front door of the main residence, and the van stops just short of knocking over the bikes.

As soon as the engine shuts down the back doors swing open, and the officers jump out in twos, all scrambling as fast as they can in the bulky outfits. Four run for the shed, four run around to the back of the house, and five approach the front door, Marcello carrying a steel battering ram with MEET MY LITTLE FRIEND written on the side.

"Open the door, Sheriff's Department, police," the driver of the van announces over a loudspeaker, adding "police" because "Sheriff's Department" may not mean anything to non-English-speaking residents.

Within seconds of the command, Marcello breaks in the front door and the officers fan out into the main room, weapons ready. They can hear loud hip-hop music vibrating through their masks and helmets. In front of them is a couch, a television with a porn movie playing, girl-on-girl at the moment, plywood tables on sawhorses, laboratory-quality heating elements, beakers with bubbling red liquid, and huge buckets full of white powder. The plasterboard walls bleed with red stains.

Red Phosphorous lab, Wyatt notes, *not Howard's style.*

Just then three bulky men in black leather riding outfits and red-stained surgical masks rumble into the main room from the kitchen area—one has a shotgun and the other two have handguns. Shock shows on their faces and they stop at the threshold when they realize they are facing officers with leveled assault rifles.

Two of the three bikers facing the officers drop their guns and raise their hands and the officers momentarily restrain the trigger fingers, but the one with the shotgun fires a single blast.

Inside the house the sound is deafening.

Wyatt takes the shot in his chest and is knocked onto his back, breath expelling, but it is only birdshot and most of the pellets are picked up by the Kevlar vest. A few feet behind him glass beakers shatter and toxic chemicals run onto the floor with a splash and a hiss.

All of the other officers instantly return fire and in less than five seconds the man with the shotgun takes eleven hits—two in the face, five in the chest, three in the legs, one in the crotch—and he backs into a wall and slides down dead, but another twenty-some bullets miss. Two of the off-mark bullets hit the bulkiest biker in his stomach, causing him to drop his hands and fall and curl. Blood from their two bodies mixes on the dirty linoleum floor.

When the shooting stops there is stillness except for the wounded biker's moans and the voice of the unscathed biker, who keeps repeating, *"Llena de gracia."*

"He just kept saying, 'Full of grace,' " Marcello, a stocky young officer with a goatee, relates. "In Spanish."

"What do you suppose that means?" another asks.

"Full of grace?"

"No, that he was using Spanish?"

"How about that he knows Spanish?"

"But the Mexicans and the bikers don't usually work together."

"Yeah, I'm not sure what the hell happened out there."

"I wonder if they're working together now."

"They're competitors."

"Mexicans don't cook here, they ship it in."

"I wouldn't read too much into it," Wyatt says from the hospital bed. "The guy just happened to be a Hispanic biker. It's not a global alliance."

St. Joseph Medical Center sits on a hill overlooking downtown and the tide flats, a large white cross glowing on the east side of the building. Through a single oval window at the end of the room Wyatt can see the city lights glitter and he can pick out where he lives, the home he will be away from for tonight. White bandages are crisscrossed over his chest and neck, covering the holes pellets were removed from.

There will be other methamphetamine-related casualties later tonight—almost a quarter of the hospital's Emergency Room admissions are related to methamphetamine in some way: burns, assaults, domestic violence, child abuse, and twentysomethings with strokes.

Ten milligrams of Vicodin is all the painkiller Wyatt rated, and

he is a little disappointed. He would like to light up a joint, but he figures his crew would not go for that and neither would the hospital staff, who have already let them stay beyond visiting hours. A group of men with guns and badges are often granted privileges, even when they are in plainclothes and look like a grunge band with their ragged pants, flannel shirts, and facial hair.

Though Wyatt sometimes feels old around them, he appreciates his crew's presence, their camaraderie. One of the things about being a cop is that you always have your crew, someone watching your back, and for this he is grateful. He would not want to be among those that go through life with their back unguarded, nor would he want to rely on Byzantine alliances as Mike does in the prosecutor's office. Mike tells his trial unit to be mutually respectful, but *they're lawyers* and Wyatt thinks this is like telling porcupines to play nice.

Just when it feels like his crew's antics might be winding down and he might have time to think, to plot, their sergeant enters the room. He is almost fifty, just a few years from retirement, wearing baggy jeans and a USC baseball cap.

"Nice shooting, guys," he says, the sarcasm instantly obvious. "Looks like you got off about thirty-five rounds and hit the target eleven times. Not even a one-in-three ratio, unless you want to count the two that hit the dumb fucker who had his hands in the air." He laughs and shakes his head. "From about ten fucking feet away."

"It was more like eleven feet."

"Yeah, yeah," the sergeant says, stepping over to Wyatt. "So what the hell happened to you?"

As soon as Wyatt saw the Red P equipment, he knew it was not Howard's lab.

Marvin lied. The fuck.

Later, in the ambulance, Wyatt figured that Howard used

Marvin to set him up. He expects the idea was that he would take out the biker rivals, and the shooting was just a bonus.

"I forgot to duck," Wyatt says, stealing the Ronald Reagan line.

"You make me look bad when you get shot."

"It's a buzz-killer, too," Marcello adds.

In 1995 the sergeant was part of a drug raid where a small-time dealer, Brian Eggleston, murdered Pierce County Sheriff's Deputy John Bananola during a gunfight by holding a .45 to the wounded officer's head and executing him. Eggleston, bleeding from five bullet wounds, including one in his testicles, thought he was dying and wanted to take the officer with him. To everyone's surprise, Eggleston lived. His survival resulted in three costly trials—the first two were reversed on appeal—and ultimately a thirty-eight-year sentence. The sergeant knows that any raid can end in the death of an officer and he is relieved that this one did not and so he is in a good mood.

"We're going to have to charge you for the vest," the sergeant says. "And the breathing mask. So you'll be going without for a while. County's cheap, you know."

"Did the other guy live?" Wyatt asks.

"The dumb fucker with his hands in the air. Yeah, he'll live."

"I want to talk to him."

"He's at Tacoma General. We already talked. Got the whole story from him and the full-of-grace guy."

"Bikers?"

"Yeah, not Howard's."

"I figured."

"So what happened here?"

"Not sure yet." He does not want to share it yet.

"You're too focused on this one target when there's plenty of other vermin in the sea."

"Vermin in the sea?"

"You know what I mean. You're taking a break."

"I wanna take a break, too," one of his crew says.

"Me, too."

"Do I have to get shot?"

And the ribbing begins again until the door opens and Mike Lawson enters, in a suit with his tie loosened, direct from the courthouse.

"Guess they'll let anyone in here," the sergeant says.

"Heard about the shoot-out," Mike says. "You guys get all the fun. Hey, Wyatt."

"Hey, chief."

"Wyatt's taking a break for a while," the sergeant tells Mike.

"Is that right, Wyatt?"

"Sure."

Mike can tell by Wyatt's deadpan expression that there will be no break.

"So, Mike, you running for prosecutor next year?" one of the crew asks. "You here looking for votes?"

"Yeah, I can't have reliable votes dying on me."

"Don't worry, I'll vote for you. And so will my girlfriend."

"She would have to be eighteen," Mike says, provoking a few knowing laughs.

Mike hates hospitals—everything about them reminds him of death: the smell, the equipment, the white jackets on the staff. He wants to ask Wyatt if he felt the closeness of death in the gunfire and if it panicked him or calmed him. Did he find Zen in the concentrated moment? This, however, is not the time.

Know your audience.

"We'll charge the cooks up in custody tomorrow morning," Mike says. "Except the dead one you guys used for target practice."

"You're going to let the dead guy skate?" the sergeant says with mock indignation, and his crew jumps on this.

"Another criminal gets off on a technicality."

"Lawyers are such pussies."

"Be careful, Wyatt's a lawyer."

"No, he's a cop with a law degree."

"Which is like a bear with a bicycle."

Mike admires their ability to channel their fear of death into laughter. He tries to imagine how weird it would have been if Wyatt died, to test the degree of grief, if only for a few seconds.

"If I die suddenly," Wyatt says, spooking Mike as he taps into his thoughts, "I'm going to come back for an official good-bye. You'll see a gray feather floating in your face and that feather, Counselor, will be me."

"A feather. Me, too. What kind of drugs did they give you?"

Two nights after the shooting, Wyatt is home.

He lies in bed staring out at the fog covering the tide flats, the mist thick right up to the loft windows, obliterating the lights and cranes of the port. Albers Mill Lofts, bordering the waterway, about a hundred yards out, appear only as a dark shadow in the haze. Pugnetti Park, even closer, is visible only as a few tree branches that seem to float unconnected in the air.

Every ten minutes the LINK, a light-rail streetcar, buzzes by and he hears the clanking on the track and the hum of the electric engines.

Though he was told the Vicodin would help him sleep, it gives him a buzz as it mixes with his adrenaline and he does not want to fall asleep and waste the high. As Winston Churchill once noted, there is nothing more exhilarating than to be shot at unsuccessfully.

He wants to plan for his next move, avenge the setup, but instead he devises a plan for victory in Iraq. Let the Sunnis and Shiites go berserk, and while they're slaughtering each other and babbling about jihad and virgins, our troops just quietly exit stage left, like characters in a *Seinfeld* episode. As for Iran, just lock up the short guy with the hobo beard, Ahmanutjob, and the world will be safer.

Shouldn't follow the news, bad for the head.

When Wyatt hears a knock, and then his front door creeps open, his hand instantly goes for his gun. He finds skin instead.

"Wyatt," Suki says as she enters, "it's me. Mike told me what happened."

He turns his head slowly, but his neck hurts so he cannot bring himself around.

"I hope I didn't wake you," she says, stepping into his line of sight, carrying a coffee cup. "But I was worried." She reaches out and holds his hand. "Are you okay?"

"Fine, just can't sleep."

"I knew you'd be awake. You're a bad sleeper."

"I didn't realize you still had a key."

"I've been meaning to return it."

"No worries. Where did you move?"

"For a few days I lived with a friend near King's Books, but pretty quickly I found an apartment near Starbucks, the one by the Spar, so I'm still not far away. I thought about Gig Harbor, but couldn't afford it."

"Gig Harbor? That's where Charles Johnson lives."

"Who?"

"The accidental Supreme Court Justice. Didn't actually campaign for the job, but voters liked the name."

"Nice name."

"Yeah, nice guy, too, except he signed off on the *Andress* decision along with that schizo Barbara Madsen, the case that reversed the convictions of almost three hundred murderers, mostly wife beaters and child abusers."

Suki frowns. "Could we talk about something else?"

"Sorry."

"You're too focused on all the crap that's wrong in the world. You know that, right?"

"I know, I'm sorry. How have you been doing?"

"Good, working at the coffee shop mostly."

"How about school?"

"I'm getting together my application for the UW."

"Good."

Glancing around, she says, "Your loft feels even more vacant than usual. How are *you* doing?"

"Fine."

"Fine except you were shot."

"The vest caught most of it." He squeezes her hand, needing the sense of something solid. "I've missed you."

"I've missed you, too." She smiles. "Are you stoned?"

"Vicodin is all."

"No pot?"

"No."

"Good. Pot's not sexy, not for a forty-year-old."

This hits Wyatt hard. "Seriously?"

"Part of your appeal is that you're this strong, upstanding, together adult. Not Tommy Chong."

"Now you tell me."

"I wanted to tell you before, but I didn't want to do it just after moving in."

"Why not?"

"For the same reason you didn't want to tell me to quit dancing. We didn't want to butt into each other's lives too much. But now I can say it as your friend."

"You okay with the Vicodin?"

"Anytime you're shot." Suki smiles. "So how did it happen?"

"Long story."

"You trying to be a hero?"

"No. Todd Beamer is a hero, Pat Tillman is a hero. I'm just trying to clean up one speck of evil."

"I have to tell you something."

"Okay."

"Howard came into the coffee shop and tried to talk to me and he said for me to tell you that he said that he was waiting for you or something and I was thinking it didn't mean anything," she says, rapidly, apologetically, "but I called you anyway, but you weren't there, so I never called back and I was still mad at you and I didn't really want to talk and I didn't know what it meant anyway and—"

"Hey, hey, relax, don't worry about it."

"You're not understanding me," she says, catching her breath.

"I get it. Howard came into the coffee shop and said something about how he was waiting for me. Right?"

"Right."

"But he wasn't there when I was shot."

"No?"

"No, I wasn't shot by Howard."

"Who, then?"

"You know what? You're exhausting me."

This makes her laugh. "Yeah, I guess I was always good at that."

"Yeah."

"Usually not with words."

"Sometimes with words."

"I didn't want to break up, you know."

"Then why did you?"

"Fuck." She sighs. "Why are men so stupid?"

"That question is out of my jurisdiction."

"Even Mike thinks you're obsessed with Howard."

"Hey, he's trying to get me killed."

"So you're going to keep chasing him until he succeeds?"

"Howard's a tweeker, he'll stumble at some point."

"So . . . if you kill the king, does that make you the king?"

"Did Mike say that?"

"I'm asking you."

"Mike's eyeing the crown, not me."

"Men." Suki shakes her head. "What's wrong with all of you?"

Wyatt's Vicodin-addled brain slowly considers this, flashing on images of elementary school, Little League sports, toy soldiers, sex, poker, apes, war, the opening scene of *2001: A Space Odyssey*, and Rebecca DeMornay and the train set in *Risky Business*, before deducing the rhetorical nature of the question.

"You look good," he says. "Your hair's shorter."

"I needed a change, I guess."

"Well, it looks good. You really look good."

He means it and she knows him well enough to feel this. They stare at each other for a long beat, both aware of the physical attraction, both aware of something additional, too.

"Well, thanks," she says softly. "It may be the last haircut I can afford for a while."

"You haven't gone back to the club?"

"It took me longer than it should have to get out of there, but sometimes it takes a while to do something even when we know we should. You don't really know something until you act on it, right?"

He nods in agreement, mind and eyes wandering.

Condensation drips down the tall windows, increasing the blurriness and otherworldliness of the tableau. Fog, snow, rain, sun, any weather change appeals to Wyatt. Murders, robberies, beatings, even full-on disasters, these, too, have an appeal for the exhilaration they can provide. He sometimes worries that he is hooked on the unhealthy.

Why can't I want peace and paradise?

Like normal people?

"Makes you glad to be inside," Suki says, following his gaze out the window. "Doesn't it?"

"Yeah. You should spend the night. Please."

She takes a sip of her coffee, tempted but trying to sense if the timing is right, if it *feels* right. His eyes follow the cup as it goes to her lips and suddenly he notices the Starbucks logo turning toward him and the image comes at him like a close-up.

HAND OUT OF THE COCONUT

After she was arrested by Wyatt on the night he missed Howard at her trailer, Amber bailed out of jail and began court-ordered drug treatment through the Breaking the Cycle Program. BTC, as it is called, is run by the Pierce County Alliance, an efficient nonprofit organization that operates out of two buildings north of the courthouse. You can spot the buildings by the chain-smoking recovering addicts that congregate outside.

Because Amber is female and only an accomplice, the judge set her bail low enough that her mother could post it through C.J.'s Bail Bonds. She has mostly complied with the BTC program—lapsing twice—and hopes that eventually she can make a plea bargain with the prosecutor, so she can win back custody of her daughter.

Wyatt asked her to meet him at the Kickstand Café not just because it is close to the Alliance buildings, but because it is next door to his favorite movie house, the Grand Cinema. The Grand, a Tacoma icon, shows independent films in cozy and intimate spaces that put Wyatt in mind of a private screening room, though he has never been in one.

Suki wants to see an arty love story—Wyatt cannot remember the title—and so he scheduled this meeting to precede the movie, slipping in work before recreation, as is his wont.

Wyatt sits with his back to the west wall, facing the door, sipping a mocha. Used books line the shelves of the walls below black and white landscape photographs. Tattered copies of *The Stranger, The Volcano,* and other papers lie on the aluminum and glass tables. An old bicycle hangs on the south wall.

Amber enters wearing a ratty overcoat, and though Wyatt cannot see her body he can see her face and it is noticeably fuller and without scabs, her teeth look okay, and her eyes do not look dilated or haunted. He quickly decides she is off meth, maybe ready to pull her hand out of the coconut.

"Thanks for agreeing to meet with me," he says, standing to greet her and shaking her hand, which she receives awkwardly.

"Sure."

"You want some coffee or anything?"

"No," she says, sitting. "No, thank you."

Though there are three other customers in the room, two are a chatty couple and the third is typing away on his laptop, so Wyatt feels he and Amber have sufficient privacy.

They exchange small talk about the difficulties of recovery for a few minutes and she seems relatively calm, albeit down, another sign she is clean.

"I want to try PROMETA," Amber tells him.

"Yeah, I hear it's the new silver bullet."

While meth saps the brain's ability to generate dopamine, causing long-term tweekers to be hopelessly depressed when they are not high, PROMETA reportedly reboots their brains to eliminate the cravings and the depression, restoring them to a pre-meth state. Wyatt is thinking of investing in Hythiam, the company that owns the patent on the PROMETA program. Rush Limbaugh and Chris Farley's family are reportedly supporters.

"Friends tell me it works, like they don't even have the desire to use anymore," Amber says. "But they're still left with all the issues that made them do drugs in the first place."

"There's ongoing counseling for that."

"I know, that's why I want to get into the drug court PROMETA program, but they won't let in people with manufacturing charges."

"That's what I'm here to maybe help with."

"Yeah?"

Wyatt nods reassuringly.

"I want my child back," Amber blurts out.

"I understand. And I want Howard. So maybe we can work something out."

"You can help me get my child back?" Her eyes well up.

"I understand this is emotional for you, but I want to talk business, okay?"

"Okay." She holds back the tears, arms clutched across her chest, holding the overcoat tight over her thin body.

"You're facing manufacturing charges now?"

"Right."

"And Endangerment of a Child?"

"Right."

"So you're looking at seventy-five to ninety-two months in prison, unless we can get you into drug court."

"What about a DOSA?"

"You would still do some prison time with DOSA, though not much."

"Any time is too much. I can't get my child back if I'm in prison."

"I can talk to the prosecutor about drug court."

"You can get me in?"

"I can't guarantee anything."

"Who's the prosecutor in drug court? Rose? I hear she screams at the judge to not let in anyone with manufacturing charges."

"I'll talk to Mike Lawson, the chief of the drug trial unit, and he'll talk to Rose."

"So what do I have to do?"

"You ready to talk about Howard?"

Amber nods and proceeds to tell him all she knows, but by now he already suspects most of what she offers: Howard is expanding, he is involved in identity theft and other scams, he has a network of tweekers working for him, he is pissing off the bikers and the Mexicans, and he is living at Brandy's house near Eatonville and there is a large lab in the barn.

"I've heard about the barn, but I can't get a warrant unless I have info from someone reliable who has firsthand info."

"Firsthand?"

"Seen something themselves."

"I haven't."

"Who would have?"

"You checked with the midget?"

"Not yet. Does the midget have a name?"

"Clay, I think. But everyone just calls him the midget."

"Has he been in the barn?"

"I don't know, but maybe. I could ask around?"

Wyatt nods. "What about you?" He studies the eagerness to please in her face. "Could you get in there? Hook back up with him? Get him to talk about the lab?"

Amber slumps and sighs.

"He knows you," Wyatt says quietly. "He trusts you."

"He doesn't trust anyone. And he's smart. You don't realize how smart he is."

Tweekers, like domestic violence victims, usually have a perverse loyalty to their man. Wyatt recognizes that if not for the

leverage of her child, she would not even talk to him, let alone set up Howard.

"I need you to get close to him again."

"That will mean using again."

"Not necessarily."

"I'll *have to* use to get back with him. If I don't, he'll be all suspicious. It's not like he doesn't know everyone is after him. And besides, I mean, you know, he doesn't spend time with girls who don't use. So . . . you'll tell my counselor it's okay that I'm using?"

This last line hits him and he leans back and contemplates the downside of this approach, frowning.

"I'll do it," she says, "I just want my child back." Tears begin. "I just want her back."

"This may not be the best plan. . . ."

"No, no," she says, "I'll do it, just tell me you'll get my child back. I know you can help." She uncrosses her arms, leans forward, reaches across the table. "I won't fuck up again, I promise, tell me what I have to do and I'll do it." As she sobs, the words spill together. "I just want her back."

"Okay, okay," he says, holding her offered hands on the table. "You've given me enough. I'll put in a word to the prosecutor."

"I'll do this if you want me to. I *will*. I can get back with him. Howard knew I wasn't just a bag 'ho, I was one of his favorites."

"I'm sorry," Wyatt says, wearing his cell phone headset as he drives south on I-5. Rain patters the roof and windshield and he cannot hear well, but well enough to pick up Suki's anger.

"I really wanted to see that movie."

"We can see the late show tonight."

"I have to open the shop tomorrow. And it opens at six a.m. Remember? Coffee junkies like to get started early."

"Later this week, then, the movie will still be there."

"That's not the point."

"Sorry, but I have this new lead I have to follow up on."

"Now? You have to follow up on it now?"

"Yes, sorry."

"We were supposed to see the movie right after your interview. Where are you?"

"I'm driving. Tweekers don't stay still long, and I know where this person is staying for the moment. I didn't want to get into it and then have to cancel on you at the last minute."

"You don't consider this the last minute?"

"Okay, good point."

"If Howard doesn't kill you, I will."

Wyatt laughs, hoping this will ease the tension.

"I'm not trying to be funny."

"I'll make it up to you." He shifts lanes into the far left, speeds up through the increasing rain. "I promise."

"I try to have faith in you, and then . . ."

"I'll make it up to you in a big way."

"I don't know, Wyatt. I really don't." Her anger segues into dis-

appointment, which is more difficult for both of them to deal with. "I'll talk to you later."

"Hold on, Suki. How about if I call you after I check this out?"

He realizes at this point that the connection is lost—she hung up. He misses the definitiveness of the dial tone that followed a hang-up when people used land lines.

He turns on KJR, the same radio station he listened to as a kid. The playlist has not changed much. After a few songs he knows and likes, he drives slowly down a dirt road through a mobile home park. Thanks to the heavy rain, everybody is inside, including the children and animals that are usually darting around in front of cars.

He has been here before investigating child molestation, meth labs, and stolen property. The litter scattered all about—tires, broken televisions, abandoned toys—represents the mind-set of the inhabitants for him.

A blue tarp hangs over the front door of a double-wide mobile home at the end of the road. Wyatt parks close, parallel to a row of mismatched garbage cans. As he steps out of his car and toward the door he can feel eyes on him.

"Open up," he says after his second knock. "It's Detective Wyatt James."

Shaking his head impatiently, he listens to the customary scurrying back and forth and then the footsteps of someone coming to the door.

"Yes?" a tall and gaunt woman says, opening the flimsy trailer door.

"I need to talk to Clay."

"There's no Clay here."

"The midget."

"I'll check and see if he's here."

"You mean he could be here without you knowing it?"

"I . . . just got home."

Wyatt gently pushes her aside as he enters.

"Someone's here, Clay," she says. "It's a cop."

Clay steps out of a bathroom door and smiles at Wyatt as though he is thrilled to see him, hands held out to his side where the officer can see them.

"We need to talk," Wyatt says.

"Leave us," Clay says to the six-foot woman.

"We can talk out in my car if you would prefer," Wyatt says.

"No, here's fine." Clay jerks his thumb in the direction of the door and, to Wyatt's surprise, the tall woman picks up a jacket from the floor and heads out silently, closing the door behind her.

"Sit down," Clay offers, gesturing magnanimously at the couch, which is speckled with cat hair and stains of undeterminable origin.

Wyatt, not wanting to ruin his blue blazer or khakis and not wanting a long conversation, continues standing.

"No, thanks."

Clay hops up on the couch and sits. A disassembled computer lies in pieces on the coffee table, next to a copy of *Barely Legal* and several empty cans of Mountain Dew with cigarette butts on the rims.

"I heard you were shot," Clay says.

"Who did you hear that from?"

"Just one of those things you hear. Cops don't get shot that often."

"They seem to in Pierce County."

"I heard the guy who shot you is dead."

"Who did he work for?"

"Bikers."

"Howard?"

"Nope."

"When did you last see Howard?"

"It's been a while."

"When?"

Clay and Wyatt look at each other for a long beat, Clay trying to gauge how much he can lie to Wyatt and Wyatt trying to look like he knows more than he does so that Clay does not lie too much.

"This is off the record," Clay says. "Right?"

"Okay."

"He would kill me if he knew I told you anything. Even if I was lying to protect him. He'd kill me for just talking to you."

"Howard's never killed anyone before. Has he?"

"No, not that I know of, but he cut off a guy's hand recently. With a chainsaw. Howard's on a run, he's got meth bugs, and he's getting worse, much worse, crazy paranoid and . . . I don't know, I'm hearing about all sorts of weirdness."

"When did you see him?"

"And you won't tell my BTC counselor, either?"

"When did you start BTC?"

"Just a possession charge. No biggie. But I hate jail, so my counselor can't know I'm, you know, associating with dealers and users."

"Secrets are safe with me."

"And you can help me with the charges?"

"Don't push it, Clay. You're just facing possession charges. Save my help for when you really need it."

"Okay, I hear that."

"So when did you see him last?" When Clay hesitates, Wyatt adds, "This is just confidential background stuff."

"Confidential, double-secret?"

"Sure, double-secret probation."

"Three weeks ago."

"Where?"

"His house."

"His house? You were inside?"

"Yeah. I'm connected, I'm trusted. That's why this has to be double-secret whatever you said."

"Does he have a lab in there?"

"Not in the house. Not that I could see. I think it's in the barn out back."

"What makes you say that? Did you see anything?"

"No, I've just heard."

"He's living with a woman named Brandy."

"Teenager?"

"No, that's her daughter, Porsche. She's twelve."

"I thought she seemed kinda young to be his girlfriend."

"You see any signs of a lab?"

"No."

"Any drugs?"

"Meth."

"Did he sell it to you?"

Clay hesitates, looks down at his small feet dangling off the floor.

"How much did he sell you?" Wyatt continues.

"Just a quarter."

"Did he have more there?"

"I don't know, I assume so."

"Did you see any large quantities?"

"No."

"Did you see anything I should know about?"

"No."

"Guns?"

"Didn't see any."

Wyatt starts to head toward the door, but turns. He watches Clay twitch for a moment.

"Clay?"

"Yeah?"

"Nothing personal, but I'm going to have to tell your counselor to run a piss test on you."

"What? You said all of this was off the record. Double-secret confidential."

I had to tell you lies to help you get to the truth.

"You know I hate jail," Clay continues. "Those fuckers are all over me." He vaults off the couch, yells up at Wyatt, face at crotch level. "They use me for midget-tossing contests!"

Wyatt steps out into the rain. Clay's girlfriend is standing under the blue tarp, calmly smoking.

"Clay will have a UA next week at BTC," Wyatt says as he passes her. "If he's not clean, he'll go to jail. His choice."

Though she stares at him uncomprehending for a moment, exhaling a stream of nicotine into the cold air, Wyatt expects she will eventually understand.

"Not enough," Mike says, sipping his tom yum soup out of a large plastic spoon, savoring the tangy flavor and warmth. Outside, the air is chilly with the frisson of snow on the horizon.

"He knows he's got a lab in the barn," Wyatt insists, his Viet curry untouched.

Mike reaches for the Blue Willow teapot and fills their cups. "No, he doesn't *know*."

"Well, *I* know."

"And you're right, but being right isn't enough."

"The midget's reliable."

"I'm not sure the midget qualifies as reliable, and anyway, he doesn't have any fresh information." Mike has this same conversation repeatedly with officers who think, quite sensibly, that they ought to be able to get a warrant for a house if there is criminal activity inside, but it is not that simple. "You know the Aguilar-Spinelli test."

"Yeah, it requires a good informant."

"A *reliable* informant, one with personal knowledge that isn't stale."

"Yeah, I know."

"Well, you've got a questionable informant: half of his information is hearsay, and all of it's probably stale."

"You just keep raining on my parade, Counselor."

"That's what I'm here for. Eat, the food's excellent."

Mike comes to Le-Le's on Martin Luther King Jr. Way almost every day for lunch, and sometimes for dinner, since he does not cook. When he discovered the place it was a dive and he liked it

that way. After more people heard about it and started coming, Le-Le and her husband painted a rice paddy mural on the walls, put the menus in plastic jackets, hung peasant hats from the ceiling, added bamboo plants, and raised the prices. Mike liked it better before it caught on, much as he liked his favorite bands such as the Replacements, R.E.M., and U2 before they caught on, but he still comes regularly.

"So what do you suggest?" Wyatt asks.

"Eat."

"Besides that," Wyatt says, having a bite.

"Nothing."

"Nothing? Are you getting Zen on me? I just want a warrant, not a fucking Zen lesson."

"Hello, Judge."

Mike confirms his attendance at an upcoming charity event the judge is supporting, and he promises the judge he will invite some lawyers and politicos she does not know how to reach but would like to see there.

"You know too many people," Wyatt says after the judge moves on, soliciting more lawyers as she works her way toward a corner table where a *News Tribune* reporter sips a bubble tea.

"People are interesting."

"Interesting is one way to put it."

Le-Le's reminds Mike of Rick's, Humphrey Bogart's café in *Casablanca*. Everybody comes to Le-Le's. Sometimes he can save himself half a dozen phone calls and e-mails by the time he leaves.

"You remember Bruce Lee?" Mike asks.

"Yes."

"A master."

"Yes."

"One of the best in the world at what he did?"

"Yes."

"Someone who understood the art of excellence?"

"Yes. Is this a cross-examination?"

"Someone we would be wise to emulate?"

"Except for the heart attack at a young age, yes."

"Well, here's what Bruce Lee had to say about your situation."

"*My* situation?"

"Your pursuit of Howard."

"Lee is speaking from his grave in Seattle?"

"'The less effort you apply, the faster and more powerful you will be.'"

Wyatt nods, seeing the wisdom of this as it applies to punching someone, or even hitting a golf ball, but not convinced of its larger application to life.

"And you believe this?" Wyatt asks.

"Yes."

"Then why work so hard?"

"Remember when I was telling you I didn't quite get the whole Nirvana concept? If Nirvana is not wanting anything, then why want Nirvana?"

"I agreed."

"Right, and I eventually quit wanting Nirvana. And so it started coming to me. And I'd like it, and then want it too bad, and it would go away. And then I'd quit wanting it so bad, and it would come back." Mike shrugs. "Nirvana is like criminals and women that way. We catch what we're not chasing too hard."

"You trying to tell me to pull my hand out of the coconut?"

Mike sips his tea. "When you stop and connect with the world, possibilities open up."

"Suki came back," Wyatt says after a long pause.

"See?"

"But I think I fucked it up again."

"Well, no amount of Zen can stop men from screwing up relationships. Buddha bailed on his wife and son and stayed a bachelor for the rest of his weird life."

TO EVERYTHING THERE IS A SEASON

Thanksgiving passes; Christmas approaches.

Mike reaches over and turns up the defroster and then the CD player, clicking on Death Cab for Cutie. He quickly refocuses on the road as the Range Rover slides in its lane. Snowflakes fall gently toward the windshield and then suddenly whoosh away in the air flow around the car.

He drives past the Bullseye Shooting Range and the Bubble Room, a bar where he used to drink after work when he and his colleagues were younger and had more time and energy and questions to discuss. Green and red lights blink around the windows.

"Stop for a cocktail, or continue on?"

"Continue on," Wyatt says. "Poker awaits us."

"The holy game of poker."

"Good for the soul."

"What's the difference between a poker room and a church?"

"Is this a joke?"

"When you pray in a poker room, you really mean it."

Ahead the road is nearly empty and the snow is falling fast enough that the pavement is covered in white. On a night like this Mike would not normally be driving. When the snow started, he was staring out at the rock garden from the kitchen where he was sitting on a stool, spacing out. After the snow started sticking, he felt compelled to venture outside.

"I keep reading these articles about how we should fight terrorism more like crime and less like a war," Wyatt says, "but I don't know about that. People would be pissed if we caught

Osama bin Laden and had to let him walk because it was a pretextual stop or there was a technical defect in a search warrant."

"You're still thinking about Howard."

"Only tangentially. You think criminals and terrorists are similar?"

"There will always be bad guys, and there will always be evil, so I guess crime and terrorism are similar in that the battle is endless, so we have permanent job security."

"Would you rather convert to Islam, or have your head chopped off?"

"The Islamic fascists hate rock and roll, so they will never prevail." Mike turns up Death Cab for Cutie. "Always bet on the good guys in the long run."

"Cool CD," Wyatt says. "Suki's into it. Glad to see you're keeping up with the kids."

"They used to play on the local scene. Pete Tyler introduced me to their Barsuk albums, and I've followed their career through the years."

Mike slows down as the snow increases, flakes swarming over the front window. Ahead of them a neon sign beckons, FREDDIE'S, shining in red cursive.

"Best poker movie?" Wyatt asks. "*Cincinnati Kid,* or *Rounders?*"

"Close call," Mike says, pleased that Wyatt is letting Howard go, if only for the moment, "but I have to say *Rounders.*"

"Best line in *Rounders?*"

"'If you're too careful, your whole life can become a fucking grind.'"

"'We can't run from who we are. Our destiny chooses us.'"

"The line about the blow job from Christy Turlington was pretty good, too, but I can't remember it exactly."

Mike pulls the Rover up into the mostly empty parking lot beside a dark rape van. The snow crunches when he steps out. Crossing in front of the Rover, he sees a Starbucks cup on the ground and, before Wyatt can notice, he kicks it under the car.

Just before they arrive at the glass doors of the casino, Wyatt's phone rings. He checks the LCD display, recognizes the number as one of his crew.

"Let it go," Mike says, sensing the call has something to do with Howard. "At least for tonight."

Wyatt flips open the phone. "Yeah?"

"Just received a report of shots fired out at Howard's lab," the hyped deputy says. "Sounds like they've got a fucking shoot-out going on, craziness, massive calls coming in. What do you think?"

"How far from the scene are you?"

"Twenty minutes, maybe."

"I'll be behind you, coming in a gray Range Rover. Don't shoot my ass."

"Roger that."

Wyatt flicks the phone shut.

"Howard," Mike says, picking up on the adrenaline vibe.

"Let's put your SUV to use."

THE SNOWS OF MOUNT RAINIER

Gunshots crack in the cold air from different directions, the echoes muffled by the trees and snow covering the surrounding hills.

Two bikers are shooting at Brandy's house from inside the barn, poking their semiautomatic AR-15 rifles with long hundred-round magazines around the doors. Orange and yellow flashes cut through the darkness. Toxic fumes from leaking anhydrous ammonia tanks cause their eyes to water and disrupt their aim.

One biker is shooting from the creek bank, the bare trees providing little cover. He is crouched down with a .50 Beowulf, a powerful variation on the AR-15, and he has a good angle on a back corner of the house and is more sparing with his shots than his friends in the barn who smoked meth just before they raided Howard's lab.

All of the bikers are using .223 hollow-point bullets, which shatter an entire window on impact and slam into the house with a scary *whap*, but do not fully penetrate walls. They came to destroy Howard's lab, which they have done. Only after he started shooting at them from the house did they decide to kill him.

Howard and Brandy fire back from shattered windows in the kitchen, recklessly triggering off shots in the general direction of the barn. They are using target ammunition and extra-long thirty-three-round magazines Howard bought on the Internet. Howard is wearing cargo pants and a T-shirt that reads JUST SAY NO TO BUGS in red letters over the black image of a cockroach lying dead on its back with a meth pipe in its mouth.

Flickering gray light from the television monitors connected to security cameras pulse in the dark kitchen, but the small and shadowy images on the screen only tell Howard what he already knows: people in the barn are shooting at him.

Though Howard went many years without owning guns because Washington State adds three years of prison for each gun if you are convicted of manufacturing methamphetamine, paranoia finally got the best of him and he bought the 9mm Glocks and now he feels his paranoia was justified.

Just because you're paranoid doesn't mean people aren't out to get you.

He purchased the guns through ads in the newspaper: cash for guns, no paperwork, no problems.

Porsche and Joe are in the living room, lying on the floor by the couch as ordered. Above them is a fresh Christmas tree, a Noble fir cut down from a neighbor's property, which is undecorated except for a zigzagging string of miniature white lights that twinkle in the dark room. Joe cannot stay still and Porsche keeps telling him he's a fool and to keep his head down.

"I wanna gun," Joe says as the shots continue.

"Fucking losers," Porsche says, face on the shag rug, not quite understanding why her life is like this, but certain it is the fault of men, *losers.*

Neighbors, not entirely unaccustomed to gunshots, are still stunned by the duration of the firefight and hide in protected corners of their houses, complaining to each other about high taxes and the lack of police in their rural community.

Howard, shooting through the shattered window at random intervals, feels at a disadvantage because the bikers have rifles and distance. He is particularly aggravated by the third biker sniping at him from the creek bank.

Brandy is on her knees at his feet reloading the Glock magazines, not thinking but just doing as she was told.

"Go into Porsche's bedroom," Howard says, "and look for the guy by the creek. Shoot him. I'm going to run for the barn."

"*What?*"

"We're sitting fucking ducks here, I'm going after the assholes in the barn."

"No, no, we're best off staying in!"

"Listen!" Howard yells. "You go into the bedroom and cover me when the fucker by the creek shoots. Now!"

Brandy scrambles off on her knees, fully loaded Glock in hand. In the hallway she jumps onto her feet and runs in a crouch, not slowing down to check on Porsche or Joe.

As Howard loads his magazine, the occasional AR-15 round flying over his head into the kitchen cabinets, Joe enters the kitchen carrying a .44 Magnum.

"Stay the fuck down," Howard yells.

Joe goes down, but still makes his way over, crawling like a soldier. Howard laughs at the sight of the small boy with the big gun.

"Where the fuck did you get that?"

"Mom's bedroom."

Howard recognizes it as the gun that was pointed at him the night he arrived. "Give it to me."

Joe pouts as he hands over the gun, the barrel carelessly pointed at Howard's stomach.

"Fucking kids," Howard says, spinning the chamber, confirming it is loaded.

"Am I supposed to just hide until I get shot?"

"You're supposed to do what you're fucking told." Though

Howard is twitching like crazy, he feels in control and focused from the lines he snorted. In retrospect he should have snuck up on the bikers, but he was so pissed—*fucking criminal trespassers*—he just broke out his meth and his gun and took care of business. "Can you fucking do that?" he asks Joe. "Can you fucking do what you're told?"

"Yeah," Joe says.

"Okay, that's a good kid." Howard hands Joe a loaded Glock, butt out into his small hand. Joe beams, lifting it, noticing the lightness compared to the .44 Magnum. "Remember, Joe, when I told you I thought you were a tough kid? And someday you'd have a chance to prove it?"

"Yeah?"

"Here's your chance. Once-in-a-lifetime, son. Once-in-a-fucking-lifetime."

Joe nods, enjoying the gun in his hand.

"I'm going to rush the barn," Howard says. "As I run out the back door, you stand up and start shooting at the front door of the barn. There's a couple bikers with rifles you're trying to hit. Shoot for their fat fucking bellies, okay?"

"Okay."

"You've shot-guns in those idiot video games, right?"

"Yeah?"

"Same idea, but the gun is going to kick back. You know what kick is? The gun is going to want to kick back toward you." Howard demonstrates with the Magnum, employing a two-handed police-style grip. "Just keep your elbows bent and let it come back a little, but not too much. Got it?"

"Got it."

"Good kid. Welcome to the real world."

With this, Howard scoots over to the back door and perches on his haunches. He shoves the Magnum into his waistband, takes a vial out of his jeans pocket, taps half of the unchopped white crystals onto the back of his hand, and sniffs it off in a swoop.

Harsh.

"Okay," he says, wiggling his nose. "Cover me."

Swinging open the door, he runs out into the backyard, barefoot, Magnum blazing in the direction of the barn. He almost instantly trips onto his face and drops the .44 as a bullet burns through a calf.

Brandy sees the flash of the shot from the dark of the creek bank and wildly shoots in that direction. Hearing the shots whizzing and hitting around him, the biker starts to slip back down the bank toward the icy water, but one of the bullets catches his arm and tears clean through and into his side.

As Joe hears the shots ringing out, he stands with the Glock in both hands and begins shooting at the opening of the barn as instructed. He does not see anybody, but suddenly there are white and orange flashes and the cabinets behind him splinter and he realizes *someone is shooting back.*

With Joe covering him, Howard crawls quickly back into the house, leaving the .44 behind. He shuts the door behind him after dragging his leg out of the way.

"Those pieces of shit shot me!"

Joe ducks down to join Howard and is shocked as he watches Howard pull his pant leg up and exposes a hole in his upper calf with blood pumping out in spurts and running down his boot.

"Get me a goddamn towel!"

After a moment more of staring at the wound, Joe grabs a

dirty dish towel from on the stove. He hands it to Howard, who loops it around his leg and ties a fast knot, which quickly turns red as the blood spreads like a blossom.

"You okay?" Brandy yells from the bedroom during a respite in shooting.

"Fucking great," Howard yells back.

"Is it over?" Porsche yells.

"Far fucking from it," Howard yells.

Sirens fade in as two fully marked Jeep Cherokees from the Pierce County Sheriff's Department pull up and stop on the road in front of Brandy's house, spaced out so one is thirty yards east of Brandy's driveway and the other is about thirty yards behind, their wig-wag lights shining on the snow, headlights on.

One of the security cameras is focused on the front of the house, a wide-angle shot, and Howard watches the arrival of the officers with mixed feelings. His chances of survival just went up, but his chance of escape just went down.

"Things are getting complicated," he says to Joe.

Two officers from each Jeep empty out of the driver's side onto the street, keeping the vehicles between themselves and the barn where the gunfire is reportedly centered.

"Sheriff's Department," Deputy Newton announces through his PA system. "Put your weapons down and come out with your hands on top of your head."

Though Newton is not sure where exactly the shooters will be coming out from—the barn or the house or the field that stretches to the creek—he thinks it best to initially address the situation with the traditional approach.

Seconds later there are several rapid-fire flashes and bangs from the barn and three of the four patrol car headlights explode

and one wig-wag light goes dark. Suddenly a firefight is on as the deputies open up from behind their vehicles with shotguns and Glock .40s. The barn, at fifty yards, is at the limit of the range for the buckshot-loaded shotguns, but distance is hard to gauge in the dark and the snow.

Sensing an opportunity, Howard stands with a freshly loaded Glock and triggers off several rounds toward the door of the barn where he can see flashes from the bikers' guns.

"Yeah!" he yells, dropping back down. "I think I got one of the fuckers!"

Joe cheers and thrusts his fists in the air.

Brandy peers over the top of the bedroom window, staring at the spot where the biker was shooting from earlier, seeing no movement. Below her sight line the biker is lying in the shallow of the flowing creek, shivering and bleeding out, losing consciousness from a lucky shot.

Mike and Wyatt approach the scene as the gunfire subsides again, Wyatt on the cell phone alerting the deputies to their arrival. Mike turns off his headlights and slows down.

"Drop me here," Wyatt says, "and turn around."

Mike has always found police work fascinating, more visceral than the formalized battle of the courtroom, and he drives Wyatt all the way up to the rear of Deputy Newton's Jeep.

"Okay," Wyatt says, "leave me here and pull back."

Suddenly shots ring out, distinctly different guns firing, and Mike and Wyatt both duck, their heads almost meeting at the center console.

"Actually," Mike says, after another exchange between the barn and the house stops, "I think I'll just stay here."

"I don't want you to get shot, Counselor."

"Hey, you're the one who always gets shot."

"Once is not always."

"You spend any more time in the hospital, I'm going to ask Suki out."

"She doesn't like lawyers."

"As far as you know."

Wyatt, not having time to banter further, checks his Glock, confirms the fifteen-round magazine is fully loaded, then quickly exits the Rover. Hunched over, he jogs a few steps across the snow-covered road to Newton's Jeep, sliding in between the deputies who are hunched down by the tires.

"What's the story?" he asks.

"I don't know. We've got a couple shooters in the barn, and apparently people in the house are returning fire."

"Howard's probably in the house. There's a lab in the barn."

Newton smiles. "Howard? You think anyone else is in the house with him?" He looks up over the hood of the Jeep.

"Could be. Woman who owns the house has two kids."

"Shit. Let's give them another chance to come out."

Once again he picks up the handset from the PA system and announces, "Put down your weapons and come out with your hands up. Now."

"The 'now' should make all the difference," his partner says, then turns to Wyatt. "Last time we tried that they shot up the car and knocked out the lights."

"We may have taken them out," Newton says. "We shot off about fifty rounds."

"Let's wait until we have backup before we try to confirm that."

"Where the fuck *is* the backup?" Wyatt asks.

"Come on, we're too understaffed to keep officers out here. This is cook territory."

"With the snow and ice," Newton says, looking up at the large flakes continuing to fall, "I'm figuring we're on our own for a while."

Slowly lifting his head, Mike surveys the scene, noting that the deputies are positioned behind the wheels of their Jeeps. He opens his driver's door and steps out behind the large front tire of the Range Rover, crouching and poking his head over the hood.

"Hey," Wyatt whispers, gesturing for Mike to keep his head down.

Mike does, turning and sitting. Just next to him is a pothole. He stares at the icy water in the pothole for a moment, watching the snowflakes dissolve on contact. The shadows of their crystal pattern linger for a split second on the surface, the amazing symmetry lingering in his mind.

The blissful sensation he hoped to recapture with the birdbath suddenly comes to him, rising from his chilly feet and through his body and into his head, and once again, for the second time in his life, he truly understands that everything is ordered, everything is connected, everything is cool.

"What the fuck are you doing out here?" Wyatt whispers, snapping Mike out of his bliss.

"Taking cover."

"Fucking lawyers." Wyatt shakes his head at the deputies. "Is anyone watching the back to cut off Howard's escape?"

"Yeah, whoever was shooting from the barn."

"Rival dealers?"

"I assume so."

"I gotta think Howard would rather give up to us than be shot by them," the other deputy says.

"I don't know," Wyatt says.

In the bedroom Brandy replaces the dish towel around Howard's leg with a clean white T-shirt, which turns red even quicker than the towel. He takes three Vicodins from his pocket and chews them down while she tightens a second T-shirt around the wound.

"Where's Porsche?" Howard asks.

"Hiding by the couch in the living room," Joe says, reloading Howard's Glocks.

"Get in here, Porsche," Howard yells.

"No!"

"Where are the car keys?" Howard asks Brandy.

"In my purse."

"Give them to me."

Brandy quickly pulls the keys out of her purse and hands them to Howard, confused but not really wanting clarification.

"Get back here, Porsche," Howard yells again.

"No!"

"Do I have to drag you back here?"

"No!"

Howard turns to Brandy. "What's that mean?"

"She's not moving."

"Shit. Okay. We'll go out there. Stay down."

Howard takes his two reloaded Glocks from Joe and starts snaking along on his stomach to the living room. Brandy and Joe follow, crawling. Their Christmas tree lights are flickering and a soft light from the whiteness outside filters through the mini blinds, closed as always since Howard came to stay.

Porsche is crying softly on the floor.

"I'm going to miss you, hon," Howard says.

Porsche scowls back at him, noticing fresh scabs on his fore-head, just like her mother has acquired of late. Brandy, reacting to the revulsion on Porsche's face, crawls over and hugs her awk-wardly on the floor.

"I'm sorry," she whispers.

Howard, sitting up beside them, admires the bright tattoo around Porsche's ankle, a bracelet of roses and thorns with drops of blood, *something to remember me by*.

"I'm looking at ten years if I surrender," he says, shoving the Glocks into his waistband and lighting up what he imagines could be his last cigarette. "And Howard Schultz isn't really the type to surrender."

"Well, you're not really Howard Schultz," Brandy says back, surprising herself.

Vaguely registering an insurrection, Howard takes a long drag of his Kool, drops the butt onto the floor. He climbs up onto one knee and uses his good leg to push himself up onto his feet.

From out of his pocket he pulls a meth pipe, which he cere-moniously slides onto the tip of the Christmas tree.

"Bo-orn is the ki-ing of methlehem," he sings.

"What are you doing?" Brandy asks.

He looks at her. *She'll always have those sad cow eyes.* "I'm going to Ireland," he says, stepping unsteadily toward the front door, pulling a Glock out of his waistband. "They don't extradite."

Brandy puts an arm around each child and brings them under her and covers them up as much as she can, shaking, anticipating the worst. As has happened many times before, it occurs to her that her latest boyfriend is borderline psychotic and a menace and no good for her or her children. She tells herself she cannot keep making the same mistake, as she has told herself so many times before.

"Wish me luck," Howard says.

"What-fucking-ever," Porsche mutters.

Howard, limping into the entry hall, does not hear. "You out there, Wyatt," he yells at the closed front door, then opens it a crack. "Come on, Wyatt. Don't disappoint me."

Hearing the voice, Wyatt and the deputies rise slightly, level their guns toward the half-open door. Mike turns and gets up on his knees, peers over the hood.

"Shit," Newton says, "is he coming out?"

"Yeah, I'm here, Howard," Wyatt yells back.

"The king is dead," Howard yells. "Long live the king. Right, Wyatt?"

"He's tweaking big time," Newton says.

"You know the drill, Howard." Wyatt stands, gun held out with both hands. "Come out with your hands up."

"Don't fucking bet on it."

Howard pulls out the vial, taps the remaining contents onto the side of the Glock barrel. He drops the vial, breathes in deeply, exhales, then sniffs up the last of the meth off the barrel, blinking and contorting his face as the crystals burn into his nostrils.

Most of his dopamine neurotransmitters have been destroyed, and his brain resembles that of a Parkinson's patient, but there are still enough neurons left for him to feel a bit of the old chemical zoom. He begins humming, *I am Superman, and I can do anything . . .*

After wiping his dripping nose, Howard pulls the second Glock out of his pants and flings the door open and runs out across the snow-covered yard toward Brandy's car, guns in hand. At first nobody shoots, Wyatt and the deputies frozen by the sudden and audacious sprint, but then Howard points his guns toward Wyatt and the patrol cars.

Nearly simultaneously they all get off shots, two of the officers with shotguns, and Howard takes several rounds of buckshot and three .40-caliber rounds—two hollow-point slugs ripping into his chest—and he writhes and stumbles, but he keeps firing his guns as he falls.

Mike stares as the muzzle blasts flare in the darkness and momentarily light up the scene in still frames. He is thinking he should duck, but he cannot pull his eyes away. Howard triggers off one last shot and Mike sees the flash just as the bullet pierces his forehead.

IT TOLLS FOR THEE

"The Bible assures us love is stronger even than death." The priest's amplified voice echoes through the dark building and resonates off the giant stained-glass image of Jesus bleeding on the cross and glowing in the light from outside.

Police and prosecutors in dark suits fill the gallery and tears flow from some, but not from Wyatt. Suki, to his left, was emotional the night before but is calm now, facing forward.

"For God so loved the world that he gave his only Son, so that everyone who believes in Him will not perish but have eternal life. God did not send His Son into the world to condemn it, but to save it."

This is only the second time Wyatt has been in a church in the last ten years and as the priest continues to tie together death and love with the ponderous tone of a Russian novelist, Wyatt's mind hopscotches through subjects, including the Holy Ghost, which he is still not clear on, and Mike and the incomprehensible void of death.

Wyatt has always been contemptuous of those who chase money or power or drugs, simultaneously recognizing that we especially dislike in others those qualities that we dislike in ourselves. His own taste for the chase, he has always told himself, is *different*. This rationalization, however, popped like a party balloon upon Mike's death.

Chasing something, no matter our target, can be one of many ways to avoid absorbing and appreciating the details of our passing lives, to avoid facing the only issue that matters, the scariest and surest issue, death. Mike was trying to tell him this, to slow

down and connect to the possibilities, but of course Mike often handed out advice, usually based on his own evolving code of conduct, and Wyatt enjoyed the conversations but did not pay Mike's counsel much heed.

There are not many advantages to being dead, but one is that people think back on what you said and give it more weight than they ever did when you were alive.

Mike seemed to know that his destiny was an early death and this, to Wyatt, suggests the death was not senseless. He clings to this belief despite a lack of proof—*it has a reason even if I don't know it.*

Very Zen, Mike might say.

Mike would, Wyatt feels, be glad to see so many wearing his preferred uniform of dark suits and white shirts.

"Could you please face each other?" the priest asks.

Wyatt pivots on the altar. Suki's veil is open around her face and though Wyatt knows marriage is about much more than physical attraction, her beauty alleviates his anxiety.

Beauty is a miracle drug.

"Will you, Wyatt Evans James, take Suki Rebecca Kubomoto to be your lawfully wedded wife?"

"I will."

Wyatt slips into the moment as the priest repeats the litany to Suki and they exchange rings, "an endless circle," and then hold each other's hands, their arms stretched between them in a V.

"Let us now bow our heads and pray together. Dear Father, in sending us your only Son, Jesus Christ the Savior, You showed us that love must be carnate."

Had to tell you lies to help you get to the truth.

"Love is not just a thought, love is flesh, love is action. We

humbly ask You now to nurture with Your love the love of Wyatt and Suki so that their love may be nurtured in others. Amen."

"Amen," responds the crowd, not quite in unison.

Wyatt did not want a church wedding and his friends and colleagues did not expect a church wedding, but Suki's mother did and so here they are.

"Before this community of supporters, according to the laws of Washington and the ordinance of God, I now pronounce you husband and wife. May God's joy, a joy this world cannot give and cannot take away, be with you forever. To signify this, you now may kiss."

They do and then turn to face the applause and a few hollers from his crew. Wyatt wanted either "I Will Dare" by the Replacements, or "I'm Not Down" by the Clash to fade in at this point, but Suki wanted "Yellow" by Coldplay or "Caring Is Creepy" by the Shins, and the latter was unacceptable to Wyatt because the Shins sold a song to McDonald's and the former was just unacceptable. They compromised on Morphine's "Cure for Pain," which plays as they step down the aisle, smiling as the cameras flash and seal their images in memory chips.

MAHALO

Hawaii's longest reef stretches out parallel to Anini Beach on the island of Kauai over a hundred yards out from the khaki-colored sand. Rolling waves break over the reef in a continually rushing white froth while the bay remains calm, the azure surface stirring only slightly, the bright morning sun glittering hypnotically off the ripples.

This, Wyatt thinks, *is solid evidence of the Holy Ghost.*

"If we evolved from monkeys," Suki asks, looking up a palm tree, "how come monkeys are still around?"

Wyatt looks at her out of the corner of his eye.

"I don't want to ever leave here," Suki says.

Wyatt cannot argue.

"I'm glad tourist season doesn't mean that you can shoot tourists."

Again, Wyatt cannot argue.

They sit on white beach chairs only a few yards in front of their vacation rental house, drinking Coronas with lime, gazing out at the water through sunglasses, paperbacks in the sand beside them.

Suki is wearing a new white-and-beige-striped bikini and much suntan lotion. Wyatt, wearing khaki shorts and a white aloha shirt, is almost color-coordinated. This is not intentional.

"How am I just discovering this place at forty?"

"I can answer that."

"Yeah?"

"Me."

He nods, sips his beer.

"Don't need much in a place like this," she says. "Don't need much at all."

"Cold beer is good." He holds the bottle up toward the sun, studies the light diffusing through the glass. "Sometimes I feel like everything in life takes too long. We learn things too late."

"Not too late. We learn when we learn."

Yet again he cannot argue. It does not seem right to quibble in the midst of so much beauty.

In the palm trees and lush foliage behind them colorful birds flap and caw and chirp. Their sounds are unlike birds in the Northwest, louder and sharper. Wyatt's senses suddenly heighten.

An airliner streaks across the clear blue sky, ascending, and as Wyatt's gaze shifts up he sees a gray feather drifting toward him. He watches it flutter, smiles after a moment.

Mahalo.